Snow monster
(*Ökötöm-kökötöm*)

KUĻÜŲ

KERKYŹŽM

GDBARDD

ol

The Junjan
Archipelago

The End of Freddy

(Rivers of Babylon 3)

by the same author

Rivers of Babylon Bratislava: Archa, 1991, Champagne Avantgarde, 1995 and Koloman Kertész Bagala, 2003 [*in English* Garnett Press, 2007]

Mladý Dônč (*Young Dônč*) Bratislava: Slovenský spisovateľ, 1993 and Koloman Kertész Bagala, 1998

Rivers of Babylon 2 alebo drevená dedina (*Rivers of Babylon 2, or The Wooden Village*) Bratislava: Champagne Avantgarde, 1994 [*in English* Garnett Press, 2008]

Skazky o Vladovi pre malých a veľkých (*Tales about Vlad for Young and Old*) Bratislava: Filmservice Slovakia, 1995

Nové skazky o Vladovi (*More Tales about Vlad*) Bratislava: Filmservice Slovakia, 1998

Rivers of Babylon 3 alebo Fredyho koniec (*Rivers of Babylon 3, or The End of Freddy*) Bratislava: Filmservice Slovakia, 1999 [*in English* Garnett Press, 2008]

Sekerou a nožom (*With Axe and Knife*), with Dušan Taragel, Levice: LCA, 1999

Posledné skazky pre malých a veľkých (*Latest Tales for Young and Old*) Bratislava: Fenix, 2002

Traktoristi a buzeranti (*Tractor Drivers and Queers*) Bratislava: Slovart, 2003

Recepty z rodinného archívu alebo všetko čo viem ma naučil môj dedo (*Recipes from the Family Archive, or Everything I Know My Grandfather Taught Me*) Levice: LCA, 2003

Peter Pišťanek

The End of Freddy
(Rivers of Babylon 3)

translated by Peter Petro

GARNETT PRESS

LONDON

first published in Great Britain in 2008 by

The Garnett Press,
Dpt of Russian (SML)
Queen Mary (University of London),
Mile End Road, London E1 4NS

© Peter Pišťanek
this translation into English: © Peter Petro
this edition: © Garnett Press

typeset in Times New Roman & Garamond by Donald Rayfield
1000 copies printed and bound in Turkey by Mega Basım, Istanbul

This book has been selected to receive financial assistance from English PEN's Writers in Translation
programme supported by Bloomberg.

This book has received a subsidy from SLOLIA Committee,
the Centre for Information on Literature in Bratislava.

ISBN 978-0-9535878-6-5

Introduction

Peter Pišťanek (pronounced *Pishtyanek*) is one of the most talented prose writers to appear after the fall of communism in Slovakia. He was born in 1960 in Devínska Nová Ves, a village now swallowed up by Bratislava, the capital of Slovakia. He enrolled in Bratislava's Academy of Performing Arts, but did not graduate. He was also a drummer in a very well known rock group. At the end of the 1980s he began to publish in the literary monthly *Slovenské Pohľady* (Slovak Views). His breakthrough came with *Rivers of Babylon* (1991), a novel that caused a sensation and catapulted him into fame. That novel was the first part of a trilogy (now all published by the Garnett Press in English), followed by *The Wooden Village* and this novel, *The End of Freddy*. Since the end of the 1990s Peter Pišťanek has worked for advertising agencies and radio and edited an influential Internet magazine *Inzine*. He has also become an expert on brandies and whiskies.

Pišťanek's reputation is assured by originality, craftsmanship and imaginative inventiveness. *The End of Freddy*, which Pišťanek declared to be his swan-song, is a magnificent finale to the trilogy: the scene now extends from the earlier novels' Bratislava and its environs to Prague and Russia's Arctic North, and to the fictional, but only too real, post-Soviet Khanate of Junja, where descendants of Slovak slaves rebel against their rulers, and the Czech state seizes its chance to acquire great power status.

The stoker turned gangster Rácz from the earlier *Rivers of Babylon* novels continues to grow in monstrous stature, just as the car park attendant turned porn-film scriptwriter Freddy Piggybank achieves unexpected glory. A host of new characters, from the primitive Junjans with their unpronounceable language, to a happy band of Czech naval officers, gives Pišťanek's novel a Dickensian richness. To the ruthless intrigues of individuals is added a wide-ranging and convincing account of rebellion and civil war. The black irony of the earlier novels is, if possible, even darker, but its Czech scenes bring in positive characters and an affectionate tone, new to his readers.

The original novel switches with virtuosity from Slovak to Czech whenever the action demands. The translator and editor have decided to render the difference (the two languages differ little more than Edinburgh Scots from London English) not by writing different forms of English (which would have had undesirable side-effects), but by printing what was originally written in Czech in the more imperial Garamond typeface.

Some guidance for the British reader…

Time and place

The novel is set in the mid-1990s, when Czechoslovakia has split into two states, and Slovakia seems an anything-goes playground for mafias and corrupt politicians, while the Czech state, now a Kingdom in the novel's imaginary world, pursues a more ambitious role in Europe. The fictional Junjan Archipelago lies beyond the Arctic Circle of the Russian mainland and, in shape, seems very like the Shetland Islands, magnified by ten and rotated 90 degrees.

Currency

The Slovak and Czech crowns were then worth about 50 to the pound.

Some characters and how to pronounce their names

We keep Slovak and Czech spellings of characters' names, but here is a guide to a few more problematic and important ones. (Junjan names, given the language Pišťanek has invented for them, will defeat even the most smooth-tongued linguist.) All Slovak and Czech names are stressed on the first syllable:

Rácz, head of Slovak mafia   *pronounce as* Rahts
Kubeš, Czech naval officer   Koobesh
Mešťánek, Freddy Piggybank's real name   Meshtyanek
Geľo Todor-Lačný-Dolniak, Junjan Slovak rebel   *pronounce as*
                    Gelyo Todor-Lachnee-Dolnyak
Mozoň, ex-secret policeman   Mozogne [*n as in Boulogne*]

Peter Petro and Donald Rayfield

Book One

Parents' hearts are with their children,
children's hearts are in the taiga.

Junjan Slovak proverb

At this point my much respected readers should be asked if they've ever heard of a gentleman called Rácz. Of course, this is purely a rhetorical question, because if the reader in his boundless kindness has already reached for this modest book, then the author will not be presumptuous in assuming that the name of Rácz is not totally unfamiliar to the reader.

This literary hero's faithful supporters and admirers will certainly be pleased to be told that, in my imagination, he is still having an excellent time. His hotels, restaurants, pizzerias, and casinos prosper just as they did in previous *Rivers of Babylon* books. He is doing equally well in other business activities. Since he is an influential man and knows how to win over similarly influential people, he has managed to privatise successfully some lucrative businesses. Take, for example, the once famous Stupava brewery that was recently going broke. Rácz bought it for peanuts and everybody thought that he was going to asset-strip it. But not Rácz. Not this time. Beer, unlike banking or insurance business, really amused him. He didn't strip its assets: on the contrary, he surrounded himself by experts and invested in new technology. The quality of Stupavar 11°, once so popular, went up. It won a prize at the Agrokomplex Fair and even got a gold medal at the Munich Beer Festival. Using sophisticated media campaigns he taught people how to drink Stupavar. And their new product, the dark beer Mast 16°? It flies off the shelves even in the Czech lands. And that is, as they say, something.

Rácz is no great beer expert. When he needed experts, he bought them. He doesn't drink much beer. He watches his weight. The slightest hint of a paunch is quickly dealt with in his home fitness room. He prefers good whisky, the best. He has been faithful to the *Chivas Regal* brand for many years, but won't say no to other reputable brands either.

"It's not only Scotland where they know how to distil a good whisky! Not just *Heevash Reygahl*!" he remarks and taps a bottle labelled Single Malt. "Malta, too! This Maltese one is quite good!"

Lately, he's acquired a taste for cognac. If you want to please him, give him a bottle of *XO*. He's sure to appreciate it.

Someone once brought him a bottle of a valuable old Armagnac. Rácz thanked him, so as not to offend the donor, but secretly gave the bottle to his chief bodyguard, Mozoň. "Rácz drinks only French cognac!" he declared condescendingly. "Armenian cognac, from what used to be Russia, is only good for ex-secret policemen."

Rácz never refuses a good bourbon, either. "It doesn't always have to be just Scottish or Maltese whisky," he says. "Even the French can make a good one. Their bourbon's not bad at all."

So much about Rácz's consumer habits.

He enjoys living in the luxury villa above the city. He's not often to be found there, however. You're more likely to find him in the Hotel Ambassador Rácz, where he has his office.

If he manages to get home early occasionally, he devotes himself to his family. It's his temple and his refuge in the rough seas of the mundane duties and worries of a major businessman and a man of power. His beautiful, intelligent wife Lenka has borne him two sons: the older, Karol, and the younger, Attila. The boys are bright; they study well. Next year, Karol will go to an élite boarding school in Great Britain.

Karol doesn't like the idea. His friends are here, and he can brag in school about his father. In England, they'll all be like him. Maybe he'll turn out to be the poorest one of all.

In a moment of weakness he confides in his father.

Rácz's eyes almost pop out of his face.

"There's no way Rácz's son is going to be a poor man!" he roars.

Then he calms down. He will put a kind, but stern mask on his face. Karol shouldn't brag about his father's accomplishments. He should brag about what he's going to achieve himself. If he does achieve anything. A bit of modesty never hurt anyone.

Karol's mother joins in. She sides with his father, but she supports her son as well. Now she's unhappy at the idea of losing him for a while. She tries to move the goalposts. She repeats that the boy is sensitive and afraid of being alone. He's eight now and even today he gets into their bed whenever he has a bad dream. Doesn't Rácz love him?

Rácz frowns. Now he has two rivals. He wants his sons to be tough, educated and manly. Not cissies. Yes, he does love Karol; after all he is his first-born son. He loves Attila, the younger one, too. And he loves Lenka, too. But Rácz's love is not soppy or soft. His love is tough, demanding, and strict. He doesn't want to feed his sons fish forever. He wants to teach his sons to catch fish. And do it better than anyone else.

Karol can't grasp that. But he senses his mother could stop things happening, including his father's decision. Didn't she tell him he was afraid of being on his own? Yes, being on his own is what he fears. He's afraid of being on his own.

Rácz laughs. Rácz has been alone ever since childhood. He was an orphan, practically. Nobody liked him. Where he comes from, everyone let him down, and, worse, hurt him. Karol needn't bullshit Rácz, his own father. Rácz looks at his wife; her look of reproach bounces back to his eyes. But Rácz has to say it straight. Karol can't use loneliness as a pretext for defiance. He has no idea what real loneliness is, he's just blathering. When Rácz arrived in the city, in *Rivers of Babylon*, he didn't know anyone there. He stuck out like a sore thumb. He lived in a little hovel behind the boiler-room. Everyone treated him like a mug. But he didn't let them. And why not? Because he's no fool. In the end he worked his way to the top. All that time he found only one being he could confide in and who really loved him. Yes, Karol's mother! She even dropped out of university for Rácz's sake. Because she believed in him. And who was he? A shitty stoker! This is how, like a little flower, he climbed out of his basement up to the light. And he finally got to where he is now. Rácz did it; now he wants Karol to do even better. Not to have to travel even one of the thorny paths his father had to take. He simply wants Karol to start where his father passes the baton to him. To take it further. And higher. So he's got to go to that school. With strict discipline. And English, day and night. That's how winners are educated, fucking right!

Karol's cheeks are puffed. He doesn't want to be like his father. He wants to be a musician. He wants to have guitar or drum lessons.

Rácz clutches his head with his hands. Why guitar? Why drums? No one in the Rácz family needs to learn a musical instrument. The Rácz family has enough money to hire people to play for them. Anytime, even at midnight. Karol will go to school, period. Other boys would shriek for joy. There are boys who study shit-all, because their parents haven't got the money. Rácz, for example, only did two years at agricultural college. That's all his education; luckily he has brains. His parents, God rest their souls, were so stingy that he had to eat his bread buttered underneath, so they couldn't see. They had a boiled egg once a year, at Easter. The leftovers on Karol's plate would have kept Rácz alive for a week when he was his age. A week!

Karol is quiet. He stubbornly shakes his head. That school, that Eton, makes you wear uniform.

"So what?" Rácz claps his hands. "SO WHAT? For Christ's sake! Rácz had to wear overalls all his childhood. Handed down from his father. Even to school. That was his uniform. In summer he went bare-

foot, in winter he wore rubber boots. He used to stuff them with newspapers, and wrapped his feet in newspaper, too, to stop his toes freezing.
Luckily, down south, the winters aren't so bad. Uniforms? That's what
Rácz really appreciates. They'll finally make a man out of Karol. No
more of those revolting baggy jeans, baggy tee shirts and expensive
trainers three sizes too big. By the way, talking about trainers, would
Karol kindly tie his shoelaces? Rácz can't stand the sight of them. He's
waiting. That's more like it. Otherwise Karol might step on his shoelace
and, since he walks about with his head in the clouds like a zombie, he
could easily fall, hit his head, and get even more stupid than he is now!
And those horrible baseball caps! The peak was meant to keep out the
sun. So why is Karol's cap turned rounded with the peak at the back? He
looks like some kind of Jew. And anyway, why does he wear that cap, if
it's a baseball cap? Does Karol play baseball? Has he ever held a baseball bat in his hand? No, he's clumsy at everything. What a bungler! In
England, that school is sure to have baseball, too. He'll learn how to play
and right away he'll find out what that cap is for.

Rácz hopes that his son will at least be happy about that. But Karol is
not the sporty type. He's still in a huff.

And Karol can kindly straighten his back, Rácz orders. They'll teach
him in that school. Twenty hours of P.E. a week. Karol needn't make
faces. There won't be any staff there, no servants, no cleaning woman
over there: Karol will have to do everything for himself. And not only
for himself, but for others, too, because the first year he will have to be a
fag for the older boys. He heard the first time. That's how it is in English
boarding schools. Bullying. But Karol mustn't let it get him down: that's
nothing compared to the bullying that Rácz put up with in army service.
Lešany near Prague. Military unit 5963, third artillery regiment, seventh
battery. That was army service! And he survived. Because he was what?
Because he was no fool, but tough and honest, as well.

Rácz smiles and lights a cigar. He puts his arm round his stubborn
son's shoulders and walks with him through the big French windows
onto the spacious terrace. With his free hand, a cigar between his fingers,
he traces an arc over the city's illuminated night panorama.

"If you cope with all that," he tells his son, "when humility, self-
denial, and hard physical and psychological demands make a better
person of you, then you'll come back here and all this will be yours."

The same way as it now belongs to Rácz.

As a sign of togetherness, he slaps his son on the back.

"May I go inside now?" Karol asks, still in a huff.

"Clear off," says Rácz: he feels let down, shrouds himself in smoke and shreds in his hand an eight-hundred-crown *Romeo y Julietta* cigar.

The panorama of the city is breathtaking. Rácz searches out the lights of the buildings that he owns and slowly calms down. He has been having difficulties lately with distant vision. Everything looks foggy. If he squints, he can see well, but he sees everything double. Rácz is beginning to worry. Could he possibly need glasses? Rácz always used to have an eagle's eyesight.

Luckily the buildings of the hotels Ambassador Rácz I and II are so prominent that the hotelier can effortlesly rest his admiring gaze on them. For a while Rácz plunges into memories. He recalls the times when he was a nobody, stoking the Hotel Ambassador. Gradually working his way up to be the king of the money-changers and a powerful man. And later buying the hotel at auction, surrounding himself with reliable people, and harshly sorting out the Albanian mafia. Yes, Rácz is a big boss, admired and feared. They all obey his every word. Word? They obey if he raises an eyebrow. It's only in his own family that he can't keep order. He's too soft.

In the evening, accompanied by two guards, he drives into town. He enters the Hotel Ambassador, walks through the lobby, and takes a look at the bar. Then he turns on the computer in his office and checks his various businesses' daily takings. One bodyguard stands outside in the hallway; the other one stands near the door, watching the antechamber on the screen. About midnight, people from Rácz's security company, *Sekuritatia*, drag in Sabadoš, the owner of a casino in the centre. He has not been paying into the kitty for his security. Rácz's people have kept an eye on him for a while and have now decided to put the squeeze on him.

Rácz asks a guard to pull off Sabadoš's belt. He beats the guilty man with the belt for a long time. When his right hand begins to hurt, he uses his left. When his left begins to hurt, too, he hands the belt to another guard to carry on. Sabadoš's back and buttocks are minced like a hamburger, he's crying like a woman.

As the guard beats him, Rácz watches him without anger. "Šolík's a kind man," he tells the victim. "If you've got kids, he'll bring them up."

Rácz really ought to have him shot, he says to the whimpering man. He returns the bloodied belt to the guard. Then he resumes his monologue. In the old days, a non-payer would be fished out of the Danube somewhere round Gabčíkovo. But it's Sunday and Rácz is as soft as bread. He couldn't hurt a fly today. He can't punish a man who's stolen from him. Who's stolen from everyone. Yet it would be so simple.

Rácz borrows a pistol from his guard and puts it against the temple of the guilty man.

"Bang and good night!" he says.

He stares into Sabadoš's cowardly piggy eyes. Rácz believes that there must be a core of good in every person. So, he's giving Sabadoš a final chance. But he'll have to pay Rácz back all the security fees, plus thirty per cent interest. Just as it says in the contract. And from now on, he'll have to keep to his payment schedule. After all, the money isn't wasted. They finance their collective security with it. If no one paid, Rácz couldn't pay, arm, and train his security people. Including Sabadoš's security. Anarchy would rule. The Albanians and gypsies would return. The Ukrainians would come, the Chechens, too, and God knows what other scum as well. Is that what Sabadoš wants?

The casino manager is a corpulent man. He has trouble getting off the bench he was tied to. He thought he was a goner. He cries with gratitude and a feeling of something radiant, all-embracing and powerful. The searing pain on his back turns to pure delight at belonging to a being who is radiant, powerful and stern, but forgiving and just. He's never loved Rácz as much as he does now. He mumbles something about temporary problems he's had, saying that he was a real idiot to throw out Rácz's accountant twice running. He'll belatedly apologize to him for that and pay for his torn jacket and broken spectacles. Also, it would be a great honour for Sabadoš if the accountant accepted a small gift from him.

Rácz is radiant.

"Now you're talking, Sabadoš," he says.

Sabadoš wants to kiss Rácz's hands, but Rácz is preoccupied with cutting and lighting his cigar.

Someone from the security team hands Sabadoš an open flick-knife and a towel. He guesses what he will have to do. He turns as pale as chalk, but bravely places his hand on the marble top of the conference table. He lifts the knife.

"No!" says Rácz unbendingly. "Not the little finger. Your thumb."

With the help of Rácz's guards, who swoop on the hand with the knife, Sabadoš gets to work. A loud crack of the bone soon announces that the good deed's been done. The casino owner is as pale as a ghost. He hands Rácz the severed joint of his left thumb. He'd like to apologize again. He needed the money, because the Junjan mafia was putting the squeeze on him. So he used the money he'd put aside for *Sekuritatia*.

Rácz goes red.

"WHAT?" he shouts.

Rácz's people are being hassled by a mafia? Did he hear right? In this city there can only be one mafia and that is the mafia of justice, order, prosperity and a rightful share of the profit: Rácz's mafia.

Sabadoš again breaks down in tears. A wave of joy is followed by a wave of despair, and the waves keep coming. Just like real life.

"These are some kind of new people," he hastily explains. "They're slant-eyed, with big lips like this, strange ones, completely foreign."

Rácz's steely gaze shifts to his security men. He points to Sabadoš, as if the latter spoke from his heart.

So, some immigrants with big lips like that bother people who pay a considerable sum to Rácz for protection, and Rácz's security knows nothing and does nothing? Is that how they work? Where are their eyes?

Rácz looks at the crestfallen Sabadoš.

"And you?" he bawls at him. "Why don't you say anything? Are you Rácz's man or not? How come you let rank outsiders fleece you? What is Rácz here for? Why do you pay him? If you're loyal to Rácz, Rácz will be a thousand times more loyal to you. All you had to do was say the word and Rácz would act. They've threatened Rácz, after all. They've spat in his face. They've shown him that he can't protect people, Rácz's people, who put themselves under his protection."

Rácz pauses for breath. He faces Sabadoš and raises his hands in a flamboyant gesture. Rácz has broken his contract with Sabadoš. He's been disloyal. The knife! Rácz wants that knife. Rácz grabs the knife, puts his fleshy and manicured hand on the table and his eyes search for a suitable place to cut.

"No!" Sabadoš shouts, pleading with him. "No! No!"

It's all Sabadoš's fault! He's guilty of lack of faith. He thought he was paying just for nothing and that if things got tough, no one would come to his aid. Now he can see that it's quite different. Mr. Rácz mustn't do that.

Rácz presses the blade on his index finger, right on the knuckle.

"Oh, my God, don't!" shouts Sabadoš and throws himself at Rácz's self-punishing hand. He pushes it away in the last moment. The knife falls with a clang. Rácz presses his bloodied hand to his chest. One of the guards runs in with a first-aid kit. With a lordly gesture of raised eyebrows, Rácz allows them to treat him.

"Loyalty is not a one-way street," he declares. "Rácz can take the consequences of his mistakes. Look, the knife's cut all the way to the bone. They can all take a look, what the fuck!" Rácz curses in Hungarian. This scar is to remind him and his employees of their duty to people who put themselves under their protection. From now on, Rácz is turning nasty. He can see things for what they are now. The civilian security service, Sekuritatia, is not worth a shit. They've all got too lax. They've got used to everyone being afraid of them. Where, for example, is Mozoň, the manager? He's at home, sitting on his arse, downing Armenian cognac. He used to stay here until midnight. Someone can call him and get him here right away. Things are going to be very different from now on. It'll be a tight ship. Crisis management. Rácz has been too soft; that was a mistake. Something will have to be done now about this new mafia. Rácz wants to see someone from this mafia with his own eyes. They can bring him a couple of these people for a look-see. Alive. Rácz will sit and wait here for one hour. If two of those — what do you call them? — Junjan mafia men aren't brought in within the hour, Rácz will start a big purge of his people. And now, everyone out! And two people can take Sabadoš and his thumb to casualty! Today they can sew pricks back on, so a thumb's easy.

Rácz is alone. He puts on a CD. The room fills with the sound of Italian opera. Rácz stretches out on his sofa and lights a Havana. All sorts of ideas run through his mind. The cut on his skin begins to hurt. A plan is ripening in his mind.

Well, that's enough of Mr Rácz for now. This book is not about him, so we shan't meet him all that often. But occasionally we won't be able to do without him. After all, part of the book will take place in his territorial waters. In any case, the reader must be wondering what is going to happen to the Junjan mafia.

At other times, however, we shall be blundering deep into waters and lands so distant as to surpass even our wildest imagination.

Oh well, off we go again.

* * *

Video Urban suddenly jerks awake. At first he was pondering about himself, his midlife crisis, and so on. He has spent his whole life waiting for something. Everything in his life seemed to him only a prelude for something bright and gloriously wonderful yet to come. And then, one day, in a magical bright moment of honest perception, he realised that the time for waiting was long past. He was horrified by the fact that his life was simply what he was experiencing at the moment. Only then did he get on with things, completely change his ways and finally begin to be content with himself. On this thought he calmly fell asleep, and when he woke up he found to his astonishment that he was sitting at the wheel of a souped-up five-litre BMW, hurtling down the empty motorway at night, heading for Prague at two hundred and thirty kilometres an hour.

Bathed in cold sweat, his eyes goggling, he cried out in fear. The micro-sleep hadn't lasted long, far less than virtual dream time, a few seconds at most. But the left wheels of Urban's heavy limousine were now ploughing into the first few yards of the dusty verge of the motorway. A dream's silky fastenings had lightly touched him, and it had flown off somewhere. Urban remembers only an intense and deliciously painful feeling of love and grati-tude wafting over him. That is how he always imagined God. He tries in vain to track it down a few times; the feeling has gone, just like an unknown and pleasant aroma vanishing.

Urban slows down. He turns on the radio and tunes it to a Czech station. News. Politics. Urban steers with one hand and uses the other to search for music. He's fed up with politics. He was even mixed up in them. But that was a long time ago. It was way back in *Rivers of Babylon*. It's in the past now. It didn't suit him. Sitting in parliament with those idiots bored him, so he got out at the first opportunity. He parted on good terms with his employer, the big businessman and hotelier Rácz. For some time he'd longed to be his own man. So he bought a few failing video stores, renamed them under his nickname Video Urban and in no time turned them round. But it was hard work. Luckily, he understood the business. He loved films.

When the Czechoslovak republic was about to split in two, he began to foresee that all the video distributors working out of Prague would need a Slovak representative. Slovakia would become a foreign country for Czechs and all the big firms would have to open Slovak branches. Everything used to be done in Prague, but now that wouldn't work. If you take the broad view, separation wasn't such a bad idea, Urban thought with relish. Idealists can pine for federation, or found "spiritual parliaments" and other idiocies. People with their feet on the ground, like Urban, have to act.

Without delay, he went to Prague and began to lobby. His cousin Tina, who lived in Prague, helped him a lot. She knew almost anyone who was anybody in the film business there. Urban came back to Bratislava as the representative of a leading distributor, Classic Home Video Entertainment. The Video-Urban hire-shop network and distributorship for Classic Home Video Entertainment sufficed to make him happy and reasonably well-off.

But then his business ran out of steam. Satellite TV got cheaper and then a new TV channel NOVA began to broadcast. What's more, there was cable TV, too. Cash flow went down. And the director of Classic Home Video kept his margins down. But Video Urban wouldn't be Video Urban if he hadn't thought of a dodge. He bought a few hi-fi video machines, a mixing deck and began to make illegal copies. He photocopied the video packaging in colour. A videocassette made by Urban was indistinguishable from the original. But this didn't work for long, either. Producers began to use coding and hologram stickers. Urban was back where he started.

But then he met Freddy in Prague: this was the conclusive inducement he needed to begin a venture which he had long ago decided on.

Usually, video films produced in Slovakia are made for the Czech market, too, and are dubbed into Czech. Slovaks tolerate Czech, but Czechs can't understand Slovak. This applies equally to porn videos made by *Freddy Vision*. Freddy uses Slovak actors for his films. Then Urban goes to Prague, rents a studio and dubs them with Czech actors and actresses. He uses the opportunity to make English-language versions, not with these actors, but with young Americans living in Prague. They'll happily do anything for money. Among them are a lot of drug addicts, male and female, and they'd have flesh cut off their bodies in front of the camera for money. "Actually, that's worth knowing," says Freddy when he hears about it.

So Urban, once again, now has working copies of new films in his car boot. He's booked a studio; he'll start dubbing tomorrow. There isn't much dialogue in Freddy's films, but what there is, is very juicy. Some actresses blush when dubbing. These are lesser known actresses, usually students of the Prague Academy of Dramatic Arts. Sometimes they also use a provincial theatre actress. Urban chooses the voices carefully: it has to be a deep, exciting voice with a rasp to it, like Eliška Balzerová's, or his cousin Tina's.

Finally, Urban gives up surfing the radio. He holds the steering wheel with one hand and uses the other to insert a cassette, the first that comes to hand in the dark. A new album by the Rebels fills the car's quiet upholstered space.

Video Urban rolls down the window and breathes in. He presents his face to the powerful cold wind that blows the scent of dusty, hoary dried hay overlaid by fresh night rain from the meadows round the motorway.

The motorway glistens. Through a veil of rain, the lights of a petrol station flash in the darkness. At last. On the left he sees the motel Střechov.

Now Prague is just a stone's throw away. Relieved, Urban indicates and turns off to the service area.

* * *

It snowed again that night. It's pitch dark. The moon's invisible. A blizzard is raging. The igloos on the coast are snowbound. The anchor cables of the boats shriek in pain.

Geľo Todor-Lačný-Dolniak, a member of the Slovak national resistance, can't sleep any longer. The snowstorm has been raging for days now. In his nervous half-sleep Geľo turns and tosses. Every bit of his body hurts. He uses the back of his hand to wipe away the spittle dripping from the left corner of his mouth and wetting the reindeer-skin pillow. The strong, hard-working hands of this former hunter, now a resistance fighter, can't help opening and clenching under the bedcovers. He'd rather be somewhere deep in the tundra, catching arctic foxes. Or waiting by a hole in ice for a walrus or seal to come out, or setting traps, counting the fur hides and, after a successful hunting trip, resting contentedly in his heated reindeer yurt among his close family, with warm food in his belly. But Geľo and his men have to freeze, fight, attack transport convoys, destroy Junjans' dwellings, kill Junjan mercenaries, and wage a guerrilla war. Slovaks have many enemies. They have to be thoroughly and mercilessly exterminated. But even that can't be done now. They have to wait for the blizzard to end, and then, back to work!

Geľo listens to the sound of the snowstorm crashing into the icy igloo's thick walls. His brain is swamped by a wave of helplessness and panic. But he soon recovers. If Geľo's boys, the Slovaks of Junja, are holed up, then so are the mercenaries working for the Junjans. They are even more paralysed, since they've been recruited from all over the world and can't handle bad weather as well as the Slovaks of Junja, who have been living here for several generations. The storms put the mercenaries out of action, and the Slovak guerrillas at least have a bit of time to rest. Sometimes that rest time drags on unbearably.

Geľo turns over again. He gives his hatred free rein. He allows it to plot a dastardly plan. He wonders how to surprise the Junjans and disturb their hibernation. He is depressed by the truce enforced by the long polar night and by the blizzard. He amuses himself for a while by thinking how to punish the mercenaries' leader, Tökörnn Mäodna, when his men capture him. But for foreign mercenaries from all corners of the world, Ćmirçăpoļ, the capital of the former Junjan Autonomous Soviet Socialist

Republic (known today as the Junjan Khanate), would have fallen into Slovak hands a long time ago. Junjans are poor fighters: lazy and cowardly. But they pay foreigners to do it for them. People like Tökörnn Mäodna. Who knows if that's his real name? Who knows what wind blew him here? He's cruel. He spares neither women nor children.

The other men of Geľo's group are also turning feverishly in their furs. They unconsciously touch the triggers of their automatic weapons, mostly of Czech manufacture, as if they were sensitive spots on the bodies of their women or girlfriends. They're dreaming of freedom.

Frolo Sirovec-Molnár is smiling in his sleep. He must surely be with his young wife whom he had to leave in the taiga with the nomadic reindeer herders, just as the other men had to. The Junjans and their mercenaries won't find them there. They're safe.

The nomads are Slovaks, too. With thousands of head of reindeer they wander to and fro over the tundra like the biblical Moses in his desert. But, unlike Moses, they have no fixed goal. For their treks they use lightning-fast sledges with sails. They follow the reindeer and appear now here, now there. They like to make extra money gathering a special kind of lichen that the coastal trading posts buy to resell round the world for use in the perfume industry. The nomads are meeker than coastal Slovaks like Geľo and his friends. But they hate the Junjans, too. They are no warriors: they do what they can to help the guerrillas by taking care of their families and of secret stores of supplies hidden in the tundra.

Geľo thinks of his wife Elena. She is with the rich herder Kresan, a relative of theirs. Geľo's brother Martin married into the Kresan family. As well as his wife Elena, Geľo has left his five children and his crippled father with the Kresans. He took only his oldest son with him. Two other brothers of Geľo, Samo and Adam, have also come to join the fight against the Slovaks' enemies.

Adam became a sniper and he fell — from the roof of a twelve-storey building in Úŕġüllpoļ, when Tökörnn Mäodna's mercenaries flushed him out. He preferred to jump rather than fall into the hands of cruel adventurers from every corner of the world. He left behind a pregnant wife, Zuzana; Geľo's wife took care of her. After final victory, Geľo will have to take care of her, too, and inherit her from his brother as his wife, and the newborn son or daughter will be his child inherited from his brother. This is the Junjan Slovak custom, for the sea or tundra often claims a good man, the head of a family.

Geľo quite looks forward to it. Particularly to honouring tradition, which animates him even more than the actual instinct to reproduce.

Thinking of Zuzana means that Geľo wakes up with an erection. When he and Sirovec-Molnár were taken on an aeroplane to the unknown world, to Prague, for negotiations with military bigwigs, they gave him a gift for her. It was a small flask with a yellowish liquid. Perfume. He believes that one day he'll have a chance to give it to her. He has something for Elena, too.

Geľo is thirsty. He clicks his dry tongue, but it doesn't help. He is reluctant, however, to climb out of his furry den and drink warmed-up water from the teapot. It's cold in the igloo and warm under the skin of a young reindeer. In his sleep he unwittingly stuck his foot out: it has turned violet and lost all feeling. He pulls it in and quickly massages it against the other foot.

The magic mushrooms that the hunters gather in spring from under the snow make them sleep well and long. You dream colourful dreams about travel in time and space. And even after waking up, the world is somehow more colourful for a while.

"Why aren't you asleep, Dad?" asks his son, Jurko.

"I can't," says Geľo.

"The blizzard's going on for a long time," says Jurko.

"True," says Geľo.

"I wonder if it blows on Tökörnn Mäodna as it does on us," says Jurko.

When he hears the name of the Junjan mercenaries' leader spoken, Geľo frowns.

"Don't babble so much, son," he warns him. "You've got an old man's mind."

"I just meant…" Jurko apologizes.

"I'm the leader," Geľo says firmly. "If I say we'll sleep, then we'll sleep. Until I change my mind. If you don't like it, you can take the dogs and go back to the tundra, to your mother and grandpa."

"I just meant…" Jurko becomes afraid.

"And quiet, or you'll wake up the men!" Geľo says sternly. "Who knows when we'll next get so much sleep? We must stock up on sleep."

The boy is quiet.

Geľo even feels sorry for him. On the other hand, he wouldn't want a babbler for a son. "When the storm's over, we'll go hunting. Just you and me," he says to make him feel better.

He lies for a while and thinks about his next steps. Finally, he climbs out from the furry bed with a sigh and, as he is, in his sealskin underpants, he gets up for a drink of warm water.

Through the howling blizzard he catches the sound of cautious footsteps and heavy breathing.

Gef'o freezes. Could it be Junjan mercenaries? They've never yet dared to come close, or in the polar night. Gef'o reaches for his gun and quietly, so as not to wake anyone in the ice house, he pulls back the bolt.

He looks at Jurko. In the oil lamp's feeble light he sees that the boy has also got up and is standing, his gun ready, by the other side of the entrance. Gef'o smiles at him reassuringly. Then he takes a deep breath and opens the first leather curtain. The cold wakes him fully. He pushes through the second curtain and now he is separated from the blizzard just by the third leather curtain. Jurko keeps his one pace behind him.

Gef'o crosses himself and steps out of the igloo. The terrible cold momentarily freezes all his body's muscles, but suddenly a massive dark object hurls itself at him with a ferocious roar and a stench of rotting fish. Gef'o fires blindly and the corner of his eye notes flashes from Jurko's gun. Several exploding dumdum bullets enter the enemy's body and rip off bits of tissue. The intruder howls and tries to flee, but the bullets have done their lethal job. His movements get slower and slower, his giant paws slowly try to ward off inevitable death; he finally stiffens.

Gef'o looks closer at the polar bear he's killed.

"Why did he come so close?" he wonders aloud.

Somewhere out in the ice a crack must have opened, he thinks. Could spring have come so soon?

The shots wake the men from Gef'o's guerrilla group. They've all come out with their weapons, ready to fight.

"Nice work," says Sirovec-Molnár, poking his gun in the white fur.

"I thought it was Mäodna's people," Gef'o explains, as if apologizing for the noisy awakening.

"And what if it were the *Ökötöm-kökötom*, the snow monster?" asked Turanec-Štefánik.

The men grow silent with horror.

"What would he do here, on the coast?" Gef'o dismisses the idea with a wave of his hand. "Nobody's ever seen him so far from the taiga."

"Let us thank God for a nice breakfast," the priest crosses himself and presses the safety catch on his gun.

Soon the bear's paws, tongue and carefully chosen pieces of rump are roasting over the fire, spreading, with a crackling sound, their seductive aroma all round.

"By God," Gef'o nods, impatiently trying the roast meat. "Don't we have it good? Who has it better?"

The men sit around the fire, casually clean their weapons and salivate in expectation.

The blizzard intensifies.

When the meat is cooked, the fighters eat. Then they quietly sit and watch each other. What can you do? The igloo is small and low, you can't even practise close combat here. The ice and snow walls would be kicked down. So, to while away the time, they tattoo each other: beautiful, colourful tattoos on their arms, legs, chests and faces. The more tattoos a Junjan Slovak has, the more respected a hunter and fighter he is.

"Men, why don't you tell us what it was like in the world, in Prague?" Čižmár-Turoň suggests.

"But we've told you the story over ten times ten before…" mumbles Frolo, as they tattoo his back with a giant bear and a red sun above it.

"So?" Čižmár-Turoň won't accept this. "When will we ever travel so far? So shut up and tell us!"

Sirovec-Molnár, his forehead propped on his arms, pretends to sleep.

Geľo sighs and starts the tale. How they travelled there and how they were fed, given clothes and housing; how they negotiated with high-ranking gentlemen in uniforms who talked to them as equals. And how these gentlemen enquired about the slightest details of the mineral grease that oozes from under the ground in the north.

"Yes, the Czechs will help us," Geľo insisted. "They're genuine friends. I liked them right away. They're almost the same as us."

That is how their days pass: they are standing by, but alert.

* * *

Freddy awakes and gets up. His feet grope for his slippers. He does it all completely automatically in the dark, so as not to wake up his wife, Sida. It takes him time to realise that Sida is making a film in Bojnice.

He goes to the bathroom. After urinating, he stands over the bowl, waiting patiently for the last drop. Like all fat men, he has a wet spot on his underpants because he doesn't shake his member enough. He turns on the bathroom light. He looks in the mirror. He's quite proud of himself. His complexes have receded into the past for ever. He started at zero, so to speak. First he had to work hard as a car park attendant, then the car park was closed down and he had no idea what he would do without it. But he found a way out. Changing into an assistant executioner's leather and latex outfit, he helped out his current wife, who made her living as a dominatrix in a sado-masochistic salon of a perverts' club called *Justina*.

He didn't make much from it, since he had a slave's inferior status, and his only sweet rewards were kicks and blows he got from the mistress he idolized. Later he progressed and began to write and produce one-act pieces in a little theatre, part of the club, for perverted dramatic shows. Subsequently, he studied film at the Academy of Arts, supporting himself by writing porn film scripts. He was born for pornography; he had a wild imagination and a rare talent for particularly disgusting detail. After getting his bachelor's degree, he threw himself into directing and gradually became to be successful. When he met his old friend Urban at a video trade show in Prague, they decided to set up a joint firm to produce porn films and successfully compete with foreign producers of smut.

Though Freddy hates Prague, he nevertheless likes to recall his trip there, some three years ago, when at a trade show of video distributors in Prague-Holešovice, he met Urban. Freddy came there as a guest of a Danish production company Sex-O-Rama. They paid him poorly, but one of the perks was being invited to places. Board, lodging and drinks were free and this was enough to give Freddy a feeling of importance and an illusion of belonging to the alluring world of porn business.

Freddy loved looking round the trade show exhibits. His pleasure was all the greater for not having to do anything. All he had to do was to represent the company. He had already done his job, he thought. Now let the others work. The ones whose job is to sell the result of his work: the young and ambitious German- and English-speaking managers. Yes, as far as Freddy was concerned, the skies were blue. Wearing a well-cut fashionable lilac jacket, a glass of sparkling wine in his hand, he would stand by the Sex-O-Rama stand and look about. Occasionally, he looked at other stands. Other firms' young, slender, dynamic female employees, dressed, perhaps deliberately, in identical outfits to stress their role as successful working women: that was something he'd always liked. He could imagine some of them in his power, in his greedy hands. Tears of shame, despair and pain would furrow those beautiful proud faces, masks of a belief in their personal importance, attractiveness and independence. Beautiful, unattainable artificial faces, made up every morning over simple country faces, would melt like icing on a cake, and the underlying unhappy grimaces, snot flowing from their noses and pale lips, would be revealed. Freddy titivated himself, guessing by their walk which of them was wearing tights, or stockings with garters, or old-fashioned stockings with a suspender belt. In fact, fetishists see the whole world through stockings and underwear. Alas, all the pleasure of this game was spoiled by the impossibility of verifying his observations there and then with his eager, damp hand. And he only needed just one lightning-fast touch. Unfortunately, that touch would be his last. He'd certainly be thrown out, official representative or not. The certainty that he'd never know the truth filled him with despair: he headed for the bar to fortify himself with his favourite drink. He was a fetishist; he liked stockings. The actresses in his films never fucked without them. Even if completely naked during shooting, they had to keep their stockings on.

Freddy was already thinking up a new script. The film would take place in this kind of erotic trade show. A man who'd just joined the firm would inspect his female boss, this same kind of severe, well-dressed beauty. She would notice and start to humiliate him with absurd orders. Finally, he'd get her on her own in a room behind the show stands, lock the door and give her a very rough seeing-to. They'd have wild inter-course while, a few feet from them, behind the show's flimsy fibreboard walls, hundreds of visitors would pass by, not suspecting the perversities going on under their noses. Her shouts and suppressed moans would merge completely with the background noise of a big erotic trade show, where dozens of porn films played simultaneously on the video screens.

A multinational crowd sat and stood at the bar. Czech, Slovak, German, English, Hungarian, and Italian could be heard. The Slovak and Czech representatives stood out in their loud garish jackets and white socks, while the foreigners were dressed in subfusc. Behind the bar two women darted to and fro, as if competing with each other.

"Freddy!" came a shout behind Piggybank. "Freddy Piggybank!"

Intrigued, Freddy turned round; a long time had passed since he'd last been addressed by the nickname he had when he worked at the car park by the Hotel Ambassador.

"Urban!" he said not without a certain feeling of joy.

Video Urban had been the one money-changer outside the Hotel Ambassador who never looked down on Freddy and never made fun of him. He always talked to Freddy as an equal. Freddy sees Urban, despite the years they have not seen each other, as something of a friend. Which is why Freddy was almost moved to see him.

"Yes, I'm happy," boasted Piggybank, when they came to the bar and Urban asked him the obligatory question.

Freddy has a completely free hand. Nobody forces him to do any-thing. Sometimes he shoots a really avant-garde film: pissing, rubber, latex, spanking, and bondage. He can get away with anything.

"Sometimes creative freedom is even more important than money," concluded Freddy with an old avant-gardist's expression, but his face showed a certain degree of resignation. In short, he was resigned to the realisation that fulfilling all his perverted desires and getting really well paid for it, too, was an unattainable luxury in his life. To be able to move in the seductive world of the porn business and to have some of its glitter sprinkled on him was in itself sufficient reward for Freddy. It was almost like a dream come true to have the chance to meet porn stars over whose pictures in the grimy and wrinkled pages of the porn magazines he only recently used to masturbate in the lavatory.

Urban did not even understand all the foreign words that burbled with such relish through Freddy's fleshy lips. What he did understand was that Freddy's talent and perverted imagination could bring great wealth to anyone who exploited him and offered him better conditions than the stupid, greedy Danes. Clearly, in his field Freddy was a real star who needed a little more motivating to show all his brilliance.

"You can have creative freedom and not be screwed, money-wise, at the same time," he told Piggybank.

Had Freddy thought of going independent? Urban could put up the capital; Freddy would bring his ideas and talent. They'd set up their own company. Wouldn't Freddy like to have his own firm, his own business?

Freddy started to pay attention.

"Porn is on the up today," Urban continued. "People go for it. You only have to read the papers."

Why shouldn't the two of them cash in on it? Why not get rich?

Freddy went red with excitement. He motioned to the bar girl and ordered two glasses of beer. Urban couldn't believe his eyes. The last time he saw Freddy pay was in *Rivers of Babylon*, just after the fat man went mad, before wrecking the whole bar and becoming, for a time, the hermit of the car park by the Hotel Ambassador. Even though beer was the cheapest item at the bar, it was, nevertheless, a noteworthy act. Urban grasped that his offer had interested and excited Freddy.

"Did you say 'cash in'?" Freddy was intrigued. "Cash in?"

Oh, Freddy'd love to!

After half an hour's conversation and another two glasses of beer, ordered, of course, by Urban, they had a deal. They would set up a limited company. They'd produce their own porn films.

Freddy knew what the public wanted.

"Men screwing women don't interest anyone now," he said sceptically. "Not even if five men screw one woman. Or if one man screws five women. Not even if they do it in a Rolls Royce, a castle, or a bathroom. Not if they screw under water or in the air. Maybe in a lavatory might work: that's people for you. Nobody's interested even in blacks. Not even in ones with long pricks." Freddy hopes Urban understands. "Black and Asian women are passé, too. Shaved cunts don't sell, either. Every other sixteen-year-old sunbathing at Golden Sands has a shaved pussy under her costume. People want things they lack courage for themselves. Anal, whipping, enemas, pissing, shitting, bondage, old whores, violence, torture, children, animals, live killing. That's today's world." Urban needn't stare at him like that: Freddy didn't invent this world.

Freddy greedily sips his beer and licks the foam off his moustache.

Urban should realise that men may think up the filth, but women are always keen to join in. Urban should note that all, even the most outrageous and perverse filth invented by a man always finds willing and enthusiastic female protagonists. "It's in the female character. If a man couldn't find a woman who'd let someone piss on her breasts and crotch, then he wouldn't think up a film where a woman lets someone piss on her breasts and crotch; that's pretty obvious. If a man couldn't find a woman to suck off an eight-year-old boy or let herself be penetrated by a pit-bull terrier, then it simply couldn't be done, and that's all there is to it. This is a basic law of the porn industry: you'll always find a beautiful woman willing to collaborate with anything."

Freddy waved his arms about contemptuously and had a drink.

"Of course, films like that will never be shown here," he continues. "They only have routine stuff here. Maybe a bit of sado-maso and preggo, but that's it."

Piggybank was licking his lips, even his cheeks, as he pontificated.

Urban couldn't understand it. A long time ago he used to enjoy having two partners, Wanda and Eva, in bed at home, but it never occurred to him to tie them down, whip them, or give them an enema. Anyway, they both ran away from him when they got a chance to go to Australia. Perhaps that's why they ran away, Urban reflected.

Urban trusted Freddy completely. He knew that, whatever else Freddy might be, he was a pro and knew what he was talking about.

Freddy was so excited by their meeting and by the new prospects opening up, that, to Urban's surprise, he paid the whole bill.

That evening they went to celebrate their meeting at Urban's favourite restaurant, the nearby *Domažlice Room*, a stylish place with old Czech cuisine and a well-stocked cellar of Moravian wines. A pleasant dinner in the company of two hostesses from Sex-O-Rama turned into an endless pub crawl across Prague. After midnight they lost both women, who were picked up by some Yanks in an Irish pub in Malá Strana.

Now they were sitting in a garden café by the Charles Bridge, seeing who could drink more tequila. Freddy never liked Prague as much as Urban, but for a man with a full wallet any city is beautiful. He watched the lights of pleasure boats going up and down the Vltava and felt wonderful. He prudently decided to let Video Urban briefly tell his own story; they could then get back to Freddy's life, which Freddy thought more important, interesting, and fascinating than anyone else's.

Urban's story had to be squeezed out drop by drop. He had to down two more tequilas to get it out. He distributes videos for a Czech firm. They keep him on a tight leash and he can't slip his lead. Moreover, by sheer accident he's discovered that the director of the firm, a repulsive Czech faggot called Hojer, is plotting behind his back to set up a Slovak branch. Without Urban. Hojer found a traitor in Urban's firm, his business manager Ján Teľacina. Maybe he likes him: Ján is a handsome boy who would do anything to advance his career, including offering Hojer his arse. The problem is, he's also infinitely stupid. In a well-fitting suit and tie he does look impressive, but, actually, he's just a car mechanic. Of course, a trained car mechanic also has a chance, Urban believes, to do something with his life. The problem is that Hojer needs Teľacina merely as a slave to betray Urban and clear the ground for Hojer, in a mistaken hope that the latter will promote him to manager of the new branch. This is just Teľacina's illusion, fostered by Hojer. Once it's all set up, a Hojer man from Prague will get the manager's job and Teľacina will go on in the business department working as a slave. But Teľacina doesn't know this. Just as Hojer doesn't know that Teľacina is a heroin addict. He even got the engineer Zdutá, who does the accounts, onto heroin, and she left her husband because of Teľacina. It's got so bad with them that they sometimes shoot up during the day in the lavatory. When Urban gets back from Prague, he'll fire them both for breach of trust. There's no law to stop him firing a pair of addicts whose next trick will be nicking videos in the warehouse. Yes, those two filthy toe-rags will be out on their necks. He won't keep them on, even if they get a doctor to say that they're clean. They've betrayed him, after all. If Urban succeeds in the venture with Freddy, he'll cancel his partnership with Hojer. Someone else can distribute his kitsch in Slovakia.

Freddy was nodding, but only half listening. When Urban paused, Freddy had his moment again. He started to talk about himself. And he talked and talked. He hadn't had an opportunity for a long time to talk like this. He told Urban everything, including how good it made him feel knowing that thousands of men lecherously watched his wife Sida in the films he makes for the Danes. He was gradually getting drunk. His outpourings turned into incoherent blather.

A few hours later Freddy was most put out by the fact that every pub where they stopped, and from which he subsequently had to be carried out like a piece of luggage, was full of the sound of Czech. Freddy was drunk. He sat with his face pressed onto the table, occasionally lifting his forehead, imprinted with the tablecloth, and feeling a need to react to the ever-present Czech element, the Czech sea that constantly surrounded them, washed over them and, by dawn, threatened to engulf them.

"You prick," he addressed Urban with his last bit of energy, "why do you speak Czech to them, when you're a Slovak?"

"Because it's a foreign language," responded Urban. "In London I don't try to communicate in Slovak, either. In Vienna I speak German. So why would I risk being misunderstood? I speak Czech, so I use it."

Freddy looked at him with glassy eyes. He couldn't understand a thing. He didn't like those bloody Czechs. Then his head dropped.

"He's not used to drink," Urban said to someone in Czech; Freddy had no idea whether it was in the same pub, or another one.

"Which hotel are you at?" asked Urban towards morning in some night casino, where billiards players were banging in the background.

Freddy thought long and hard. Several times he fell into a light sleep, and then his head collapsed between the glasses of Guinness.

"No sleeping here, sir" someone objected in a night bar on Wenceslas Square.

At the time Freddy's head was propped on a table, his eyes were closed and he was dribbling onto the carpet. A voice came from above, over Freddy. It was polite, but authoritative.

"Hotel!" Urban was shaking him on the pavement where he had half-carried him. "What's the name of your hotel?"

"International," said Freddy. "Or Intercontinental?"

He was being driven somewhere in a taxi. He heard Urban's voice on a mobile phone.

"He's not staying in the Intercontinental," someone said: it sounded like a court judgement.

Voices conversed softly in the dark. Freddy thought it was about him. He pulled himself together and blabbed a few words. He needed to vomit. The taxi stopped and Freddy vomited on a roadside lawn.

"Better now?" he heard Urban behind him.

He silently nodded with tears in his eyes. Urban gave him a tissue and helped him into the car. The taxi moved off. On one hand, Freddy wanted it to slow down, as his head was spinning. On the other, he wanted it to speed up, so as to get to bed sooner.

He woke up as Urban dragged him past the hotel reception; as soon as he felt the cool, slightly mildewy touch of the hotel bedclothes, he passed out.

In the morning he awoke in the same position. At first he wanted to die. Any kind of thought led to an attack of nausea. He was afraid to open his eyes. When he plucked up courage, he found a note on his bedside table. He had to close one eye and screw up the other: "WHEN YOU'RE OK, CALL MY MOBILE." The number was written down.

Freddy lay there like a dying man. Around eleven, a chambermaid knocked at the door, but Freddy just shouted out something wildly, as much as the pain under his forehead allowed, and cursed. It took him the entire morning to pull himself together. Only then did he call Urban. He knew that it was a splendid idea to set up a company and go independent, and there was no need to hesitate.

FORBIDDEN PLEASURES: The Best of Freddy Vision— dubbed into Czech: 120 minutes.

The cassette has four short films. The first one begins with a club's two cleaning women who, instead of washing the floor, get off by torturing each other. But their female boss catches them in the act... she lights candles and the performance begins: hot pincers, whip, handcuffs, chains, punishment cross, rack, and hot wax all leave their marks on the tormented bodies. The second film shows a slave tortured, using similar instruments. The focus is on the torture of his balls and penis. In the third film, a policeman puts a very young girl in prison on a false charge. In a cell with a lesbian and a randy policeman, she suffers one humiliation after another. In the cell, we witness her strangulation, bondage, and gagging, beating and, above all, constant humiliation. In the fourth story a young village boy riding a bike is hit by a car and kidnapped. His two brutal female kidnappers drive him to their own torture chamber where he undergoes sophisticated torture. The boy manages to free himself and the roles are immediately reversed. The kidnappers now beg for mercy as they are brutally tortured, pissed on, shat on and sodomized again and again by the randy and, as it later turns out, utterly perverted primary-school pupil. The kidnappers cannot expect anything but prolonged torments and a death, not at all undeserved, from unspeakable torture and humiliation.

Order N°: 1820 0129

31

Price: 999 Czech Crowns
Price for club members: 950 Czech Crowns
(From the sales catalogue of *Freddy Vision*)

* * *

Freddy found coming up with a title, logo and corporate culture for the new company the most interesting task.

Westerners come here to shoot films because it's cheap, Freddy claimed. The films are unbelievably crappy. Viewers aren't really interested in more and more luxurious settings and ordinary fucking. Nor are they interested in the minor variations: sex in a Rolls Royce, in a castle, in a fancy restaurant. People want something unusual in the actual fucking, not in its location. People are not interested in seeing more and more beautiful women and more and more beautiful and exclusive settings. Where will it end? Soon they'll be screwing in the presidential office under the clock that you see in the New Year's presidential address. And then what? Freddy knows what to offer people. He'll offer them filth. The foulest filth you can get on a porn cassette. Filth with beautiful women is the right combination. Are we any worse than the westerners? Are our women uglier, our imagination inferior? No, no and no. Only we don't have the stars. So we'll create some. A few years ago nobody had ever heard of Hungarian and Czech porn stars, someone had to create them, too. So let's make our own Slovak porn stars. We'll have several genres. Straight fucking will be called *Simply Fuck*. Then we'll have a series for the piss fans: *Champagne Avantgarde*. The shit series will be known as *Caviar Avantgarde*. The sado-masochistic one we'll call *Perversum Universum*. Child pornography, and we want that, too, as it's increasingly fashionable and popular, will be called *Lolita Parade*. And the series of bestiality porn can be called *Animal Instinct*.

Given his new, successful life, Freddy finally went to see a doctor for a complete health check. To know how things stood. He got surprising news: The blood clot on his brain that caused his childhood tantrums had been absorbed over the years and had vanished without trace. He was totally healthy and normal. That made Freddy happy. He had always known that he was not mad. Now it was official, on paper.

Soon all that was in the distant past. Urban scraped the money together and the first cassette in a *Freddy Vision* series was on the market. It was pretty filthy, so it flew off the shelves. Nobody minded the lack of hi-fi stereo sound. Soon Freddy and Urban were rubbing their hands. They didn't have to wait long for a second cassette. Urban and Freddy had made it not just in the domestic market, but in Europe, too. They had become successful European-style porn producers.

Less than four years have passed, and Freddy is a fabulously rich film producer. His and Urban's *Freddy Vision* has several dozen employees. Apart from a big crowd of actresses, actors and independent crew members. The videos of *Freddy Vision* and *Perversum Universum* brands are among the most hard-core and most sought-after porn on the domestic market. Some titles have even been banned from distribution in Slovakia and the Czech Republic. Freddy and his partner don't give a toss; they have a grateful public in Germany and elsewhere.

In one society magazine Freddy was even called a European porn king. Then he ran from one office to another with a copy in his hand. Every one of his employees had to see the published photograph. In a quiet but solemn voice Freddy declaimed the whole column dedicated to his person. After he'd run round all his company's offices, he locked himself in his study that he shared with the ever-absent Video Urban. He opened a papier mâché globe which concealed a rich assortment of nicely flavoured drinks and poured himself a full glass of Cointreau: to celebrate. He liked this liqueur's inimitable orange aroma, sweet taste and, incidentally, very high alcohol content, which made it a classic distillate. It was superb on ice and, paradoxically, it was an extraordinarily refreshing drink. When he'd downed the Cointreau and crushed the ice, he made a new mark on the label, wrote down the date and put the bottle and the glass where he'd got it from. For a long time he stood in front of the mirror, his fists clenched. Alfréd Mešťánek was a European porn king! And that was just the start. Well, he'd show them all!

The water boils for coffee. Freddy quits his memories, makes a Turkish coffee, and adds cream and a few spoonfuls of sugar. Cup in hand, he enters his study and turns on the light. He sits down at the computer. Before he turns it on, he checks his watch. It's almost five. Freddy likes to get up this early and sit in his pyjamas for a few hours, writing a new script until the time comes to go to work.

Fresh damp air blows from the nearby pond. After his parents died Freddy had complex renovations done to their house, and he and his family moved into what is now a luxury villa. He likes living there. Each tree and each stone remind him of his childhood. The house is big and spacious. A pool, a fitness centre, and a small wine cellar are tucked away in the basement. But there have been no visitors there yet. Freddy is stingy and doesn't invite anyone. They can all buy their own drinks.

Recalling his years at the university, studying scriptwriting in Bratislava, arouses mixed emotions. He had to write real scripts then. Their
professor, a popular and successful scriptwriter, made them all write
similar, formally perfect scripts. Now he's a successful artist, Freddy
doesn't have to do anything. He sketches the action in a few lines and
improvises the rest while shooting. Actually, if you come to think of it,
Freddy earns his daily bread easily and joyfully. He's loaded. He has a
fine wife, pretty and respectable, at his side, and they have a beautiful
healthy child. Life can sometimes be wonderful, really.

The main character of the forthcoming film is, of course, his beloved
Sida. Using the pseudonym Siedah Strong, a cruel smile on her made-up
face and a whip in her hand, under Freddy's direction she's become a
porn star of European renown. She's a success. All the more so since she
has never had sex in any of her films: she only tortures and punishes,
while the juicy sex is always provided by her female assistants. Freddy
reflects: should he let her finally have real intercourse? That would be a
sensation, something totally new. It would be like Wilma, the legendary
Dutch porn star of Color Climax Corporation's zoophiliac works, letting
herself make love to a man. Interesting.

The new film will take place at the time of the Holy Inquisition.
Freddy hasn't a clue about the period, but he's not inhibited: he's never
cared about historical accuracy. Perhaps Siedah can even use her legendary SS-style leather cap. Freddy writes a part to suit her when he makes
her a cruel judge-inquisitor who uses various methods to interrogate
several young, well-built men suspected of witchcraft. Everything takes
place in the gloomy location of a mediæval torture chamber. Siedah has
beautiful assistants but they are terribly cruel. Their job is to find out if
the young men really are in league with the devil. They find out by
sexually exciting the men in various ways. If the young men turn out to
be male witches, it will be proved by their over-developed sexual organs
and marked virility. Of course, they are devils incarnate.

Freddy has worked out this much. He just doesn't know how to end
it. But he's not interested in the ending today. There's plenty of time for
that. Today he has to think up a title for this new opus. He types the first
that comes to mind: STRONG INQUISITION. He pauses and mulls his
idea over. He runs it mutely past his lips a few times. The sense is good.
It suggests that this is another film in the series starring Siedah Strong.
At the same time, the target group will be attracted by the dark practices
of the inquisition. But the sound, the sound of it! It's too long and there
are too many syllables, too many sibilants. Sida has enough of them in

her screen name already. Freddy thinks about it. Then he writes:
STRONG JUSTICE. He rubs his hands in satisfaction. This is more like
it. It has the screen name "Strong", and that's a guarantee of quality.
There's also a hint of the courts, and that means strictness. In fact, there's
twice as much strictness now. Freddy frowns. Unfortunately, there are
more sibilants than ever. Freddy clenches his fist. He drinks his coffee.
The title is wrong. It sounds like a bad western. Freddy reflects once
more. Then he writes: ANAL JUSTICE. Yes, this could be it. The title is
unambiguous and apt. Anal sex is in fashion now. Men like it. They like
to watch. They don't dare do it themselves. It either repels them, or they
don't get hard enough to penetrate the rectum. Or they may be too shy to
ask a woman to offer her buttocks. Or they ask and are rejected. Freddy
looks worried. What if there's been too much anal sex recently, he wonders. Will the target group be attracted? Is the word "anal" still a good
enough magnet? In the end he decides it is. Now he has to include at
least one anal sex scene, and it's done. Besides, what if he used young
transsexuals, instead of young men? They'd act the beautiful witches
until the moment they undress for torture. Then the young girls with gorgeous breasts would turn out to have big hard penises under their skirts.
Hmm. Freddy tries to imagine it. The computer fan hums in the dark.

To be a rich, successful artist is lovely. And magically easy.

ANAL PAIN, dubbed into Czech, length: 60 min.

*Another superb film in the popular Siedah Strong series! The post-
man brings to a perverted dominatrix's underground torture chamber a
wooden crate holding two very young female sex slaves. These girls are
the daughters, kidnapped and tied up, of a powerful drug dealer. The
sender of this arousing package demands the harshest punishment
possible for the girls. A superb serenade of pain for two slaves and one
crazy dominatrix follows. The torture includes the use of various SM aids
and some of the unlikeliest objects. Whipping until the first sign of blood,
breasts and lips beaten with a stick, nipples tortured, and anal torture
with huge objects. Whipping the back, burning the most sensitive places
with hot wax. The cameraman documenting the torture to send to the
parents later can't hold back anymore and in the agony-filled conclusion
joins in torturing the half-dead victims to satisfy his secret desires. You
won't believe how flexible a young girl's sphincter muscles can be and
the kind of things it can take in! Enjoy the SIEDAH STRONG series,
known to the specialists round the world, particularly to connoisseurs of
female pain and extreme humiliation meted out by a female hand!*

Order N°: 1813 0034
Price: 699 Czech Crowns
Club Member Price: 650 Czech Crowns.
(From the catalogue of *Freddy Vision*)

* * *

Urban stands at a high round table in an empty corner of a snack bar. He is drinking a lethal dose of coffee from the vending machine and studying the blurred image of his pale face in the window opposite the petrol station.

The microwave oven bell rings and Urban takes out a hot sandwich. He eats gingerly so as not to burn his lips. His cousin Tina's fridge is sure to be empty; by day she grazes in vegetarian restaurants; she might have a peach, or a bunch of grapes in the evening. No square meal for him in her house.

Soon he's speeding towards Prague. As he passes the motel Pruhonice on the right and a moment later a water tower on the left, an indescribable feeling seizes him. He is back in his beloved city again.

Once, when he was a little boy, his father took him to a railway station.

"Daddy, where does this track end?" Urban asked.

"Nowhere," his father replied.

"What do you mean: nowhere?" the boy couldn't understand.

"Well, it's a kind of network," his father said, "it doesn't have an end."

When Urban, then a university student, first came to Prague for a sports festival he arrived at Masaryk Station, then called Prague-Central. Urban saw the huge buffers of the railway terminal. So this was where the track ended. Or began, depending which end we look at it from. From that moment on, Urban sensed that Prague was an extraordinary city which would one day mean a lot in his life.

He sharply slows down to one hundred and fifty. He passes over the Nusle Bridge and rushes towards the station and the Hlávka Bridge. He can see, on the other side of the Vltava, the black towers of St. Antony's cathedral emerging from the heavy rain. "I'm home," he thinks, overcome by emotion. Soon he is driving up glistening Veletržní Street and Milada Horáková Avenue. He crosses the Letná and turns into Střešovická Street. He climbs the hill, passes the imposing houses, and drives round the pretty church finally to park in front of a two-storey art-nouveau villa overgrown with ivy. This is where his cousin Tina lives.

Urban pulls his travel bag out of the trunk and unlocks the gate.

* * *

What can one expect from an ox, but a pound of flesh?
Junjan Slovak proverb

Zongora wakes up the same morning next to Sida Mešťánek in a hotel room. He needs a while to grasp what has happened. So he has, after all, actually become her lover. And it didn't even take that much effort.

He admired her from the very start, when he borrowed *Mad Angel of the Torture Chamber,* one of her first films, in a video shop. In his feverish masturbatory fantasies he imagined himself as her partner in a porn film. This desire finally came true when they offered to star him with Sida in a film, *The Goddess of Vengeance.* And although his first raging orgasm was lit by two lamps and watched by an omnipresent camera eye that couldn't miss even the smallest drop of the white hot liquid dripping down Sida's face, neck, and breasts, it was beautiful. And the presence of Sida's husband, in the director's chair somewhere behind the reflectors' white-hot boundary, gave it a peculiar perverted charm.

"You were quite good," Mrs Mešťánek told him later the same day opposite the studio building in a bistro, where all the company's creative team and the actors in Freddy's movies liked to go for an aperitif. Zongora was alone in the bar, celebrating his baptism by pornographic fire, and Sida dropped in to have a coffee with her women friends.

"Really?" Zongora rejoiced.

"It made me, like, come," smiled Sida with the shy expression of a schoolgirl taught by nuns. She turned round. "But don't tell anyone. I don't want my husband to know. He's insanely jealous."

Zongora puffed himself with pride. Knowing there was an exciting conspiracy between Sida and himself made his pulse race.

"Can I order you anything?" he asked, barely able to speak.

Sida looked at her friends, who had now taken a window booth.

"Why not?" she smiled coquettishly.

"What would you like?" the barman asked.

"Another beer for me," said Zongora and turned to Sida. "And you?"

"I'll have a Margarita, please," Sida told the barman, sat down on a bar chair and crossed her legs. "But with Cointreau, please."

"Perhaps we can be on first-name terms," she suggested after clinking glasses. "I always think it's silly to be formal with someone who's just come on my face…"

And so they called each other by their first names and chatted for a while about unimportant trifles and then Sida left to join her friends and Zongora left to get ready for the afternoon shift in the Slovnaft refinery.

After that, Zongora acted in several more films; the pleasant conspiracy and friendly tension between them deepened. In time, Zongora felt a desire to seduce her for real, with no camera or film crew looking. What they did when the camera was running, to a script by her husband, didn't satisfy him. Having sex for a film and for oneself are two different things. In a porn film, the woman has to make her genitals face the camera all the time; that makes it quite tiresome for her partner. Even when changing position, the first consideration is whether the viewer can see it, since he is buying or renting the film. So the repertoire of positions is quite poor. No long foreplay, since that's boring. Porn actresses don't have time to get ready for sex, so they must lubricate themselves artificially. Even the arousal of their nipples is simulated with the help of clear varnish. That was why Zongora wanted more and more to do it with Sida in private: romantically, slowly and with pleasure.

After a long day shooting in rented rooms and the Red Stone Castle's torture dungeon, he invited himself to her hotel room and opened a bottle of sparkling wine that he'd brought. Another bottle followed the first and finally they both quite naturally ended up in bed. To Zongora it was clear from the very beginning: he gave her an intense pleasure, which her husband, that perverse and impotent fat slob, could never induce.

For a while he tried to make out the outline of the objects in the dark, but then he gave up. Darkness without an importunate omnipresent neon light has an unusual effect on him. In the Slovnaft dormitory there is bright light even at night. The reflections from the burners bounce off the room's walls and ceiling. You hear incessantly the sound of machinery, the hissing of steam and the buzzing of transformers. A repulsive stench from the asphalt plant permeates the room. Here, the night forest rustle and a cool moist breeze come through the half-opened window.

Zongora is overwhelmed by a pleasant sensation of victory. Wealth is within his grasp. Soon he'll live like this all the time and not have to think about his holiday ending in a couple of days and him going back to the Slovnaft oxygen plant, to the machines and stupid colleagues who'd never understand any of the great things that he's experienced here. Right after shooting he'll see Mešťánek and ask him to increase his fees. He'd like to leave Slovnaft and devote himself to filming. He no longer feels like being a part-time porn actor, alternating between the seductive world of porn and the unbearable factory.

He turns round and presses against Sida's back. His youthful body reacts to the pleasant feel of soft female skin. Sida, half asleep, senses that Zongora wants to penetrate her. She moves away.

"No," she hisses.

She raises herself and gropes for her watch. She looks at its phosphorescent dial. "Oh God, it's almost three!" she says.

Zongora puts his hand on her crotch from behind.

"I said no!" Sida gets angry.

"Why not?" Zongora insists in low voice. "We'll do it once more and then I'll go."

"No," says Sida. "We're doing cum shots today and if you come now, you'll be dry on location. Freddy will fire you. Is that what you want? What kind of a pro are you?"

Zongora pulls back. He can't argue with that. If he came now, his ejaculations would have less power and range in front of the camera, and his dream career of a porn star would be over.

"The production team will be up soon," Sida reminds Zongora. "Better clear off to your room. If they find out you were here, you're finished in this business. Make do with what you've got, and do as I say."

Sida utters the last sentence in a conciliatory voice, and as a sign of her favour she massages Zongora's erect and eager penis a few times. Zongora sighs, puts on his dressing-gown and carefully opens the door, checking the corridor. Then he slips into his room like a snake.

As soon as he falls asleep, the phone wakes him up.

"Good morning, this is reception," he hears. "You asked to be called at half past five?"

"Yes," says a sleepy Zongora.

"Well, get a move on," says the voice briskly, "it's six twenty."

Shooting starts at seven, so that the rooms can be tidied and opened for tourists. No tourist will suspect, from looking at the mediæval torture chamber, what kind of scenes were shot there just a few hours ago.

If Zongora wants to make it, he only has less than an hour to wash and have breakfast.

He puts on a tee shirt. He looks at himself in a foxed mirror hung on the inside of the wardrobe door. He flexes his biceps and smiles with satisfaction: the build-up of muscle mass continues as before. He locks his door and goes down to the dining room.

It's a typical socialist-era hotel dining room with a thick, worn carpet, yellowed tablecloths and an omnipresent smell of kitchen, beer, stale cigarette smoke and mould.

Zongora takes a plate and serves himself from the buffet: cheese, butter, eggs, and rolls. Then he joins the two actresses with whom he is going to shoot today. They're drinking tea. His ten hard-boiled eggs on a plate make them giggle.

"How's it going, girls," Zongora asks jocularly. "All had a bath?"

The porn stars give him a haughty look.

"What is it?" Zongora asks. "Not hungry?"

The girls curl their lips. Zongora decides that they're still young and inexperienced chicks. Compared to them, he's an old porn pro.

"At least have a yoghurt," he suggests.

"Are you mad?" one of them says. "We're shooting anal today… you think I want to shit on location?"

"Okay then," Zongora shrugs. "I'll give you a food supplement. You just have to be good at catching. Ha, ha, ha!"

He throws a radish in the air and instantly catches it with his mouth.

The girls finish their tea and, grimacing with scorn, leave the table.

The director appears in the dining room. He's a stocky greying forty-something, whose teeth shine white against the beard he's dyed charcoal black. He joins Zongora. He looks tired, but perhaps only to emphasize his boredom with routine.

"Good morning," he says and smiles when he sees what Zongora is eating. "So, today we shoot scenes eight and ten. Read the script?"

"Of course," mumbles Zongora.

"So you know what to do," says the director. "It's the interrogation and torture scene."

The director looks into the papers he's holding.

"The action takes place in the gloomy atmosphere of a mediæval torture chamber," he reads. "Siedah has assistants: they are beautiful, but terribly cruel. Their role is to find out if the young man is really in league with the devil. They find out by exciting him sexually in different ways. The man being interrogated is a magician, which he proves with his conspicuously developed sexual organ and expressive virility…"

The director sighs. "When I think that my graduation film at the Film Academy was an adaptation of Kafka!"

Zongora is unimpressed. He has no idea what *kafka* is. He is stuffing his face with hardboiled eggs, certain that they'll increase his potency.

"Look, let's not complicate things," the director suggests. "We'll shoot it in two or three hours, and we're done. Let's switch scenes. First we do the anal, and then the cum shot."

Zongora shrugs.

"I don't care," he says with his mouth full.

"Well," the director laughs. "You should. I'd like to know how you'd get it up to do an anal after a cum shot."

"Any time," says Zongora with confidence. "Any time."

The film location in the castle torture chamber is suggestively lit. Sida is with the make-up girl. She has dark shadows and demonic lines painted round her eyes. Then the make-up artist uses darker tints to add colour to the nipple aureoles.

Sida's helpers are already made up. They've withdrawn into a corner, warming each other up anally by using a vibrator lubricated with lotion, to make the sphincter muscles stretch well for the camera. It saves the girls pain and Zongora, alias Luigi Longo, and the director time.

"Oh, well," sighs Luigi and starts to change into a leather harness. "Another working day ahead of us!"

* * *

Kubeš shouts and then jerks his body on the bed, listening for a while. There is no ripple of the sea, no sound of the engines a few metal decks below, and no humming of air conditioning.

The girl next to him wakes up.

Outside the window it's early morning and the cars on Palacký Bridge rush one after the other, pooling their efforts to create once again a typical Prague morning rush-hour traffic jam.

"What's happened?" she asks sleepily.

"I dreamt I was back at the sea," says Kubeš.

He gets up and opens the window.

"You and your sea," says the girl, as if she resented his not dreaming about her.

"Our boat fished out a container," says Kubeš, closes the window and climbs back under the covers. "There was a bad spirit, demon, or something. He took over the whole crew. Only strong people could resist him."

"Could you?" asked the girl.

"Yes," says Kubeš. "He followed me into the street, we were in port by then, but I managed to get away from him."

"Are you a strong person?" the girl asked.

"I suppose so," says Kubeš.

The girl cuddles up to him.

"But it does eff-all for me now," says Kubeš.

"What is it you don't like?" the girl wonders. "This way we can be together every day."

"When I applied to Naval Academy," says Kubeš, "I thought I had an unusual, exciting life ahead of me. I really enjoyed it. Now, less than five years later, it's all up the spout. They abolished the Czech merchant navy and sold the ships. And now I have a thrilling life, working a sightseeing boat. And I should be glad I got the chance to do that. What bloody luck!"

"But it can be quite nice to take tourists on the Vltava," retorts the girl. "And you're home every evening."

"It's awfully nice," says Kubeš. "Always the same thing, always the same itinerary. I'm tied to Prague on a chain, like a dog to its kennel."

"Don't give me that," says the girl. "I know you love Prague. After all, you seduced me with your talk about Magic Prague, Mysterious Prague."

"Well, Prague is beautiful," Kubeš admits. "But not when you have to sail round Kampa and Charles Bridge again and again, carrying five loads of Krauts a day. Sometimes I feel like pissing on those smart tourists and sailing, just like that, down the Vltava and Elbe to the sea. I love the sea."

The girl is silent. Maybe she'd prefer Kubeš to express as much passion for her, but he doesn't. She loves him, yet she isn't quite sure if the reverse is true. She likes being with him and doesn't want to lose him.

"Isn't it because you had a girl in each port?" she asks coquettishly.

"Oh yes, the ports," smiles Kubeš. "Valparaiso, Rio de Janeiro, Aden, yes. But I was too stupid to appreciate it. Sometimes when we got to a port I'd even volunteer for on-board duty and didn't even go ashore."

"Valparaiso, Rio," sighs the girl. "I know them only from geography lessons. I might like to visit them some day, too."

"Most of the time we had only the sea around us," says Kubeš. "We were always staring at water. The biggest thrill was passing another ship."

"So, actually, it must have been pretty boring," says the girl. "You really don't know even now if you liked it or not. That's why you booze."

"I don't," says Kubeš. "A few beers after work aren't worth mentioning. I bump into my mates on the river all day long, we honk at each other, and we pass each other, all of us skippering boats loaded with Krauts. And it all happens under the shitty, tacky panorama of Prague Castle and the Charles Bridge. So we have to get together in the evening and have a chat, don't we? I sailed with Honza Libáň on the *Banská Bystrica*.

And I hear that crooked bugger Viktor Koženy's sold the ship to the Chinese. But you can't say there's any heavy boozing."

"Every day you smell like a beer barrel. And yesterday, too, you came home pissed."

"Well, we were celebrating," admits Kubeš. "It's been three years since we were laid off by the Czech merchant navy. Some blokes are even worse off than me. And that says something."

"Look here," the girl says angrily. "Why are you always complaining? Have you got a job? You have. Are you on a boat? You are. You're even a captain. So why do you complain all the time?"

"A boat!" Kubeš laughs sarcastically. "A boat? Calling *Mayor Pfitzner* a boat is like calling a pontoon a cruiser!"

"It's all the same to me," says the girl. "They are all boats as far as I'm concerned. In fact, I've seen a real boat only in a film. *Titanic.*"

"Well, that was a ship," says Kubeš. "A real ship, but a stupid film."

"I happened to like it," says the girl. "Look, have you ever been drowning? I mean, when a ship sinks?"

"No," says Kubeš. "But once it came very close."

He swallows several times in the dry air.

"And what did you do when you were at sea so long?" the girl asks.

"Always the same," says Kubeš. "We looked after the ship, the cargo, the engines. We fixed problems. There's always something broken on a ship. I was in charge of navigation."

"What's that?"

"Ensuring the ship goes in the right direction. I was navigating officer."

"And in your free time?"

"There wasn't much of that. We watched videos, read, played games. I had my computer, so I played computer games: Wolf, Doom, and so on."

"And what about sex?" the girl asks. "Did you masturbate a lot?"

"Sometimes," Kubeš admits.

"What do you mean by sometimes?"

"Well, once every three or four days," Kubeš says.

"And what did you think about when you did it?" the girl asks.

"Different things," Kubeš says. "I imagined I was sleeping with the girls I saw in porn magazines I browsed."

"And did you imagine real girls, too?" asked the girl. "I mean someone you knew?"

"I did," Kubeš says. "Yes, of course."

"And since we've met, have you thought of me, too?" asks the girl with silent hope in her voice.

"Well, of course," says Kubeš and kisses her. "In my imagination I did things with you that you'll never find out about."

"Go on, tell me," says the girl. "Just for once, tell me, to see if I could handle it."

"Why should I?" Kubeš smiles.

"Go on, tell me," says the girl. "You tell me and then I'll tell you if you could do it to me for real."

Well, here we can leave Captain Kubeš and his girlfriend to my dear readers' imagination. We now know, roughly, that Kubeš was a Czech merchant navy officer, and after its demise and the sell-off of the entire fleet, he returned to Prague where he had a number of jobs before he found work with a private company running sightseeing cruises along the Vltava in Prague and its immediate vicinity. After a few hard months selling tickets and working as a deck hand, he finally became captain of the sightseeing boat *Mayor Pfitzner*, and his existence seems secure. That is, as long as crowds of tourists keep flooding Prague.

* * *

Cousin Tina is awoken by the sound of Urban's car. While Urban unlocks the gate, cousin Tina dabs perfume on her temples, neck and décolleté.

Tina moved to Prague from Slovakia with her parents when she was still a child. The father was a diplomat. At least, so Tina thought until the magazine *Reflex* published a short table of the Secret Police command structure. Her father was quite a bigwig there. By now, Tina was an independent fashion designer, trying, with a fellow student of the College of Applied Arts, to get into business under the new conditions after the Velvet Revolution.

Her first husband was an administrator of the Pragokoncert, a real swine. He stole whenever he could and took bribes. After the revolution he was kicked out, and never got over it. He constantly drank, his breath stank of beer, and he was extremely stingy. He started beating her and once he almost drowned her in the bathtub, when she was having a bath. Since then cousin Tina has only used the shower. She can't recall if she ever loved him.

She admits that she too has changed a lot. "Before the revolution I must have been a screwed up little twat," she once told Urban. "I can't understand how I could have liked the things I used to like. And the people? Don't even ask!"

Her first husband left her with a spoiled brat of a daughter whom she locked up at the onset of puberty in a luxurious boarding school in Switzerland. Luckily, she has the money to afford it; unfortunately, she has no choice: her work tempo and lifestyle really threatened to let her daughter end up a slut. At least she can use her money to bring her up.

After her divorce, cousin Tina was at first really on the rocks. She rented a modest room in the south of the city and knitted avant-garde sweaters. She offered them to people she knew in art galleries. Oddly enough, cousin Tina's production sold well, and soon she bought a knitting machine and increased output. Then she joined a former fellow-student from college, started a limited company and hired first two, then four knitters. She and her friend failed to get on, and went their separate ways. Determined to go into business on her own in future, she set up a new limited company. She gradually moved her firm and herself closer to the centre. Once she was in the Vinohrady quarter and could see Wenceslas Square in the distance, she realised that she'd won. To celebrate her success, she remarried. Her second husband was a friend, a successful theatre director. The marriage lasted less than a year. As a pretext for divorce, Tina named her husband's uncontrollable predilection for alcohol and women. Since the marriage was childless, the court gave them an instant divorce.

Cousin Tina made up for failure in private life by professional success. After Vinohrady, she might have moved to the city centre. Surprisingly, she rejected the centre, even though she was offered a superb location in Rytířská Street. Instead, she bought spacious basement rooms in Letná, near the Hotel Belveder, and equipped her permanent workshop there.

Today, several dozen Ukrainian slave-knitters, all dressed in flowery aprons, work for the *Atelier Tina* company in the big airless basement. They work in the basement; they even sleep there on three-tier soldiers' bunks. They almost never go out. Some have been working for cousin Tina for years, but still haven't been further than the street corner.

When Tina received a lucrative offer to sell her knitwear in America through the Sears catalogue, she bought new machines, divided her workshop area horizontally with a metal grid and recruited dozens more slaves.

They were all illegal. The Ukrainians work a whole month in twelve-hour shifts, two weeks by day, two weeks by night. Then they go home for a month. For that time, new compatriots, rested and full of energy, take their place. This way two sets of workers, each comprising two shifts, alternate.

The impressive villa in Střešovice was bought by cousin Tina for a song from a retired man who, in a fit of anger, dispossessed a son who had emigrated and hadn't lifted a finger for his father. For the money he got in cash by selling the neglected building with a rather spacious garden, the retired vendor set out on a trip around the world and died somewhere in Brazil with two naked mulatto women in his arms.

Cousin Tina is a businesswoman straight out of a Dickens novel. Of course, she doesn't see herself as a businesswoman. She is lucky to have made a good start after her business partner left, and today her firm runs almost by inertia. Just occasionally she goes and bawls out her executive manageress. Otherwise, she spends whole days in her studio and draws models, or in the huge overgrown garden, an elegant straw hat on her head and shears in her hand. Her hobby is cutting flowers, drying leaves and putting them in huge glass jars in which doctors used to keep embryos in formaldehyde. She calls this "spending her life among flowers". She also likes to be seen by others as a fragile flower. She is unhappy if she is considered a rapacious beast, noble, but still utterly perfidious.

Now Tina lies on her bed and looks into the dark with wide open eyes. She strains her ears, and her inner vision follows Urban's every step: as he unlocks the gate, opens the house door and enters the hall, and climbs the stairs to her floor. As he hesitates for a moment at her bedroom door.

The door flies open, the sharp light comes on and Video Urban is standing in the middle of the room in a well-fitting suit, his tie at half-mast, a suitcase in his hand.

Tina pretends to be sleepy. Features that once expressed youthful eagerness have been aged into a predatory expression by the ensuing years and experience. Her narrow nose is now pointed, her eyebrows lifted asymmetrically into a charmingly scornful look. The eyes are still big, but have changed from blue to dark violet. Where innocence and graceful girlish naïvety once shone, today only a cold desire remains to grab from life as much as she can. The wide lips that once freely offered themselves have hardened into a resolve not to let anything be taken away any more. And all that is covered at this night hour by a thick layer of cosmetic night mask.

"Good evening," says Urban. "So here I am!"

Urban approaches the bed and kisses his cousin on her night mask.

His cousin makes a gymnastic twist with her eyebrows.

"This noisy arrival is quite pointless, if you've come empty-handed," she says reproachfully.

"You said empty-handed?" Urban is surprised and takes out of his suitcase a longish package whose contents are promising.

"Oh," cousin Tina smacks her lips and takes the gift.

Video Urban sits down on the bed and inhales her body odour. Cousin Tina unpacks the parcel and opens an oblong case inscribed Cartier. It's a diamond bracelet.

"You shouldn't have," says cousin Tina. "Not this…"

"Don't take it like that," says Urban. "I was buying a CD in Paris and they didn't have any change, so they packed this instead."

"Oh, shut up," says Tina visibly excited. "This must have cost an entire fortune."

"When you're found out," Urban says, seduced by the aroma radiating from cousin Tina, "you'll sell it and right away you'll have money for your pension, as well as the fine."

Cousin Tina immediately puts the bracelet on her slender wrist. She stretches out her arm and observes at its maximum reach how well the jewellery suits her.

Urban moves closer, kisses her fingers and then runs his mouth along the entire length of her arm. Cousin Tina gently pulls away.

"Well, I don't know now," says Urban, looking at his watch.

"What don't you know?" asks cousin Tina.

"If it's worth going to bed," says Urban. "It's almost half past three."

"It's worth my while," says cousin Tina. "You do whatever you like."

"Really?" Urban asks. He leans on one elbow and with his other hand caresses the rather small breast that peeps over her nightdress neckline.

"I bet you're wearing only a nightdress," he says.

"No," answers cousin Tina. "Underneath I wear my chastity belt."

"Really?" Urban asks. "A metal one?"

"No," says cousin Tina. "*Always Ultra.*"

Urban reaches under the cover to make sure.

"Don't be silly," says cousin Tina. "I have to be in my office by nine. I've an appointment with the editor of *Cosmopolitan*."

"We'll make it easily," says Video Urban.

"No! I don't want this to become a habit."

"What habit?" says Video Urban in astonishment. "The last time I was here was two months ago."

"Don't you have any girls in Bratislava?" cousin Tina asks. "Does your poor relative from Prague always have to help out?"

"You know I only want you," says Urban.

"I don't know that," says cousin Tina. "I think you'll take anything and that it's very nice for you to have someone for unproblematic screwing in Prague. Since you spend so much time here, right?"

"Well, you shouldn't have said that," says Urban. "You've really hurt my feelings, you know?"

He tries to undo the nightdress, but she frees herself from his arms.

"I said no!" she says. "Not now."

"When, then?" ask Urban.

"If you ask in that silly way, then never!" cousin Tina blurts out. "Look, don't make a habit of it. I'll find someone one of these days and you'll be out. So don't expect anything, and take everything as temporary, like a gift out of the blue."

"Quite," Urban agrees, and presses his body to hers.

Cousin Tina pushes him away.

"Look what a pathetic sight you are, cousin," she says in disgust, pointing to the bulge in his trouser crotch. "And you've only just arrived."

"You can't have heard of morning erections," Urban responds, but gives up any more physical attempts. "This is how the male sexual organ shows it's ready for sexual intercourse."

"Of course, the female sexual organ shows that it's not ready," counters cousin Tina.

"Luckily," Urban says, "a man's sexual organ is willing to be entertained by another suitable female organ."

"Look, why not take a cold shower? And open the window in your room before you do," says cousin Tina. "I forgot to tell Mrs Pecháček you were coming. So the room hasn't been aired for two months. Good night."

Mrs Pecháček is, as cousin Tina says, "a nice lady who comes in to help". Urban of course calls her what she is, a servant. Why pretend to be a democrat where there's no need to?

"Good night," says Urban unwillingly and goes to bed.

"Well, for that bracelet she really could at least give me a hand job," he thinks later in an ice-cold shower. "But I'll have her," he finally tells himself, as he falls asleep. He wouldn't be Video Urban if he didn't.

* * *

Ever since Rácz interrogated the two Junjan gangsters he'd captured, some of his good mood vanished forever. What he found out from them would dismay any responsible administrator with long-term plans for his city, region or country. Yet these were not underworld leaders, but just run-of-the-mill enforcers. They made it clear to him that he had no chance in the business, as the Junjan mafia was strong, the strongest in Europe, and the smartest thing Rácz could do would be to apologize to them and immediately release them. They in turn would put in a good word for him to Gôdöğonñ Sürgünn, the Junjan businessman and *de facto* head of the whole family. Because what Rácz has to do is to visit Gôdöğonñ Sürgünn and acknowledge his dominance. The mighty Gôdöğonñ Sürgünn would mercifully take into account the position that Rácz used to enjoy and would let him keep a sufficient number of smaller privileges. Similarly, his payments to the common treasury would not be that steep, since Rácz's businesses make so much profit that, even after giving up a third, he'd still have a lot left over.

Rácz would not listen to any more of this. Some immigrant wants to steal from him everything he's built up with these two hands and this head? Where the fuck do these people come from, if they think they can shove Rácz aside like a beginner? You can't do this to him. Big mistake! Big mistake! Rácz sorted out the gypsies, the Albanians, and in between *Rivers of Babylon* and *The Wooden Village*, he sorted out the Russians, Chechens, and Ukrainians too, and not a word was written about it, and now they think he can't get rid of these new ones?

Rácz had heard enough now. Without anger, but without a word of explanation, he personally shot both Junjans with his new nine-milli-metre pistol with a silencer as thick as a sausage. They hadn't expected that at all. They felt very sure of themselves under Gôdöğonñ Sürgünn's protection. Only as Rácz started slowly screwing on the silencer, did they realise in horror that even Gôdöğonñ Sürgünn couldn't help them here.

Unfortunately, Rácz couldn't order their corpses to be taken away and burned in the boiler-room as he used to in the old days. He had the boiler-room converted two years ago to gas, so the Junjans ended up that night in a meat grinder of a rendering plant that, of course, also belonged to Rácz and was the first stage in producing delicious *Bobby* and *Mick* food for our four-legged friends.

"That's where they'll all end up," Rácz bragged to his men. "In dog biscuits."

It didn't help him to restore his equilibrium. Quite the contrary: one Junjan wet himself before he died, so the hypersensitive Rácz had to get his favourite carpet cleaned. The second one sprayed blood and brains over his brand-new Doctor of Social Sciences diploma that he'd just bought from a private Luxemburg university for a horrendous sum.

The very next day he had Mozoň summoned. Nobody knows what transpired between the two of them; before the conversation he threw everyone out of the office and told his security team, Mozoň's immediate subordinates, not to listen outside the door.

After half an hour Mozoň left the office with a torn ear and a bloody nose. Rácz came out after him.

He'd come to an agreement with Mozoň, Rácz told his men. The job of security service *Sekuritatia* director is hard and demanding, especially in these hard and demanding times. Mozoň (alias Silent) has been demoted to hotel detective. From now on, the acting director of *Sekuritatia* is Rácz. A war that won't be easy or short has to be prepared for.

* * *

If only there was just the Khan in this world and not his underlings, too!
Junjan Slovak proverb

And this is how it proceeded: first Rácz ordered an attack on and beating of Krčmárik, a member of parliament who had previously stopped Rácz privatising the Tatra Foothills Freezing Plant. Meanwhile Rácz found out that the Krčmárik he'd beaten up was only a minion of the Minister of Food, who was a minion of Gôdöğonň Sürgünn — officially a Junjan businessman dealing in fur and tinned fish, unofficially one of the godfathers of the Junjan mafia located in Europe.

Gôdöğonň Sürgünn was tense and out for revenge. He was fighting for dominance in Central Europe against the Budapest Junjan godfather Cmüngürül Gabdźâ and the Viennese Üngurtt Tököroll, and was having little success, so he had no stomach for protracted wrangling. Worse, he'd lost two men, vanished without trace. Rácz was stopping him taking over the city, so he decided to deal with him summarily. Unfortunately, he underestimated him. Both Sürgünn's hit men, whose task was to murder the mighty business tycoon, ended in the Danube with their feet concreted in tasteful plastic bowls.

Shortly after that, a bomb went off in the office of Sürgünn's firm *Junja Fish & Food*. It happened at night, so the explosion just wrecked the building and blew out the windows in all the nearby buildings.

A retaliatory bomb exploded in Rácz's Hotel Ambassador, this time in the evening, so the few people present in the lobby lost their lives. Among them was poor Mozoň, who was sitting in the lobby, made up as a negro, watching through a hole in his newspaper what was going on around him, as his poorly-paid position of hotel detective required.

The member of the parliament, Krčmárik, was scared shitless, as they say, and fled to Austria, where he meant to hide. But Üngurtt Tökö-roll, informed of all Slovak parliamentarians' and government crooks' movements, got him even before he reached Vienna. When he found that this member of parliament, ex-communist, now rabid nationalist, was only a useless, uninformed puppet, he was dismayed and disappointed, so he tortured him a bit and sent him back to Bratislava, via the Danube.

The Minister of Food recognized the bloated drowned man fished out near Gabčíkovo as his man: he judged this to be Rácz's work. Without consulting Gôdöğonñ Sürgünn, he ordered Rácz to be shot. The sniper fired around noon from the rooftop of the Manderla Building. The moment the gun went off, Rácz bent his head down to a lighter one of his bodyguards helpfully proffered to light his cigar. The unlucky bodyguard lost his life: the bullet aimed at Rácz found its way into his brain. Rácz's other bodyguards ran to where Rácz noticed a split-second reflection of a sniper's telescopic sight. They found only an empty cartridge case and no trace of the sniper on top of the Manderla Building. He had fled somewhere over the roofs, or hidden in the building.

Ordinary people long to have heroes of their own, so they turned the funeral for Rácz's bodyguard, a sadistic psychopath whose education was five years of elementary school, into a spontaneous demonstration against the wiles of government privatisers. Rácz backed up this demonstration with suitably chosen media activities. He, too, was a government privatiser, but that was under the previous government. That government was less rapacious than the present one, therefore it was better. Which means it was good. Rácz's dead bodyguard, who used to beat his own mother, almost became a symbol of democracy.

A day later, somebody used a shotgun to kill Sürgünn's son, a well-known Bratislava playboy, just as he was getting out of his Porsche 911. Rácz was a bit puzzled, since he wasn't behind it. But who was?

Then came Saturday and Sunday, and everybody went off to some lake or other. On Monday things started again. Bombs exploded and wrecked a number of cars parked in front of the *Masex* trust that had been privatised by the Minister of Food's wife. Gôdöğonñ Sürgünn, heart-broken by his son's death, had felt the need to punish the Minister of Food for acting out of hand. By now Gôdöğonñ Sürgünn had begun to cruise the city in a bespoke armoured car ordered from the USA.

Rácz disliked a foreigner with drooping lips cruising round a city that he had long considered his own. One day a commando with anti-tank weapons ambushed Sürgünn and riddled his luxurious armoured limousine full of holes. And everything in it, too.

Üngurtt Tököroll and Cmüngürül Gabdźâ attended Sürgünn's funeral at a crematorium. The next evening they had a secret meeting in the Hotel Junior. Each brought about a hundred underlings. The meeting centred on an opulent dinner and an agreement on dividing up influence in Central Europe.

The Junjan gangsters were just eating their first course when at least fifty kilograms of Semtex, packed in paper bags filled with nails, exploded inside the air-conditioning pipes in the restaurant ceiling. Nobody finished the crab cocktail in mayonnaise or the well-chilled champagne.

Rácz was not taking half measures. The amount of explosive could have flattened all of Eastern Slovakia Steel Works (now US Steel). Štrkovec Lake immediately doubled in size. The hotel no longer existed and emergency crews of divers spent three days pulling out of ruins anything with the vaguest resemblance to a corpse.

The police response was tough. This was more than misbehaviour by ministers, gangsters, members of parliament, or ex-secret policemen. The Minister of Police, a party colleague of the Minister of Food, took a personal interest in the investigation. Rácz became a suspect, though no evidence was found against him. Anyway, he had a cosy relationship with the previous Minister of Police. The latter had retrieved documents about the present Minister of Police's pædophile activities, including nice photos of various friendly encounters with eight-year-old prostitutes.

Rácz had the documents copied and made sure that the minister found an envelope on his desk. The minister took a quick look at the photos and the copies of invoices for underage flesh that he had charged to his office: he came to his senses.

The investigator was taken off the case for incompetence. Very soon, he had a fatal heart attack. A second investigator was swamped by paperwork. Evidence vanished. Finally, he died of a heart attack, too. The case was shelved.

After this mass execution, the Junjan mafia finally understood what the Albanian, Ukrainian, Russian, Chinese and Chechen mafias had long understood: that Rácz was boss in this city. Heavenly peace reigned. And ordinary people soon found something else to chew over in the media. Ethnic conflict in Junja escalated into real civil war. The whole world focused its interest there.

* * *

When Kubeš receives a summons to the Ministry of Defence, at first he is afraid that he is being called up for military manœuvres. He did his military service under the communists, in the eighties. He's in no mood for fooling about in a uniform.

Fortunately, his reception at the entrance is already proof that there is some other reason. The warrant officer at reception takes Kubeš's summons, pushes the intercom button and announces to some unseen person, "Mr Kubeš has arrived."

Soon a lieutenant in braided uniform appears.

"Please follow me," he tells Kubeš, politely, but formally.

Kubeš can't believe his eyes. What's happened to the crowds of sweaty, greasy duty officers in shiny trousers that he remembers from his military service? Everyone's attitude here seem different, as if they'd graduated from Anglo-Saxon military colleges. Stunned, he follows the officer, who takes him to a room where a number of people are already sitting or standing.

"Please sit down and wait for a bit," he says. "We're about to begin."

Kubeš takes a look round. As well as himself there are seven or eight other men roughly his age. Two of them are in Czech Elbe-Oder river fleet uniform. The others are also obviously sailors. Kubeš take a closer look. He sees by the window his friends from the Prague sightseeing boat fleet, Honza Libáň and Franta Skopšík. He greets them and goes up to them. Then he notices a man standing with them.

"Mikuš!" he says.

"Kubeš!" says the man.

The former messmates of the Naval Academy hug each other.

"I haven't seen you since Odessa!" says Kubeš. "The last time I heard about you, you were on the *Zlín*."

"The *Zlín*'s history," sighs Mikuš. "Like all our sea-going navy, in fact. I was on it until the last moment, even after it was sold. I thought the new owners would keep me."

"The *Zlín* was sold to the Koreans, right?" Kubeš asks.

"Yes," says Mikuš. "But they weren't interested in us. We're still not cheap enough for them. Russians will do the same for half the money, or even a third. I work now in southern Bohemia, on soil improvement."

"That's no fun, is it?" Kubeš says.

"Certainly not," Mikuš agrees. "If I could catch that Kožený, I'd make him eat his own balls. But at least I have a place to sleep: a trailer. How about you?"

"I still have a vessel," says Kubeš. "On the Vltava. I'm captain of the *Mayor Pfitzner*."

"You're kidding," says Mikuš in disbelief. "What kind of a vessel is it?"

Kubeš, Libáň and Skopšík burst out laughing.

"Next time you come to Prague, buy a ticket," Libáň tells him. "Sightseeing cruise boat on the Vltava. The panorama of Prague Castle and Vyšehrad. It's like the Captain Corcoran."

Now all four laugh in unison.

A man enters the room. He's about forty, slim, with prematurely grey hair and blue eyes. He is dressed in civvies, but one look tells you he's a military man.

"Good day, gentlemen," he says in a stentorian voice so that all the hushed conversations in the room cease. "I see you're in an excellent mood. Thanks for accepting our invitation. My name is Sosna. Jiří Sosna. That should be enough to start with. But I'd like to get to know you."

He approaches the navy officers individually and shakes their hands. Each one tells him his name.

"You must be curious why we've invited you," says Sosna. "It's simple. You're all former naval officers, serving in the now non-existent Czech merchant fleet. You're all graduates of the Naval Academy. Mr Kylar and Mr Drličiak," Sosna lifts his head, seeking someone out, "have even got two degrees each. I'm here to offer you an exceptional chance in life. Perhaps some of you, after the demise of the Czech merchant fleet, enjoy working on dry land and dreaming of the sea. My offer is for those who want to go further in life than being captain of a clapped out rust bucket of a tugboat on the Vltava or Elbe."

The visitors say nothing.

"I'm offering you something you can't even imagine," says Sosna. "If you sat here a whole day and night and tried to guess what it was, I guarantee that none of you would guess right. It's a tremendously important, but also very risky business. Your reward will be very good money. I repeat: very good money. But not just that. Most of you will certainly be motivated by the chance to take part in something great that will earn you the respect of the entire Czech nation, the respect of the whole world and a career which none of you has even dreamt of."

Sosna makes a dramatic pause.

"Anyone who feels," he says, "for any reason, that he doesn't belong here can leave. Anyone dissatisfied with his present life, but lacking courage, can also go. Only those who want to get ahead in life should stay. Right. Gentlemen, you have ten minutes to make a decision. When I come back, if anyone's still here, we'll discuss the matter in more detail."

Sosna turns on his heel and leaves the room, which is humming like an angry beehive. When he returns in ten minutes, everyone is still there. A hint of a smile plays on his lips.

"Follow me, gentlemen," he says and opens the door of a large conference room.

"I've already told you my name," says Sosna. "Now I will add: I am an officer of the Czech navy with the rank of Rear Admiral."

The room fills with whispers.

"Yes, you heard right," smiles Sosna. "In the Czech navy. It's a bit odd, isn't it? Well, gentlemen, the historical importance of the Czech State as well as its place in the global framework will soon change radically. If all goes well, we shall be among the world's most important countries. The Czech Crown has already identified certain areas of strategic interest, and to defend them in the future it will need a functioning navy. That is why it has been formed. So far, only on paper. All of you sitting here with your jaws dropped, gentlemen, have the chance to be members. Founder-members!

For a moment Rear Admiral Sosna enjoys their shock. "The Czech Navy consists for the time being of a number of vessels under cover of civilian registration and, most important, of a submarine fleet," he continues. "This consists so far of one submarine, to which two more will soon be added. It all depends on the speed of the refit. These are submarines of German manufacture, U-XXI series."

Sosna motions to an assistant, who draws the curtains and starts a projector. On the screen appears a photograph of this type of submarine.

"Well, it's not the most modern war machine," Sosna admits. "Despite many improvements, there's no denying this submarine dates from the end of World War II. For the time, however, it was a very advanced fighting vessel, and for our purposes these submarines are more than adequate."

Again, Sosna pauses dramatically, then shows his strongest trump card.

"You must be wondering what you'll get for this," he says. "We offer you the opportunity to become an officer in the Czech navy with the rank of Sub-Lieutenant on a salary of twenty-five thousand crowns monthly. Further promotion in the service depends on you. Each promotion in rank will give you an extra five thousand crowns a month. Some of you are already lieutenants from military service and will start at thirty thousand crowns. For every hour spent in combat you will get extra operational pay of fifteen crowns. A month at sea will add another ten thousand crowns."

The gathering hums like a beehive.

"And moreover," says Rear Admiral Sosna, "immediately on signing the contract, you each get a thirty thousand crowns signing-on bonus and two week's paid holiday. Just think: you begin your new job with a holiday."

The naval gathering can't hold back and bursts into jubilant applause.

"As far as combat action is concerned, gentlemen," Sosna continues, "basically, this will not be direct combat: anyway, the likelihood of direct combat is virtually zero. Therefore, lack of experience of combat action on a submarine won't be a problem. What is needed is your experience of routine naval operations. What you'll have to learn, you'll learn in the training session you'll get in the near future. The credit will be yours if the standing of our Czech motherland at the global level radically changes. We shall train you theoretically, using simulators. Your progress during training will be carefully monitored. The two best trainees will be promoted to the rank of commander and will be given the post of submarine commander. Others will have to be satisfied for the time being with subordinate posts. By the way, as soon as the mission has succeeded and is declassified you will all be sent to the USA for real practical submarine training. We are counting on having a naval fleet whose power will match the importance we shall have in future reallocations of spheres of influence. Therefore, each of you will be rewarded according to your ability and merit. You will be the pioneers and nobody will be able to take that away from you. Well, I think I've said enough for today. The rest you will learn directly from your instructors on the course. I have to mention one more thing, though."

Sosna makes a dramatic pause and then he starts in a lower voice as if someone might be eavesdropping: "All the information I have given you is strictly secret. It requires absolute discretion. Otherwise, severe punishment will follow. Since this is extremely important business of absolute priority in the Czech Military Secret Service, all other considerations have to be set aside. I have to warn you in advance that we shall ensure that not only will anyone who talks disappear from this world, but so will everyone to whom he reveals the secret and, moreover, everyone suspected of having learned this secret by accident. So entire families could disappear, entire circles of friends. That's how important it is to us. Think about it, gentlemen. And now, please let's move to signing the contracts."

Sosna nods to an aide, who brings a file of documents.

"Once more, gentlemen: if there's anyone who's reluctant, he may leave," says Sosna. "We won't take offence. But he has to forget everything he's seen and heard here."

Nobody gets up to leave. They all look determined. They made their decision long ago.

"I didn't think you'd let me down," says Sosna, almost moved. "Long before we sent you the summons, I studied your personal files. I looked at your faces on the photographs. It's as if I've already talked to you all before. It was I who finally chose you from a hundred naval officers of the former merchant fleet. And I'm not mistaken. Together we'll form the steel core of the Czech Navy."

Sosna clenches his fist and lets it fall on the desk.

"And now, gentlemen," he says in a friendly tone, "while my assistant gives you the contracts, I should say a few words about myself. I was born in Plzeň. In 1949, when I was three years old, my parents emigrated to the United States where I grew up, had my secondary and university education and joined the Navy. I fought, among other places, in Vietnam. After the Persian Gulf War I went into the reserve and started a business. For business reasons I came to my motherland where I had an offer I couldn't refuse. The Minister of Defence asked me to build up and to lead the navy. I accepted the challenge so as to be a part of something that is only starting, something that I can, with your help, influence. You can bet your life that together we can do it. I want you to know that I am here for you."

The fist falls on the table again.

"And now, read your contracts carefully," says Sosna. "If anything's not clear, come to me."

Rear Admiral Sosna sits down and opens a file.

Kubeš looks at his friends. The offer is so tempting that there's no need for much talk. He peruses the contract. It's set out in great detail; the signatory undertakes to serve the Czech Navy for ten years. The usual stuff, more or less, as anywhere else. The need to keep important facts secret is stressed.

The sailors silently sign the contracts and are given the signing bonus.

"At first you will serve without uniform," says Sosna, "but that doesn't mean that you won't behave in a military fashion. Remember that. On the contrary, membership of an élite in the Czech armed forces obliges you to follow a strict code of military honour. I suggest that none of you delay: give notice to your present employers today. Do it either by agreement or within a month. If there are any problems, tell us. We'll requisition you from your employers as persons vital to state security. We shall all meet on the fifteenth of September in Lešany near Prague. You will receive precise instructions. That's where your accelerated military training will take place: your military service was a long time ago and military habits will have to be revived. And then accelerated submarine training will follow. Gentlemen, I congratulate you on the best decision you've ever made in your lives."

With these words, Sosna clicks his heels and marches out of the room, followed by his aide holding the contracts.

After this, nobody can reign in the brand-new submariners with money in their wallets. In a short operational meeting they agree where they'll drink to the sudden change in their lives.

"*On the Watch* opens only after three in the afternoon," Skopšík shouts louder than anyone: he used to live in Dejvice and knows his way about here. "And it's a dump. Let's go to the *Riga*. It's been open since one."

And that's where they go. The élite of the Czech Navy noisily leaves the ministry building.

"Man, I'd like to know how I'm going to explain this to my wife!" Skopšík laughs, though it is now no longer a joke.

"Well, I'd like to know how, too," says Kylar. "In the morning I left as an administrator of the Water Supply Board and in the evening I come back as a navy submarine officer. There's an enigma for you."

* * *

> We were six brothers. We kept dying and perishing: only seven of us remained.
>
> *Junjan Slovak proverb*

For Geľo Todor-Lačný-Dolniak it all began long ago, early one morning two years ago. First, an unbearable blizzard raged for about three weeks.

As soon as the blizzard abated for a few days, the hunters from the Slovak settlement of Habovka set out for the bay. They put the sealskin cases with their guns over their shoulders and set off for the ice floes where the wind and sea currents formed pools of water. Experienced hunters could tell by the reflections in the sky how big these pools were and how far away. Huge pools looking like giant lakes with icy shores were no good for hunting: it was hard to pull a dead walrus out of them.

The hunters, camouflaged in white polar-bear fur coats, sat somewhere by the edge of the pool, smoked their pipes, drank their alcohol, watching for prey, never taking their eyes off the water. A walrus only rarely appeared. But the moment he poked his hairy snout out of the water, a shot would ring out. The prey would start to paddle its fins, hide for a while under water and then surface, dyeing the water with its blood.

For three days, the hunters returned almost empty-handed. On the fourth day a strong freezing wind blew offshore again. It was dangerous to stay on the floes. The hunters hurried back. The wind blew in violent gusts and the reindeer yurts almost vanished in the blizzard. You could hear cracking floes moving in from the sea. The walruses were far away.

Famine struck the coast. In the men's house they talked only about hunting walrus. Nobody was interested in foxes any more. It's pleasant to hunt for fox fur on a full stomach. You can buy a lot of goods for the fur. Nobody dies for want of goods. But you can't live without food.

As soon as the blizzard died down for good and the winter set in, the ice field closed up. The edge of the open sea moved further from the shore. Stars came out at night. In the morning the impatient hunters grabbed their leather kayaks and set out to the sea to hunt.

Fragile vessels with sails made of plastic sacks sailed off to the horizon. Experienced hunters navigated flawlessly. Soon they found walruses. The hunt went on till noon. People waiting on shore could hear the gunshots echo: the sea surface carried sound an unbelievable distance.

It was afternoon when one of the children yelled. The kayaks were nearing the shore. One of them was so low in the water that it nearly sank. Six sealskins filled with air were bobbing in the water, keeping it afloat. Hunters dressed in furs were bailing it out. Others sat up to their waists in water. They calmly paddled and wouldn't let the kayak come onto the ice until their friends threw them a leather rope. Only when they were on the shore you could see why the kayak had almost sunk. It had three walruses in it. All the other kayaks had one or two walruses. The hunt was a success.

Not only people, but dogs from all over the settlement rushed to the ice field. They sat in a motionless semicircle, their heads facing the meat, licking their chops. They showed their impatience with an occasional long howl and a snap of their teeth. The least patient ones dashed at clumps of snow formed by blood and hungrily ate them.

Since the blizzard started, no one had fed the dogs. They ran round the settlements, freezing and mangy. Snatches of hair stuck out only on their sides. They fought viciously over discarded bones. Others ran deep into the tundra. They turned feral and hunted for marmots and shore mice. Now they sensed that the fast was over and showed their joy in their own way. When the hunter is sated, his dogs do well, too. When the hunter starves, they starve, too.

The men dragged the walruses to the reindeer-skin yurts. The dogs followed in their tracks. Knives appeared in the hunters' hands. With skilful movements they began to skin their prey and joint the meat.

The women came eagerly out into the street. They took the walrus skins and started working them: a thick layer of fat had to be scraped off.

A huge fire was lit in the clearing in front of the yurts. Pieces of meat roasted. With a loud spray, the fat burst out and dripped down. Old and young Habovkans ran round with greasy faces. They couldn't get enough of the meat. The dogs were resting with full bellies. They panted, and their squinting slant eyes watched their masters singing merry songs.

In the evening, a thanksgiving Mass was celebrated in the priest's yurt. The priest's wife had to boil a big cauldron of tea: they had probably never had so many believers here before. Many could not even fit inside the yurt. They stood outside.

The parish accordionist Treful'a was aware that this was no ordinary event and added to his music all sorts of extras, so the priest was sometimes thrown and lost his thread in his sermon. He talked of our Lord Jesus Christ and the fishermen. He compared them to today's exploits.

The believers sang with feeling and sincere thanks in their souls. Their voice rose from the snowbound coast through the fragmented clouds, up to the stars freezing in infinity.

When Geľo Todor-Lačný-Dolniak woke up next morning, he did not realise that today his carefree journey through life as a simple hunter and fur trapper would end and he would begin the life of a fighter for the freedom of the Junjan Slovak ethnic minority.

The day before, after Mass, he decided to set out to Stormy Tooth, to check his traps and take a barrel of mineral grease from the hot asphalt lake that never froze. The Todors' yurt had run out of it, and he had also promised a barrel to the priest.

Geľo got up early: the battered old Russian alarm clock showed two-thirty in the morning. His head ached a bit after the feast that had gone on late into the night, but when he had a sip of brandy, the pain in his forehead went away.

Over his thin underpants made of reindeer-calf skin with the fur inside, Geľo put on sealskin trousers and comfortable and ornamental boots. He couldn't remember if he put on a warm jacket and the sealskin vest over it, or the sealskin first and the jacket on top. It was a long time ago. Over everything else he wore a thick ankle-length fur coat.

He put a huge fur hat on his head. In the yurt it was semi-dark. Of three lamps only one, the smallest, was still burning. The moss steeped in walrus fat burned with a stench and quiet sputtering. The winter was long. The mineral grease had run out a few days ago.

They were all still asleep. Geľo went to the children's corner, screened off by a leather curtain the height of a man. He grabbed his eldest son, thirteen-year-old Jurko, by the shoulder and shook him.

"Get up," he said. "It's time."

The youngster quickly opened his eyes.

"Right away, Dad."

"Get dressed quickly," his father told him. "I'll feed the dogs in the meantime. I'll be outside."

Geľo took his axe, climbed through a narrow opening in the yurt's leather wall and from a storage room made of snow blocks he pulled out a huge lump of frozen walrus meat. He began to chop it into small bits.

It was dark everywhere, but thanks to the radiant snow you could see far into the distance. The morning was quiet and man's voice would echo a long way. From the ice hole a freezing wind blew.

The dogs woke up, gathered and began to shake the freshly fallen snow off their backs. Geľo began to feed them. He called out the dogs by name and threw them pieces of fat meat. There was no shortage of it now. Geľo himself had shot two walruses.

The sledge was ready by the yurt's entrance. Jurko came out already dressed and began to untie the long walrus-leather leash and tack with nooses over a foot apart. The nooses would each harness a pair of dogs.

Gel'o's father, head of the clan and once a great hunter, also shuffled out. He complained of rheumatism. He began to advise Gel'o how to feed the dogs. In the old days you threw the meat to the dogs differently. Gel'o should do so. This isn't how to do it. Gel'o wanted to put his hands over his ears, but he was holding the bowl of meat. So he gave it to his father.

"You feed them, if you're so wise," he said deferentially.

He came to the sledge. He turned it so the runners were on top.

"They're rough," he told his son. "Pour water over them."

Jurko ran into the yurt and soon returned with a teapot full of water. He quickly dipped a piece of polar-bear skin in it and spread it over the runners. A thin layer of ice formed.

Gel'o looked at it in the light of the lamp and said:

"Too thick. Should be thinner. We'll lose it on the bumps."

Grandpa finished feeding the dogs. He returned to the yurt mumbling something. They could hear him outside complaining to anyone around of his humiliation.

There was an echoing tinny noise. In front of the yurt appeared the priest with a long rifle and an ammunition bag. In front was an empty three-hundred-litre barrel that he was kicking ahead of him.

"Praise be..." said Gel'o.

He didn't go to Mass in the priest's yurt, except for yesterday, but he did go out hunting with him. He was doing something to save his soul.

"The good Lord has given us a nice day," said the priest. "You can see far into the distance."

"Yes, Father," Gel'o agreed. "Yesterday you talked divinely well and wisely."

Jurko took out a knife and quickly scraped off the layer of ice down to the wood.

"I'm glad when the word of God falls on fertile soil," said the priest. "And you, Gel'o, I'd like to see at services more often."

Gel'o blushed. He took a piece of bearskin and smeared the runners himself.

"This is how it should be done," he told his son and turned the sledge back on its runners.

Jurko poured the rest of the water into a bottle and handed it to his father.

Gel'o put the empty barrel on the sledge and sat down in the front.

The priest sat down in the back, on the place of honour. Covered by a bearskin, he leant on a whalebone backrest.

"Are you dressed warmly?" he asked Jurko.

Jurko nodded and opened his jacket to show the fur vest underneath.

"Then sit down," said the priest.

The boy quickly settled down in front of him.

"Mush!" shouted Gel'o.

The dogs jerked the sledge and ran off. They had set out on a long trip to Stormy Tooth.

Day was breaking. The ice and snow were not white, but kept changing colour according to the thickness and angle of the sun's rays.

"Hey, it's beautiful on the snowy plains," Gel'o said in praise.

The sledge rushed like a wind. Gel'o had bought pedigree dogs from Inkirunnuit dog breeders. He paid eight or even more fox skins for each dog. Now he was breeding good quality dogs himself. There was no better dog team on the coast. Nobody had better dogs than Gel'o and his family. Gel'o had traded with migrant herders for a long time. A long time ago, in the bad times of hunters', fishermen's and herders' collectives, he would take to the tundra leather belts, walrus skins, shoes, and always brought back a quantity of red and arctic foxes. Some he was forced to give to the collective, and some he sold on the side in the town.

Gel'o preferred exceptional dogs, huge with a long stride. They had to be all the same size so that they could run in each other footprints. Moreover, Gel'o would harness up to forty or fifty dogs at a time and had an enormous sledge. With a sledge like that you could carry big loads.

Imperceptibly, the sun had climbed high above the horizon. The ice shone thousands of colours until it burned their eyes. Gel'o reached into his vest and pulled out an ornamental wooden mask covering half of his face, with a narrow slit across it at eye-level. He put it on and fixed it with a leather strap.

"Jurko, your mask!" he ordered his son, who reached for his mask, sighing reluctantly as he obeyed. He knew that many a hunter on the coast had gone blind by not wearing the mask. The sun burned as it refracted through the myriad of crystals all round. It was getting worse and worse every year. There was not much the unfortunate victims could do except throw themselves into an ice hole and drown, if they didn't want to live off scraps that compassionate people threw them.

The priest put on his sunglasses.

"People seldom got blinded by the sun in the old days," he remarked. "The old people don't remember anyone going blind in the old days."

"A lot has changed," Geľo said. "So should a lot of other things, but they haven't. The Soviet regime went away and we thought we'd be better off. We're not. Hüğottynünđ Ürġüll, who was First Secretary of the Central Committee of the Communist Party of the Junjan Autonomous Soviet Socialist Republic, became President of the Junjan Republic, but he abolished it and turned Junja in a Khanate. And he had himself crowned Khan. It's shitty politics, excuse my language, Father!"

"Daddy, but why are we here?" Jurko asked.

"What do you mean, why?" Geľo is puzzled. "Because we have to check the traps near Stormy Tooth."

"I didn't mean that," Jurko objected. "How did we Slovaks get all the way beyond the Arctic Circle? The priest at catechism class said that we used to live somewhere else."

"Well," said Geľo, "our forefathers came here from far away."

"Where from?" Jurko wanted to know.

"I don't know," Geľo admitted. "The priest can tell us, if he knows."

He looked back at the comfortably ensconced priest.

"You'd have to use good dogs for many moons to get there," said the priest from his cosy lair. "But first you'd have to cross the sea on a huge kayak."

"You must be babbling, Father," Geľo disagreed. "Are you telling me there are more countries beyond the sea?"

"Of course there are!" said the priest.

"Whoa!" Geľo said astonished. "Can the world be that big?"

"That big!" said the priest. "And somewhere very far away," the priest pointed with his hand in its fur glove somewhere far away, "is the Slovaks' land. Some of them live there to this day."

"Are you telling me that there are Slovaks living somewhere else?" said Geľo, even more astonished. "Not just here?"

"There, too." said the priest. "They say that they don't have winters like ours. Most of the year, there's no snow."

"What do you mean: no snow? What happens to it?" Geľo is surprised.

"It melts," the priest said, "just as when you boil tea in a kettle."

"And the sea isn't frozen either?" Geľo wants to know.

"It isn't," agreed the priest.

"So how do they hunt seals and walruses when there are no ice holes?" asked Jurko.

"That I don't know," the priest shrugged. "But apparently, it's as warm there as if you'd lit two fires in a yurt."

"And where did you find all that out, priest?" Geľo was amazed by so much information.

"From my grandfather," said the priest. "His grandfather, my great-great-grandfather, still remembered the Slovak land."

"So why are we here, if Slovaks live over there?" said Geľo angrily.

"Our ancestors weren't doing well in their country," said the priest.

"No wonder, if they had no walruses or seals," Geľo joined in. "The fools hunted them out and there were only shore mice left to trap."

"Whatever happened," said the priest, "the Slovaks decided to sail overseas, not here, but to a completely different country. Just to survive. That was when the Junjan Khan needed slaves. So he bribed a foreign devil captain who deceived our forefathers and offered to take them on his huge kayak across the sea much cheaper than any other foreign devil sailor. Well, instead of taking them where they wanted, he took them to Junja. But that was a long time ago, many dozens of winters ago."

"So we're slaves, are we?" asked Jurko.

"We used to be," said the priest. "Our forefathers were slaves. Well, they had to work very hard for their masters. But more and more escaped north. Here, to the snow plains, and even further, to the northern islands. The last of an almost extinct northern people lived there, and they helped our people. They taught them how to survive and everything. Later, the Junjan Khan abolished slavery and pardoned runaway slaves. Then the Russians came, overthrew the Khan and set up Soviet power. Junjans joined the Bolsheviks. But our people did not go back south to the towns. They stayed here. Some became hunters, others fishermen, or reindeer herders. Junjans founded hunters', fishermen's and herders' collectives to keep on squeezing them, but they had a little bit of freedom, all the same, even if for each Slovak arctic fox trapper there were five Junjan officials and their families. But we had freedom. Because a Slovak is like that: his character is as meek as a dove's, but he'll give his life for God and his beloved freedom."

"And what about the town Slovaks?" Geľo asked. "When I went to Úŕġüllpoļ to buy a hunting rifle, I saw them."

"The town Slovaks are poor people," said the priest. "The Junjans treat them like dirt. They've got used to humiliation. They do the meanest work: they take out rubbish, sweep the streets, and clean lavatories. Here, on the coast, they couldn't survive any more. I'm afraid the Junjans have managed to kill their Slovak pride over the years."

"When you went to Úŕġüllpoļ, did you go by train?" asked Jurko.

"How else? Of course I did," said Geľo. "Day and night, all the way to the south coast. You were very little then."

"Well, I'd like to ride a train, too," Jurko fantasized. "It must be great."

"It's bad in the town," said Geľo. "Here on the north coast, Slovaks breathe freely. This is what our nation is like: we don't start anything new and don't abandon anything old. As God has commanded us."

Geľo blushed lightly. His last remark was made only to show respect for the priest.

"The Junjans are God's children, too," said the priest. "They were created by the Almighty, too."

"But he can't have been thinking when he did it," said Geľo.

"He could have made fewer of them, too," the priest agreed.

"They're a mob of thieving gangsters!" Geľo got worked up, sensing that the priest had given him a green light. "They steal from the traps. If I catch one, I'll put both his hands in the iron jaws, pull down his britches and let him turn into an icicle."

"The Soviet regime collapsed," said the priest. "The collectives fell apart, but the officials are meant to live on money from our taxes. Junjans, unlike Slovaks, don't have to pay taxes. But the officials don't get their money. The tax collectors, the ones who come to our settlements, keep it. They spend it on drink and gambling. So the others thieve to survive. There are a lot of clans of officials living here on the coast: take the Glebąârs, or the Eńjors from Gargâ settlement, for example. They're big clans who've lived for generations off the collectives. They are born parasites. They need victims to keep up that way of life. They've been brought up like that for generations. That's what they are."

"But if no one stops them robbing us," Geľo put in, "then no one can stop us punishing them for it. We, too, are what we are."

"The law's on their side," said the priest.

"It's a bad law," Geľo snapped. "Junjan law."

"That's what it says in their constitution," said the priest. "The only full-fledged citizens with full privileges are the Junjans. We Slovaks are second-class inhabitants. We don't even have their citizenship."

"What do I need their citizenship for?" Geľo got upset. "I want to be left alone. If I ever catch a Junjan stealing from me, then, as God is my witness, I'll cut his hands off and throw them in the ice hole."

"Keep calm, Geľo," said the priest. "God's law is clear: whoever slaps your face will have his head broken. An eye for an eye, a tooth for a tooth. That's what our Lord Jesus Christ told us. He used to crucify his enemies on the cross. Revenge meant everything for him. That is why Slovaks honour the symbol of the cross. And God's law is, for a Slovak, above the law of any Junjans."

"But what can I take from them for the fur they steal right out of our traps? Do you live in this world, priest?" Geľo got angry. "Even if I crucified their family to the third generation, what would I get? Didn't they steal Sirovec-Molnár's traps? And Cižmár's dogs? And what about the accordionist Trefuľa? Tell me, how many accordions he had to buy, after all those they stole from him? And it could be worse, of course! If Hüğottynünđ Ürġüll could bring back the Khanate, he can bring back slavery, too. Then we'd be given to the clans of officials and everything would go back to the collective farm times, or even worse."

And so Geľo Todor-Lačný-Dolniak and the priest went on arguing politics and venting curses for a long time. No wonder, for the journey to the Stormy Tooth had many miles to go. The whole day passed in pleasant conversation. The evening came and our travellers had to find a place to spend the night. Being tough, resilient children of nature, they slept under the open sky, on the sledge, wrapped in fur. They assigned turns to keep watch and went to sleep.

Here the author would like to stop for a short explanation. The Junjan Slovaks' native language is Slovak, but an archaic nineteenth-century Slovak. The Slovak migrants used a language spoken in Slovakia when Slovaks were forced to settle the Junjan islands. Over the years, the Junjan Slovaks' language has been enriched by so many Russian, Junjan, and Inkirunnuit expressions that my dear reader would find exact transcription of our characters' dialogue hard to understand. So we have the Junjan Slovaks speak a contemporary, almost literary Slovak, at most seasoned with a few unusual expressions to bring out the idiosyncrasy of their dialect. That is all. The author is grateful for your understanding.

In the morning, Geľo, Jurko and the priest continued their journey. Finally, on a blindingly white plain a rocky cliff emerged in the distance. It was in fact the shore, since the plain which our characters had crossed was the frozen, snowbound surface of a sea inlet. If they'd decided to travel along the coast, the journey would have taken twice as long and involved traversing the settlements of several clans of Junjan officials, and that would have ended badly. A cleft hill jutted vertically up from the range of cliffs. That was Stormy Tooth.

The first trap was empty. Only a missing bait, spots of blood on the snow, and a piece of skin showed that someone must have emptied the trap before them. The priest pointed quietly to footprints in the snow.

"Two men," said Geľo.

"Junjans," said the priest, examining the footprints. "Look at the shambling walk."

Geľo took his glove off and touched the side of the footprint.

"Fresh," he said. "The edges are still powdery."

He got up and put his gloves on. His eyes behind the slit in his mask burned with righteous anger.

"Let's go to the next trap," he ordered.

It didn't take long to see that the unknown thieves were travelling ahead of them in the same direction. Geľo stubbornly urged the dogs on and the sledge flew over the shining snow. Every now and again, Geľo stopped to examine the tracks ahead of them.

Each time he came back, he was calmer. His anger was turning into icy vengefulness.

"There's just the two," he said to the priest. "And they have only ten dogs, at most. We'll catch them. Today's not their lucky day," he added.

The priest nodded.

Geľo drove the dogs like a madman.

"Mush! Mush!" he shouted.

They found the second trap emptied, too. They just flew by the third one. Geľo didn't even give it a glance. Obviously, all the pelts were on the thieves' sledge. They had just saved him work. His eyes were glued to the two glistening tracks vanishing into the distance ahead.

Finally, after many hours, they spotted a far-off black dot. Geľo whipped his dogs and sped up. The sledge flew over the icy snow.

"They're heading for a Junjan settlement, for Gargâ," said the priest.

"I knew they were Junjans," Geľo shouted, to drown out the swish of the runners. "A Slovak would never do that. We have to get them."

The dogs flew like a gale. Despite all his rage, a good feeling came over Geľo: he had the fastest team on the north coast.

The thieves were speeding, too, but their dogs could not cope. The dogs in the Junjan team were stolen, badly fed and often abused.

The pursuers got so close that they could see the two men on the sledge. Suddenly, one of them picked up a rifle and took aim.

"Watch out!" the priest, who had the best view from his high seat, yelled just in time.

There was a shot and Jurko's fur hat flew off.

"Ouch!" he shouted and ripped off his mask. Drops of blood were running down his face.

"It's only a scratch!" he said. "My mask's saved me!"

Geľo was livid with anger.

"Mush!" he shouted and began to whip his dogs furiously. The sledge sped up. Geľo reached for his rifle. He aimed carefully and fired. One Junjan spread his arms, dropped his rifle and fell off into the snow; soon he was far behind his sledge.

Geľo's sledge caught up with the Junjan's, and rode alongside it.

"Take out the lead dog!" he ordered Jurko.

Jurko aimed and fired. The first dog in the Junjan team howled, kicked up its legs and fell down. The other dogs dragged it for a while, but then slowed down and finally stopped.

Geľo stopped his dogs with a stern command. He got up and, rifle in hand, approached the Junjan. The Junjan was shaking with fear and raised his hands. It was Özgett from the Glebâ̧âr officials' clan. Geľo knew him from the collective farm. The man he'd shot must have been his brother Ötögögonn. They were an inseparable pair of thieves.

"*Mokasündryjje*! Mercy!" shouted the arrested thief.

Geľo silently knocked him down with his rifle butt and grabbed the package of frozen fox pelts.

"Look, priest!" he shouted at the priest. "Look, my pelts!"

However, the priest was far away, bending over Ötögögonn's body.

Geľo stubbornly counted the pelts and took them to his sledge. Then he started shooting the Junjan's dogs. His face was stony and inexorable. Silently, he fired, then loaded, fired and loaded. He aimed well; each dog fell with a sinister howl. When he'd done the dirty work, he sighed.

Meanwhile, Özgett had recovered consciousness. One eye, struck by the rifle butt, was ringed with blood. He sat on the snow, trembling and mumbling something in his native Junjan. He thought that he was next.

"Shut up!" Geľo screamed and hit him once more with the butt. The thief collapsed by his sledge. He said something in Junjan. It sounded like a complaint, or a plea for mercy.

"I've not finished with you yet, by any means," Geľo shouted at him. "So shut up, or speak Slovak!"

The priest returned.

"He was alive," he announced. "So I baptized him. I'll baptize this one, too."

On hearing that, Özgett stopped pretending not to understand Slovak. After all, in all those years of cheating Slovaks in the hunters' collective *Üngütür ököltott* (Glorious Dawn), he must have learned something.

"Mercy! Mercy!" he began to shout, wringing his hands. "No baptize! Our spirits will have terrible revenge on me!"

"Shut up!" Geľo shouted at him and hit him with the butt a third time. The Junjan collapsed into the snow.

"Oh, sorry, Father!" he said to the priest. "Can you baptize him if he's unconscious?"

"Makes no difference," said the priest. "He doesn't need to know about it. Little children don't know they're being baptized, either."

The priest went on with his work.

When Özgett recovered consciousness, he was a Roman Catholic Christian. He was shaking all over, trying to slither away. Only the noise of Geľo reloading his rifle stopped him.

"You deserve death, really," said Geľo. "But I'm a Christian and so are you now, basically. I'll let you live."

The priest nodded.

"That's right and proper, Geľo!" he said.

"But I'll take your sledge in compensation," Geľo went on. "You stole it somewhere, anyway. And my son is a grown man now. He'll be needing a sledge of his own. I can see you stole it recently. It's still in good condition."

"That's right, too," said the priest. "An eye for an eye, a tooth for a tooth, as is written in the Holy Scripture."

"Does it really say that?" asked Geľo happily.

"And what's going to happen to me?" Özgett asked.

"You can go where you like," said Geľo. "If you're lucky, you'll get back to your people. If not, then you won't. You'll freeze and the bears will eat you. Or the snow monster will. Let's go."

Geľo attached the Junjan's sledge to his own.

"Let's get a move on!" he shouted.

The team started to run over the snowy plain. The Junjan ran behind them for a while and shouted that he'd rather be shot.

"Waste of a bullet!" Geľo yelled back. "You'll croak here anyway."

The priest was content.

"Two new souls saved in one day!" he congratulated himself. "That doesn't happen so often. Oh, it's good to snatch the people from hell!"

They spent the next night on a plain with a gorgeous view of the ice fields and the sea with far-off ice floes. And over all that, against a dark sky, the Sandy River constellation shimmered as if at arm's reach.

The next day they set out early in the morning. Again, the wind kept blowing and in the afternoon a blizzard struck. The journey to the asphalt lake took a little longer. Soon our travellers noticed the horrid wooden and stone totems that lined the way to the lake.

When they reached it, Geľo took out a Russian-made hand pump and filled the barrel with a stinking black liquid that oozed from many holes in the ground and spread far and wide.

"If anyone set fire to this lake," he said, "the whole globe would catch fire from inside."

"That's why Slovaks are duty-bound to guard and keep this secret," said the priest. "No Junjan and no foreign devil will ever dare come."

"Because of the terrifying totems alone," said Geľo.

"Yes, they were a very good idea, by God," the priest agreed. "Even though I'm no follower of idolatry. Virgin Mary, Jesus, and the Lord God, that's fine. But no spirits, no."

Geľo firmly tightened the lid of the barrel, picked up it up and loaded it as if it were feather-light onto the sledge. Then they filled another barrel and were soon on their way.

It was evening when Jurko smelled smoke. Soon they caught sight of the first yurts of Habovka.

* * *

Little is easier to understand than an eaten egg.
Junjan Slovak proverb

Ever since childhood Video Urban and his cousin Tina have had a strange relationship. There was a peculiar tension between them. As a child, Urban was the darling of his family and his uncle; Tina's future father could play cowboys and Indians with him for hours and took him on trips round Košice, where they lived. Urban remembered his uncle, then a sergeant on leave from military service, visiting them once in uniform. He brought little Urban some lapel badges. When he came back from military service, uncle had found a girl in the town of Michalovce. He had less and less time for Urban, which the latter took badly. Although his uncle's girlfriend took a liking to him, little Urban's childish egotism saw her as a barrier between him and his much loved uncle. When Tina was born, Urban was six and just starting primary school. He instantly stopped being the family's spoiled only child, and everyone, including his parents, focussed on little Tina. Little Urban was sidelined. He made a few attempts to recover his former standing in the family. His biggest mess-up was simulating appendicitis. They finally took his appendix out, to be on the safe side, since he went on simulating too long. That put him off any more attempts: his illusions were over. His childhood was finished, but not Tina's.

The more cousin Tina grew, the more Urban disliked her. She was an annoying, snivelling brat. Sometimes his parents made him play with her. His child's egotism stopped him showing her the love and patience that his uncle had shown him years before. Instead, he tormented her and subjected her to various horrifying experiments.

Then his uncle got a new job and moved with his family to Prague. The two families corresponded sporadically. From time to time uncle and would bring his wife to celebrate New Year with the Urbans, and sometimes the Urbans went to celebrate it in Prague. Tina stayed at home in Prague, and Urban in Košice and later Bratislava. He had a fixed memory of his cousin as a stupid, taciturn cry-baby.

Once, at the end of his studies at the College of Applied Arts in Bratislava, he came home for the weekend: in the living room sat his uncle, aunt and a pretty girl. "Tina?" asked Urban, taken aback by her looks.

It was his cousin, and she was sixteen.

In the evening, Urban rescued her from the company of the "oldies" and, with his uncle's and aunt's consent, took her to a disco at the local community hall. He discovered Tina to be not only very charming but an intelligent and perceptive person for her age. He found her somewhere to sit and bought two coca-colas. They danced for a while, slow dances too. She held him round the neck, and they were wrapped round each other like lovers. That was how you danced in those days. Tina could move in a way that switched on a flashing warning light deep in his body. He had to pull away from her so that she wouldn't notice his youthful erection.

"Let's go and sit down somewhere," Tina suggested. "It's awfully noisy here. Anyway, this music's getting on my nerves now."

They were in a garden restaurant near the railway station. Urban ordered a bottle of red wine, as his cousin looked eighteen already.

"So what kind of music do you like?" he asked her.

"Real music," she replied: Urban right away fell in love with her soft Prague accent. "Music with something to say. Prague Selection, OK Band, Žentour. And Mišík, though he's old. But his lyrics are good. I listen to all kinds of music."

For a while they talked about literature. Cousin Tina knew much more than Urban. She came up with names that he'd never even heard of.

They finished the wine. Actually, Urban drank most. Then they walked the old-town streets. By the Hotel Slovan they turned off uphill and headed for the cathedral. Then to the theatre and back down the other side of the square. Urban would have liked to take Tina to dine at the *Tokay* restaurant, but he didn't have the money.

"Aren't you hungry?" Tina asked.

"Yes," Urban replied. "But I'm broke."

"I've got a bit," said cousin Tina said. "We'll buy a hot dog."

Their relatives stayed at the Urbans the whole weekend: that was time enough for Urban to fall madly in love with cousin Tina. When he found out that his uncle was about to take his family, this time with Tina, to France for six years, he fell into despair.

He didn't have the courage to tell her that he was madly, desperately in love with her. There were barriers: she was so young and innocent. And besides, they were blood relatives.

He said good-bye to Tina, kissed her on the lips, and on Monday morning took the train to Bratislava: he had crumbled like a biscuit dipped in milk coffee.

Of course, once he got into university, a carefree student environment buried his weekend love in new loves; but the memory of her pretty and radiant appearance stayed. He followed her career at a distance.

After she came back from France, Tina went to the Prague College of Applied Arts. Urban was no longer a student by then: he got himself thrown out of the theory of culture course and worked as a window dresser in the *Prior* department store. That was, of course, only a cover: in fact he made his money in Bratislava as an unlicensed taxi-driver and then as a money-changer and pimp. Anyone interested in knowing more about this should read *Rivers of Babylon*: it's explored there in detail.

Then the Velvet Revolution broke out and Urban came across Tina's photo in the Czech weekly *Young World*, featuring her as a member of the strike committee at the College of Applied Arts. She was far more beautiful than in the awful wedding photos that Urban was shown by his parents when he went home. Video Urban knew that Tina had married a man twelve years older and married before. His father and mother went to the wedding in Prague, but Urban, although he was invited, made his excuses.

A few years later, when Urban was acting director of Rácz's holding company, he was invited to a fashion show in Prague by a company called

Atelier Tina. Since Urban planned to visit Prague for negotiations with a federal ministry, he arranged things so that he could come to the show. The invitation was for two, but Urban didn't then have anyone he felt like taking. His cohabiters, Wanda and Eva, were unsuitable. In any case, Urban was now thinking how to dump them neatly. So he went to Prague alone.

He was not at all impressed by the fashion show. Long knitted dresses, especially worn with heavy boots, could not excite him. He knew they were the fashion then, but he disliked them. He preferred watching the women present in the room. He saw Helena Vondráčková and, near her, Kateřina Kornová. Then there was Magdaléna Dietlová who, despite being an old bag now, still looked quite sexy. He also saw minister Macek with a girl. He almost missed seeing the models call the dress designer up to the podium, when everyone began to clap.

The designer was cousin Tina. She was dressed in a long knitted dress, too, but it was so tight that you could almost see her appendicitis scar.

After the fashion show there was a reception to which he was invited, too. As he cautiously left the lift and went into the reception room, he immediately noticed Tina. Surrounded by hangers-on, she was accepting congratulations. He approached her.

"Hello," he said.

"Hello, cousin," she replied. "We haven't seen each other for ages."

"Congratulations," he said. "It was excellent."

He gave her a rose he'd bought on Wenceslas Square beforehand.

"Did you really like it?" asked cousin Tina.

"Really," said Urban. "I did."

He embraced her in front of everyone and kissed her on the lips. Tina was a bit thrown. To collect herself, she began introducing Urban to people around. Urban shook hands and mumbled polite phrases.

Tina took his arm and used the subtle pressure of her hand to navigate him ahead. Subdued music began to play.

"Get me a glass of champagne," she told him. "I'll powder my nose."

"I beg your pardon?" Urban didn't understand.

"I need a pee," said cousin Tina and vanished.

Then they stood on the terrace and watched Prague's night panorama. On the one side they could see Wenceslas Square topped by the Museum building. On the other side the castle was lit up.

"You're very beautiful," Urban said. "How do you do it?"

"Moderation in all things," said cousin Tina.

"In all things?" Urban asked, and put on ladykiller look number six.

"In all things," said cousin Tina. "But of course, not today. Today I want to have fun. This is my evening. Today, Prague belongs to me."

Cousin Tina pointed to the city panorama.

"What made you think of me?" Urban asked.

"I read about you in *Reflex*," she replied. "In an article about Slovak businessmen. So I said to myself, as we've not seen each other for so long…"

"You're wearing a fantastic dress," Urban said.

"Thanks," said cousin Tina.

"But why wear those clumping great clogs with it?" Urban wondered. "I don't know much about it, but classic pumps would go better with it, wouldn't they?"

"Not at all," retorted cousin Tina.

"Don't they hurt your feet?" Urban was interested. "They look like ordinary cheap work boots."

"They're luxury brand-name ladies' boots," said Tina. "They cost a bomb."

"Then you must excuse me," Urban yielded. "It's just that in those boots you remind me of Pipi Longstocking. And don't your friends resent your spending all this time with me?"

"They don't need me to entertain themselves," said cousin Tina.

"And your… er… boyfriend?" Urban sounded her out. He knew that she'd already been divorced twice.

"At the moment the position is vacant," said Tina. Then she came closer to Urban.

"I don't know if you'll understand me," she said. "This is a terribly important moment for me. I've been waiting so long for it. And I'm happy you're sharing it with me. I was always interested in you. I kept asking about you. You probably don't even know that in my teens I was madly in love with you. Before we left for France, we went to visit your family in Košice and you took me to a disco. Do you remember?"

"No," said Urban and smiled.

Inside, he froze up completely. Everything came back to him. Including the moment in the express train from Košice to Bratislava when he felt like jumping under the wheels of the train as he realised that somebody other than him would have her first.

"I was about fifteen then," said cousin Tina. "I came very close to killing myself in France. It was the books I was reading then, and the music. I listened to Mišík: *The music played, she cried.* It was about me."

"That song 'Obelisk' had a different subtext, I think" Urban retorted, fighting back emotion. "I saw it as joy and sadness after losing virginity."

"Perhaps," said cousin Tina, "but you hadn't tried anything on yet."

They both smiled.

"I was desperate, too, because we're blood relatives," said Tina. "So even if you had feelings for me then, it would still have been hopeless."

"Cousins can do it," said Urban. "It's not incest."

He smiled.

"It's nice at least to think about it, though," he added.

Tina smiled too, and drank her champagne. She felt a need to make light of it.

"Oh well, it was calf love," she said.

She pressed his arm fleetingly.

A waiter brought a tray to the terrace, and Urban took another two glasses of champagne.

"Do you have a cigarette?" asked cousin Tina.

"Only cigars," said Urban. "Would you like one?"

"Why not?" said cousin Tina, determined to enjoy and celebrate her triumph to the hilt.

"But don't inhale!" Urban warned her, as he lit their cigars.

"I'm really very happy I wiped the floor with those bitches," said Tina, focusing into the distance. "Those envious evil vipers!"

Urban didn't ask which bitches in particular she had in mind.

"They're all in it together," said Tina. "Those old whores of the normalisation period. They used to design uniforms for Bolshevik youth festivals and today they won't let anyone into the business. They're a mafia. But today I've shown them all who's best."

She finished her champagne and calmly smashed the glass on the blue tiles of the terrace.

"Call the waiter," she ordered Urban. "I feel like more champagne."

Urban found her Slovak with a strong Prague accent powerfully exciting. Her gently lisped 'sh', 'ch' and 'zh' were simply devastating.

The waiter came straight back. Urban took the bottle off the tray and looked at the label.

"Would that be acceptable?" asked the waiter with a touch of irony.

"Piper Heidsieck?" said Urban. "Why not, it's fine for glugging…"

He poured for himself and Tina.

"Where are you staying?" asked cousin Tina.

"At the Intercontinental," said Urban.

"I'd like you to see me home," she said in a resolute tone. "And you can sleep at my house. There's enough space. My daughter's away on a 'school in nature' programme. You can sleep in the nursery. But I still need to relish my triumph a bit. Let's go and join them. I want to enjoy seeing their mugs."

For the whole evening and most of the night Urban smiled and, his face showing a lively interest, listened to the opinions of various people about splitting up Czechoslovakia. Everyone who learned that Urban came from Slovakia felt impelled to tell him that they were against the split. The more they had to drink, the more sentimental they were. In extreme cases, some tried to speak Slovak, which they fancied to be Czech spoken with a Russian accent. As the only Slovak present, Urban soon felt like a majority stakeholder in a defunct federation whose collapse everyone regretted. After two years they still seemed to be chewing over events.

"Pay no attention to them," a melancholy drunk told him later in the lavatory, as he was washing his hands. "I hope you won't get offended and take an axe to them."

Video Urban was on the point of being offended, but the drunk clapped him on the back.

"But you wouldn't lower yourself," he said. "I was joking. They're little Czechs, and it makes them squirm to see you, a Slovak, come here in a Versace dinner jacket. They'd have loved to see you in a creased high-school graduation suit, standing meekly at the cold buffet, begging for a cigar. Then they could feel sorry for you, because they love THAT SORT of Slovak. I bet that every one of them has told you that he knows a Slovak. How typical of Czechs! They each know one Slovak. Listen, let's get a drink, and leave your beautiful relative for a moment to her admirers."

He introduced himself at the bar: Tomáš Kaluba, a builder. They shook hands. Kaluba introduced him to his wife, who hosted an alternative radio programme whose long name meant nothing to Urban.

"Probably because you can't get it on your radio," said Mrs Kaluba.

The new friends had a drink.

"Everything you see here was made by my company," said Kaluba, looking over the room with a proprietorial eye. "The building belongs to a steel company, but an Italian rents the top. And he gave me the job. I specialise in renovations. You buy, rent, or inherit an old house, a mouldy cellar space with nothing but mess and rubbish and in a few weeks I turn it into a perfect restaurant, or a boutique. Your cousin Tina could tell you all about it. She's a good friend of ours. The little villa in Střešovice that I'm renovating for her is like surgical work. To my health!"

After this round it was Urban's. Then Tina came, greeted Kaluba, hugged his wife Marie and pulled Urban away from the bar.

"Let's go home," she said. "Where's your car?"

"Where it always is," replied Urban. "In the garage under the National Theatre."

They walked down the romantic, crooked, and poorly lit old-town streets. At each shadowy spot cousin Tina pulled him by his white scarf towards her and fastened her lips to his. It was romantic, even though Urban was a bit unsure if it was spontaneous, or the alcohol at work. After a while he forgot his scruples and enjoyed what chance had sent his way. They kissed like pubescent youngsters and their hungry fingers met in various configurations, and their enlarged silhouettes flashed against the cracked walls of the grotesquely leaning houses.

"Where to, dear lady?" asked Urban as they got in the car.

"Mánes Street," said cousin Tina.

"Where is it?"

"In Vinohrady. I'll navigate."

Luckily, no policeman stopped them. They got to Mánes Street by a roundabout route. Urban searched a while for a big enough parking space and then let Tina guide him to the attic flat where she then lived.

Once home, cousin Tina poured a glass of cognac.

"Help yourself," she offered Urban. "The ice is in the freezer."

Urban chose bourbon with ice and slowly mixed his drink.

"So you really liked my dresses?" asked Tina.

"Yes, it was an interesting show," said Urban, changing the topic and taking a sip. "Though I didn't see much. I was standing in a bad spot."

"And what about this dress?" asked Tina, stroking her waist with both hands.

"It could have been shorter," said Urban expertly.

"How much shorter?" asked cousin Tina. "This much? Look!"
She pulled her dress up a bit, so Urban could admire her slender calves.
"Hmm," he said.
He was embarrassed, because he could see how this would end.
"Or like this?" asked cousin Tina and revealed her knees.
"Fine," nodded Urban.
His cousin pulled her dress up to her long thighs.
"Yes, I like miniskirts," Urban assented, and, since he felt it was his turn to do something, he put his glass on the table.
"How do you like a mini?" Tina asked artlessly. "Like this? Or this?"
The sight of her very long legs amazed Urban. He went to her and pulled her dress even higher. Then he realised why under her tight-fitting knitted dress he had failed to see any panty lines. There were no panties.
Knowing that Tina had been naked under her dress all evening and that only he was now seeing it with his own eyes nearly cost him his sanity.
He pounced on her wildly, blood relative or not. They wrestled a while before he pulled her dress over her head and flung it in a corner. Tina was stark naked, wearing only earrings, bracelet, necklace, and a flesh-coloured strapless bra fixed below her breasts. Her hot skin emitted a wildly alluring scent that could make a man demented. Urban took her in his arms, carried her to the sofa and lay down next to her.
"Let's not be silly," said Tina, panting. "We're related, after all."
"Cousins are allowed to," said Urban and was himself surprised that his voice also echoed his heartbeat. "The Bible says so, too."
"Where?" cousin Tina asked. "In what book?"
"I can't remember now," said Urban.
"It's incest," Tina warned him.
"So be it," said Urban: his hands stroked her breasts and all her body.
Cousin Tina was shaking with excitement, or perhaps with the cold. The window was open: the room filled with cold moist air from the Rieger Gardens. Tina hinted that she wanted to undress Urban, and lifted up his shirt. Urban kissed her mouth and breasts in turn, while discarding his bow-tie, cummerbund, shirt, shoes, trousers, socks, and boxer shorts. How lucky, he thought, that instinct had told him not to put on his comfortable favourite long johns. Cousin Tina's fingers ran feverishly through his hair while his mouth and hands concentrated on her knees, inner thighs and, finally, her moist open crotch. Before he realised, he was in her.

"NO!" sounded Tina's last psychological barrier.

"Yes," whispered Urban.

In panic, Tina jabbed her nails into his shoulders and tried to get out of his embrace with violent twists of her hips. But Urban didn't let her get away so easily. His erection pinned her like an impalement. Tina's last escape attempts gradually changed into passionate copulative movements.

"But don't think it means anything," were her last words before she lost her self-control. "It doesn't mean anything at all."

And then she turned into a half-crazed orgasmic she-devil who at one point felt compelled to awaken all Mánes Street with her howls.

Since then, their relationship has been the same: neither fish, nor fowl.

* * *

Maybe it was at this very time that Elena, a strong and wide-cheeked beauty with a pretty face, a black tattoo round her eyes and thick jet-black braids, was hastily untying the wet leather straps of her husband's boots. Geľo had just come back from Stormy Tooth. He was lying on his back and watching her silently. Elena took off his boots and fur socks, pulled off his sealskin trousers and put them behind the screen to dry.

Semi-naked, dressed just in thin reindeer-calf underpants with the fur inside, Geľo sat down on a soft reindeer pelt. His face was wide, simple, and kindly. The sun had tanned it brown: only round his almond-shaped eyes was there white untanned skin, thanks to his sun mask. His eyes shone quick and bright, belying his simple features. His jet-black braided hair, greased with walrus fat, hung in two plaits over his chest and two down his back. He looked at Elena and pulled her towards him. She yielded, bared her crotch and used her hand to help him inside her.

A little later, Geľo half-sat, half-lay in the men's corner, alone. He was pleasantly tired. He stroked his mighty muscles as if getting ready for a fight. His wide chest, powerful neck and huge sinewy arms hinted at his extraordinary strength. When his chest muscles rippled, a tattooed herd of walruses began to move. Geľo liked amusing his children with this trick when he was in the mood. And he almost always was.

There wasn't a man on the north coast who could out-wrestle Geľo. Geľo liked wrestling. He often made his compatriots accept a challenge to a match. But he was always an honest and chivalrous rival.

The men's corner was spacious. Three lamps burning mineral grease gave a lot of heat and light. Above them hung teapots and a pot of fresh walrus meat. On the cross timbers hung smaller objects: a statue of the Virgin Mary carved in walrus ivory and a filigree carved cross. These objects protected the Todor yurt from misfortune.

Near the fire, on reindeer pelts sat a wizened old man, Geľo's father. He had the same braids as Geľo, but they were grey. He had an extra pair of eyes tattooed on his forehead, which made his face look pensive.

"You've got us into trouble, again, Geľo," he said. "As if we hadn't enough already! Why are you always quarrelling with those Junjans?"

"Father," Geľo said patiently, "those swine robbed all our traps south of Stormy Tooth. Should I have put up with it?"

"We must bow our heads," said the old man. "They're the masters here."

"How long do the Slovaks have to submit, for God's sake?" Geľo raged. "They nearly killed my boy."

"You stuff your head with all these mad new harmful ideas," shouted the old man. "Before you young men started to rebel, the Junjans left us in peace. If anything happens to Jurko, it will be your fault."

"I will always rage against unfairness and injustice," said Geľo. "Why do Junjans, with all their privileges, need to steal from us, too?"

"Because it was ordained by God," said Geľo's father.

"Strange that the priest has never mentioned that," remarked Geľo.

"Because he's infected by worldly ideas, too," his father retorted.

"Nothing's ordained by God," Geľo interrupted his father. "Everything's ordained by people. And if people won't change it, nobody will."

"Well, you certainly won't change it," the toothless old man cackled contemptuously. "Dolt!"

"If you handed the leadership of the clan to me, many things would have changed long ago," said Geľo. "We'd certainly not be so helpless against the clans of officials."

"Well, you'll have to wait for that to happen, my son," said the old man. "I'm still in charge here. I give the orders."

"You ought to hand over power to me," said Geľo. "People laugh at me. You're sixty-five years old; I should've been head of clan long ago."

"You're not grown up enough," said the old man. "Your body is mature, but you have the brains of a ten-year-old. You're short-tempered and full of hate. You'd lead the family to disaster. I don't want war with the officials' clans. I've always yielded to the Junjans, and always will, if you want know. For our clan's peace and prosperity; for your good, too."

"But you can't go on yielding for ever," Geľo said angrily. "You know what the Junjans are like: give them an inch and they take a yard.

You're old and weak; you don't hunt any more. But if you did, you'd know what is going on at the coast and you'd think differently."

"Who's old and weak?" shouted his father. "How dare you talk to your father like this?"

Geľo's father got up and made a few clumsy warm-up moves with his arms. He worked up a sweat and his face went all red. He was breathing heavy. He quickly started to put on his furs.

"Where are you going?" Geľo asked.

"None of your business," snapped the father.

"Only there's a strong wind blowing off the mainland," remarked Geľo. "It could blow you away."

"Don't worry about me," retorted the old man. "I'm going where you won't be allowed to go for a long time yet: to the men's house."

The old man put on a hood and climbed out into the cold.

Geľo clenched his fist. He was the general laughing stock. Other old men in the settlement had long since handed leadership of their clans to their sons: Čižmár, Sirovec-Molnár, as well as Sirovec-Adamčiak, even Bartoščík-Horný and Chalupa-Hluchý. Only Geľo was still a youth with no rights. And he was a family man. How shaming!

Every Saturday evening the elders of the individual clans met in the men's house. The tradition was that, as soon as a man became a clan head, all the other men of his generation in his clan would be admitted, too: brothers, cousins, and so on — but not until then. Otherwise, they had to make do with the status of youths and meet in the youth corner.

It was good in the men's house. The clan heads sat there and talked about the week's events, deciding a common approach and, with the help of moonshine, which they distilled from flour and sugar, adding special fungi and herbs, they set off on long trips in time and space. Geľo's father was the oldest hunter in the men's house. So Geľo and his brothers would have been the oldest youths in the youth corner, had they not been too abashed to visit it and mix with fifteen- to nineteen-year-old lads.

Geľo preferred instead to spend time on long hunting trips, on exploratory treks to find new hunting grounds and trade outlets. So he was well travelled and knew many settlements on the coast and in the tundra.

He was, for example, a welcome guest of nomadic herders, Slovaks who lived deep in the tundra. They bred reindeer and skilfully rode sail sledges, moving from place to place at lightning speed. Like the coastal Slovaks, they avoided the Junjans. They, too, had been forced for long years to stay in herders' collectives. On their long travels they had to drag along numerous parasitic families of Junjans who had enslaved them. But when the Bolsheviks withdrew to Russia, the tables were turned.

Overnight, the capricious absolute masters became slaves of their former slaves. But the Junjans were a dead loss as slaves. They were useless. For a time the nomads used them for rifle target practice, but even then they proved useless: they couldn't or wouldn't run fast. There was no fun or thrill in shooting them. Not even on night target practice, when the Junjans ran clumsily to and fro with lamps hung round their necks. Soon the nomads ran out of Junjans. The survivors were finally left in the tundra to the mercy of the cold and the wild wolves, as big as calves.

It was much the same in the fishing settlements scattered over the various islets. The fishermen got rid of Junjan officials and their families very simply: they took them out to the sea and threw them into the water.

After Hüğottynünđ Ürğüll's coronation, Junjan oppression worsened again, but only in the towns. In the open tundra, on the coast or the islands, among Slovak fishermen, there was really no one to poison their lives or avenge the murdered officials. Relative freedom reigned. Except for Junjan tax collectors, of course.

Geľo had three brothers: he was the oldest. Then came Martin, married into the Kresan reindeer herder family and now living with the nomads somewhere in pastures far off in the tundra that took up the entire centre of the island.

Brother Samuel was now married but still lived in the yurt with his parents and Geľo's family. The youngest, Adam, still single, was living with them. He had an eye for Zuzka Chalupová, daughter of the local blacksmith. She was quite willing. They could marry when the ice broke.

"Something has to be done," said Geľo to his brothers after his father had gone. "We're the laughing stock of the whole settlement."

"Not just the settlement!" Samo shouted. "The whole coast! Nobody has seen a man that old going to a men's house. A man of that age should be sitting in the yurt chewing skins."

"Everyone our age meets in the men's house," Geľo said. "Their fathers handed power over to them long ago. And what about me? Do I or don't I inherit the clan rights?"

"Our father was given power when he was sixteen years old," noted Adam. "At least that's what old Čižmár said."

"And what about you?" Samo prodded Geľo. "You're thirty already and you're still considered a youngster just like us."

"Something must be done," Geľo said and his anger surged up to his brow. "Something must be done, for God's sake," he added darkly.

* * *

The night was silent and still. The moon shone brightly. Old Todor-Lačný-Dolniak walked home from the men's house. He was a bit high: the effect of the herbs and fungi had not quite worn off. He saw everything in weird colours and the trek made his mouth dry.

He stopped on the coast, near a viewing point. From the pocket of his fur coat he took a bottle and had a sip. He watched the ice field for a while. Beyond it was a dark ribbon of unfrozen sea. Over that ribbon was a dark sky.

On the other side, where the mountains rose up, the entire firmament was sown with clear stars. From time to time one of them fell with a swoosh and was immediately extinguished.

The old man took a pipe and tobacco from his inside pocket. He filled his pipe and lit it.

Lights began to play over the sky. The Sandy River that crossed the whole sky shone brightly. From zenith to polar star, long bands of light ranged, like walrus-leather ropes tied from yurt to yurt. Various shades of colour played on the sky, all burned and inflamed by ribbons of flame.

"The ancestors are having a big holiday. They've lit a lot of fires," said the old man.

The heavenly fires did not last long, though. They went out and soon the moon, surrounded by radiant stars, shone in the sky. Small stars kept falling down. One of them whistled nearby, above old Todor. It flew by and went out somewhere in the south, in the tundra.

"It's the ancestors throwing old lamps they don't need any more out of the yurts," said the old man.

The old man smoked; clouds of smoke rose to the freezing heavens.

Suddenly, out of the darkness, three figures ran out. One hit him on the head with a wooden pole, so that he lost consciousness.

When he came to, he was lying, almost frozen, in the snow. He tried to get up, but was so badly beaten that he could hardly move. He crawled with his last strength to the lower end of the settlement, to the yurts. He dragged one of his legs behind him. At the first yurt, he banged at the frozen skin at the entrance and again fell into unconsciousness.

When he came to for the second time, a neighbour, Sirovcová-Molnárová was nursing him. Her husband Frolo, the same age as Geľo, was looking on, giving the old man something to drink.

"Who did that to you?" asked Sirovec-Molnár, concerned.

"I don't know," the old man could barely speak. "There were three of them. I got the first," he lied. "The other two got me."

"Who'd want to do such a thing?" said Frolo, bewildered.

"Were they Junjans, perhaps?" asked Sirovec-Molnár's father, a short one-eyed old man. He was sitting in the corner and, together with his old wife, enthusiastically chewing a skin.

"Keep out of it, father," Sirovec-Molnár turned on him. "Just chew faster, or you'll both go to bed with no supper." Sirovec senior felt embarrassed in front of Todor-Lačný-Dolniak, since he knew that the latter still wielded power with a firm hand in his own clan.

"Stop it, son!" he retorted, offended.

Sirovec-Molnár paid him no more attention. In a firm voice, he gave orders to all the members of the clan:

"Andrej and Fraňo, go to the Todors quickly and tell them to fetch the old man. Matej can make a splint: it looks as if he's broken his leg."

From his bed of fur the old man watched. He felt odd, even though he had no pain. He was caught out by his own helplessness.

Geľo came straight back with Samo and Adam.

"What happened, father?" Geľo asked him. "Who attacked you?"

"It must have been Junjans," said Samo.

"Did you see them?" asked Adam, avoiding his gaze.

"I did, but I couldn't recognize them," said old Todor-Lačný-Dolniak. "They had sun masks on. And they clubbed me to the ground."

"You said you hit the first one and he fell," said Sirovec-Molnár.

"Yes," the old man agreed, and blushed. "I just hit him like this and he fell… the two of them carried him off and ran away."

"Oh, you are strong!" Sirovec Molnár's wife cried out in admiration and then suddenly fell silent.

"I'm sure it was Junjans," said Samo. "They found Ötögögonn and Özgett and came to take revenge."

"Whatever happened," said Sirovec-Molnár, "If you hadn't been gallivanting outside, to and fro, but stayed at home, in the warm, like all the other old people, you'd have come to no harm. What business is it of yours to go the men's house at your age? You should have handed power over the clan to him, to Geľo." Geľo lowered his eyes and blushed. Frolo Sirovec-Molnár spoke from the heart, but it still shocked him. The naked truth revealed seemed to pinpoint him as the perpetrator of the nasty act.

The old man was quiet. He drank moonshine and closed his eyes.

Carrying him to the Todor yurt raised howls of pain from the old man, no matter how careful his sons were.

In the yurt, a high bed made up with the softest of furs was waiting for him. The women cooked a pot of the tenderest reindeer meat.

"Will you have a drink, father?" Geľo asked.

The old man's eyes were shut; he didn't answer.

* * *

Nobody ever found out who had attacked old Todor-Lačný-Dolniak.

The old man got back on his legs, but now he could walk only with a stick. His back was slightly bent, his leg had healed crooked. He bore his fate stoically, even though he sometimes mumbled in his corner. He had an inkling who was guilty, but dared not shout out about it. He valued above all the food ration that he would otherwise have lost.

Public opinion in Habovka settlement was on the side of the Todor-Lačný-Dolniak brothers. No matter how the beating occurred, the old man should have handed the clan leadership to Geľo long ago.

As if naturally and by the whole settlement's unanimous agreement, Geľo became head of his clan. A week after the old man's beating, the Todor-Lačný-Dolniak brothers put on their best clothes and precious hand-embroidered boots and set off to the men's house for the first time.

They were expected. Men welcomed them with laughter. There was no end of backslapping. Everyone knew what Geľo had had to put up with and do to make things happen in the traditional customary way. The clan leaders made space for the newcomers. Nobody said a word about old Todor-Lačný-Dolniak. The men had even organized a small welcoming ceremony for the brothers. Soon came the moment for gifts. Every one of the men wanted to honour their new friends in the men's house and had brought a small present. One brought a fishing hook, another a pack of tobacco. But most men gave the brothers plastic bags. "Rubber pockets" (as the Junjan Slovaks called them) were a precious gift. In the life of the inhabitants of the Junjan archipelago these bags played an important part because of their many uses. You could wrap food in them before storing it in an ice larder, or wrap your feet to keep them dry in your boots. Junjans also used them to send their very old relatives to the People Above, as it was much more tasteful to use bags than to strangle them with a leather strap. Of course, this was something Slovaks would never consider doing. Junjan Slovaks had great respect for their elders. If someone could no longer take care of himself, the worst they would do was to take him, lightly dressed, out of the yurt into the freezing cold, to die on his own. The priest was against even this, but he didn't have any helpless old man or woman to take care of. His father, the former priest, was murdered by the Bolshevik Yasin, the permanently drunken political commissar of the hunters' collective *Üngütür ököltott* (Morning Glory), in the campaign to eradicate superstition and the occult.

After the gifts came the agenda's next item, which Geľo, Samo and Adam had been looking forward to: travelling in time and space. When the familiar bottle came and started its rounds, the brothers exchanged happy looks. What they had been waiting for so long had now arrived.

Geľo's first sip was as bitter as seal gall. After the second sip, heat spread round his mouth. The heat increased and then suddenly stopped, as if switched off. Two men had to hold him down to stop his spasms of jerking and writhing. But Geľo was now unaware of it. He was trying to get out of a dark space, a kind of giant, dark yurt. He was escaping through some half-solid obstacles. His head kept hitting something like pelts hanging from the ceiling. Everything around trembled like the ice floes cracking in the spring. Over it all was a dark universe with stars like lamps. There Geľo flew, free as a bird, with a heart full of exaltation and with tears of happiness that flowed down his weathered cheeks.

* * *

Urban is an enthusiastic patron of Prague restaurants and pubs. His favourite place is a wine cellar called the *Domažlice Room* on Strossmayer Square. He is also one of their favourite customers. He goes to the *Domažlice Room* with his friends, or sometimes alone. It's a traditional Czech restaurant where nothing can surprise him, unlike the time that Tina and he went to a Japanese restaurant, Shusui in Malá Strana.

They were waiting for their meal. At the next table someone had ordered a very exotic dish: when it came, the tray was carried by two Japanese waiters followed by a Japanese singer with a fan in each hand. The singer danced in an absurd, jerky way, ceremoniously bowing in all directions, opening out the fans and singing a strange song in a high throaty voice. Urban noticed tender pink slices of some fish on the plate. The customer started eating, but right away his eyes popped, and he suddenly stood up, clutched his throat with both hands and collapsed on the floor, gasping for air. For an instant his hand appeared above the table as his fingers, bent in a spasm, raked the air; then he pulled down on himself the tablecloth, the filigree little Japanese plates, bowls, glasses and trays.

The other customers in the restaurant sat on tenterhooks. The meaning of this event was an enigma to them. Everyone, including Urban, waited to see what would happen next. Cousin Tina put her hand in Urban's, squeezed it hard and said nothing, while she waited. Two waiters ran in, picked the customer up and put him back on his chair. The customer's head dropped forwards, his arms hung by his side. He was dead. One of the staff ran into the kitchen and quickly ran back, followed by the chef.

"This is like a Kurosawa samurai film," said cousin Tina. "They run to and fro there, too."

Video Urban had a silent foreboding of what would follow.

The chef approached the dead customer and carefully looked him over. Then he ran back to the kitchen.

Urban smiled encouragingly at cousin Tina. He pressed her hand to show that everything was all right.

It was not.

The chef soon returned, but this time holding a filleting knife. He knelt on the floor and a waiter positioned himself behind him and raised a meat cleaver: the biggest meat cleaver that Urban had ever seen since he'd watched *Bad Taste*. The chef, his eyes goggling, yelled a few rapid sentences in his mother tongue and then, without warning, stabbed his belly with the knife. He gave a shout of pain and shock, as did the most of the customers watching him; then he began to twist the knife round his guts. Finally, he moved the knife to where most people have an appendix. The chef's jacket was instantly covered in blood. The chef's head drooped. He raised it with his last ounce of strength and said something in Japanese, whereupon the waiter cut off his head with a well-aimed blow.

The head rolled under one of the tables: the customers jumped away from it as if it were a smoking bomb.

"That's probably enough," Urban said to Tina, and threw his napkin with a firm gesture onto the table. "We'd better leave."

Nobody tried to stop them at the door.

They came out onto the street and headed for a taxi rank.

"We won't go back there," Urban said when he recovered. "Why do they burden us with their problems?"

"The service there was awfully slow, anyway," said Tina. "We'd probably have to wait forever. And now they could only offer us a cold supper."

* * *

From time to time cousin Tina organized dinner parties for people close to her, her best clients and friendly fashion journalists. Originally, the dinners were held in various élite restaurants round National Avenue and Wenceslas Square, but Urban finally persuaded her that "his" *Domažlice Room* was the perfect establishment for this kind of event, and also much cheaper. So even now, when he came to Prague to have his films dubbed, he would come to one these dinners. Tina introduces him everywhere as her cousin, a successful businessman from Slovakia.

"What kind of business are you in, Mr. Urban," the editor of *Cosmopolitan* asks him during the aperitifs.

"In film," says Urban.

"Are any films made in Slovakia?" the *Harper's Bazaar* editor asks incredulously.

"Certainly," Urban says.

"My cousin works in video films," cousin Tina rushes to his aid. "They're short films, educational films, and so on."

"Really?" the exalted lady editor seems impressed. "That's fabulous. How refreshing!"

The co-owner of the *Domažlice Room* appears in person, to make sure that everything is fine. Urban knows him and so invites him to join them at their table. The owner hesitates, but then accepts.

"What will you have, Pavel?" Urban asks him.

"If I may, scotch on ice," says the restaurateur, still a young man.

"One scotch with an ice cube for the boss," Urban orders.

They are just bringing in the dishes. Most of the guests ordered Stuffed Steak à la Lamminger; some ordered Poacher's Game Bag; cousin Tina, a vegetarian on principle, went for the mushroom omelette. The food is perfect, and everyone uses superlatives. So the guests express an interest in meeting the chef who's cooked these remarkable dishes.

The chef, a chef's cap on his head and wearing a double-breasted jacket with black buttons for the occasion, is personally summoned by the boss, and is greeted by the guests' applause.

"This is Jarda, our master chef," says the boss, after they all drink a toast to the blushing master of gastronomy. "He's been with us for several years. He worked here when my father owned it."

"And did your father…" asked Tina, "pass away a long time ago?"

"Dad?" Pavel laughs. "Dad's doing fine. He only gave up the *Domažlice Room* and runs just his two other restaurants: the *Pivoj* and *Houbar*."

"He's the very tall gentlemen with a blond moustache who was standing by the bar an hour ago," says Urban.

"Of course, all I do is watch who's standing at the bar," says cousin Tina and looks back at Pavel. "Your father must have a lot of faith in you to let you have such a famous traditional establishment."

"He didn't let me have it," says Pavel. "He sold it to me. To me and my quiet partner Robert. You must know him, he works here, too."

"Oh, is he the fair-haired lad with a ponytail, right?" asks Tina.

"Yes, that's him," says Pavel.

"That's how I remembered you," said cousin Tina. "The dark one with the beautiful eyes and the fair-haired one with the ponytail."

Pavel doesn't know where to look.

"There, you see," says Urban, "now you've finally been introduced."

The chef finishes his drink and apologizes for refusing another drink, as he has a lot of work in the kitchen.

"Did you know I used to come here as a student?" asks Tina, when they sit down again and Pavel orders another round of whisky. "But we didn't eat much, we used to come more for wine."

"Well, we had a good kitchen even when my father was in charge here," said Pavel. "The menu hasn't changed much since then."

Everyone, including cousin Tina, browses through the menu.

"You might be interested to know," Pavel tells Urban, "that we had the menu designed on a computer by a good friend from Bratislava. He comes here, too, but not as often as you. Perhaps you know him: Peter Pišťanek, a well-known writer."

"I don't," Urban shakes his head. "He's probably not that famous."

"You know," says Pavel, "there are restaurants, hotels, canteens, snack bars which keep their reputation for years. But it's still true that it's far harder to regain a lost reputation than to build one from scratch."

"No doubt about that," agrees Tina, lost in Pavel's almond eyes.

"Under the old regime," says Pavel, toying with his engagement ring, "there was a popular slogan: if you don't rob the state, you're robbing your family. That went for restaurant kitchens, too. And some employees, even owners, of private restaurants go on like that today, cheating their clients."

"Unfortunately," says Urban.

"Why unfortunately?" Pavel asks. "It's only short-term. In a competitive environment, those businesses are bound to go under. People can choose where to go. And soon even the memory of those restaurants will vanish. Here, just down the road from us, there was a restaurant called *The Rabbit's*. It was old and famous, too. But the owner relied on getting busloads of Germans. That kind of customer comes, eats, or doesn't eat, what he's given, and he's never seen again. If a restaurateur doesn't look after his steady customers, he might as well pack up. And that's what happened to *The Rabbit's*. The buses stopped coming, ordinary customers had long stopped coming: they had to close down. Now it's an electronics shop.

"I wonder how you can cheat in that kind of restaurant," says Tina.

"Well, there are various ways," says Pavel. "Cooks can work all kinds of miracles. Raw meat can weigh less when raw, or you use different cuts of meat. A favourite trick is swapping expensive cuts for cheap ones. For example beef tenderloin can be replaced by sirloin and sirloin by rump steak.

"Terrible," says Tina. "But I couldn't tell the difference, anyway."

"But I could," says Pavel. "If you're making a dish with more than one kind of meat, like Moravian Sparrow, or Szegedi goulash, you can use more pork flank and less shoulder. And if the flank is nice and from the top, it can all replace shoulder. Pork haunch, especially if you dice it first, can be replaced by pork shoulder. In a Playboy's goulash, not many customers can tell if the meat is rump, or good front-end beef with the sinews taken out."

"True, I don't suppose many could," agrees cousin Tina.

"Or," Pavel recalls, "if there's some leftover tomato sauce, the next day it can be turned into Gypsy roast beef. If you have some old cheese left over, it's used for Dutch steak, various sautés, or is used to sprinkle on other dishes. Or take frying oil. Sometimes they fry in used oil bought from confectioners. That's an old trick: old oil is much cheaper than fresh and can be used for quite a time."

"And how do you know so much about it, Pavel?" asks Tina with a smile.

"Look," says Pavel. "I run a restaurant. I have to know all their tricks so that I can recognize them and stop them in my business. We're not into money laundering, we care about keeping our customers happy."

When Urban and his cousin Tina were in a taxi on their way home, Urban could not help making a caustic remark to Tina:

"Odd, you were so taken by his talk about meat. I thought you were definitely a vegetarian."

"So I am," said cousin Tina. "But the boy spoke so nicely that I could have listened to him all night."

"Careful!" says Urban. "That boy is happily married and has a child."

"That's doesn't make him ugly," says cousin Tina.

"Could you listen to me all night?" asks Urban.

"You couldn't discuss your work so enthusiastically," says Tina. "Then, what would you talk about? Your video business where girls screw dogs?"

"That's only temporary," says Urban, ashamed. "It gets on my wick, too. But there's money in it. When I make as much as I need, I'll drop it."

"That boy Pavel," says cousin Tina, "was talking all night about doing good to people, giving them the comfort and joy of good food and drink. He was talking about tradition, about what he'd learned from his father and grandfather, about pride in his company. And you? All the time, all your life, you've only tried to cheat. You've never done anything properly, nothing to make you happy or absorb you. You've always only gambled. So, please don't be surprised if I take you as I see you. Prove to me that you're different. Prove to me that you've got somewhere, that you've risen to a higher level. I mean spiritually. That boy Pavel is no intellectual, but spiritually he towers higher above you than you probably can understand."

Video Urban is stunned into silence. He didn't expect such a telling-off. He tried to take Tina's hand and intertwine their fingers, as he always does coming back from somewhere, but his cousin moves her hand away.

"Show me you're developing," says Tina. "Do something. You're nearly thirty-five. You can't waste your whole life like this, doing things temporarily, as you are. I really like you; really, I do, because I know that, inside, you're totally different. Occasionally something from inside you surfaces, in a kind of eruption. It takes my breath away. Those are beautiful moments. That's the real you, in my opinion. If only I knew how to unlock you, if I had the key. I so desperately want to trust you, Urban."

Urban is embarrassed listening to all this in the presence of a taxi driver who pretends he can't hear a thing, but who has pricked up his ears. Cousin Tina, of course, can't even see the taxi driver. She behaves like a queen shamelessly undressing in front of lowly servants. And this is something about her that gets on Urban's nerves.

"And you do all that with that awful fat slob Mešťánek, or what's his name," says Tina, shaking with revulsion after a moment's silence. "You only have to look at that man to see he's sick. His hands are damp, as if he kept them in his underpants. How can you have a friend like that?"

"Freddy isn't a friend," says Urban. "He's my business partner. And that's a big difference."

"And the way he looks at me all the time!" says cousin Tina. "He always looks at my legs. I don't want to meet him again."

"But he doesn't come to Prague that often," Urban defends Freddy.

"Then I don't want to see him when he does," says Tina. "Not even by accident. He doesn't even try to hide those looks he gives. God knows what he thinks about when he looks at me like that."

Well, you know how it is," says Urban. "You're the type that attracts kinky looks."

"I can't imagine any woman desperate enough to go to bed with him," says cousin Tina.

"Would you believe," smiles Video Urban "that his wife is one of Europe's most famous porn stars? And she's damned pretty."

"You must show me what she looks like when we get home," says Tina. "I'm really curious to see her."

At home, Urban puts on the video of *Goddess of Revenge* for Tina, who follows with interest Freddy's wife Sida in various unsavoury situations. Tina is frankly repelled by this kind of spectacle, but, on the other hand, finds it strangely intriguing and alluring. For Video Urban, the situation is extremely exciting and erotic. Shots that he's seen hundreds of times on the screen excite him unusually in this new context. He begins to kiss his cousin in her armchair and slowly undresses her. Tina makes only a token resistance as if the repulsive spectacle had removed all her usual defences. So, finally, Urban makes passionate love to his almost apathetic cousin on the living-room carpet while the screen emits the sporadic moans of tortured girls and the whistling of a cat'o'nine tails.

* * *

After his visit to the Ministry of Defence, Kubeš is naturally more interested in the news about Czech foreign policy. He hunt for articles about international events. He even cuts the articles out and saves them.

He is particularly proud of this story from an old issue of *Flash*:

Not Just Our Survival, but Our Coexistence is at Stake

Ever since the beginning of the civil war in the Junjan Archipelago, Geľo Todor-Lačný-Dolniak, aged 37, has been at the head of the Slovak National Revolutionary Front. The Front aims to form an independent Slovak state to replace the present Junjan Khanate. Todor-Lačný-Dolniak was fighting the Junjans even before the war. As a fur-trapper, he refused to pay exorbitant taxes to the Soviet tax commissars and was gaoled and tortured several times for his refusal. He can be said to be one of the initiators of the civil war, for he took part in the first of the Slovaks' spontaneous punitive campaigns against the Junjans. At first sight, he reminds us of Jánošík, in one of the famous Frič films starring Paľo Bielik. His black plaits hang over his giant chest and his straight back. He looks impressive, even in a baggy suit and garish tie, because of his statuesque two-metre tall body and the impressive tattoos on his face and hands. The same goes for his deputy whose name we are not allowed to know. He arrived in the Czech Republic suddenly on a lightning visit, supposed to stay secret. Nobody from the Ministry of Defence, who hosted the two rebel leaders, felt any need to announce it to the media, so ours was the only reporter to succeed in interviewing the mysterious guest. It's better not to ask about all the things he had to do to get this story.

Q: Why do some Slovaks in your organization use terrorist methods to fight the Junjans? How do you justify Slovak radicals attacking Junjan civilians, too?

A: Look, our statistics show that there are at present some three thousand Slovaks, mostly young people, kept in labour camps. Among them are women, too. They are all innocent. They just happened to have the bad luck of being where the Junjans were carrying out arrests and had to fulfil the planned quota for a labour force to collect lichen. So are you surprised that the Junjans are hated? When a radical kills a Junjan, he is certain that he's doing his duty. It's not the Slovaks' fault. You can't consider this terrorism. Terrorism is when the Junjan régime sends mercenary squads to subdue the trappers' settlements in the north and the mercenaries shoot at anything that moves. The response of the radicals is then to blow up railway tracks used by the mercenaries.

Q: Could you briefly describe the organization of the resistance's armed movement?

A: We attack over the entire archipelago. As the Junjans and their mercenaries, mostly Russians and Ukrainians, are afraid to follow us to the tundra and the northern coast, we have to get them in the cities. We attack at lightning speed and then vanish. Our bases are fishing and hunting settlements on the coast, as well as settlements of nomadic reindeer herders deep in the tundra. We don't have many weapons, and they are mostly hunting rifles. Military weapons have been captured from the Junjans and their mercenaries, by attacking their stores and patrols.

Q: When we compare your compatriots with European Slovaks, there seems to be a big difference: most Carpathian Slovaks before the break-up of Czechoslovakia wanted only autonomy, not independence. Why do you reject everything except independence?

A: As far as I know, in the former Czechoslovakia repression was never so harsh. There were no attempts to limit the birth rate of Slovaks. Slovak trappers, fishermen and reindeer herders in the former Czechoslovakia certainly didn't have to pay the taxes we had to. Besides, there are no real Slovaks living in Europe, except for some strange mixed race for whom the Slovak cause is remote and foreign. They have proved it in their foreign policy by their support for the Junjan government. This is distinct from the Czechs, who support our fight. The European Slovaks are probably afraid that Junjans might make them get visas when they visit. We, the real Slovaks, have no interest in autonomy on paper. We want good neighbours, but our fight is for survival. We can't wait in the hope that someone will give us something. History has clearly shown that nobody grants anyone freedom, if they're not forced to. And we understand that here, in the Junjan archipelago, we shall either live as a free and equal people, or we shan't live at all.

Q: What is the purpose of your visit to the Czech Republic?

A: A short holiday and shopping for a hunting rifle. Why do you ask?

At this point the interview was broken off: despite his waiter's uniform, our reporter was unmasked by security and then escorted from the hotel dining room in an extraordinarily summary manner.

* * *

Video Urban stayed in Prague for several days: work had unexpectedly ran into problems. The content of the films that Urban had brought was so outrageous that the owner of the dubbing studio reneged on the contract. He didn't want trouble with the law. So it took Urban time to find a new studio where he could have the films dubbed into Czech and English.

Of course, Urban is thoroughly enjoying this forced extension of his Prague stay. By day he works and negotiates, and in the evenings he goes for long walks alone or with his cousin Tina to Hradčany, Malá Strana, or Kampa. Cousin Tina welcomes these walks; she likes walking round Prague. They stop in every café they like and order a coffee or a pastry.

In a few days Tina will be celebrating the fifth anniversary of the founding of her design company *Atelier Tina*. Video Urban, as an organizational wizard helps to organize the celebration. To make it a bit different, this time Urban rents a Vltava excursion boat for the evening.

The celebration starts at half past seven in the evening. Until eight they have welcoming drinks and wait for latecomers. Then the boat sounds its horn and weighs anchor by Jirásek Bridge. Slowly and majestically heading south upstream, the boat passes Vyšehrad. Cousin Tina, wearing a simple grey mini suit, and visibly moved, welcomes her guests with a few words and, to the accompaniment of a constant barrage of camera flashes, wishes them a pleasant cruise.

Then comes a fun fashion show. Various personalities from Czech cultural, sport, and society life model Tina's older creations from her previous design periods and, at the end, her newest collection. There is no point mentioning all the prominent models, it would make more sense to list who was not there. But why reopen old wounds?

After the fashion show, comes the free, unstructured part of the event. A jazz trio supplies the music: piano, bass, and drums. On the upper deck there is a well-stocked bar, well patronised from the start; on the lower deck there's a cold and hot buffet. Some members of Tina's fan club have accepted invitations, too, and she has to divide her time among them all. Urban, who alone knows the truth, finds this amusing.

He is just consulting with the captain about the next stage of the excursion boat's itinerary when Tina comes to the bridge. Her eyes flash typical champagne fires. Video Urban introduces her to the captain, whom Tina invites downstairs to join them for a drink.

"I shouldn't really, dear lady," says the boat's captain. "Thanks, but I wouldn't like to get in trouble."

"They wouldn't fire you," says cousin Tina.

"They certainly wouldn't," says the captain. "I wouldn't worry about that. In any case, this is my last cruise on this boat."

"Do you intend to smash us onto the rocks and perish?" asks Tina.

"Not that," smiles captain. "But I'm leaving the firm tomorrow."

"Fancy that!" says cousin Tina. "And what don't you like about it? It's such a beautiful profession."

"It is, especially when I have the pleasure of meeting such charming passengers," says the captain. "But I'd like to go back to sea."

"Are you a sea captain?" cousin Tina is astounded.

"I used to be an officer on a sea-going ship," says the captain. "But then the Czech merchant fleet was sold, and I had to take this job. But I've found a new job. Abroad," he add quickly.

"That's a pity," says cousin Tina coquettishly. "Who's going to take us on Vltava cruises?"

"They'll find someone," says the captain, smiling. "Those three years have been enough for me."

"Well, you should come with us and drink a toast," says Tina. "This is a big day for you, too. After all, you have a helmsman."

"Yes, you're right, probably," says the captain, who buttons up the modest, but neat uniform originally designed for railwaymen, puts on his cap and follows Tina and Video Urban downstairs.

"Are you all right, cousin?" asks Tina. "Have you taken a vow of silence?"

"Maybe you should drink less, Tina," says Urban tensely and quietly.

But Tina hasn't heard: she just addresses the company assembled on the upper deck.

"Ladies and gentlemen!" she shouts, and her every gesture and her posture is imbued by the certainty that she looks fabulous in her suit. "Let me introduce you to Captain Kubiš, the man in charge of this vessel."

"Kubeš," the captain corrects her.

"Kubeš," says Tina. "Captain Kubeš has just told me that this is his last voyage and tomorrow he goes abroad to follow the call of the sea."

"Bravo!" someone shouts out and a few guests applaud.

"So let's drink to the success of Captain Kubeš!" shouts Tina and takes two glasses of sparkling wine from a waiter in sailor's uniform. She gives one to the captain. The jazz trio plays a fanfare that gradually turns into an old hit song, *Captain, where are you taking that ship?* made famous by the *Semafor* theatre. Some people join in the singing.

"And won't you miss Prague?" Tina asks Kubeš after the song and the applause. "I couldn't go away for so long."

"I shall," smiles captain. "But not that much. I'm not leaving for good, after all. I'll always be happy to come back here."

By now the boat has got as far Modřany. It turns round and heads back to the city. Darkness has fallen. As the boat slowly sails through the city, the passengers watch the street lamps coming on.

"It's a beautiful city," says the captain. "You know, I'm certain that Prague is a giant receiver, accumulator and radiator of cosmic energy."

"How do you mean?" asks Urban.

"Whoever enters its force field will never be able to live without it," says the captain. "And anyone forbidden to visit it for a long time will end his life in torment and die of longing, like, for example, Angelo Maria Ripellino, an Italian, the author of *Magic Prague*."

"I love Prague too, but I've never heard that," says Urban. "Do you believe it?"

"I didn't see it that way before," says the captain. "I was born in Prague, you know. And then I studied abroad, or sailed the seas... and every time I came home I had the strange feeling that something was flowing into me, some force. And that charged me with energy."

"Yes," says Tina. "I feel exactly as you do. Every time I come back here from anywhere I always feel something taking me over, the city claiming me with thousands of gentle fingers, putting them in my eyes, ears, my mouth, my nose, everywhere."

"In every orifice, in fact," Urban sustains his lightly ironic pose. "Could it be the Prague smog?"

"Look, you love Prague, too," says Tina. "So why the irony?"

"Oh, I love it, no question" says Urban. "But I don't look for irrational explanations. Living here is just different from living in Bratislava. There are a lot of beautiful cities and, if you insist, a lot called magical. Paris, for example, is another city whose air you have to breathe. And London?"

"That's quite different," says the captain. "Prague is simply unique in its way. Old Prague. Do you know, looked at from above, its architecture is a cleverly organized, astronomically oriented developing structure?"

"Seriously?" Tina is astounded.

"Of course, the question is: is this organization conscious or just spontaneous, automatic and basically unconscious?" says the captain. "But some indications clearly confirm the first possibility, particularly in its foundation period. Further development of the architectural structure was involuntary but still seems to be governed by some coded ontogenetic experience."

The boat is sailing by Mánes and the National Theatre. Cousin Tina looks with respect at Castle Hill, all lit up.

"Look, St Vitus's cathedral!" says the captain. "How many meanings are encoded in just its ground plan!"

"How many?" eagerly asks cousin Tina.

"That'd take too long to describe," says the captain with a smile. "There's a book called *Praga Mysteriosa*. It can help you discover the hidden mysteries yourself, or together with your cousin."

"You must tell me about it one day!" sighs Tina. "I could listen to you forever!"

"*Praga caput regni,*" says Kubeš, looking at the towers of Prague and the illuminated Charles Bridge in the distance ahead of them.

"What does that mean?" asks cousin Tina. "I've often heard that, but I must confess that I don't know what it means."

"Prague destroyed by rain," Urban attempts a translation.

"Prague, queen of cities," Kubeš corrects him. "Or, rather, mother of cities."

"Of course," says Urban meekly. "I was only joking."

Before the weir between Kampa and Charles Bridge, the boat stops and drops anchor. Smiling, Video Urban takes out his mobile phone, calls a number and issues a order. The park between Werich's villa and Sova's mills conceals a team of fireworks men who will start a festive fireworks show. Against the dark sky, with a garishly illuminated Malá Strana, golden, red, and green sparkling fountains of fire race over the sky.

"Wow!" shouts cousin Tina and claps enthusiastically.

When the company leaves the excursion boat, the captain naturally and unobtrusively falls in with Tina and Urban.

"All the same, it's an odd feeling," he says, as the three of them walk along Rašín Embankment towards the National Theatre. "I was so much looking forward to leaving this job one day, but now I have a strange feeling. On the one hand, I'm happy I've found something I'm qualified for, but on the other hand, I'll probably miss those little Prague boats."

They sip Czech sparkling wine from glasses they took from the boat. When they finish, they leave the empty bottle and glasses on a stone balustrade above the river and continue walking. "People are never content with what they have," says Tina, "and always want something else."

"Yes, that's how it is," agrees the captain. "You know what? I'd like to invite you for a nightcap. Will you have the last drink with me?"

"Why not?" says Tina and turns to Urban. "Let's do it, right?"

"What's still open now?" Urban thinks aloud. "Yes, *Beránek's Refreshment Room*. But we'll have to cross to the other side."

"I don't want to go there," says cousin Tina. "It's full of smoke. I vote for *Slavia*. At least they've got air conditioning."

"Yes, that's a good idea," the captain agrees.

Of course, the *Café Slavia* is closed.

"Nothing doing," says cousin Tina. "It wasn't meant to be, I suppose. We shall certainly meet again. Can we drop you off in our taxi?"

"No, thanks," said the captain. "I live in Smíchov. The underground gets me there in five minutes."

"Well, then we'll see you to the underground station," suggests Tina.

They turn round and slowly walk back, to Palacký Square.

"You know," says the captain after a while, "I have the feeling that we haven't just met today but have known each other for years."

"Yes," says the cousin Tina. "I have the same feeling."

Urban feels a bit of a gooseberry and hangs back at least a few steps.

"It's a pity you have to go abroad," says cousin Tina. "I've never heard anyone talk so interestingly about Prague. When you come for a short holiday you must call me."

"I'll certainly do so," says the captain. "Now that I know you, it's not going to be so easy to go."

And so on.

He says goodbye with a long handshake.

"So long, mate," says Urban, shaking his hand, too. "When you get back, you must visit us and tell us more. And we'll buy that book."

He uses the plural on purpose, so the bloke doesn't get any ideas.

The captain runs down the stairs. Halfway down he stops, turns round and waves to them. Then he vanishes in the underpass.

Tina is moved.

"As if we were seeing a friend off to do military service," says Urban to lighten the atmosphere.

"Call a taxi, please," says cousin Tina. "My mobile's dead. And don't get jealous, please."

"But he was making a pass at you in front of me," says Urban. "How can I not be jealous!"

"You're my cousin, not my husband," says Tina. "And anyway, it was quite different. Everything was on such a high spiritual level that it couldn't have affected you."

"Should I take offence now?" asks Urban, bewildered.

"It's a pity you meet some people only when it's too late," says Tina, and Urban ponders what she meant by that.

"Just have your fun, my girl," he thinks. She can have esoteric discussions with other men, but when she feels like good-quality sex, it will be with him, the ever ready, dependable and discreet Video Urban.

* * *

Kubeš drives out of Prague on Sunday afternoon. He takes the Brno motorway. After a few kilometres, he turns off towards Velké Popovice. The ineffable beauty of the countryside he passes through enchants him. Every now and again he stops the car and revels in his surroundings. He stops for lunch near Žampach, in the Hotel Troníček, which he reaches by leaving the highway and going all the way down to the river Sázava. The hotel dining room reminds him of restaurants in port cities of England and Scotland when he was in the merchant fleet. It is old, dark, and meticulously clean. From outside comes the roar of the weir. Kubeš orders steak with lingonberries and a small Gambrinus beer. Then he resumes his journey: over the steel bridge near Kamenný Přívoz in the direction of Lešany. He has a detailed map of the Sázava region, but just to be sure, he asks in the village pub in Lešany about the way to the military base.

"You want to see the military museum, do you?" says a man in overalls sipping his beer in front of the pub. "There's no military unit there now. Almost no soldiers any more. I'd know about it, I used to work there. I was a civilian buildings caretaker. Now there's a museum of military technology."

"I know that," says Kubeš.

"And is that where you want to go?" asks the helpful villager.

Kubeš nods.

"Look," the man explains. "You head down there until you hit the fork at the pond, then you turn left towards Krhanice. And to get to Krhanice you turn onto this narrow road before the bridge over the Sázava. You'll see a sign 'Military Museum'. That road takes you to the old base. Got it?"

Kubeš thanks him, start his Škoda Favorit and moves off. He drives slowly, looking round. The old military base's sleepy village look fills him with mixed feelings, idyllic and depressed. As if generations of soldiers, who all these years lived, suffered, drank beer, went AWOL, and drove to exercises, had left in this location some eloquent but unidentifiable trace. And the entire area was steeped in the smell of camouflage uniforms, blank ammunition, duty assignments and black boot polish.

Soon in the distance, at the end of a lane, he spots buildings. This is the Museum of Military Technology. He sounds his horn at the gate. An elderly man comes out, clearly a retired local earning extra as a museum receptionist. He looks at Kubeš with suspicion. He checks his documents.

"Well, you go to the mobilisation warehouse," he mumbles and opens the gate. "Go straight down this road, round the canteen and stores, to the other gate. You show your papers there. We're just museum staff here."

The receptionist shows him the way to go and the asphalt road that cuts through the thick pine wood around the barracks.

Visitors to the museum use this narrow road. Kubeš drives slowly. He passes by a sign warning museum visitors that the area further down is guarded and not part of the museum.

Mobilisation warehouse, Kubeš thinks. What an excellent cover for a secret training facility of any kind, including the navy!

At the second gate stand military policemen in camouflage uniforms. A glum second lieutenant checks his documents, then salutes him.

"All in order, naval lieutenant," he says quietly, so that visitors to the museum can't hear him as they take refreshment at the snack bar.

"Aha, so they've already given me naval rank," Kubeš realises with mixed feelings. It felt the same when he was promoted sergeant during his compulsory military service, after he had graduated: he pretended to be angry, but actually he was proud of his promotion.

"Go straight down and stop at the first crossroads," says the second lieutenant. "Turn left and stop at the first building. That's headquarters. Report to naval captain Vacula. He's the quartermaster and registrar. Welcome to the Museum training base, sir!"

Naval captain Vacula is a jovial and sociable alcoholic, like most headquarters dry-land rats.

"Listen to me, my good man," says Vacula in a voice that suggests that he is now repeating something he has said several times this day. "Every one starts at the rank stated in his military ID. You went home after basic military service as second lieutenant in the reserve. And three years ago you were promoted to lieutenant. Have you been on manœuvres?"

"No," says Kubeš. "They just sent me a promotion notice."

"Oh well," sighs Vacula. "You're now naval lieutenant engineer Kubeš. Of course, you realise your rank is secret for now. Here's a comparative table of naval and army ranks for you. You'll note some variations in it."

Vacula hands back his military ID and adds a photocopied flyer.

"You can study this later," he says. "Now go and settle in, my friend. Go up the hill, and the last barracks before the medical centre is the officers'. You came by car? You can leave it parked behind the kitchens. You won't be needing it for some time. The barracks duty officer will show you your room. Then you'll get your uniform and kit. And afterwards you can take a look round. You might like to look at the museum, too, it's quite interesting. But you have to get a move on, because a little welcoming party starts in the officers' mess at seven."

"Where's the mess?" asks Kubeš.

"When you leave this building, then just opposite, across the parade ground," says Vacula, "on the ground floor is the mess. That's where we'll meet. Don't forget, at seven!"

Kubeš parks as instructed, takes his bag from the boot and sets off to find the officers' quarters. As he walks, he studies this leaflet:

List of Ranks in the Czech Naval Fleet

Navy	Army Equivalent
Admiral of the Fleet	Full General
Vice Admiral	Colonel General
Rear Admiral	Lieutenant General
Commodore	Major General
Corvette	Captain Colonel
First Captain	Lieutenant Colonel
Captain	Major
Commander	Captain
Lieutenant Commander	First Lieutenant
Lieutenant	Lieutenant
Second Lieutenant	Second Lieutenant
Warrant Officer	Sergeant Major
Petty Officer	Sergeant
Leading Rating	Corporal
Seaman	Private

All the barracks in a row were flat-roofed, single-storey buildings, just renovated and painted green. On the other side of the street was another row of identical buildings. There must have been a big military presence here in the past. Kubeš enters the last of the green barracks. He is met by cool air and the smell of paint, disinfectant and boot polish. He can hear the sound of running water in the washroom.

Well, here I go, he thinks as he puts his things into a tin locker. Luckily, the room is not full of bunks. It reminds him more of a hospital room than of military accommodation. There's no one in the room, but personal objects strewn on the beds suggest that the owners are not very far away. He can hear the sound of voices and a ball bouncing. Somebody is playing volleyball behind the barracks.

Kubeš gets up and, after all, goes to take a look at the museum. He wants to be alone for a while and think things over.

* * *

The officers' welcoming party deteriorates into an unbridled drinking binge. Kubeš remembers standing in the middle of the square-bashing ground with Skopšík, Libáň and Mikuš until three in the morning and shouting confused orders at the moon. They'd finally realised they were in the army and behaved accordingly.

Had they known what was awaiting them in the days to come, they'd have been more careful and have retired at ten.

Reveille is unusually rough. Vice Admiral Sosna — who merely dipped his lips in bourbon the night before, and left before midnight — goes in person from room to room, mercilessly shoving the future naval officers and their sleeping bags off the beds.

"Move it, move it, gentlemen!" roars a warrant officer with big veins on his neck. "Get into your track suits and form ranks for a warm-up! Let's get going! Let's get moving!"

Kubeš is so disoriented by it all that he obeys blindly. He wakes up properly only when he is on a third run with the others round the barracks. Everywhere around him he sees white and green faces and droplets of terminal sweat spraying everywhere; nobody can get his breath back, and some are kneeling by a ditch, vomiting.

"What the fuck have we got into?" says Libáň, shocked and gasping for breath. "I'm not doing this shit!"

"For the money they give us," Kubeš gasps, "I'll do one more run…"

The run is over.

"Attention, men!" orders a tall young man in a tracksuit, a whistle on a string round his neck. "Follow me in rows of two! One! Two!"

Muttering, all twenty future navy officers obey. It takes time for them to mingle and calm down.

The young man faces the trainees.

"First row, take four steps forward!" he orders. "One! Two! Spread out at arms length!"

He parades in front of the trainees. Some are still out of breath.

"Gentlemen, my name's Buzina!" he says sternly. "First Lieutenant Buzina." (His surname sounds like *buzík*, queer.)

He waits with stony calm for the odd suppressed giggle to stop. Not many giggle, since most trainees are still fighting oxygen deficiency.

"Just so as you know, I'm heterosexual and married," adds Buzina.

"That means nothing," Skopšík whispers in Kubeš's ear. "I know queers with two children."

"And I have two children," says Buzina. "But what should interest you is that I'm in charge of physical training for this touring circus. And it's my task to instil in you in the next two months at least a semblance of physical readiness. Naturally, I count on your cooperation. Before we get into gymnastics, I'd like you to note that you began to earn your pay fifteen minutes ago. So try to do something for the money."

After another fifteen minutes of torture, Buzina dismisses them to their rooms. This is followed by personal hygiene, then putting on uniform, and afterwards they muster for breakfast.

The breakfast is substantial, though not very appetising. A military meal. Of course, Kubeš shows a good appetite. He's firmly committed to succeeding. After all, he has no option. They've all signed contracts and are subject to military law.

The situation in which he now finds himself still seems like a dream from which he can wake up at any time. He remembers coming back from the military many years ago — as a student abroad he had to do two years — and having constant nightmares of being forced back to his military unit. In his dreams he had never finished basic military service and had to put in extra time. He had to go as he was, wrenched from civilian life. Now the dream had come true.

After breakfast the novices have to change into camouflage and a captain takes them over for drill, marching them round the parade ground for two hours. It's bearable because, although boring, it's a lot of fun doing it. And even captain Macháček has some sense of the absurdity of human life, so the two hours pass quickly.

They gradually get into it. Their bodies recollect, way back from basic military service, reflexes they've pushed to the back of their minds for only a few years. A reservist needs less time than a novice to get the hang of military drill.

Sosna joins them at the end of drill. He musters them into two rows, tells them to stand at ease, and briefly explains the daily routine of their intense training. Above all, he stresses the need for secrecy and the banning of any leave outside the area, namely Krhanice village.

"I'd hate more than anything to see you in Prague," says Sosna. "I'd like to have a man-to-man talk with you about making Prague a taboo subject for all of us for the next two months. I do have to go to the ministry from time to time, but I promise not to abuse this. During your training I'll live here, at headquarters, and will eat what you eat. We can do it together. You must realise that you will have to learn in two months what cadets in naval officer training in advanced naval powers take years to achieve. I'd also recommend that, when you do eventually get leave, you move about in small groups. I'd suggest that no more than four people should go out together. Look, there are a lot of pubs nearby. I'd ask you to spread yourself out among them, if you have to go. No large group pub crawls. As far as the public's concerned, you're civilian museum employees. That is why you will wear civvies and nobody will touch your over-long hair. For the time being."

Sosna smiles.

"You'll go through tough training here," he continues. "None of it is unnecessary or senseless hassling. Everything has deep significance. Keep in mind that nobody wants to humiliate you or insult your dignity. You're well-paid professionals: take it like that. I'd also like to note one important thing: I want you to address each other formally not just as serving officers, but also when you're off duty. I realise it's an unusual request, but perhaps you won't find it so hard. Even Holmes and Watson knew each other for years but addressed each other formally."

Sosna detects a muffled protest.

"I'll tell you why I insist on it," he says. "I won't deny that all your scores are being kept. You are constantly being evaluated and awarded points, even as you sleep. The top two of your group will be submarine captains. The others will be warrant officers and chief engineers. The only secure posts in your group are those of ship's medical doctors lieutenant Dr Ondriáš and sub-lieutenant Dr Svatý. Nobody gets pally with the submarine captain. So far we don't know which of you will become one. That's why we'll address each other formally, so that it won't be hard to switch later. This is an order. You'll get used to it. Well, that should be all for now: we'll see each other in specialised training. Captain Macháček, carry on!"

After the drill session, the unit goes to a classroom in the headquarters building. Captain Dr Jíra, a military historian, is already waiting for them.

"Although we Czechs have no sea of our own, we do have a rich submarine tradition," Dr. Jíra starts his first lecture. "In the Austro-Hungarian naval fleet during World War One, the Czechs formed the basis of the ships' qualified crew. That applied to submarines as well. A long time has passed since then, but it's a tradition the Czech navy will build on."

Then follows a factual history of submarines as weapons, with examples of combat missions.

Some of the audience can't bear it and fall into a deep sleep. Captain Jíra ignores them. He concentrates on those who listen with interest.

Then the future naval officers change into service uniform and are mustered for lunch, whose quality pleasantly surprises Kubeš.

After lunch there's an hour's free time. Most trainees spend it lying on their bunks. The free time is very short. As soon as the future naval officers fall asleep, a warrant officer is there to call them to muster. Their garb is workmen's overalls. Sosna, also dressed in black military overalls, is awaiting them. He leads them through the pine wood to a big hangar.

"Gentlemen, what you're about to see inside will probably surprise you," he says before entering the hangar. "You'll spend the most of your training time here. Everything else, drills, physical training and theory is grey stuff. Eternally green is the tree of praxis."

"And your brain," mumbles Libáň.

Sosna slides the hangar door open and the trainees catch the breathtaking sight of a real submarine, loftily enthroned on steel supports.

"Has anyone ever been in a submarine?" Sosna wants to know.

A few hands come up. "Where was it, Mr Rajter?" Sosna asks.

"In Odessa, Vice Admiral," says Rajter. "In the Black Sea fleet museum. They have a Shch- class submarine at anchor."

"And you, Mr Mikuš?" Sosna enquires.

Kubeš can't help admiring the man's phenomenal memory.

"In Cuba," says Mikuš. "In a Cuban submarine. On a friendly visit."

The men break out laughing.

"Well, yes," says Sosna. "Cuba. Havana Club. Well, this is the German class U-XXI, one of the last models before the end of the war. Gentlemen, this is a submarine that could have given the Nazis victory in the Atlantic, if it had appeared two years earlier. Its original designation is U-XXI, but for Czech Navy purposes it is designated P-45/M. 'P' stands for *ponorka* (submarine), 1945 the year it was produced, and 'M' modification of the vessel. This one is of course a simulator. All controls and regulators go via an interface to a computer so we can simulate every kind of situation."

Sosna walks round the vessel, which looks like a beached whale.

"The Czech Navy has acquired two seaworthy submarines of this type," he says. "They are now undergoing a full refit in dry dock in Latvia. By the way, the P-45/M was the world's first real combat submarine. That means this vessel could move under water for a long time, and not just keep that option for times of danger. It was more comfortable for the crew than previous submarines. The interior was quieter, and there's even a refrigerator on board for food, a shower cubicle, and other features. You'll see for yourself. Of course, most interior fittings for the crew have been replaced by modern ones. So, anyone hoping to see a fridge of the Thousand Year Reich period is bound to be disappointed. And now, please, follow me."

Sosna climbs up to the platform round the submarine roughly at deck height. He nimbly climbs into the conning tower and slips into the opening.

The trainees follow him one by one.

The twenty future submariners have to spread out in a narrow space along the vessel. Luckily, Sosna's voice carries well through the submarine.

"We're now in the submarine's command centre," Sosna points around himself. "Above all, this is the captain's, duty officers' and first mate's work space. Could anyone tell me in one word what is typical of any submarine?"

The trainees are quiet.

"It's the symbol of a submarine, really," Sosna hints. "A symbol of its deviousness, if you like. Does anyone know?"

"Torpedoes," Libáň says confidently.

"No," Sosna smiles. "Destroyers have torpedoes, too, so do torpedo boats and aeroplanes. Any other suggestions?"

"A periscope?" Kubeš asks, talking to himself.

"Louder, please!" Sosna shouts. "Yes, a periscope! You know, the submarine is the most treacherous of all warfare devices. And a periscope is a submarine's eyesight. A submarine can see, but stays mostly unseen. Notice that when you see a film and the director wants to suggest action in a submarine, they show a man with a periscope.

Sosna pushes a lever and a shiny column in the middle of the bridge slides up with smooth buzz. Sosna pulls its handles out with a snap and presses his eyes to the eyepieces, which have a black spongy frame.

"Take a look," he tells the trainees.

Nobody can resist the chance to look through a periscope.

"It's dark now, of course," says Sosna. "In training you'll see enemy ships on its computer screen. Now follow me. We'll go from front to back."

And so the trainees start at the very front. They learn that the torpedo section of the P-45/M submarine is equipped with a hydraulic self-arming mechanism which can arm all six torpedo tubes in about ten minutes, less time than a VIIC class, the commonest German submarine, took to arm a single tube.

"Of course, this information is irrelevant to you," says Sosna. "On your combat mission you'll be carrying something else in this section."

Touring the submarine takes two hours: from the torpedo section to the crew quarters and mess, the officers' quarters and mess, the captain's cabin, the radar and sonar stations, the command station, the non-commissioned officers' quarters, mess, kitchen, washroom and lavatory ("This is a simulator, gentlemen, please don't use the lavatory.") and then the diesel-electric engine room, and the rear torpedo section.

"Compared to submarines of the earlier class, P-45/M has triple-capacity electric batteries, which give it an enormous underwater radius of action," says Sosna. "A snorkel allows it to recharge the batteries under water. It needs at most three to five hours to recharge. Travelling at a speed of four to eight knots, it needs charging once every two to three days. This makes the vessel far less vulnerable. Well, that'll do for today, gentlemen."

As they leave the submarine, the bright light surprises Kubeš. The submarine was dim, even though the light was on and all the service openings were wide open for ventilation.

Back in their quarters, the trainees change into service uniforms and muster for dinner. When they get back from dinner, they have the order of the day. After that is free time. They can leave the barracks. This, however, is only a theoretical opportunity that nobody takes. They all collapse onto their bunks and soon the barrack echoes with rhythmical breathing.

Only Kubeš cannot get to sleep. He wonders what the mysterious beauty that he so fatefully met in Prague at the last moment might be up to. And what about his ex-girlfriend whom he left the day he came back drunk from the *Riga* tavern? Or did she leave him?

Kubeš feels as if he has spent at least a week here, not just two days. "I'll make it," he thinks. "I have to," says a second voice. "I have to be better than the others. The very best." He falls asleep with these thoughts and wakes up in the morning to the ringing of his alarm clock.

The days come and go, one after the other. After a week the strenuous drill no longer seems so unbearable. Their bodies overcome the first attacks of muscle fever and demand high doses of exertion. First Lieutenant Buzina no longer takes morning exercises: the leader is always one of them, whoever's on the rota. Similarly, morning drill, an important part of any disciplined army, reverts to a reasonable level and now the trainees issue their own orders for their regular drill hour.

For specialised training, after the first lectures for everybody, they are divided into two separate teams, depending whether they are meant to become warrant officers or chief engineers.

Part of the warrant officers' simulated training is a commercial computer game *Silent Hunter 2*, whose software has been modified to transfer all its data to displays on the bridge. The same goes for controlling the directional and depth steering mechanism, flooding and clearing the submersion tanks, controlling the periscope, and every other submarine control. All sounds in the computer game are amplified, so the sound experience is a realistic rendering of a diesel engine, the buzz of electric motors, the noise of a destroyer passing above the submarine, the hull cracking under pressure in very deep water, or exploding depth charges. In training the trainees learn various tactics for evading surface vessels if they are identified and consequently pursued. These are all defensive tactics: none of them is offensive.

"This is what your real combat mission will be like," explains Sosna. "You won't have any effective means of defence. No torpedoes. Only a double-barrelled 88mm cannon on the deck, just in case. So you'll depend above all on your cunning and ingenuity. Your victory will consist not in sinking your opponent, but in successfully evading him."

Nevertheless, Sosna kindly allows them occasionally, at the end of a demanding training day in the simulator, to fire torpedoes and sink a few virtual enemy vessels.

"That's only for fun, of course," he never omits to mention. "And as a kind of reward, since you've done particularly well today. You were sunk only three times after lunch and managed to escape eight times. You seem to be getting better, gentlemen. So let's have another go and this time with torpedoes. Show that destroyer who's boss!"

But it isn't only specialised training that turns them into soldiers. In parallel they get classical army training, centred on reconnaissance and diversionary tactics. Their instructor is paratroops Major Dvořák.

"The fact that you're submariners," he tells them at the first meeting "doesn't mean that you'll be stuck in a submarine all the time, even though it's the best place to be. A submarine crew has to be able to survive for some time under combat conditions off-board, too, in the real world, if you're reconnoitring unknown terrain, freeing and rescuing prisoners or hostages, transferring military material, or even — touch wood! — dealing with a submarine wreck and recovering the crew on foreign soil. Briefly, my aim is to teach you how to fight away from your fighting ship, on dry land with a gun, a knife, and your bare hands. You've all been through the training and know what I'm talking about. So, gentlemen, let's not waste any more time and get down to it. We don't have much time."

There is little time and even less free time. Reckless pub crawls, downing endless glasses of beer, are now only a fantasy. They're all glad, when, after the order of the day, they can throw their tired bodies on a bunk and rest.

Only a small core, notably Kubeš and Libáň, regularly change their clothes after their day's work: they put on track suits and say they're going for a run, but take off along the forest path over a hill called Polygon to the pub in Lešany where Kubeš asked for directions two weeks ago.

Their long hair and moustaches arouse no suspicions among the pub's patrons, who take them for weekend chalet owners from Prague on holiday. After two or three glasses of beer, they run back and refresh themselves with sleep before another demanding day.

Naturally, the men constantly ask themselves questions about the real nature of their mission. They try to work it out from the training they get. If a mystery hangs in the air, various guesses and hypotheses are inevitable.

But Sosna is silent. Smiling, he refuses to say a thing.

"You'll know everything in good time," is his invariable response.

The following days continue the tough training, and the lectures on the submarine navigation, tactics, and missions. The trainees are quite unaware how quickly two months have passed.

Then comes the time when Sosna, at the order of the day, announces the two best trainees who will be submarine captains: one is Kubeš; the other Kylar. Both are immediately promoted to the rank of lieutenant commander. Libáň and Drličiak are named first warrant officers with the rank of lieutenant commander. Skopšík and Machovský are second warrant officers. Kraus and Bílck are third warrant officers. The engineering trainees are given ranks according to their scores.

"From now on, you are Crew A and Crew B," says Sosna. "On board you'll find detailed instructions. You will report from tomorrow accordingly. In a few days, your warrant officers and non-commissioned officers will join you and will be attached to your crews. You will pass on to them all that you've learned over these two months. Of course, we'll be here to help you. But the men will be only as good as you make them."

After this assembly, a mass migration of people takes place. Officers from Crew B move to the first floor, while officers of Crew A take the ground floor. Each submarine commander has his own room with a desk and a safe built into the wall. Similarly, warrant officers and engineers now live in their own three-bed rooms. In the evening a small celebration, with all the instructors present, takes place in the officer's mess. Although the next day is Saturday, the first real free day since the beginning of the intensive course, nobody stays up late. Over the last two months even the biggest party animals have learned the value of sleep.

The next day Kubeš wakes up at six, unconsciously expecting reveille. It doesn't come. They're all catching up on lost sleep.

Kubeš gets up, changes from his canary-yellow pyjamas into a tracksuit and goes for a run to the Polygon. At the edge of the wood he runs uphill and then slows as he climbs the path. His nose takes in the autumnal forest's fragrance. Looking at the tall yellow grass Kubeš remembers a tactical exercise they underwent with Major Dvořák, his mouth full of dust and sand, and his lungs fighting for a breath of fresh air. You could have wrung their uniforms out, they were so wet.

At the top, at the highest point of the Polygon that is unnamed point 360, Kubeš stops to catch his breath. He looks back. The military base and the museum are below him, in the beautiful Sázava valley. The encroaching autumn has stripped the surrounding woods of foliage, and the buildings are all clearly visible. In the distance, on the other side of the river, above the railway, you can see a quarry; to its right is a hunting castle and the slope of Priest Mountain. The Sázava valley is beautiful country, and in autumn it is the most beautiful place in the world.

On the other side of the Polygon, Kubeš runs down into the village. In the grocer's near the little castle, he buys a newspaper and ends up in *Pavel's Pub*, with pork brawn and a beer.

* * *

On Monday morning, Sosna summons both submarine commanders and their first officers to join him in the crisis room.

"I shan't waste your time with pointless preambles," says Sosna. "The time's come to tell you about the mission that we've prepared you for."

Sosna walks up to a big map.

"This is the Junja archipelago," he says. "It lies beyond the Arctic circle. All the details of its geography, population, industry, and political situation you'll find in a file in front of each one of you. I assume that, if you read the papers, you'll have some knowledge of the present situation. For our purpose we need now to focus on two important facts: first, some of the population is of Slovak origin and the Czechs have backed their fight for independence ever since the conflict broke out."

Sosna makes a dramatic pause, as if considering whether he should mention the second point.

"The second fact is one that you will not find discussed in the press," he continues after a moment, "and it concerns our own wellbeing, rather than our relationship to this fraternal nation. From casual remarks by Junjan Slovaks who came here on a visit, our intelligence analysts learned interesting facts. We therefore secretly sent a group of experts to the Junjan archipelago to carry out a geological survey. Their findings have made a big impact on our military secret service: under the archipelago are the world's biggest oil deposits. Luckily, they are so deep that no satellite has found them. On the island of Öggdbardd, the biggest and the main island of the whole archipelago, oil comes to the surface. The locals of Slovak origin have for generations travelled there for fuel. Gentlemen, when drilling starts, Kuwait and Saudi Arabia can pack up. They're finished! According to preliminary findings, this is the purest oil ever found anywhere. Luckily for us, the local population of Slovak origin have managed to keep the existence of these deposits secret from the Junjans as well as from their former Soviet rulers and the present fascist regime. The Czech Crown believes that it is necessary to help the Junjan Slovaks attain independence. It is a moral issue and accords with the Masaryk-Havel traditions of the Czech State. Besides, there's oil and other natural resources, right?"

Sosna shows them another map, showing the sailing route.

"Your secret combat mission is to transport in two submarines type P-45/M humanitarian help for the Slovak resistance: medicine, food, weapons and ammunition. After the victory of the democratic Slovak forces in Junja, the reason for the mission's strict secrecy will lapse and you will be able to admit publicly your assignment to the Czech navy's submarine fleet. Until then, not a word is allowed. Your combat mission will be performed in civilian clothing; neither submarine will have national or other identification. In any emergency, the Czech Ministry of Defence won't acknowledge your mission and so it is in your own interest to avoid situations where you could be discovered, so you won't be acting the hero for no reason."

The vice-admiral passes cigars round.

"This is the most secret and most dangerous mission in the history of the Czech military and secret service as such," he says, "including World War Two and the assassination of Heydrich. This is why you will have to keep the mission's goal secret from your crews until the last moment. Submarine Number 1 will sail with its cargo on February 1st. Which crew mans it will be decided by your scores, as before. That seems to be all for now. Any questions?"

The four men are shocked into silence.

"This looks like a very simple mission, sir," says Kubeš. "What's the catch?"

Sosna laughs.

"You've earned a point, Mr. Kubeš," he says. "Naturally, there's a catch, and I won't hide it from you. I'd have told you even without prompting from Lieutenant Commander Kubeš. Well: the extraterritorial waters round the Junjan archipelago are patrolled by Russian navy ships. Russians keep out of the conflict, they observe strict neutrality, but, in fact, what they're doing round Junja is really a naval blockade. Our information is that helicopter gunships and torpedo ships check all ships headed for the archipelago. You'll have to break a blockade. That's why the submarines."

Sosna gets up, to show that the meeting is over.

"You'll make it, gentlemen," he says and, against regulations, shakes the hands of all four men.

"We expect the warrant officers and non-commissioned officers to join us this afternoon," he says. "I'd like you to be their superior officers and commanders straight away. And now, gentlemen, off to work!"

* * *

Life is cruel and merciless: even a dead man is two days' work.
Junjan Slovak proverb

When the Soviet system collapsed in Russia, the hunters' collectives in the Junjan islands disintegrated. The real workers, the Slovak trappers and hunters, sensed that the Junjan officials no longer had any backing. The officials were not shot, as they were by the nomads, nor were they tipped into the sea, as they were by Slovak fishermen. The trappers just stopped delivering pelts to the trading posts. They preferred to work the pelts themselves and sell them in the cities, or to adventurous Norwegians, Swedes or Americans whose ships strayed too close to the shore in the summer. Only now did the Slovaks realise how valuable white and blue fox pelts and reindeer skins were. An American would pay as much as two or three paper dollars for a pelt, depending on quality. And those paper dollars would buy in Űŕġüllpoļ or Ćmirçăpoļ more goods than the Slovak trappers had ever seen before.

The *Üngütür ököltott* (Morning Glory) officials had no one to exploit and were left without support. The permanently drunk Bolshevik commissar Yasin cleared the settlement warehouse, loaded it onto a ship and went back with his sidekicks to the motherland. Gargâ's Junjan officials were helpless without their Russian Bolsheviks. Russian ships stopped bringing tinned food, vodka, tobacco, coffee, and diesel for the electric generator. The decline was irreversible. The Junjans began to starve.

Some decided to raid nearby Slovak settlements and make them hand over food. The Slovaks knew that times had changed, kicked the Junjans out, fired in the air, beat them with sticks and set their dogs on them.

For Junjan settlements, hard times had come. Some, the younger and more capable, left for the cities. Only the stupid, old, and helpless were left behind in the settlements. They lived on shore mice and fishing. Now and again they stole something from the Slovaks, but the latter soon began to keep an eye them. They left nothing outside even at night, and moved everything into their yurts. Their dogs guarded their natural ice-block refrigerators outside.

Gargâ settlement lay under a hillside on the steep shore. Former collective farm officials lived there. Their yurts were poor and jerry-built. Some were large, with a domed roof, others were small, roofed with cardboard and plastic bags. In the middle of the settlement was the collective's once proud fur-trading post. Of the huge one-storey warehouse building only the massive foundations and remnants of the installations were left. Plywood insulation panels, bits of corrugated iron roof, columns and all the interior equipment had been taken by the settlement's inhabitants. The huge diesel generator, left to rust, had not been moved. It was no use to anyone, and, besides, the Junjans were afraid of it. Even now, cold and motionless, it stuck out in the chilling wind like a big black shadow. The Junjans made a big detour round it.

At one end of this scattered settlement stood pointed yurts patched with burlap, old pelts, and pieces of sealskin. This is where the oldest or laziest inhabitants lived.

It was night and a wild storm blew in from the sea. Özgett Glebąâr stumbled up from somewhere between the seashore and the frozen tundra. Icicles hung from his beard, moustaches, and eyebrows. He kept falling and getting up and a rattle came from his chest. He used his last ounce of strength to crawl to the first yurt and collapsed against a piece of corrugated iron over the entrance: he and the iron sheet crashed inside.

The people at home were then all drunk on industrial alcohol they had stolen somewhere. It tasted good and it relieved the pangs of hunger and cold. They lay prostrate on the floor, breathing heavily. None of them noticed Glebąâr's entrance. Özgett Glebąâr grabbed a bottle and took a swig. His cracked gnawed lips began to hurt. He cursed wildly and smashed the bottle against the floor. He ran like a madman round the dark yurt and hit his head on a succession of teapots and cold lamps hanging from the ceiling. The blows on his head, added to the heat from the alcohol, soon stupefied and pacified him. He stopped in the middle of the yurt, his fist raised in an angry gesture. Without a word, he crashed close to the family and fell into a sleep as deep as theirs. His posture still expressed the leap he took as he lost consciousness.

* * *

Before he became a porn star, Zongora lived in a Slovnaft refinery dormitory. He was a passionate body-builder and collector of porn magazines. He wanted to be more in life than a technician in an oxygen plant.

For some time he yearned to become a money-changer and for a while he even felt like one. He dressed like them: he wore baggy black trousers and a gaudy shirt. He always wore white socks and black moccasins. He had to compromise on the leather jacket and bought an artificial one from the Vietnamese. He couldn't afford real leather, but at a decent distance, you couldn't even tell fake from real leather.

He hung about the Hotel Ambassador Rácz, where the small-time money-changers gathered. He followed their moves anxiously and admiringly. In their presence he behaved as if he belonged. The money-changers accepted these admiring yokels, but only after their work hours. They sometimes used him for sending messages to their colleagues, a job he carried out enthusiastically. When he did it, he felt he was taking part in the exciting life of a superior class of people to whom he felt attracted. He felt that he belonged with them. All that ended with the coming of mobile phones. In the evening, the money-changers got into taxis and went to the all-night casinos and other entertainments. Zongora had no money for gambling or brothels. He had to do a night shift or go to the dormitory to sleep. Waiting for a bus at the stop in his white socks and black moccasins, he looked odd. A money-changer's outfit was meant for sitting in a bar, waiting in front of a hotel and driving round in your car or a taxi. It did not fit certain occasions. Travelling in dusty and plebeian public transport was definitely one.

To his younger colleagues Zongora pretended to be a member of some secret brotherhood. Occasionally, he brought into the smoke-filled changing room and the always noisy workplace an echo of the attractive, alluring world of rich gangsters and their dolls, of bars and hotel lobbies.

Zongora longed to be more, but he lacked knowledge. He was just strong and his body was well tuned. This is not much if a man is stupid and untalented. Perhaps he could try for a career in pornographic films. He would make extra money, but, above all, he could fuck for free and eventually get into something better.

In some pornographic magazine he read that a basic criterion for choosing porn actors is penile length and ejaculative quantity and range. As for the first requirement, Zongora was amazingly well endowed: his proud thirteen inches towered up at times of maximum excitement. And the range? He experimented once in the dormitory shower. At least an ounce of semen sprayed a good six feet. Zongora concluded that he was a good candidate for the job of male porn star and decided to act.

In Zongora's life it all began with an ad whose text he put together with much effort and secrecy during his night shifts. He published it in the magazine *Perverse Sex:*

Young man, 19 yrs/13 inches seeks lady partner 40-50 with own flat for purpose of fantastic sexual pleasure. Neglected, passionate and very perverse lady welcome if interested in oral, anal, fisting, pissing, and IQ.

When the magazine printed his ad, Zongora's chest was puffed with pride; this was the first time that a text penned by his own hand had appeared in print. He read his own ad several times in a row, even though he knew it by heart: he had spent so long composing, editing and rewriting it. Imagining his sexual life taking a new, positive direction, he almost had a hard-on.

Several women wrote back. Zongora arranged to meet them but never made himself known. None of them were the neglected ladies he dreamed of: in fact, they were over-aged women who really had let themselves go.

He had also set the maximum age of his potential lovers too high. When he imagined a fifty-year-old he thought of a well-preserved woman like Ivana Trump or Catherine Deneuve. Alas, such women do not put ads in dubious magazines, or reply to them. None of the women who turned up resembled the touched-up, photoshopped beauties in porn magazines, such as *Mature Sluts*, that he relied on so much.

Instead, only tired, fat, and poorly dressed housewives came to meet him under Tesco's bell tower. They were short of breath, sweaty and flushed as they thought that they were going behind the backs of their old men, who wore yellowing underpants and had greasy locks of hair to mask their glistening bald patches. Zongora was disgusted. He ran away and let his potential partner pace about under the bell tower, looking around nervously and blowing her fringe off her forehead.

He always took refuge inside the supermarket. He walked the air-conditioned floors. He unconsciously feared that the woman he'd spurned was also walking those floors. He was terrified by the thought that she might miraculously discover his identity, and flush him out now.

It did not take him long to realise that this was no way to go about it. He decided in future not to try meeting women through advertisements. He was still aroused and tempted by ads of the type: *I am looking for a well-established gentleman with hard equipment. I don't know the meaning of the word taboo. I approve of whipping, oral, and scat. Signed: Standard,* but he was inwardly scarred by his bad experience.

He wholeheartedly threw himself into sexual adventures offered by the proximity of the male and female dormitories near Slovnaft refinery.

I want to know the unknown, so I'm looking for an opportunity to act in porn films and perverse type photo sessions. O, A, S/M, fisting, pissing, scat, preggo, clinic, bondage, very young girls, latex, rubber, plastic, everything interests me; I stop at nothing. I am 23, 13 inches.
Signed: Fees unimportant.

Even this second advertisement got no reply for a long time. He almost lost hope. He did his shifts in a bitter mood and thought for entire days how to get out of his degrading ordinary worker's position when all around him were bagging the products and perks of early capitalism. Zongora was well aware that he was not very bright. A leaving certificate from chemistry trade school, the absolute peak in his life, was not the best capital for the era that was dawning. Moreover, he knew what it cost him to get that certificate and he did not even think of getting school matriculation. And he had no capital to start a business with, as he came from a simple working class family, so modest and honest that it stayed in poverty for that very reason. And even if he had any capital, he was cowardly and wouldn't take risks. Besides, he was lazy.

The only thing that nature had endowed him with was a well-proportioned body, which he improved by regular exercise and building. He started with weights in army service. At first, he had no particular aim, just a desire to kill time. After leaving the army, he brought his weights to the oxygen plant. From then on, during his shift, every hour when he recorded technical parameters and emptied the oxygen compressor separators, he did a set of exercises. That made eight sets a day. So Zongora had a well-developed body, but not enough to make him a professional body builder. His facial expression was far too stupid for modelling.

He chose to exercise as a means of killing time in any way he could; he did nothing and envied cleverer men, like his colleagues Végh and

Czanner, for example. They spent the long shifts chatting about growing oyster and button mushrooms one day. They discussed every aspect of production problems until it got on Zongora's nerves. He wanted to nod off, and they were stopping him. He did his best to make fun of their prattle. But when the enterprising pair rented an abandoned limestone quarry between Nová Ves and Devín and began their planned mushroom growing, Zongora nearly exploded with envy. What really hurt was that they hadn't invited him to join them. After hours and hours of discussion he felt that, despite his negative attitude, he had a share in their venture, which was why he was so surprised and bewildered when Végh and Czanner one day suddenly handed in their notice and left to follow their dream. They had sorted everything out officially and left Slovnaft filled with optimism. Zongora felt left in the lurch when the two so suddenly became businessmen. To the very last moment he was sure they would take him into their new radiant future, even though he was lazy and ignorant, simply because he was there at the start.

A few years later, Czanner visited the oxygen plant: he had come to Slovnaft to buy polyethylene foil. While his employees were loading, Czanner sat in the communal room, his mobile phone on the battered table, drinking coffee made for him by one of the technicians. He had put on weight and grown nice moustaches. He was doing well. He had broken up with Végh and joined forces with a nobleman, a real prince. Together they privatised a small cannery and their brand *"Méltóságos konyha*, Noble Kitchen"* of sterilised meals was sold worldwide, competing seriously with Uncle Ben's. Zongora nearly died of envy; he, too, was buying jars and frozen packages with a label showing a moustached Hungarian aristocrat in an unbuttoned hussar coat sitting at a groaning table. Zongora, too, liked the witty advertising with the slogan: "Hungry as a prince?" But not even in his dreams could he have guessed that these were the products of a former colleague whom he spent years working shifts with and whose smelly boots he had put up with for years.

While Czanner was explaining how down in southern Slovakia they raised pigs exclusively on acorns and how in an abandoned quarry somewhere in Central Slovakia they grew mushrooms, he could stand it no longer. Swallowing his despair and hatred, he grabbed the ear muffs from the table and instead of listening, went to the machine room with its humming compressors. To calm down, he gathered the oily rags kept by the moving pistons of the air compressor and took them up to the skip. In front of the building's metal door Czanner's Chrysler was parked. That was too much for Zongora. He looked at it for a while admiringly, but then scratched it ruthlessly with his key.

But fortune finally smiled on him, too. He found an ad in OKM, an erotic magazine. A film company was seeking suitable actors for its porn films. Applications with a brief biography and a picture of the whole body (men had to include a picture of their erect penis) were to be sent to the editorial office. Zongora took his own picture and sent in an application. In his biography he included the following: "I very much want to become a porn star and am willing to do scatological sex, too."

This must have worked: soon he got an invitation to an audition.

A famous company called *Freddy Vision* had organized the audition. Besides Zongora, there were some thirty hopefuls, women and men, all young. The audition members sat in armchairs and at the side on a tripod stood a camera to film the audition. In front of the camera was a big double bed, which is where the crucial part of the audition took place.

The selection committee head was a corpulent man with jerky movements and a bossy manner: obviously the owner of the company. The committee also included several personalities known to any consumer of pornography. Zongora was a consumer, and he could not keep his eyes off Siedah Strong, a popular porn star. There was also Bruno Tatarelli, a pure-bred Italian porn star, of gypsy origin, from the nearby village of Lozorno. Zongora almost pitied him: he knew that when he unpacked his tool, Bruno with his ten inches would have tears in his eyes.

"I'm the Freddy of *Freddy Vision*," the committee chairman introduced himself. "But always Mr Mešťánek to you. So let's get going!"

Some young people had come in pairs, a boy and a girl. Freddy was not interested in their doing it together: he split the couple up. He tried out the girl with another man and made her man have sex with another woman. Not all candidates agreed to be split up.

"Get out!" Freddy shouted. "Out! Someone who can only fuck one partner has no place in our business! Do you think I'll write screen plays just for you? You think you're Tom Cruise and Nicole Kidman? Get out! You think you're a famous couple? Get lost! Out you go!"

Another candidate blew it when he had a huge ejaculation just at the sight of his partner, chosen by Freddy—a beautiful mulatto girl who had just turned up and was offered a contract while still in her clothes.

"Get out!" Freddy shouted. "And wipe it properly after you, and then leave! A rag? We don't have rags. Does anyone have a rag? Nobody has one. Why are you gawping? What's your tee shirt for? Wipe it and go!"

A girl was thrown out for refusing anal sex ("Anal is the foundation of pornography, didn't you know that? Get out!"). Another hadn't shaved her legs properly ("With depilatory products now available, it's a crime to run around with legs covered in fur! Out you go!"). A third refused to have sex without a condom ("Just for your sake we'll start using condoms, right? If you're afraid of getting infected, join the Salvation Army, not the porn business! Get out!").

Another girl didn't fancy having sex in front of so many people. She was under the impression that porn was produced in an intimate setting, with the director and cameraman present, at most. Freddy was quite beside himself with rage, for otherwise the girl was very attractive.

"Get out!" he roared. "Film yourself masturbating at home! Pornography is mass culture. Thousands of people will see you fucking. Thousands will know the inside of your vagina intimately. And you're too embarrassed to undress in front of this committee? Out! Out!"

These scenes happened in front of the other participants, whose numbers were steadily diminishing. Some fled even before their turn came; others were so flustered that they couldn't even get a hard-on.

Freddy was merciless. He took pleasure in humiliating candidates and making them suffer. They all had to undress completely; women were allowed to keep their stockings and shoes on.

"What? Tights?" Freddy was raging. "Has anyone ever seen tights in a porn film? Are they at least crotchless? No? Where did you buy them? In a prosthetics shop? Get out! Out! Wait a minute, stop! You have a nice behind. Take them off and wait, we'll try you out."

Zongora sat and watched it all very closely. But he never gave in to despair. He knew that when he came before the committee and showed them his well-trained body crowned by his proud thirteen inches he would not be rejected. Watching semi-naked men and women being humiliated gave him an obscure pleasure and kept his heart beat at the right speed. Moreover, he liked these cruel professionals and couldn't wait to become one of them. He knew he'd been one of them from birth. Besides, he was excited at the thought of showing himself naked to Siedah Strong and two other porn actresses on the committee.

Therefore, when his turn came and he achieved a steely erection in front of everyone, his eyes bore into Siedah Strong's. He sensed rather than saw the jaws of all the committee members dropping.

Nor could Siedah keep her eyes off his thirteen-inch club with its bright red polished head slowly dripping clear liquid, the so-called drop of desire, provoked by looking at the naked girls who silently obeyed every humiliating order from the committee chairman.

"Well," said Freddy, looking at the committee members. "Have any of you ever seen anything like that?"

His answer was a mass shaking of heads.

"Fine, we'll look at you in action," said Freddy. "Where's the black girl? The…" he consulted his papers, "Jana Tokárová? Is she here?"

A beautiful mulatto raised her hand.

"Well, I'm curious to see you do it," said Freddy, slobbering with lechery. "You both know what to do, right? Right, camera, please!"

When Zongora saw her, his member grew at least another inch. Out of impatience, not gallantry, he helped Tokárová remove her clothes,.

"First, show us some foreplay," Freddy ordered.

"Excellent, that's very good. And now penetration."

Bewildered, Zongora stayed kneeling over Tokárová. The mulatto radiated heat and the fragrance of some exotic perfume.

"What do I have to do?" asked Zongora.

"Put it in her," said Freddy.

"Oh God," whispered Tokárová, yielding as she looked at Zongora's member. "But, for God's sake, slowly and carefully!"

Zongora entered her some of the way and began to move.

"Jesus and Mary," said Tokárová.

Zongora felt an insistent itch round his tailbone. He was about to come.

"Are you taking anything?" he asked the mulatto.

"Like what?" Tokárová did not understand.

"Contraception," said Zongora.

"Yes, of course," said Tokárová. "But you needn't come inside me, if you don't have to…"

She had barely spoken when Zongora pulled out of her and in a mighty hot spray spattered her, the bed, the carpet, the camera, and even the inquisitive cameraman.

The committee members looked disappointed.

"Ah!" yelled Freddy in despair, with the expression of a football fan whose favourite player has blown a clear chance, and clasped his hands.

However, Zongora was smiling. He had another trump card up his sleeve. He used his hand to squeeze the last drops out onto Tokárová's brown belly and then he again inserted his pulsating member into his shocked partner. His astounding erection was not diminished at all.

"Good, that'll do," Freddy spoke up, as Zongora noticed Tokárová's breathing getting faster and deeper and her muscles beginning to contract rhythmically. So he did not stop, but kept moving inside her until he felt the pressure down there relax and Tokárová collapse helplessly onto the bed. Her spread-out long brown arms and legs kept twitching in spasms. Then he felt he was starting to come again: he sprayed her a second time.

"Excellent," shouted Freddy, when the two of them had recovered and begun to towel themselves and then dress. "Excellent. Welcome to the *Freddy Vision* team! You're hired. The rest of you can go home. We'll have a look at the films and let you know!"

Zongora got dressed. He looked at Tokárová. She was really pretty.

"How did you get this beautiful skin?" Freddy asked the mulatto. "Are you of gyp… I mean, Roma background?"

"My father came from Gabon," said Tokárová. "He came to study medicine here and…"

"Jana Tokárová," Siedah Strong interrupted, and for the first time Zongora heard her real voice, not that of the Czech actress who dubbed her. "That name's no good. You've got to have a name with an international ring to it. From now on, you'll be Naomi Africa. Naomi. That's what you look like."

"And what about this little bird?" Freddy asked, pointing at Zongora.

Sida shifted the gaze of her painted eyes to Zongora.

"Zongora sounds stupid, too," she said. "From now on, you'll be Luigi Longo. That's more to the point."

"Yes," said Zongora. He liked this name.

"I only hope the premature cum shot was caused by stage fright," said Freddy, "and under normal circumstances, you'll last longer."

"Yes, certainly," said Zongora.

"But since you don't lose your erection even after ejaculating," Sida joined in, "we'll overlook it. Not many men have a talent like yours. Some men start to droop even before they come." She gave Freddy a defiant look; he averted his eyes and cleared his throat.

"Starring Naomi Africa and Luigi Longo," he recited, outlining with hand gestures the lead titles on the screen. "I'll make stars out of you and I'll get you to Cannes for the porn Oscars."

* * *

Disguised as ordinary merchant sailors, on false civilian passports, the submariners arrive in Gdansk under the command of the newly promoted

Commander Kubeš. The passports were not really forged: the proper authorities had issued them. Only the names and dates were untrue.

They don't stay long in Gdansk. They board a smaller merchant ship flying a Polish flag and sail off.

Kubeš, with a few sailors in his crew, stands on the bows. Others are on the lower deck, sleeping off a hangover they got on the express train. Kubeš breathes in the air and smells the fresh sea breeze. When he licks his lips, he can taste salt. He can't take his eyes off the sea's choppy surface. His nostrils flare in sweet awareness, "At sea! At sea, finally!"

"Well, gentlemen," says Kubeš to his men. "Finally back at sea. I don't know about you, but nine months ago, I never dreamt of such a thing."

"Nor did I, captain sir," says Petty Officer Zrno, a cook. "I thought we were stuck on dry land for good. But you know what I like most?"

"What, Zrno?" Kubeš asks, not commenting that the cheerful cook has decided to promote him a rank.

"Well, I'm pleased we're getting an active service bonus from ten minutes ago, sir," says Zrno.

They all laugh.

"What are you going to do with all that money?" asks Kubeš.

"I'll have to think of something, sir," says Zrno. "Maybe after the ten years I've signed up for, I'll go into business with my brother. We'll open a small tavern, or a restaurant, something like that."

Kubeš turns back to gazing at the sea. To hell with *Mayor Pfitzner* and its panorama of Prague Castle, he thinks. Prague is beautiful, but the sea is even more so. He's finally in his element. He got his chance and will use it to the full. He'll conscientiously do his duty by the man who gave it to him.

Sailing from Gdansk to Riga takes two days. When they drop anchor, a representative of the Czech navy is already waiting for them. Without delay they board a bus with their bags and are taken out of the city to an industrial zone where the private docks discreetly leased by the Czech navy are located. They pass through multiple security checks and then enter the secret area. There, on the mole, is anchored a huge light-grey vessel, so intimately familiar to the crew members. It rocks gently on the waves. The conning tower has no number, name, or registration.

"Its cover name is *Kamýk*," says the representative. "That's what the Admiralty decided. P-45/M-01 is called *Kamýk*, 02 is *Albatross*, and 03, still in dry dock being refitted, is *Seagull*.

"Nice names," says Honza Libáň and steps on the gangplank connecting the submarine deck to the mole.

"And no military talk, please," warns the representative. "Behave like civilians. You never know who's watching you from the sea. Quickly board the vessel, settle in, and get into open sea as soon after sunset as possible."

The crew obeys. They board the vessel, stocked in advance with everything necessary: food, water and equipment. Before Kubeš, Libáň, and chief engineer Rajter sign the inspection certificate, they carefully check every inch of the vessel. Only when totally satisfied do they put their signatures on the document.

"So, break a leg, gentlemen," says the navy representative as he leaves the vessel, "and come back in one piece!"

Kubeš waits a while, leaning on the conning tower parapet. Then he turns to Libáň, his first warrant officer. "Report all stations ready to sail."

"Yes, sir," Libáň clicks his heels.

The dockers untie the ropes and the submarine weighs anchor. The *Kamýk*'s stern slowly moves off the mole.

"Slow reverse!" commands Kubeš.

He shivers when he realizes this is his very first command on the *Kamýk*. He hears his command repeated in the lower deck. Then he hears the muffled but deep sound of the diesel engine, a vortex appears behind the stern and the vessel begins to back up.

"We're off," says Libáň.

"Finish the manœuvre, Lieutenant Commander Libáň!" says Kubeš and lights up a cigar.

"Yes, sir," says Libáň and turns to the microphone. "Stop the engine!"

The vortex stops for a while.

"Steering ten points left. Slow forward. Course 310."

"Course 310, sir," says a voice from the tower, leading rating Petrovič, the chief steersman.

"Steady forward," says Libáň.

"Steady forward," they repeat on the lower deck.

Kamýk is now headed for Cape Kolka the middle of the Gulf of Riga.

Libáň steadily issues one command after another.

Kubeš takes a puff of his cigar and blows the smoke against the darkening sky. He lets himself face the wind to be braced by the sea spray. He watches the seagulls, woken by the engine noise, circling the boat's wake.

The *Kamýk* is starting to cut through waves rushing towards it from Saaremaa Island and the deck under the tower is awash.

"Clear the deck!" Kubeš orders.

One by one, sailors vanish through the doors in the side of the tower.

"Deck clear, sir," Petty Officer Schäffer, the bosun, reports from below, and disappears onto the lower deck.

Kubeš watches him, then lifts his head and goes on observing the circling seagulls.

Second warrant officer Skopšík and third warrant officer Kraus begin to devote all their attention to their binoculars.

The lights of the city recede and against the city back ground the lights of docked ships can no longer be seen. The seagulls begin to fall back behind the *Kamýk*; their screeches voice disappointment that the submarine's wake has no edible refuse. The sea gets choppier.

Kubeš throws away his wet cigar. He wraps himself tighter in his coat. It will be some five hours before they get their boat out of the Gulf of Riga and shallow waters and are able to submerge. Kubeš will feel safer with fifty metres of water under his keel.

"I'm going down," Kubeš tells Libáň. "Let me know when we pass the last buoy of the fairway."

"Yes, sir," says Libáň.

Kubeš goes down and paces the length of the boat. Clearly, long hours spent in a simulator have borne fruit. All the crew knows what to do. He pauses in the engine room, where, fascinated, he watches both engines.

"Commander: the last buoys," says his intercom.

Kubeš goes up to the bridge.

"Manœuvre station watch is over," he says, his eyes focussed on the phosphorescent sea. "Move to regular cruising mode. Shift A keeps watch."

He looks at Libáň and Kraus.

"There's no more to do here, gentlemen," he says. "The radar can see further than you and your binoculars. Forget about submarine folklore. Let's go inside and have some tea."

* * *

The crew members who are off-shift don't get tired even after midnight. What they have been preparing for in all their training at the Museum base has become reality. Only at two o'clock in the morning, when shift B takes over, do all the men, except the watch in the command centre and the engine room staff, lie down on their bunks.

Around six in the morning, on the left, that is, east, a pale green circle appears. When it turns yellow, Lieutenant Commander Skopšík, the second officer on the watch, announces down the tower:

"Commander, daybreak!"

Kubeš climbs up. Duty officer Skopšík reports and tells him the submarine's position, bearing and speed. The commander patiently says nothing. He's checked their position with his GPS and considers the report a mere formality. So does Libáň. But this is a ritual performed by mutual agreement. After the report, Kubeš goes back down into the submarine.

Skopšík also steps into the tower. In the command centre Kubeš leans on the map table. In the underwater steersman's place sits Petty Officer Záruba. To his right is Petty Officer Koniarczyk, in charge of rear steering. Behind them is the chief engineer, Lieutenant Rajter.

"Tower hatch locked," says Skopšík from the tower.

"Prepare to release air," the chief engineer commands.

The men at the air tanks report:

"First tank!"

"Second tank!"

"Third on both sides!"

"The fifth is all right!"

"The air tanks are ready!" reports Rajter.

"Flood them!" the first warrant officer shouts down to the command centre.

"Flood them!" repeats the chief engineer to the men near the tanks.

Záruba turns the underwater steering wheel to the "down" position and the man next to him turns the rear regulator to "rear middle". The air tanks quickly shut down, water enters the tanks and the submarine tips downwards — the first tank is flooded a bit earlier — and then starts to sink into the depths. Fifteen metres down, the chief engineer shouts:

"Emergency tanks!"

Compressed air expels water from the emergency tanks with an infernal noise. At thirty metres, the chief engineer stabilises the boat. He reports to the commander:

"Vessel stabilised!"

"Turn off air pressure!" Kubeš orders. "Dive to forty metres! Both engines easy forward, condition weightless."

The chief engineer repeats the command, balances the boat with the balancing tanks, levels out and communicates with the steersmen. When the boat dives to fifty metres, the steersmen work independently and Rajter only corrects them when necessary.

At this depth, the boat does not pitch any more. Everything is wrapped in silence, broken only by the hum of the electric motor resonating through the boat's hull.

"Vessel at forty metres, sir," says Rajter. "Zero tilt."

Kubeš looks at the compass.

"Course 225," he says.

"Course 225, sir" says the chief engineer after a while.

"Maintain course and depth, Mr Rajter," says the commander.

"Maintain course and depth, sir," nods Rajter.

"Take over, Mr Petrovič," the commander tells the chief steersman and then turns to Rajter. "Come to my room in ten minutes. All the officers, except for the shift that's asleep. Make sure."

Kubeš's room is luxurious. The walls are panelled with walnut-grain wood and the floor is decorated with a rug that visually improves the gap between the wooden table and the bunk, which is more like the cot Kubeš had in Lešany.

Kubeš leans back in his armchair and motions to Skopšík, Kraus, Rajter and Kolesa to sit down. So they sit on his bed.

"I think it's time you knew what our mission is," says Kubeš.

There is a knock on the door, and Kubeš quietly curses:

"Get the hell in and make sure you clear off quickly, too!"

The door opens, revealing the expressionless face of Vrba, the cook.

"You ordered coffee, sir," he says, offended.

Kubeš nods and makes room on his table for the tray. He patiently waits for the cook to pour the coffee into cups, close the door and vanish: only then does he continue:

"I imagine that you've all guessed what the mission of this trip is. We're taking humanitarian aid to the Junjan archipelago. Look at the map. Some-where over here: we'll find out more precisely just before we reach the Junjan archipelago. Slovak guerrillas will try to keep the unloading point secret to the last moment, so that the handover of the goods doesn't become a trap. Precise coordinates will be communicated by radio. It will be encoded according to our codebook. Any questions?"

Kolesa takes a breath.

"Yes, Mr Kolesa?" Kubeš asks.

"No, nothing," says Kolesa.

"But you wanted to say something," Kubeš counters.

"Yes, I did," Kolesa admits. "I wanted to ask what will happen to us if it is a trap."

"We'll be shot on the spot," says Kubeš, watching Kolesa without moving an eyebrow. "Or tortured, lieutenant. Or taken to a labour camp and used to gather that famous lichen of theirs. Any other questions?"

The men are silent.

"If you carry out my orders to the letter," says Kubeš, "we shall complete our mission successfully and return safely. I promise you. Please keep this information secret. We'll tell the rest of the crew about it when we're in the Atlantic. I don't want them worrying too much. All clear?"

"Yes, sir," the officers say.

"That will be all," says Kubeš and dismisses them.

* * *

The *Kamýk* crosses the Baltic at cruising speed: underwater by day, on the surface at night. Around Skagerrak it enters the North Sea and then continues north, to the Atlantic.

At first all the crew members, including Kubeš, bang their heads when they walk upright; but anyone who hits his head a few times quickly adjusts and walks with a stoop. At the same time, they all also learn how to squeeze through the round hatches of the watertight compartments. Every day they have lots of opportunities to practise, better than in the Lešany simulator. They were not motivated then: now they are.

One morning, Kubeš comes down from the bridge. Lieutenant Commander Libáň is standing by the map table, drinking his morning coffee.

"Good morning, commander," he says. "In about an hour we'll be in contact with the supply ship."

Bosun Kreuzeder adjusts his GPS receiver.

"Mr Kreuzeder, give me our echo-sounder depth," Kubeš orders.

"A hundred and twenty, chief," says Kreuzeder.

"Everyone to diving stations," Kubeš commands.

The steersmen quickly take their places and start the dive.

"Dive to ninety metres!" Kubeš shouts loudly, to be heard over the roar of expelled air and of water entering the diving tanks. "To the seabed!"

As soon as the alarm sounds, the engine room, electric motor room and command centre go through a number of procedures. The engine room crew stops the left engine, disconnects it from the electric equipment and closes the intake and exhaust valves. As soon as the diesel is turned off, the electrical crew turns the electric motors on. All intake and exhaust pipes are closed. The diving tank crew opens all tanks except the rear one.

In the command centre, Rajter watches the desk's warning lights that tell him about shutting down pressure and opening the diving tanks. When Kubeš orders a dive to ninety metres, he opens the rear tanks as well. The *Kamýk* dives nose down until the hum of the electric motors stops. They feel a light bump and the submarine settles on sand.

"Lieutenant Commander," Kubeš turns to Libáň, "Gather all the men at quarter to five in the front storage space." Bosun Schäffer stands at the entrance and counts them to make sure everyone is present. The space, now the torpedo equipment has gone, is large. The men could play mini-football in it. They each look for somewhere to stand. No one moves and the only sound detectable is the hull scratching against the sand. It sounds unusually loud in the silence.

Kubeš enters the room. He has been preparing his speech for some time now, but what he is about to say is shorter and quite different.

"Sailors," he says, stressing every syllable. "In an hour we meet a super-tanker *Carabella*. It's a Czech navy floating submarine base. Before we rendezvous, I'd like to say a few words about our mission."

The room is dead silent. A drop of dew falls noisily to the floor.

"I imagine that you've all guessed that we're sailing to the Junjan archipelago," says Kubeš. "We're taking weapons, ammunition, and other things for the local Slovaks who have risen up against their exploiters. They have nobody else but you in the whole wide world."

Kubeš pauses, looks at the floor, then lifts his gaze to the crew.

"I shan't tell you," says Kubeš, "that our mission is simple, but I believe it's feasible. The hardest part will be breaking the Russian blockade of the archipelago. We have to do it by stealth, since we don't want to provoke international conflict."

The men look at their captain tensely. Kubeš again scans their well-lit pale faces. He sees his men are astounded, but also relieved that the mission's goal, that they had so far only guessed at, has been confirmed.

* * *

As evening falls, they meet on the open sea, where the North Sea meets the North Atlantic, the elderly, Liberian-registered super-tanker *Carabella* that serves as the Czech navy's floating submarine base.

The *Carabella*'s entire crew is already waiting on deck and gives the visitors a hearty welcome.

"Welcome aboard, friends," says a stocky moustached man in a civilian sweater and a baseball hat. "Which of you is the commander?"

Kubeš comes up to him and salutes.

"Lieutenant Commander Kubeš," he introduces himself.

"Captain Jiří Molnár," says the tanker commander. "Welcome to our floating submarine base. Allow me to introduce the officers."

After the introductions are, Molnár gives Kubeš a sealed envelope.

"Here are your detailed operational objectives," he says, still unable to take his eyes off the submarine.

"A beautiful boat," he says. "And how practical everything on board is! Finally, I'm proud to be a Czech again."

"But I'm still puzzled how you could have kept all this secret," says one of the *Carabella*'s officers.

"There's no guarantee that the secret has been kept," Kubeš laughs.

"As far as I know, all three submarines were bought via third parties," says chief engineer Rajter. "Their original end-use was research by a private scientific institute studying an unspecified South American country. They were headed for the scrapyard, anyway. When we told the Latvian firm to strip the ships of all military gear, torpedo equipment, cannons and so on, their suspicions vanished: they weren't interested who was buying them."

Molnár nods. He looks over the submarine's slender hull gently swaying on the waves.

"I must say," says Molnár, "it's not a very nice feeling to go into combat carrying nothing but pistols and a few machine guns."

"That's all we'll need," says Kubeš. "We shall avoid contact with the enemy. In the worst case, we'll use our speed under water."

"As far as speed's concerned, I wouldn't be so optimistic," Molnár says. "Firstly, the specifications are fifty years old, and secondly, this machine is a an old banger. I'm not saying they haven't spruced it up, but still: even a complete refit can't make it younger. Metal fatigue."

"I'm quite sure we won't have to use maximum speed," says Kubeš, "and that everything will run like clockwork."

"I believe so, too," says Molnár. "Well gentlemen, let me invite all the officers to our officers' mess for a little celebration. According to the operative plan, you set sail at one in the morning. So your crew can start by loading the goods. And now to dinner, gentlemen!"

It's a magnificent banquet. Captain Molnár personally serves the reticent submariners. He offers dry sparkling wine. Despite his excellent mood, Kubeš constantly runs off to check on the progress of loading.

An hour after midnight, fully loaded, the submarine *Kamýk*, manœuvring neatly, disengages from the *Carabella*. It is heading north.

* * *

As we said, cousin Tina is a slave driver by vocation. Naturally, she considers fashion design to be her life's major achievement. She sees herself as an artist and never mentions the existence of her underground slave factory, not to kith and kin, not in press, radio, or television interviews. If urged to say something about the source of her income, which obsesses journalists, then she euphemistically says she is "financially independent". She owns three brand-name shops in Prague, one in Brno, one in Karlovy Vary and two on the Catalan coast. Her products fly off the hangers. Of course, no one cares where these lovely things come from. Perhaps they all think she knits and sews her creations personally in the evenings.

Tina is romantically inclined and has little interest in her slaves' appalling living conditions. Her extreme, pathetic and false altruism finds other objects. She can easily give a tramp in the underground a thousand crowns to start a new life, or spend twenty thousand on a shelter for homeless animals, but she counts every penny spent on her knitters, and, in principle, any request for a rise is met by dismissal.

"If anyone's not satisfied," she says, "then they never will be. She can go back to Ukraine; twenty more are outside the door waiting for a job."

Cousin Tina has a cohort of males who are in love with her, desire her, and would do anything in the world for her. She cynically keeps them in this sorry state and exploits it. She deliberately doses them with drops of hope and despair, as required, to keep them always at hand and hot with expectation. If she sees someone's enchantment and love waning, she gives him a hint that in the near future there's a chance… Briefly, cousin Tina knows how to deal with each one, and plays them all like an organ.

She styles herself as a fragile beauty disillusioned by life, one who has for a long time not wanted to have dealings with anyone, but who is now eager for a powerful new force: a relationship with someone who is the world's finest man. Such a man will inherit paradise on earth. She would show him that she was not only a being with an unfathomably deep soul, but also an uninhibited and inventive lover. The problem is that every man considers himself to be the world's finest man.

Cousin Tina is fair. She gives each of her fans the feeling that he is the one nearest to becoming her chosen one.

No, he doesn't have to be a slim intellectual: she has a weakness for solidly built and rather simple men, or so she tells the dull, big man who will then be able to rearrange in one day all the furniture in her villa, satisfying Tina's unquenchable desire for constant change.

The right man needs no muscles, he just has to be a thinker, or so she tells an economist with a hen's chest and pebble-lens glasses who does her accounts and tax returns out of pure altruism and in hope of sweet rewards.

A highly placed City Hall official has an interesting hobby which impresses her. Yes, Tina is also totally obsessed with collecting beer labels. Nor will she fail to emphasize that of all the men she knows he has the highest rating, tactfully omitting that this is due to commercial premises on National Avenue, ideal for a designer fabrics boutique.

But another highly placed man, a police officer, is certain that he's the man closest to Tina's heart, and thus to her driver's licence, which she lost after a trivial crash on the highway.

Tina has done her sums. She knows that she wields absolute power over her fan club only as long as she stays an immaculate solitary saint, a slender and beautiful promise on legs. Occasionally, she makes an obscene comment to prove to an admirer that for all her spiritual asceticism, she is a sexual being, too. She realises that nobody can combust spontaneously for long. So, if she senses that a man of great importance to her plans could be lost, she softens up and offers him everything, including full intercourse. But to offers of a long-term relationship, naturally, she reacts hypersensitively: there's nothing she craves more than to have a long-term relationship with the man in question, but she has to sort things out in her head. She needs time. But they can stay good friends for now.

Oddly enough, few people are as calculating as cousin Tina, yet no one has seen through her play-acting as a scatter-brained beauty torn by her emotions. Her fan club is still convinced that she has been sleeping alone for years on principle, that she has no intimate relationship, that she is saving herself for her future lover. Nothing will soften her resolve on this point, not even blackmailing declarations of love with every conceivable stupidity dictated by the despair of an infatuated man: from offering to murder his wife and children, to suicide from despair.

"A dry whore," a thwarted Urban sometimes mutters, but then rebukes himself for ingratitude. He has less cause than anyone to complain of his beautiful cousin: if he is not rejected, and he seldom is, then it's worth it.

Urban realises that if the cohort even suspected that everything cousin Tina so coyly refuses them, she actually grants to him, a blood relative, they would all take offence and drop her. She might even make new enemies. There is no worse enemy than an aggrieved potential lover, fed for a long time on copious doses of hope and understanding, who is suddenly shunted aside by an apparent outsider. Such humiliation always calls for revenge.

Worse, if there were no fan club, Urban would have to move the furniture, mend the roof, cut the hedge, mow the lawn, clean the pond, mend the carburettor, file tax returns and recover the confiscated driver's licence.

So he prefers to bite his tongue and put up with his beautiful cousin's moods. He still gets more from her than the unhappy admirers who will never be able to have their own happy end.

* * *

Kubeš lies on his bunk, dressed, thinking. The *Kamýk* is just a few hundred miles from its destination, but everything threatens to be ruined by a stupid mechanical problem. Rajter and his mechanics are doing all they can to fix it. Kubeš can see Admiral Sosna's stony face: the thought of turning back seems unendurable to him. He kicks his feet off the bunk and gets up again. Mindlessly, he runs his left hand over thirty days' growth of beard on his face, picks up his cap and puts it on. He passes through the command centre and looks at the four men on duty. Then he turns round and goes to the rear section of the submarine, to the engine room. Even though it is ventilated, the room is very hot. His worried look settles on the right-hand engine: it has died.

Lieutenant Kolesa turns to Kubeš and wipes the sweat off his face.

"I think it's going well, sir," he shouts.

"Will it take long?" Kubeš roars into his ear.

"I can't say exactly, sir," Kolesa replies. "Five, maybe seven more hours."

Not fully reassured, Kubeš goes back to his cabin. This engine breakdown has made him ponder all the problems to be expected on future voyages to Junja. He sits on his bunk and tries to imagine what form the Russian blockade of the island takes. He thoughtfully observes the strange movement that his jacket, hanging on a hook, makes as the boat pitches. He has studied his data so thoroughly that he could draw by heart a detailed map of all the islands in the Junjan archipelago, but he looks at them again, looking for any new detail that he has forgotten to remember.

"Commander: daybreak," his intercom announces.

Kubeš checks his watch. It's six thirty. Yes, time to go to the bridge and get some fresh air before diving. He puts on waterproofs and boots and approaches the ladder in the command centre. Kraus reports a slight change of course, otherwise nothing unusual has happened.

The sky is overcast and the waves are capped with foam. Icy spray hits him in the face, so he pulls the hood down over his face.

"Will the diesel be working soon, commander?" asks the third officer.

"Yes," Kubeš answers dryly and aims his binoculars at the brightening horizon. The clouds break, showing areas of clear sky. Kubeš lets the binoculars fall on his chest and observes the stars turning pale against the ever brighter sky. Then he turns to Kraus.

"We'll dive in a moment," he says.

They both clamber down to the command centre. Kubeš goes to the intercom and pushes the button.

"This is your commander speaking," he says, and his amplified voice echoes through the entire submarine. "Gentlemen, the Junjan archipelago is very close. Soon we'll find ourselves within operational range of Russian ships. Engineer Rajter has to finish repairing the right-hand diesel engine, and then we'll immediately head for the Russian blockade. If we're lucky, we'll sneak through unobserved. If not, we'll have to play a cat-and-mouse game with the Russians. Somehow or other, we'll get to Junja and then use another way to get back. Of course, if we are to survive, all my orders, and those of all our officers, simply must be carried out precisely."

As Kubeš speaks, he observes the faces of the four men in the command centre. He sees tense, grimly determined faces. None betrays any unwillingness or inner disagreement. Kubeš has in his crew either only superb sailors, or only superb actors, he thinks.

"We have on board a few dozen self-targeting anti-aircraft Stinger missiles for the Slovak guerrillas in Junja," says Kubeš. "Two of them have been re-programmed by Engineer Kolesa to hit surface or naval targets. If the Russians really fuck with us and get us in a corner, we'll show them."

Kubeš hopes that it never gets to the point of using these weapons, but neither does he want his crew to feel totally defenceless.

Kubeš can hear, despite the barriers between the compartments, his words generating noisy approval and applause.

"Anyone who has nothing to do, I mean not on duty, or in the engine room, should now go to their bunks and get some sleep," Kubeš goes on. "No videos in the mess room! The men on watch will wake the cooks at three p.m.; we'll eat at five. During the approach manœuvre, there'll be no hot food, only sandwiches that men can eat at their posts. Everyone gets a bar of chocolate, too. We'll be saving electricity, so all lights, unless needed, will be turned off. Nobody should move more than necessary, so we use less oxygen, as we may be diving for several days. No noise! We'll be very deep down, but the Russians' instruments might detect us. We shan't surface; the batteries will be recharged via the snorkel, if needed."

Kubeš pauses and then adds:

"It's in everybody's interest to be well rested and in good form: that's why we have to sleep now. Good night!"

Then they dive.

Kubeš goes to his cabin, closes the door over its high threshold, and takes off his cap. He falls into his bunk and remains lying there for a long time, not thinking about anything. Then he gets up and runs a hand through his hair. His eyes fall on his open notebook on a table. He sits down at the desk and opens the ship's log. He begins to write:

22.2. South-westerly, 7-6 knots, overcast. Overnight, boat moves southwest Junjan archipelago (see tracker record). In the morning, set coordinates as per GPS and a dive.

He puts his fountain pen away. He should now mention the broken bearing in the right-hand engine crankcase, but he'd rather not. He takes his jacket off, stretches out on the bunk and turns his light out. Light comes through the ventilation opening in the door of the captain's cabin, but then someone turns the light off in the corridor, leaving only the night light on. The cabin is immediately plunged into darkness. Occasionally the noise of repair work on the engine comes from the engine room.

In the rear, behind the partition of the command centre, five feet from the cabin, Kubeš can hear the watch whispering in a monotone. Here and there is the gurgle of water in a pressure tank and the conning tower.

Kubeš opens his eyes and tries to estimate how long he has been dozing. He listens hard, but he can hear no noise from the engine room. He hears only the murmur of the men on watch nearby. He cannot wait any longer, gets up, puts on his shoes, draws the curtain and quietly goes towards the engine room. The coughing and movements of men turning on their beds behind the plastic walls and doors prove that he is not the only one up. As he quietly passes the open door of the warrant officers' cabin, a few heads are raised to see who is walking by.

It's almost dark in the engine room; only a small lamp illuminates Rajter's face bent over the engine room log. Immersed in his work, he doesn't hear Kubeš come in and only straightens up when Kubeš taps his shoulder and quietly asks: "Has it all worked out as you thought?"

"Yes, I think the problem's solved, sir," says the chief engineer. "We'll know for sure only this evening, when the engine's running."

Kubeš frowns.

"Look, no joking, Mr Rajter," he says. "The engine has to work and properly, too. You know very well that I'll be asking the engine to do the impossible. It mustn't fail before Junja and certainly not on the way back. If you're not utterly sure, better tell me while we have time. Is that clear?"

"No worries, sir; the engine will work fine. I see no reason for another breakdown," the chief engineer assures him very calmly.

"Good, Rajter, that's what I needed to hear from you," comes Kubeš's conciliatory reply.

Rajter's answer calms him a bit and yet astounds him. Apparently, the idea of sailing into the Junjan archipelago area with improvised repairs to an engine did not bother the engineer at all.

Kubeš lies down in his cabin and promptly falls asleep. After reveille and dinner, most crewmen return to their bunks: they've nothing to do.

Kubeš, all three warrant officers, steersmen Petrovič and Sebera and the electronic systems operator, Anděl, are in the command centre. The submarine is running at a depth of one hundred metres.

"Sir, we'll have to ascend higher," says the chief steersman Petrovič. "The seabed is rising and soon we'll get to the shelf slope."

The submarine proceeds blindly, by the map, as the sonar is turned off, since there may be enemy vessels about.

"Rise thirty metres," Kubeš orders.

"It's dark now up there," says Skopšík.

The men are quiet. Their expressions are grave: the mission is now affecting their nerves. Kubeš sits with his legs up on the map table. Bosun Anděl is wearing earphones, searching for noise. He turns round and reports: "No noise of ship screws, sir."

"Fancy that!" says Kubeš. "I was expecting it to be teeming with Russian ships. And there aren't any."

He gets up and nervously paces the command centre.

"Or maybe they're all sitting overhead with their engines off, waiting for us to surface," Libáň jokes.

"That's easily checked," notes Lieutenant Commander Kraus.

All eyes discreetly turn to the commander.

Kubeš thinks for a while, then reaches in his pocket for a cigarette and puts it in his mouth.

"Surfacing stations!" he says.

The words have an immediate effect. The general tension eases, the white lamps are turned off in the tower and the red light is on.

"Surface to periscope depth!" says Kubeš.

The pumps come on, Petrovič corrects the balance as the boat rises to the surface.

"Periscope up!"

Kubeš turns the shield of the cap back and circles the periscope. Clearly, there is something suspicious, as he keeps turning the periscope and observing the surroundings.

"Zapletal, did you clean the optics?" he asks loudly, not taking his eyes off the viewer.

"Yes, sir, I cleaned and tested them carefully," replies the petty officer.

"Interesting. It looks as if somebody's covered them with a white veil," says Kubeš. "Surface! Periscope down."

He turns to Libáň.

"It's night now, after all, isn't it? I'm not mad. It's not possible for it to be so bright outside. And there's not supposed to be any moon."

The periscope descends the shaft. The first warrant officer opens his mouth to say something, but changes his mind. The hissing of compressed air in pipes and along metal walls is drowned by water bubbling up, flowing through the flooding openings: all noise is drowned by Libáň's voice:

"Tower hatch is open!"

Nobody rushes up. Everybody is looking at the radar screens.

"There's nobody around us for miles, in fact," Kubeš shakes his head. "What sort of a blockade is that? What can you say? Russians..."

Libáň slowly opens the valve of the air duct from the tower to the bridge, to equalise inner and outer air pressure.

Compressed air whistles out of the boat through the pipe. Kubeš takes his binoculars, a gift from Sosna, off the hook, puts them round his neck, climbs up the ladder, opens the hatch and jumps onto the bridge. A cold wind hits his face. An unusual diffuse light surrounds the boat. Kubeš looks in surprise at the sky; Libáň and Kraus climb up as well. The northern lights gradually turn to all the colours of the rainbow.

"Good: we should have realised," says Kubeš, sounding annoyed, as if the Russians had let him down. "Extend the air pipe. Dive to snorkel depth. Both engines half power ahead!"

* * *

At about ten in the evening, the *Kamýk* surfaces on the North Atlantic's freezing waters and rocks on the waves by the shore. The watch climbs to the bridge. After them, Kubeš climbs out, too.

The weather is freezing. A wind is blowing from the northeast, 6-7 knots strong. It's a gale. It's just before high tide. The tide comes at a speed of one knot from the southwest. Wind and tide from opposite directions make the sea full of unexpected dangers, currents, vortices and so on.

Kubeš knows that the shore is close: it showed on the radar. It can't be long before they see it. He is satisfied to note that, as they approach the coast, the wind slackens. He carefully cleans his binocular lenses and searches in the sector where he hopes to find dry land; from the left to the middle. There is nothing to be seen, though.

Petty Officer Koniarczyk has unusually sharp sight. But even he can't see anything.

It has to be here, thinks Kubeš. He saw it on the radar screen. Or was the coast under snow? In that case, the visibility may be lower than one mile and that can be dangerous both for crew and guerrillas. The radar has to be turned off, so that the enemy can't get their bearing. Unknown, changing currents could push the submarine onto ice floes or rocks.

Kubeš is about to give an order below, to ask about the depth below the hull, when Koniarczyk reports: "Land on the horizon, sir."

Kubeš looks through his binoculars. Petrovič's navigation was not bad at all, he thinks with relief. The land that he sees is at an angle of forty-five degrees on the right. It's indistinct and its features merge with the night sky and the sea. This is Junja, close by and wrapped in deepest darkness.

"Coast in sight," he reports downstairs. "Slow ahead!"

The submarine stops about half a mile from the shore. Water spray drenches Kubeš's binoculars. While he wipes them with a chamois leather, he carefully observes the outline of the rocks on the right and tries to get a general picture of the coast. On his right Koniarczyk peers into the darkness, on his left is Libáň.

"I think we're at the right spot," says Libáň.

He points his hand at the characteristic shape of a hill above the bay, reminiscent of a sleeping walrus.

Kubeš tries to survey the coast thoroughly, hoping to find yet another visible point to help them locate their boat even more precisely. They both spent a lot of time on planning the operation, so they remember the topography of the area well. In the darkness one hill looks like another.

"Look, Jan," says Kubeš and points further. "Every hill looks like a sleeping walrus, with a little bit of imagination."

Libáň is quiet. The shore ahead seems deserted. There are no signs of life. Suddenly, around the limit of the impenetrable darkness, a tiny light comes on. Soon a fire is roaring and some hundred metres from it another one joins it.

"Two fires!" Koniarczyk shouts. "It's the signal."

"Well then, we've come to the right spot," Kubeš nods. "They're waiting for us."

"I'd like to have their eyes," says Libáň. "To spot us in that darkness and snowstorm they must really have eagle eyes."

"They're hunters," says Kubeš. "They depend on their eyes."

"But even so…" says Libáň and shakes his head in disbelief.

"Launch the motorboat!" orders the commander. "Watch B will be the first to deploy. They'll be armed; it could still be a trap."

Four sailors in a rubber dinghy vanish into the darkness with a farting engine noise.

"Now we'll see who gets sea-sick," says Libáň looking at the waves tossing the boat as if it were made of paper.

Kubeš descends to the command centre. He calls in first warrant officer Bouček.

"Is everything ready for handing over the goods?" he asks him.

"Yes, commander," nods Bouček. "We're ready to off-load. As soon as they bring their boats, we open service hatch C8. It'll go like a dream."

"So get ready," says Kubeš. "We'll free up some space tonight."

"We'll be able to play football," says Zrno the cook, who's brought the command centre a pot of hot coffee in one hand and cups in the other. "Coffee, commander?"

"Did you put sugar in it?" asks Kubeš.

"Sugar and cream," says Zrno. "Specially for you."

Kubeš and Bouček each get a cup.

"This will be a long night," says Kubeš.

The submarine gently rocks on the choppy surface of the bay. The men on the bridge vainly peer through their binoculars into the darkness.

Before long, they hear the familiar sound of the outboard motor. The boat brings two guerrillas. Kubeš welcomes them and shakes their hands. The guerrillas speak a particularly incomprehensible kind of Slovak, but in the end they all understand one other.

"Our kayaks will be here shortly," says a guerrilla introducing himself as Sirovec-Molnár, apparently a chieftain with a full mandate. "They'll take all the cargo to the shore. We have put out guards, but the area's clear. I think we chose the right spot."

Indeed, by the side of the submarine appear a few dozen boats crewed by strange little people dressed in furs.

"May I invite you on board, Mr Sirovec?" says Kubeš.

"Call me Frolo, for God's sake!" says Frolo Sirovec-Molnár, and good-naturedly slaps his shoulder.

"Well, in that case, I'm František, but you can call me Franta. Can I offer you a glass of anything?"

"I'll offer you one; let me!" says Frolo Sirovec-Molnár, takes a bottle of clear liquid from his fur jacket and hands it to Kubeš, who doesn't want to look soft and so puts the bottle to his mouth and takes a sip.

"I distilled it myself," says Sirovec-Molnár. "From the best flour and sugar."

Kubeš is not used to such powerful distillates. For a moment he is completely knocked out: his breathing stops and he has no voice.

Frolo Sirovec-Molnár takes the bottle and drinks from it. Then he passes it round those officers who are unluckily on the bridge at the time.

Unloading the crates goes smoothly. The kayaks, loaded way above their gunwale, vanish into the darkness, and others come from the shore.

Not even four hours pass before Bouček reports to the commander that all the goods are unloaded. Kubeš says goodbye to Sirovec-Molnár who boards the last kayak.

Then Kubeš goes down to the command centre. He inspects the hold. It really is empty.

"Well, senior bosun Bouček," he says, "You're now a passenger on our boat. The cargo hold is empty, so we have no duties for you. Would you like to stay ashore?"

"I'd rather not, commander," says Bouček. "I'll find work on board."

"I'm sure you will," says Kubeš. "We're not used to passengers here. Now, gentlemen, we're off to our friends on the *Carabella* for more cargo."

* * *

If it weren't for Sida, Zongora's dream of instantly becoming a great porn star would have evaporated in the humiliatingly small routine roles that Freddy started him off with.

"A young man has to begin at the bottom," Freddy declared when Sida told him to give Zongora a more important role. "He can get used to film world first, so he doesn't get so randy that he shakes like a leaf."

And so Zongora had to start from scratch. Although he got a fine stage name, Luigi Longo, he still cleaned up the stage after the shooting of piss and shit films. Only later did Sida secure him his first role of doorman in the film *Anal Castle*. But in that film he doesn't copulate, he only wanks. And he cleans, too, first in front of the camera, as part of his role, and then after shooting, when the camera is off.

Gradually, however, Freddy, under Sida's influence, gives him bigger and bigger roles. Finally the day comes when Freddy gives him the main role in the film *The Goddess of Vengeance.*

For his small roles in earlier porn films, Zongora got only a pittance, but that was fine as a bonus to his worker's salary. He couldn't splurge on that pay, but he was happy to have a foot in the porn industry, his long-standing dream. Some admire the work of ambulance drivers; others prefer lorry drivers. Zongora was impressed by people in pornography. And becoming one of them was for him an achievement in itself. But it was only a temporary achievement: he was aiming higher.

The Goddess of Vengeance brought him a substantial fee, compared to the modest sums he had been getting. So Zongora began to think about resigning from his long-term day job. After *The Goddess of Vengeance* came *The Crazy Angel of Torture Room II,* and then a real full-feature porn film roughly based on de Sade's notorious *120 Days of Sodom.* In this seventy-minute, uro-scatological, pseudo-pædophile and fetishist work he had the main role. His fee was more than all the money he'd ever seen in his life. He could finally leave his austere room in the Slovnaft barracks and rent a studio flat in Petržalka, a suburb of Bratislava. The new place was just as bleak, but it lacked the noise of distant plants, the hissing steam, the stench of tar products, or the sighs and farts of fellow boarders to whom Zongora no longer had anything to say.

He can't talk to anyone. He looks at his colleagues in the oxygen plant with the condescending expression of a man fortunate enough to get a look behind the curtain of boring, pathetic everyday life. "What do you know, you poor buggers?" he thinks, sneering at their everyday hustling for cheap thrills: family, children, trips, watching films, going for a walk. Luigi Longo aims higher: a luxury flat and perhaps in the future a little villa with a swimming pool, a good car, Porsche or Ferrari, holidays in the Mediterranean, just what he always wanted. He's got used to judging everything around him from a pornographer's point of view. He buys a bunch of radishes at the grocer's and can't understand what keeps the beautiful young shop girl in these dusty, dirty, smelly premises. Why doesn't she cash in as a porn actress? She'd be sure to make much more money than here, selling carrots and fruit juices.

So the time comes for Zongora to leave Slovnaft. His male porn star career is coming along nicely and the security of a permanent job at Slovnaft no longer has the appeal it had only recently. So he gives notice with a light heart and leaves. He doesn't even say goodbye to his colleagues: he's never been very close to them and they, too, were estranged from him when they sensed that, underneath, he despised them — unlike Czanner the businessman, who always buys something from Slovnaft and never misses a chance to visit the oxygen plant where time has stopped. Czanner is stupid and will never be one of the élite. Zongora will leave at the end of the workday and will never come back.

Anal Castle (The Castle of Sin)

The castle owner and his wife put on a special dinner for a business partner. The business partner and his wife arrive in a Porsche. A doorman lets them in. After a short welcome, dinner is served. At dinner, the partner's wife asks the castle owner to show her the hothouse. There, the castle owner undresses the woman (leaving her, of course, in a black corset, black stockings and pumps). For a while, he penetrates her genitals and anus with various exotic fruits that he grows. Soon they begin to engage in passionate sex: anally, of course. After anal sex in various positions, the partner's wife fellates the castle owner. He sprays her face with semen. Meanwhile, the lady of the castle shows her husband's partner their precious collection of erotic art. Viewing this collection so excites the partner that he tries to rape the lady of the castle. She hardly resists, but the business partner can't get an erection. So he tries to satisfy her with cunnilingus, while she unsuccessfully tries to make him hard by masturbation. Finally she takes a lump of salami off the table and masturbates with it. The business partner takes a corn on the cob, spreads butter over it and puts it in her anus. The doorman spies on them through a keyhole. He can't hold back and starts to masturbate. His huge ejaculation makes a mess on the floor, but the doorman has to put his trousers on and flee, since the castle's owner and his partner's wife are returning from the hothouse. Traces of all sexual activity vanish and a dignified, if over-formal politeness reigns again between hosts and guests. Only the lady of the castle notices a huge pool of semen on the floor behind the door, as she serves coffee. Since she has nothing at hand to wipe it off, she discreetly licks it up with her tongue.

(From Freddy's notebook)

* * *

It took the shaman from the settlement of Gargâ a long time to revive
Özgett Glebąâr. From then on, the Junjan's eyes burned with frightful
hatred. The very same day he organized a revenge raid on the Slovak
settlements. Some of the Junjans joined Özgett out of boredom, others
hoping to steal something in the chaos. Nobody cared about Özgett and
even less about his brother. But any chance to harm Slovaks was welcome. All the men in the punitive posse ran out onto the snow and put
together the dog teams at breakneck speed. They hollered vindictively
and joyfully: after days spent dying, something was finally happening.

The vengeful raiders did not dare attack Habovka. It was quite a long
way away, and also quite populous. So they decided to attack a smaller
fishing village, Hanová. The population of Hanová counted at most forty
inhabitants, belonging to three families.

The weather stopped raging and from the greyish mass of sea a
moderate wind blew. It was a good sign: Hanová's men would be fishing
and only women, children and old men would be left in the village. With
wild and excited shouts the revenge raid set out. Death to Slovaks!

When they came back a few hours later, the inhabitants of Gargâ
welcomed them as heroes. The raid was a success. The Junjans brought
on their sledges a cargo of food on which they could survive for many
weeks. Besides, there were fur, tools, and a few Slovak women, who
were yelling madly. They would not accept their slave status.

Özgett was still shaking with rage. He felt he had not yet sufficiently
avenge his brother's death. Something worrying that Junjan soul had not
yet been appeased. On attacking the Slovak village Özgett worked his
rage off on a young woman who was working skins in front of her yurt.
He raped her violently right in the snow. The Slovak woman fought back
ferociously, so he had to knock her out with a punch. When he'd
satisfied his needs, he saw that he had not just knocked her out, but killed
her. The blow was so strong that it broke her back. Excited by the sight
of blood oozing from the Slovak woman's nose, he got up and searched
for his next victim. His kinsmen were looting and sometimes killing any
woman or old man who tried to stop them. Özgett, too, took something
from the yurt of the murdered Slovak woman. He took a fancy to two
guns, a rifle and a shotgun, hanging from the ceiling. He smacked his
lips with satisfaction. He grabbed a fistful of shotgun cartridges and
headed for the exit. He ripped open the curtain and went out.

The Junjans killed and looted hastily. They all knew that the shots would be heard by the men hunting seals at distant holes in the ice floe. So they killed the Slovaks' dogs to hinder the pursuit and only then, weighed down by looted food, weapons, tools and female slaves, did they hop onto their sledges and race from the scene of the crime.

When Hanová's men got back from the hunt, a scene of destruction met their eyes.

"The Junjans," shouted those women and children who had escaped capture or death. "The Junjans came and killed and looted."

Grown-up men cried like small boys. They clenched their fists until their knuckles went white. Some drew blood from their wrists, as they bit into them in mad fury. Everyone's voice cried for revenge.

"First we must look after the wounded and put out the fires," proposed Ondrej Šebo, the oldest hunter, whom all the others respected as the settlement's uncrowned chieftain. "We won't be able to catch them now that our dogs have been killed. But revenge is not a fox; it won't run away. Go to your tasks and do what has to be done."

In the evening there was a meeting in Šebo's yurt. By then they knew exactly what the Junjans had wrought. They had left fourteen dead. Four young women were gone. Their men were going mad from despair and helplessness. They insisted on setting out on a punitive raid.

"Who will benefit?" Šebo tried to dissuade them. "If you want to stop them being screwed, you're too late: they've been screwed long ago. If you want to free them, you need a cool head, not this madness."

"Revenge is a dish best eaten cold," agreed an elder of the Kyselica family. "We'll visit our Slovak brothers in Habovka, Horná and Dolná Náprava and Krempná, too. We'll seek their advice and then we'll decide what action we'll take. But we won't let such a crime go unpunished."

And that was what they did. They immediately set off to see their Slovak brothers in nearby villages and settlements, and crossed the sea in their kayaks, visiting Slovak fishing and hunting settlements scattered over the smaller islands. They told everyone of their suffering.

They all drank tea with them and even moonshine was put on the table, but everyone advised them to be very cautious. Not all were ready to risk their safety, although the injustice cried out. That's what Slovaks are like: they won't fight a fire until it burns their arses.

"So what?" an elder from Krempná advised. "You'll find new women. And your women won't be so badly off with the Junjans. You know Junjans like their women plump. At least they won't go hungry."

"You're a Slovak and you tell me that?" Kyselica-Kuna shouted at him, got up brusquely and left the hearth. All the other Hanová elders followed his example to a man.

"Oh, you're a bad Slovak," Šebo-Kováč told the Krempná elder and spat on the ground in front of him. "There's not an ounce of pride in you. Your cowardice is indecent, even for a Slovak."

"What you call 'cowardice,' I call 'sense'," said the insulted Krempná elder. "We've always had these minor squabbles with the Junjans. We understand your pain, but what you propose is rebellion."

"Yes, it is about time the Junjans found out that there are no Russians here to protect them," said Kyselica-Kuna. "If you are not with us, then so be it. Get back to your furs and don't stick your nose out."

The men from Hanová filed out of the yurt through the hole in the wall with dignity and, as a sign of disgrace, the last of the hunters did not pull down the leather curtain behind him.

"Well, I say!" murmured the Krempná elder.

The men from Hanová fared differently in Habovka.

When they told the gathering in the Habovka's men's house what had happened to them, the clan heads leapt up and their hands spontaneously reached for weapons.

"Damn them!" Geľo Todor-Lačný raged. "This calls for revenge!"

And a group of excitable younger men immediately joined Hanová's.

The same happened in Dolná Náprava.

Before daybreak a punitive expedition came to Gargâ on several dozen dog sledges while the Junjans still slept. The Slovaks poured mineral grease everywhere and set it on fire. When the Junjans ran out from their burning yurts and huts, the Slovaks easily got them with their rifles. The priest dashed among the dying, baptizing as fast as he could.

The fighters brought back all the women they'd rescued who'd been abducted by the Junjans. Only one did not return: Fero Topoľský-Cigáň's wife, who, the rescued women testified, preferred to stab herself with an iron skewer rather than be dishonoured by a lecherous Junjan. He dishonoured her anyway, but by then the poor woman was no longer aware of it. Fero Topoľský-Cigáň exacted a terrible revenge. He tied the Junjan identified as the culprit by the Hanová women with a long leash to the dog sledge and, a wild expression on his face, he drove his dogs into the snowy taiga. The Junjan at first tried to run, but then his legs gave way. He slipped, and the unhappy Fero dragged him to death, still roaring curses. He left the disfigured corpse in the taiga and returned to Hanová the next day, half-mad with unsated desire for vengeance.

When he entered the men's house, where the Hanová and Habovka men were celebrating their punitive raid, everyone fell silent. They feared Topoľský-Cigáň's frost-cracked, wind-burned face.

"Is there a God, priest?" Fero Topoľský-Cigáň asked the priest.

"Why do you ask?" asked the priest. "If there were no God, there'd be no us. The fact that we're here is perfect proof that God exists."

"And why is He here if He lets such things happen?" asked Fero, reaching for a bottle.

"God doesn't always pay attention," said the priest. "That's why we have to be on guard. And if we fail, then it's an eye for an eye and a tooth for a tooth. That's what Christ said. That's why we're Christians."

"And how do you know this so well?" wondered Fero.

"From my father," said the priest. "And he got it from his own father. We've been a priestly family ever since our forefathers came here. Our great-great-grandfather used to be a priest in the old Slovak country. That was why they used to call him Sexton, here in Junja, because of his priestly profession. That's been our name ever since."

"Sexton," said Kyselica-Kuna. "An odd name. What does it mean?"

"Churches were big yurts made of stone where services were held," said the priest. "And the sexton was the highest priest in such a church."

"So you're from a high priest's family," nodded Fero. "But tell me, where do you get all those stories of yours? How do you know so much about Christ?"

"There used to be a book once," said the priest. "It was called *Holy Scripture*. But it hasn't been seen for ages. So we pass these stories from generation to generation. My father didn't get round to telling me all of them, as I was only a boy when the drunken Bolshevik commissar Yasin beat him to death. And so I had to find all those stories with my heart. My father comes in my dreams and teaches me all the holy things."

The men are astounded and full of veneration.

"Christ was a great fighter," the priest said, "and he left no wrong unpunished. Revenge was sacred to him. He had anyone who hurt him crucified. So we Christians wear the symbol of the cross to put fear in all our foes. And Slovaks are God's chosen people. Moses was a Slovak, too. Kamil Moses-Červenka of Horná Náprava is a distant kinsman."

"If that's how it is," said Geľo Todor-Lačný-Dolniak, "then it's time to declare holy war for the Slovak nation's rights. We've spent a long time in slavery and bondage, but no more! We shan't be put off our aim. Therefore we'll set out against the Junjan settlement of Gbb'bnää. We'll do to them what we did today to Gargâ. Who's coming with me?"

Geľo's faithful followers all raised their hands.

"But the people of Gbb'bnaa haven't hurt us," said a Hanová elder.

"But for some reason they make me angry," said Geľo. "Men, do you remember the kayaks we found full of holes last year, when the whales were migrating? Well, I say that Junjans from Gbb'bnää did it."

The men got worked up. Anger and moonshine went to their heads. They picked up their weapons again.

"Junjans will find out what Slovaks are," raged Geľo.

"What does Christ say about that, priest?"

"He says that you think rightly," said the priest. "Christ taught, 'Never hide or swallow your anger. Spread my teaching and anger will be your helpmate'."

"Amen," said Geľo and loaded his gun.

It was not so easy, though. The retaliatory raid, provoked by Junjans, on the former officials' settlement Gbb'bnää was meant to be a surprise, but many Junjans managed to escape in boats by sea. These refugees alarmed their compatriots in other Junjan settlements round the former fur-trading posts and they made war on the Slovaks.

To save his family, Geľo had to take it to a secret place, the reindeer herder Kresan's camp. And the other men from Habovka, Hanová and other places did the same. They themselves left Habovka and withdrew deep into taiga. They became homeless outlawed fighters. Their only law was that of revenge.

As a reprisal for the massacre at Krempná, two Junjan settlements were massacred by Slovak guerrillas, since these settlements harboured government soldiers. They had been sent in by the Junjan Khan to suppress the rebellion. The army suffered great losses in combat with the wild Slovaks who were prepared for anything, being used to the terrain and its deadly conditions. The rest of the army ran away in panic. So the Khan invited foreign mercenaries to join his army and clear the guerrillas from Junja. At the head of this army, even more cruel and resolute than the Slovak resistance, he placed a man who had perhaps taken part in every putsch, civil war and rebellion of the last fifteen years, a man of mysterious origins and unfathomably devious intelligence, known in Junja by the name of Tökörnn Mäodna. This very well paid mercenary became a serious opponent for the Slovaks, but Geľo Todor-Lačný-Dolniak did not give up so easily. His ally was the wild taiga and the broken terrain of the northern coast from where he launched devastating raids against Junjans and their government mercenaries.

It soon turned out that the civil war in Junja had a charm and specific quality that made it attractive to journalists from all over the world. They gathered here in large numbers and, as is usual in such circumstances, focussed the world's fickle attention on this insignificant little spot of land way beyond the Arctic Circle.

Among the journalists were also Czechs, who easily crossed the lines and often managed to get confidential information, not least because, unlike American or German journalists, they could understand a little of the local Slovak dialect.

The Czech journalists were the first to write about Junja and show marked sympathy for the Slovak resistance, and this was gradually taken up by journalists from other countries. The Czech public's and government's sympathies finally resulted in an invitation to the leaders of the rebellion to make a short visit to the Czech lands. This was not announced publicly, but intermediaries knew that Todor-Lačný-Dolniak and Sirovec-Molnár had flown to Prague to discuss, besides moral support, the possibility of material help for the rebellion.

* * *

Video Urban, too, came across the geographical name Junja for the first time only in a newspaper report of some shooting incident between local inhabitants and settlers. All the Slovak and Czech press at first kept a dignified distance from this unknown land far beyond the Arctic Circle. No one really knew anything about the country at all. The world press portrayed the indigenous people as the goodies, at first as brave, honest fighters, something between Apaches and Chechen patriots. Their enemies were portrayed as bloodthirsty foreigners having problems assimilating. Then the papers for the first time named the baddies' leader: Geľo Todor-Lačný-Dolniak. That was strange: an odd name to find beyond the Arctic Circle. Could he be an émigré adventurer, Urban wondered. Later, the paper printed more news about the Junjan fighting, which by now had turned into a veritable bloodbath. At first the impression given was that the enemy, the destroyers, was the Slovak minority. Slovaks abroad. But how had they got there, Urban wondered.

The most surprising fact was that as the world slowly learned the full truth about the fighting in Junja, the position of the Slovak Press Agency remained, in agreement with the Slovak Republic's official position, pro-Junjan. To confirm this, the Prime Minister invited Okhlann Üncmüñć, Chairman of the Supreme Council of the Junjan Khanate, to visit

Slovakia. The joint statement of both sides was as follows: "The Slovak Republic considers events in Junja to be an internal affair of the Junjan Khanate and condemns efforts by the Czechs to influence events by overt and covert support of anti-government terrorists who happen to be ethnically similar to the population of Slovakia."

This was typical of the Slovak ruling class's unerring diplomatic incompetence. After practically every West European country, including Hungary, but not so far the Czechs, had unilaterally introduced a visa regime for Slovaks, it was a sure way of losing the Czechs' good will, which was based on sentiment.

"Shit!" Urban laughs in despair. "And I voted for those pricks!"

Urban is not amazed. He'd be surprised if the corrupt Slovak government behaved in any other way. Even his anger has an element of resignation and a kind of gallows humour about it. He can see it clearly: we'll screw things up with the Czechs as well. The borders will close and we'll need a visa even for a trip to Brno. But until then, he'll be on the other side of the border. When the iron curtain comes down between Slovakia and the Czech state, Urban will already be in Prague. If only Freddy Piggybank weren't such a dimwit, they could move the whole company to Prague and just laugh it off. Business in Prague is done differently; life's much better there, too.

In the tabloid *Plus 7 Days* he reads some geographical and surprising demographic facts about Junja:

The Junjan Khanate is spread over four large and fifteen small islands. The central island is called Ögdbaardd and has two towns: Űŕǵüllpoļ (its international name, in Junjan the name is Űŕǵüll-khan-khalla: the city of Khan Űŕǵüll), which is the capital, and Ćmirçăpoļ (Ćmirçă-khalla). These are the only two big towns on the islands. They comprise about one fourth of the Junjan population. The rest is spread out in settlements that originated as Soviet fur and fish processing plants. Other large islands are called Kerkyżżmm, Külüú and Mgdräag. The Junjans are of unknown origin, but their language suggests they are descendants of the original Finns and Norwegians interbred with Lapps, Huns, and Tatars. How they got to Junja is a mystery; all that is certain is that this happened in several separate waves around the 12th century.

The Junjan archipelago's indigenous population was the so-called Inkirinnuit, or People of the North, distant kin of the Chukchi and the Innuit. But the Junjans killed them off. Survivors of these peaceful tribes welcomed Slovak refugees from Junjan slavery and taught them how to survive successfully in the tundra and on the coast. They gradually merged with the Slovaks and vanished as an ethnic group. This is why so many Junjan Slovak men and women even today look quite exotic.

Officially, the Slovaks are a national minority, but in reality, thanks to their industriousness and fertility, they have been the majority for quite some time. About a quarter of the Junjan Slovaks live in towns, a quarter are nomadic reindeer herders and the rest live in hunting and fishing settlements scattered over the north coast of Öggdbardd and the islands. Although their population is twenty times larger than the Junjan, officially, they are a national minority with no rights. They don't even have citizenship, let alone representation in the Great Council.

The only thing of interest in Junja from the economic point of view is a special kind of lichen that grows only on some northern islands of the archipelago. For most of the world's leading producers of perfume this lichen is indispensable. If Junja stopped exporting lichen, it would lead to a crisis in the perfume industry and most famous brand names would cease to exist or would lose their famous quality.

Amnesty International and other human rights organizations regularly protest against the Junjan monopoly, because, according to uncorroborated information, slaves imprisoned in labour camps harvest the lichen. Hitherto, protests and demonstrations appeared to be organized and financed by the competition: purveyors of lower quality lichen.

Junja is also notorious as the origin of a criminal organization, the infamous Junjan mafia, who operate in countries of Central and Eastern Europe, and whose ruthlessness and unparalleled cruelty oust other notorious criminal organizations from Ukraine, Chechnya or Kosovo.

Urban also met at a party an old acquaintance from his time in politics. This man still worked as a government official in the Ministry of Foreign Affairs. He told Urban a lot of funny stories. Okhlann Üncmüñć's visit to Slovakia, for example, was full of amusing events.

After his speech to parliament, the Chairman of the Great Council stopped by the automatic coffee machine in the hall. "*Ündzzmardžž!?*" ("What's this?") he asked his bodyguards. Nobody knew.

The Slovak Prime Minister worked out what the guest was asking and hastily replied. "An automatic coffee machine," he said. His interpreter translated it into Russian, which Okhlann Üncmüñć luckily understood slightly. "*Kazhetsya avtomatt?*" asked the guest of honour in Russian, both hands miming the firing of a machine gun. "*Na kofye?*"

The Slovak Prime Minister shook his head. *"Nyet,"* he said. For Junjans shaking one's head is a sign of agreement. The obvious contradiction between what the Slovak Prime Minister said and did put Okhlann Üncmüñć in a grim mood. He fixed his slanted eyes on the liar. *"Nu vot kak (Well, then)?"* he asked impatiently. Without explaining, the Slovak Prime Minister took a plastic cup, put it in the machine, and pushed a button marked: COFFEE WITH MILK. Before the amazed Chairman of the Supreme Council and his bodyguards, the Prime Minister stirred his hot refreshment with a wooden stick and drank it.

That was all Okhlann Üncmüñć needed to know. He went for the automatic coffee machine with the determination of a citizen of a country where every morsel of food is a struggle. In a flash, he learned how to work the machine, and drank cup after cup. He handed used plastic cups to his underlings who piled them up and put them away in plastic bags. As he drank, Okhlann Üncmüñć irritably gestured at them to go and pick cups from the nearby rubbish bins, too. After all, plastic cups are among the most precious possessions in Junja.

The whole programme of the visit was in ruins, drowned by innumerable cups of milky coffee and hot chocolate.

Okhlann Üncmüñć was a bottomless vessel. He drank without a pause, with grim determination. Not even monstrous stomach rumbles, coming from under the Junjan statesman's badly made jacket, could change his resolve to drink the machine's entire contents. He achieved this after an hour and a half. Then, belching and rolling his eyes, Okhlann Üncmüñć continued the friendly visit according to protocol.

At the end of the friendly visit, the Slovak Prime Minister and the Chairman of the Supreme Council signed an agreement on mutual cultural and economic help.

* * *

WILD THINGS: The best of Freddy Vision Vol. 2.
Length: 120 minutes.
Porn king Freddy of Freddy Vision offers us in the second volume of this instalment of "The Best of…" a sample of four unusually rough and perverse short films. In the first one, a young boy and his two girl friends hiking in the mountains witness strange goings-on. In the mountains they find a semi-naked blonde left hanging head down by a thick rope. What's it all about? Then, right behind their backs they hear the heavy breathing of a modern slave driver about to stop his victim being rescued. The

supposedly hanging girl tortures the boy; both girls are bound, whipped and raped. The film's ending will please all admirers of group scenes of bondage featuring naked young girls and a boy. In the second story, two mysterious masked bandits grab a young girl in a school. The evildoers are not as interested in getting maths lessons as in sadistically outraging the young girl's body. Bondage, clothes pegs on their breasts, spanking with a whip and sticks, impalement on a huge vibrator are all part of the programme in a musty underground cell devised by these two madmen full of hatred of women, especially of young girls. The third story takes place on a luxury ranch — a ranch of human animals, a farm where women are treated as horses. In this exciting performance, we witness very unusual dressage of beautifully developed women-mares, humiliation where every wrong step is punished with a long whip. Five girls gradually change before our eyes into absolute slaves, obedient animals bereft of all vestiges of human will and dignity. The fourth story is about a young thief who breaks into a flat. Unfortunately, the flat belongs to a sadistic dominatrix who catches him in the act and decides in her own way to stop him doing similar things in future by beating it out of his head, and his body. There are unique shots of burning and crushing of testicles, fist in the anus, and hanging on hooks through pierced nipples.

Order N°: 1820 0173
Price: 999.00 Czech crowns
Club member price: 950.00 Czech crowns
(From the *Freddy Vision* catalogue)

Freddy has been badly hurt. He detected that there was rather more to Sida's and Zongora's relationship than that of mere colleagues. It began when Sida started to stand up for Zongora even when he messed up or made a professional mistake.

"Do you really think," Freddy shouted in front of the whole crew at this self-appointed lawyer for Zongora, "that if someone has a thirteen-inch prick he doesn't have to arrive for a shoot on time?"

"No," Sida answered. "I'm only saying that Luigi's simply a star and you have to have different criteria for him."

"What do you mean a star?" Freddy raged. "Only a year ago he was an ordinary worker at the Dimitrov factory, or somewhere. Who got him out of there? And now he gives me this attitude? He's nowhere near being a star yet. Mister thirteen inches is still a big zero!"

"But just think," Sida reminded him, "how much money this zero has earned you. Just think of that and treat him as a human being."

"As a very unreliable human being," Freddy said angrily.

Sida and Luigi have evidently taken to each other. Perhaps they have even fallen in love. In Freddy's company Sida is morose and dismissive. She comes alive only when Zongora is around. Her eyes begin to gleam; her lips turn red and become enlarged. They meet secretly and make love, as if they did not get enough in front of the camera. Like any man in love, Zongora, too, would like somehow to make his relationship public and shout about his happiness to all. The laws of conspiracy, so binding for the more rationally minded Sida, are alien to him. Who knows why men are like that, why they need to brag about everything? Finally, even the birds in the trees are talking about it.

And as is traditional, Freddy is the last to find out. A kindly soul in the company whispered it to him. At first, he can't believe it. His Sida? His fine wonderful wife Sida, with whom he shares so many pleasant memories? A whiff of menace has crept into Freddy's soul.

In the evening, Freddy brings his suspicions into the open. He, suspects that Sida's and Zongora's relations have become more than a normal professional partnership.

Sida almost chokes on her food. She fires back: how could Freddy even imagine it? Inwardly she curses Zongora's stupidity and carelessness in letting the whole company know how badly he's fallen for her.

"And what about that sighing and moaning in front of the camera? You never moan with me," Freddy complains.

"I just fake it," says Sida. "I always do it that way in films, don't I?"

"And why don't you ever fake it with me?" Freddy asks.

Sida flares with quite unfaked anger. She shouts at Freddy and brings up everything she has kept back for so long. How he gets on her nerves with his suspicions, how he never gives her any attention, how he doesn't hug her, or show her affection, how he gets off on her in a few seconds so that even if she wanted to moan, she wouldn't have time even to take breath. She's a neglected wife and no one in the world would find it odd if she took a lover. She is surprised she hasn't done so yet, and yet she has to listen to these humiliating and absurd accusations.

Freddy is stumped. On the one hand, he's glad that his wife has refuted his accusation. He wants to believe her. On the other hand, the doubts gnawing at him have not gone away.

"Look," Freddy says calmly. "I love you…"

"Really?" Sida, listening ironically. "And how can I tell?"

Freddy jumps up, napkin in hand and foam on his mouth.

"HOW CAN YOU TELL?" he roars. "By the fucking jewellery and fur coats that I buy you. By making you into a world-class porn star. By all that I do to make you famous."

"You do it all only to make your money, anyway," says Sida.

"MY money?" Freddy is baffled. "You mean OURS, don't you?"

The food turns sour in his mouth. He throws down his cutlery, gets up and bangs the door as leaves.

He walks alone round the pond till midnight, meekly submitting to the myriad mosquitoes that hungrily attack the unprotected parts of his body. So even the ungrateful environment is sucking his blood, he thinks as he morosely watches the pond's calm surface.

Freddy's suspicions, even after a few days, remain. The fact that the two have sex in front of the camera is fine. After all, Freddy scripted it. The fact that Sida massages and sucks Zongora's prick, while he licks her crotch before they do it normally and anally does not bother Freddy. That's the profession. It's a job like any other. If anyone thinks that porn is carefree fun, then try it! The money's hard earned. In short, it's a business like any other. But private life is quite another thing. In private, only Freddy can have Sida. Only he is her husband.

The suspicion that Sida and Luigi may be meeting and making love in secret, even in their free time, is hard for Freddy to bear. He is almost insane with jealousy. He cannot track every step Sida makes; as a famous porn star she has a lot of social commitments, media interviews, promotions, work on the side. Freddy is too stingy to pay to have her followed. And so Freddy does his work only with great self-denial. They have to finish *Anal Justice* at any price.

Just before the film is finished, Freddy is in such a state that he does not know whether he feels like this because of overwork or jealousy. When they're shooting a scene in a torture room, with Zongora tied to the rack and Sida whipping him, Freddy, as director, thinks that the lashes of the whip are too gentle and seem unnatural.

"Harder!" Freddy shouts at Sida. "You must do it harder!"

They repeat the shot. Sida swings her arm again and the leather straps fall on Zongora's back with a whack.

"That's too gentle," Freddy roars. He jumps off his director's chair.

"Give it to me!" he tells Sida and takes the whip from her hand. "This is how to do it."

Fear shows in Luigi's eyes. He sees Freddy's glassy look and a strand of foam hanging from the corner of his mouth. Before he can say a word, his back and behind are cut with the first blow.

"This way," shouts Freddy and hits with all his might. "This way! Like this! Like this!"

Luigi cries out with surprise and pain. Afterwards he cries continuously. The whip has cut his skin, and is now ripping out fibres of subcutaneous fat and muscle. Everything around is instantly spattered with blood. And Freddy looks like a meat packer in a slaughterhouse.

Finally the crew intervene. The cameraman and the soundman grab Freddy, and the lighting man takes the whip from Freddy's hand. Freddy's eyes are bloodshot and foam pours from his mouth. He hangs in their arms unconscious. He has fainted from being so overwrought.

Zongora is hanging on the rack. He, too, is unconscious. His eyes are turned up, covered by an opaque film and his swollen tongue hangs out of the side of his mouth. His head has fallen sideways.

"Shit, just what we needed!" shouts the production manager. "What a cock-up! Somebody untie him!"

Sida and the other women look after Zongora. They gently take him off the rack. It looks like a *pietà* in a Renaissance painting, but for the wailing women in sexy underwear and leather accessories. Zongora comes round and sighs with pain. Someone pours whisky into his mouth.

Freddy also comes round, in an armchair where they set him. He looks round with a dull expression.

"Is that what you wanted?" shouts Sida in front of everyone. "To lash out at a defenceless man? Why not do it when he wasn't tied down, when he could defend himself? You disgusting coward! I hate you!"

Freddy is quiet. He looks around in resignation; he seems unaware of his wife. He reaches into his chest pocket and takes out a leather-covered metal flask. He takes a sip. He doesn't offer it to anyone else.

"No, best not to call a doctor," says the production manager supervising Zongora's treatment.

Zongora faints as they wash his back with whisky and bandage it. He regains consciousness after a while. He watches Freddy. Freddy coldly returns his gaze. The two will never be friends again, that much is clear.

The same evening, Freddy acts the modern aggrieved husband and moves out of the house. He takes a room in the Hotel Ambassador-Rácz. It's the only hotel he knows, so he feels a little bit at home there. When he unpacks the necessities he has brought with him, he locks the room and goes for a walk in the city. Every corner round the hotel reminds him of something. He goes to see his old car park that once, in *Rivers of Babylon,* had to make way for a wooden village. But there is no trace of any wooden village there today; the car park is back. Freddy follows the parking attendant for a moment, as he sits in his modern booth, controls the entrance and exit barriers and collects money. For heaven's sakes, if only Freddy had this modern booth and gates then, a long time ago, he'd have made much more money. Nobody would run away without paying or being fined. They'd have to break down the barrier.

Freddy momentarily regrets the money that he missed making then, but then he recovers. Today, after all, Freddy is much wealthier. Why open old wounds? He walks on. There's no need to return to the past.

Freddy's in a bad mood and decides to improve it with a good dinner. He'd rather call Urban and complain to him, but Urban is in Prague again. And so he dines in the *Tibava* wine cellar, which is a part of the hotel complex. It's late, but Freddy does not feel sleepy. Finally, after downing two glasses of whisky, he gets himself to sleep.

The next day he goes to work as usual. The morning begins with the porn actresses raising hell. They'd like bigger fees. They feel underpaid.

Freddy curses. All he needs is for them to bring a trade union into his production company. And yet they're lucky that he's a person of character. But is he a person of character? He's a stupid prick! He pays them such incredible sums that all the other porn magnates laugh at him.

He even knows people who never pay women anything. They simply kidnap women they fancy, force them, or drug them to do in front of the camera whatever they invent, including the most degrading and disgusting filthy things, and then they just kill them. And they do it in front of the cameras, to get some profit from it. And after their death they'll shoot a film with them for a highly and narrowly specialised clientele. Such females thus have multiple uses. Like a sheep that gives milk, wool, and meat. And what does Freddy do? He pays like there's no tomorrow. But this is the end of it. Fees will not be increased

The girls retort that they don't even know how their pay's arrived at.

Freddy shrugs. The girls need a price list for acts performed? They want to be like doctors? That's no problem at all. A price list will be drawn up today, so that all performers can calculate their fees. Gross, of course. How much of that they pay the state and how much they have left doesn't interest Freddy.

Freddy locks himself in his office and works hard. The price list is ready by lunch time. Freddy has it printed out on the laser printer and posted in the office areas, dressing rooms and photo and film studios.

Let them all read it! He's spent hours working on this price list. Everything's been thoroughly calculated. From now on, all the girls will be paid accordingly.

Basic hourly rate: 100 Slovak crowns;
Hourly rate for technical pauses: 20 crowns;
Additional:
Simple sexual act: 0 crowns;
Oral: 200 crowns;
Anal: 500 crowns;
Bondage: 700 crowns;
Penis in vagina, another in anus (sandwich): 1000 crowns.
Two penises in anus: 1600 crowns
Fist in vagina: 2500 crowns;
Fist in anus: 3000 crowns;
Whipping until blood is drawn: 3500 crowns;
Fist in vagina and another in anus at the same time: 3500 crowns.
Other items: by agreement.

The price list gets the notice due to it from the company employees.

"And what about the men?" one of the porn actors asks Freddy. "Haven't you thought about the male actors?"

"Male actors should be glad to be so lucky," Freddy tells him brusquely. "For every male in work, there are five waiting on the street. By the way, you're fired. What for? For asking stupid questions. Pack up and get lost. Oh, has no one told Zongora he's fired, too? No? Well, I repeat: he's fired. When he comes, the guards can throw him out."

Pleased with himself, Freddy goes back to his office and sits down at his desk, turning to the script he is working on.

Wicked Schoolgirl

Mother (Wanda Desire) and her schoolgirl daughter (Ariana Anal), come after school to see the headmaster (~~Luigi Longo~~ Bruno Tatarelli) begging him not to fail the daughter. The headmaster is adamant until the mother takes her blouse off and shows him her naked breasts. The headmaster relents, but, pretending to be shocked, points at the daughter, saying that such things should not be shown in front of a child. The child smiles perversely, lifts her little dress and shows she has no underwear. The headmaster seems more fascinated by the sight of the daughter's childlike genitals than by the sight of the mother's breasts. The visitors notice, so the girl takes her clothes off, unzips the headmaster's fly and begins to masturbate and suck him in turn. Meanwhile, the mother also takes her clothes off and joins the daughter. The headmaster is also undressed and the mother offers him her vagina. He prefers to have sex with the daughter. The mother won't agree: the daughter is still a virgin. The headmaster say he knows a way of not breaking her daughter's virginity. The daughter smiles and kneels with her back to him. The headmaster takes her from behind anally. At the same time the mother lies under her daughter and performs cunnilingus on her. The daughter does the same to her, as their position makes it feasible. Then they change position. Now the headmaster has anal sex with the mother, face to face, performing anilingus on the daughter. The mother's and headmaster's tongues meet on the daughter's behind and crotch. Soon the headmaster ejaculates with classic loud moans of relief. Woman and child get dressed. The headmaster suggests meeting the next day. He promises that the daughter now has good marks guaranteed until the end of her school days.

(From Freddy's notebook)

* * *

The Good Lord decided to make a poor man happy: he
drove reindeer into the tundra and helped the man find them.
Junjan Slovak proverb

"Mr Rácz is expecting you," Freddy is told by a rather dubious-looking man in his thirties with a jacket bulging under his left armpit. He opens the double doors wide.

In the room is a huge desk at which the hotelier Rácz is sitting. Round him, three more men of suspicious appearance, but in well-tailored suits, lounge comfortably in armchairs.

Freddy crosses the long carpet and stops at the desk.

"Good day," he says.

He looks at the hotelier.

"I'm grateful you've found time to see me, Mr Rácz," he adds.

"Friends of our friends are our friends, too," says Rácz. "I'm sure you know of the long fruitful friendship between your business partner Urban and myself. We seldom meet now, but our friendship survives."

Freddy realises that he may have made a mistake by deciding to act himself instead of asking Urban to intervene.

Rácz sizes up Freddy for a while. Then he motions with his hand to a chair placed in front of the desk.

"Please sit down," he invites Freddy.

Freddy blushes. He accepts the proffered chair. He politely declines to take a cigar from a wooden humidor that the hotelier offers him.

"Thanks, I don't smoke," he says. "Sorry," he adds unsurely.

Rácz cuts the end of the cigar. He places it in his mouth and lets a bodyguard light it. His eyes half-closed, he puffs on it.

His movements are deliberate and unhurried. The hotelier's whole personality radiates the austere, but benevolent calm of a wealthy and powerful man who knows no obstacles.

"It's come to my attention that you've graced our hotel with your presence for a few days," says Rácz, takes the cigar out of his mouth and inspects it closely with a pretence of interest. "It's a great honour for us if a famous personality like you shows a preference for our hotel instead of the comfort of his own home."

Freddy swallows a few times and clears his throat.

"Well," says Rácz. "What's brought you to us, Mr Mešťánek?"

Freddy clears his throat again. Then he begins to tell him the whole story. At a few points he blushes. At others, he displays righteous indignation. He presents himself as an upright artist and businessman who has long been harbouring a snake in his bosom. He gave an ambitious young man a chance, and this is how he's been paid back. Freddy recognises his only mistake: he got too carried away by work. He neglected his family hearth. He portrays Sida as an slightly unworldly artist, good at heart, but romantically inclined, and now a slightly straying wife and mother whom he has already magnanimously forgiven. After all, it's all the fault of that demon, the vile seducer, Zongora the home-breaker.

Rácz listens quietly. His eyes are firmly fixed on Piggybank's face shining with animated, just indignation. At times, he subtly and solemnly nods to let the narrator know that he follows the thread of his narration.

Rácz's men also listen quietly. Freddy is a little embarrassed, talking in detail of his family life in front of this audience. But the longing for revenge is stronger than shame. Freddy knows that only Rácz and his men can help punish Zongora. So he swallows his pride and takes an even harder stance against his wife's lover: yes, Zongora will have to pay in blood and tears for these shameful moments, too.

Freddy describes Zongora as an ordinary plebeian, a thoroughly perverted parvenu: even his performances in Freddy's films are for him a way not to solve financial problems, but only to satisfy his dark desires.

"He likes showing his prick, pardon the word, that's all," Freddy ends.

Silence reigns in the room after Freddy's monologue.

"And how can I be of help?" Rácz asks after a moment: until then he has been listening, his hands thoughtfully clasped to his mouth, and has been furtively making a few notes on a piece of paper. The hotelier's steely eyes bore into Freddy's face.

"Why have you come to see me?" asks Rácz.

Freddy seems put out by this question. He stutters.

"I'm asking, because you've never needed Rácz before," the hotelier continues. "How many times you've celebrated various premieres and as a producer you've had many prizes, including the Porn Oscar, if I'm not mistaken…" Rácz pauses for a moment to give Freddy time to appreciate his detailed knowledge, then continues, "but you've never invited me to any of your parties. Rácz wouldn't say that he'd be sure to come, he'd rather not, but it's the gesture that counts. Or take last year: Rácz was celebrating his thirty-fifth birthday. Congratulations came from all over the world. There were three baskets of telegrams. Did Mešťánek congratulate Rácz too? No."

Rácz puts on an embittered expression. As if it really bothered him.

Freddy almost falls off his chair with embarrassment and a vague feeling of horror. Not even in his dreams did he imagine that his audience with the powerful hotelier would take this direction.

"And at the same time, it's not so long ago," Rácz continues, "that both of us, Rácz and you, were just nobodies."

He used to be a stoker; Mešťánek was a car park attendant. What? Does Mešťánek think that Rácz has forgotten? No, he's forgotten nothing. Today, of course, they're both among the élite. Rácz is the most powerful man in the city; Mešťánek has achieved success in the arts. Rácz is of course aware that it's only dirty pictures, but he doesn't dismiss that at all. Quite the opposite: Rácz, as someone who's made it virtually from zero, can appreciate anyone who's good at his line of work. And Mešťánek is good, that much he knows. Rácz doesn't follow these things, but others, who know about such things, have told him.

Freddy smiles uncertainly and pretends to shrug off this praise.

"Never, all this time," continues Rácz, has Mešťánek needed any-thing from him. He never wanted to be his friend. So why come to Rácz now? Mešťánek is not the first man in the world whose wife went whoring. Would Mešťánek like to know what Rácz would do in his shoes? He'd take that wife and tie her to the fence and beat her so long that she'd crawl on the floor and shit tomato paste. And that bloke? He'd kill him with these two hands. Rácz lifts up his thick, but carefully groomed hands. "But first, he'd cut his balls off, roast them, and make him eat them," he says, "and his prick, too."

Freddy nods in agreement. He'd have liked that. But that would still be not enough punishment for what Zongora has done.

"Well," Rácz continues, "Mr Mešťánek, however accomplished he is, seems to be a big coward. That's why he's come to see Rácz, to get him to punish the son of a bitch. After all, why not? Why should Mešťánek sacrifice his career, his work and his wealth for a prick who's screwing his wife? That's what all this is about, right?"

However, the hotelier does not wait for Freddy's answer and goes on. "The problem is just that Rácz is not actually a friend of Mešťánek's. It's not that Rácz wouldn't want to be one. He'd value friendship with such a famous man very highly; quite the contrary, it's Mešťánek who's never cared to be friends with Rácz. So he can't help Mešťánek at all. He only helps friends. He wishes Mr Mešťánck a pleasant rest of the day."

Shocked, Freddy realises that Rácz is no longer paying attention to him, but burying himself in papers on the desk. A man in his thirties comes up to Freddy from his left; it's the man who showed him in. He gently presses Freddy's shoulder and points his other hand at the door in a broad gesture. "This way, please," he says. Freddy looks at Rácz again.

"I want to be your friend, Mr Rácz," he says with determination.

"Are you serious?" Rácz's face expresses doubt and one eye looks up from the papers. "But being Rácz's friend is not that simple. Rácz's friendship is cruel, harsh, and demanding. Rácz may happen one day to ask a favour in return."

"Anything you like," declares Freddy firmly. For Alfréd Mešťánek it will be a great honour to consider himself a friend of the great Mr Rácz.

Rácz gets up and walks round his desk.

"In that case," he says, "Rácz accepts."

His lips clenched, he extends his hand to Freddy, a bit too high for a simple handshake. Freddy hesitates a moment, but behind his employer's back Rácz's gunman hints what Freddy has to do. Freddy takes the hotelier's manicured hand in both of his and kisses it, bowing his head.

"Thank you, Mr Rácz," he says.

"Oh, drop the 'Mr Rácz'!" smiles the hotelier. "My friends call me boss. And sit down, Freddy. I can call you Freddy, can't I?"

"Yes, boss," says Piggybank and again takes his place on the chair.

"For my friends, Freddy," says Rácz, "I'm always ready to do anything. And I will for you, too. As I said, I may need something from you, too. So I'm listening. If I understood you well, you want me to get rid of your wife's lover."

Freddy is stunned, because, even though he understood his status of betrayed husband very well, he never dared to call a spade a spade.

"Yes, boss," says Freddy.

"Should I have him killed?" asks Rácz clearly.

Freddy thoughtfully shakes his head.

"No," he says.

"So what should I do to him?" Rácz asks wondering.

"I want him to suffer more," says Freddy and blushes.

"To suffer?" Rácz laughs and puffs at his cigar. "We can let him suffer. If he gets it in the belly, like Steinecker the Mushroom, he'll suffer for hours."

"No," objects Freddy. "I want him to suffer much longer."

"I see," says Rácz and, intrigued, nestles down in his armchair. "Any suggestions, Freddy?"

Freddy gets up, goes round the desk and bends down to the hotelier, whispering something in his ear.

The men in the armchairs become more attentive: their hands slip under their jackets. Rácz calms them down with an offhand gesture and listens with interest to Piggybank.

When the porn king has finished, Rácz begins to laugh.

"That's a magnificent idea!" he shouts. "Magnificent idea! Damn it all," he swears in Hungarian, "Rácz loves tricks like that."

"Of course, all the expenses are on me," adds Freddy Piggybank, flattered by the hotelier's praise.

"That does simplify things," the hotelier nods his assent. "The point is that no one will have suffered so much since the world was created."

The mood in the room has improved. Rácz is smiling with contentment and slaps Freddy's back.

A bottle of whisky and a box of cigars are conjured up on the table.

Rácz pours out personally.

"*Heevash Reygahl*," he says meaningfully and raises the glass for a toast. "Rácz's favourite brand."

Freddy takes a sip and takes a cigar. Rácz lights it up for him. Freddy takes a drag and almost shits himself.

"A real Havana," says Rácz.

He sends his underlings away and sits on the desk right opposite Piggybank. Rácz, he starts, doesn't like to see such a little cunt mess with a man like Piggybank. How come Piggybank hadn't yet beaten the shit out of her and that prick? Rácz checks his notes: "Zongora hasn't had his balls cut off yet?"

Freddy says he has a calm temperament and disagrees with violence.
Rácz nods: Piggybank's just a plain shitty coward, a useless jerk.
"Yes," says Freddy and lowers his gaze. "Something like that."
"You weren't in the army, were you?" asks Rácz with understanding.
Freddy shakes his head. He wasn't. He had a blue-book exemption.
When he was a child, a vein burst in his head after he found out that his
parents had taken the money he'd saved by sweating blood to buy a
rubber dinghy, and spent it on a sweater for him."
"Just as I thought," says Rácz. "A spoiled city boy."
Rácz can tell at first sight who hasn't been in the army. He did his
service. He spent two years there, for heaven's sakes! In Bohemia, near
Prague, in an artillery regiment. But he didn't complain. He did what he
had to and had peace and quiet. He could go out every evening; he
always got a pass. They even wanted to make him lance-corporal, but he
wasn't having it. He didn't want to order his friends around. He was
happy to be uncrowned king on the floor where they had their rooms.
Freddy can't quite make sense of all this, but says nothing. Rácz
interprets his expression as the need for a drink. He feels a hospitable
instinct and pours Freddy a glass of whisky.
If Freddy wants to have a special adventurous experience, Rácz has
something to offer him. People of Rácz's and Freddy's social class have
various ways of having fun. Some like tennis, some squash, others golf.
There are people who do bungee jumping. Rácz has a hobby, too.
"What kind of hobby?" Freddy is curious.
"There are a lot of us," says Rácz mysteriously. "We're all business-
men, managers, even a famous football player. We have a club. Very
secret. We call it the Adrenalin Club. We accept a new member if a permanent member recommends him."
"And what do you do there?" asks Piggybank, his spirit soaking up
the excitement of mystery.
"Various special things," says Rácz. "High-risk things."
"Dangerous?" Freddy enquires.
"Very dangerous," agrees Rácz. "You could get killed at any time.
But ordinary bungee jumping is nothing compared to it. Have you ever
thrown yourself head first down a thousand-metre deep mine shaft, tied
to a four-hundred-metre rope? Rácz enjoys that, because he wants to stay
fit. You know, spending days in the office, managing a company, does
your head in. I need to relax now and again. But fuck golf or squash!
That's for queers. Rácz needs real thrills. And we do other things, too!"
"Like what?" Freddy says eagerly.

"We model ourselves on the Lord of Terror, Fantômas," says Rácz, lowering his voice. "For example, we put on masks and attack international trains. We get on at a stop and, when the train's moving, we rob everyone in the first class, and then we jump out when it's still moving. But no violence: we're gentlemen robbers. 'Sorry, dear lady, but I need to take your purse.' 'Excuse me, sir, but your watch is of vital importance to me.' No, Rácz doesn't invent these lines, but one of us gets a real kick out of saying them. You wouldn't believe how much money people take on trips. Sometimes we jump a goods train and rob it. Electronics, car parts. It all comes in handy. It's exciting and it brings in lots of money, too. This isn't for the shit-scared. Well, interested in joining?"

Freddy reflects. He's always yearned for good friends, for a gang. As a boy he badly wanted to make friends with the children from the brickyard where he grew up. But they didn't want him. He was fat, clumsy, and didn't own a bike. When he decided to build himself a bicycle, boys of his age stopped being a bike gang; instead, they began to smoke their first cigarettes, secretly drink beer from the factory snack bar, touch up girls from the brickyard settlement and meet them in the acacia woods surrounding the nearby kiln pit. Freddy had always dreamed of friendship, but nobody ever wanted to be friends with him.

But Rácz's offer gives him pleasure, consolation and excitement.

"Look," says Rácz. "Right now you're a shithead. But Rácz will make a man of you. Because he believes in you, fuck it!"

Freddy blushes and modestly, though pleased, lowers his eyes.

Rácz nods. Freddy can't grass on Rácz, because then it will come out who put away Zongora. No dirt ever sticks to Rácz, as he employs a whole bunch of lawyers who do nothing but spend entire days clearing Rácz's path. But Piggybank would get twenty years, because he'd take the rap for everything. No, Rácz isn't threatening him. He's only explaining why he's such a friend as to offer Freddy a chance to become a man: a real man. After two or three such jobs he'll be a hard enough man to stop any woman pushing him about him ever again. Is it a deal?

Freddy clears his throat. He needs time to think it over.

Rácz nods tolerantly. He quite understands. Nothing should be done without thinking it over. But Freddy had better not think for too long. He must realise what an honour and opportunity it is for him. And he needn't worry about Zongora. Rácz has his channels.

* * *

After visiting Rácz, Freddy goes home after a long absence. He is full of energetic anger. His head cleared as he came back from seeing Rácz. He took the full measure of his own pathetic ineptitude and humiliation. Now he finally understood. For a few bright moments he saw himself in his true colours, as other people had hitherto seen him. The scales of illusion fell off. From now on it will all be different! He's not a total idiot; if he were, he'd never have had such a career. He's hard working and resilient. He's even managed to lose weight. Well, true, in recent successful months he's put it back on, but with the proper motivation, he'll lose it again. Yes, it will all be different from now on.

Sida is at home. Freddy tried to avoid her at work and if he met her by chance he passed by her silently, while his employees whispered excitedly. Now he brusquely orders her to undress. Sida forgave him long ago and is under the impression that this is a new ploy. She sheds her clothes with a smile. Freddy lets her keep her illusions. He silently puts up with her provocative movements and her deliberate, drawn out disrobing. He watches this striptease and, instead of wildly pulsating excitement, terrible hatred boils up inside him.

When Sida is finally naked, Freddy gives her face such a slap that she falls to the floor. Freddy grabs her by the hair and hits her face with his fat hands for so long that tears mingle with her blood. Blood drips on the carpet from her cracked lip. Sida is so shocked and scared that at first she doesn't fight back at all. She's never known Freddy to be like that.

When she falls on the floor, Freddy kicks her a few times. Then he opens the closet and takes out the hippo whip that he gave her years ago. He starts to beat her all over, though he is a bit more careful than he was with Zongora. He knows that a real gentleman never whips a lady's face or genitals. There are other body parts big enough to beat.

Sida crawls on the floor to get out of reach of Freddy's blows. She succeeds for a while, crawling on all fours, but then a fierce blow pushes her on her side. Freddy holds her down with his foot. All his jealousy flows into the quivering tip of the whip. Freddy beats her and at the same time cries with pain. He knows that each blow irrevocably distances him from the family happiness he took so much trouble to build.

Sida is now speechless. She doesn't move, she only moans helplessly. Freddy hears a quiet burble. A little puddle of fear spreads over the wooden floor from between Sida's legs. Oh, no! This oak floor cost him a fortune. And now it will be ruined.

Freddy grabs her by the hair. He wants Sida to repeat after him that from now on she will be his faithful wife.

Sida sobs and clears her throat. Tears flow from her eyes, blood from her mouth, and snot from her nose. Her back and behind are on fire. Now she knows the beating is over, and that Freddy won't kill her. She sees that the beating was just a prelude to this theatrical scene of making vows. She's determined to do anything to stop him hitting her again.

Freddy repeats his demand.

Sida nods. Through her swollen lips she slowly articulates words: "I will from now on… and so on."

"Not 'and so on'!" rages Freddy and lashes Sida's thigh with the whip. "Faithful wife! Careful mother! Housewife!"

Sida nods.

Nodding's not enough, she must repeat after him, he orders her. From this moment she's finished professionally. Porn is out forever. Siedah Strong is dead! She's a housewife. She will cook, wash, and darn. She will bring up her child. And bear him more children. In quick succession. Lots of children.

"Dead…" Sida concurs.

Now he's going to the hotel Morava for a beer, says Freddy. Just like other guys. When he gets back, the house will be in perfect order. Dinner will be ready. Hot food. Or else!

Freddy's unsmiling lips are clenched.

Sida nods humbly.

Sida can't rely on Zongora's support, Freddy says with relish. She can forget about Zongora.

Sida becomes animated. She was never interested in Zongora except for his body. But after what Freddy has said, she's beginning to believe that she's in love with him.

"What have you arranged to have done to him?" she screams.

Freddy is enraged that right from the start Sida is certain that he wouldn't be able to sort out her lover by himself: that he couldn't beat him up, but only *arrange* for him to be beaten up. He furiously grabs the handle of the whip until his knuckles go white.

"I don't want to kill you," he says. "From now on you'll do what I say. I'll show you who's the master here."

Freddy remembers his visit to Rácz. He stretches out his hand to her. Sida can hardly see with her swollen eyes, but realises what she has to do. She covers the back of Freddy's hand with blood, snot and tears.

Freddy throws the bloodied whip away and takes his jacket. Now he's going out for a beer, as he said. By the time he's back, everything will be cleaned up and the food will be cooked. From today the household help is dismissed. Freddy and Sida will be like any normal family. He will bring home the money. Lots of it. Sida will take care of the house. If she doesn't know how to cook, it's high time she learned.

Freddy leaves the flat and bangs the door behind him.

* * *

Freddy Piggybank is jerked awake by the growl of a radio transmitter. For a moment he looks around in bewilderment until he realises where he is. He's sitting on the back seat of Lanštiak's Renault. Dozing in an awkward position has left a bad taste in his mouth.

The evening Freddy took revenge, he got back from the pub to find the house empty. Sida had taken the child from kindergarten, packed up and left. She took her documents, all her cassettes and porn magazines. She took the car, as well. On the fridge was a note: DON'T LOOK FOR ME, YOU IMPOTENT. YOU'LL NEVER FIND ME ANYWAY.

First thing next day Freddy rushed to the bank to freeze the account, but too late. It was empty. Fortunately, Freddy had another account which Sida didn't know about.

Freddy has suffered ever since. He misses Sida less than the money and the child. He asked Rácz to help find them, but so far unsuccessfully.

Freddy has lost interest in his company. He's been spending whole days in nearby pubs. He got drunk, cried and showed everyone a picture of his child. After a few days he wiped the tears from his eyes and got off the bar stool. Life goes on. He will have to learn to live with the fact that no one will shed a tear when his eyes close. He has enough money; he does not have to lift a finger till he dies. The company runs by itself. Recently, a few talented directors have appeared, so Freddy has no worries about who will come after him. He can drink as much as he wants, he can go on a trip around the world, he can fly off to the Bahamas, buy a yacht and disappear in the Pacific: it doesn't matter.

Video Urban came back from Prague and quite naturally took over all responsibility for running the company. Freddy has stopped going to the office. Only occasionally he comes to have a word, or rather to pour his heart out. With Urban he gossips about Rácz, with Rácz about Urban. That's Freddy: an in-your-face bloke who always gives you the truth.

After an alcoholic period came a fitness period. He began to spend most of his time in a fitness centre round the corner. Weights, running belt, sauna, pool, twice over. It didn't take long, and his body got rid of all the toxins, alcohol and excess fat. But memories he couldn't get rid of. At idle moments Freddy liked to wallow in sadness and misery.

As he's wallowing now. He keeps swallowing, but the lump is still there. He's lost his family, he was betrayed and robbed by an unfaithful woman. He only wanted a tiny bit of happiness on this earth. Everything he did was for his small family. Everything! Every month he directed at least ten hour-long porn films just so that those closest to him had everything they could dream of. And what was his reward? Betrayal!

Since Bratislava at night was too small to provide an audience for his complaints, he goes to Prague to cry. Czech barmen and waiters have more patience and value more highly a customer who, even if he spends his evenings crying and complaining, spends money like water.

Finally he went to see Rácz and told him that he was interested in joining his highly exclusive Adrenalin Club. Rácz took him along to a meeting and introduced him to the other members. Freddy passed the initiation ritual, became a member, swore an oath and threw himself headlong into adventures that smelled of risk, death, and imprisonment.

Suddenly he was a member of a gang, what he had longed for ever since childhood. The club members are bored wealthy men like Freddy. They get their thrills from reckless, even insane activities: bungee jumping on a four-hundred-metre rope down a thousand-metre dark abandoned mine shaft, flying head down in pitch darkness and experiencing indescribable feelings of mortal fear; jumping out of an aircraft without a parachute, followed by a parachutist with a parachute who, during freefall, catches up with the adventurer and ties the two together, so they both land with one open parachute; driving at full speed on a highway with no headlights in total darkness; jumping on goods wagons and looting them while the train is moving; robbing shocked first class passengers on international Eurocity and Intercity express trains.

This highly risky, often criminal activity gives the bored rich men excitement and their blood a hefty dose of adrenalin, as well as much-needed physical exertion. It rouses their dulled nerves. They do anything prohibited. Each pretends to be a Fantômas. The police hunts for them, but no one suspects that this is a gang of men from the best society.

Freddy feels good in the club. It's a highly conspiratorial society, much like the freemasons.

"I understand," says Lanštiak into the transmitter. "Over."

He turns to the men in the car.

"So the Octavias are in wagons three to eight," he says. "The electronics are in nineteen. And twelve to sixteen are full of sand."

The men are visibly relieved.

"It's going to be child's play," says Otto Učok. His voice sounds tired and clearly disappointed.

Freddy hopes the men missed his micro-sleep and micro-weeping.

"Not like last time, when we jumped onto canvas," he says.

"Oh, fuck, that was something," Rácz remembers, chewing on a cigar. "Just like a trampoline!"

"And you didn't know what was underneath," recalls Lanštiak, starts the car and puts it in gear. "If there'd been machinery there, packed to the top, we'd be history!"

The men drive to an abandoned viaduct over the railway. It is totally dark all round. The lights of a far-off village shimmer in the thin mist.

"I'd love to steal a locomotive from a depot," says Freddy. "I'd crank it up full speed and then jump out. And if I could watch at the same time the damage it did when it crashed into something!"

"Great idea," says Rácz. "We'll have to think about that one."

"It'll be here in five minutes," says Lanštiak. "So break a leg, gentlemen! I'll wait for you under the viaduct at the seventieth kilometre."

His voice has a note of disappointment, since he can't be with them.

"Cheer up!" Učok tells him and opens the back door. He places his foot, shod in a heavy army boot, on the wet road. "Next time you'll draw a different lot," he adds. "You'll see action and maybe I'll be the driver."

The men get out of the car. They put on rucksacks full of tools, and pull masks over their faces. They quietly close the doors. Lanštiak steps on the accelerator. The Renault, its lights off, vanishes round a bend.

Freddy strains his eyes, but can't see a thing. He hears a buzzing noise: it comes from Učok who's put on a helmet with infrared goggles. Freddy does the same. He turns on the infrared reflector on top of the helmet and focuses the lenses. The countryside is bathed in greenish light. The moon is behind a cloud. The village lights do not reach here. He grabs the cold, dewy rail. He peers deep down. Only after a moment do his short-sighted eyes get used to the distortion of the night-sight instrument, and he notices down there a pair of shiny ribbons: the track.

They silently wait for the train. Finally engine lights appear. Soon an endless goods train is rattling beneath them.

"Ten, eleven, twelve," Učok counts the wagons. "Let's jump, men!"

Freddy closes his eyes. He hurls himself into the abyss-like depth, a bit to one side, to avoid the overhead power line.

The landing into a gravel-filled wagon is a bit harder than he'd expected, but he's used to it by now. But he still has to catch his breath.

Rácz lands nearby. As he does so, he sprays Freddy's face with a handful of gravel. Freddy wipes his eyes and jumps up. He takes a look behind. Učok waves at him from the next wagon.

"Everything's fine," shouts Rácz, drowning out the train's rumbling.

Freddy points forward. "Let's get to those wagons first!" he shouts. He begins to climb from wagon to wagon. He does not look down at the track, which sways wildly. Rácz and Učok hold firmly to the sideboard. They wait for Freddy to jump so that they can jump, too. There are five more shaking wagons ahead before they reach their goal for today.

For Freddy, the goal is clear: forget, forget, and forget!

100 % WATERPROOF
After a game of mixed doubles, two couples are taking a shower. A blonde decides to go somewhere. Her partner asks her where. "I want to take a pee," says the blonde. Her partner suggests that she pee here, in the shower. The blonde pees on her partner. The brunette's partner hears the sound and decides to take a look. He sees the blonde crouching and peeing into her partner's mouth. He likes it a lot. He'd like to see it close up: he's never seen a woman peeing before. The blonde's partner is already excited. He has an erection. He sends the brunette's partner to get the brunette and pee on him. The brunette's partner comes to the brunette and tells her about it. Meanwhile the blonde's partner starts to have sex with the blonde. The brunette comes and pees on all of them. Then she kisses the blonde, while the brunette's partner pees on their heads. The blonde and her partner change their position: now the partner lies on his back and has anal sex with the blonde, who crouches on him, facing him. She uses both of her hands to spread her lips and pees in rhythm to intercourse on his belly and chest. In the meantime, the brunette performs fellatio on her partner while peeing in his mouth. A dog comes by and pees on the couple having sex. And so on. Everything ends in wild geysers of piss and sperm!

(From Freddy's notebook)

* * *

One day the porn actor Zongora, known by his stage name Luigi Longo, vanishes without trace, never to be seen among the living. Only a few people know that he was anæsthetized and secretly, at Freddy's expense, sent to the Arab mini-state and oil emirate Shut-al-Banja. Here, until his merciful death, he will be an erotic slave in the homosexual and also sadistic Emir Tariq ben Yusuf ibn Muhammad's secret male harem, a place full of other desperate men like Zongora. There is no question of escape or suicide, only despair remains, as painful as the red-hot desert round them. This is the revenge that Freddy has devised for the man who hurt him where it hurts most.

But enough of Zongora. He disappears from this book. Why mention a person who no longer has any meaning for us?

Freddy finds his newly awakened desire for adventure can't be fully satisfied by the sorties the Adrenalin Club puts on. Something else stirs in him. Something self-destructive. Unlike his colleagues, he has a quality that makes him immortal: knowing that if he's ever caught and put in prison, he'll just be glad. Finally, there'll be a change in his dreary life. Something will finally change. He's not afraid of prison. If it gets bad, he'll kill himself. Nobody's got any hold over him. He can't suffer more than he's suffering now, anyway.

He acts like a boy in a school story book who wakes up one day to find everyone, including his parents, gone. He can do anything he likes. At one time Freddy was quite taken by that edifying story. Every time he walked down the village in the evening, looking at well-lit windows, he chose houses that he would enter once the people vanished somewhere. The house of a noted aeroplane model builder Ebringer took first place.

Now he was rediscovering that delicious feeling; moreover, he had realised that people need not stop him doing anything. They don't have to vanish: they can stay. Freddy can do whatever he wants, anyway.

He had long ago discovered the excitement aroused by evil, and had exploited it in his porn films. Now he's excited by even more intense delights than the virtual delights offered by pornography. He has broken all bounds and now goes in for risky ventures. He has got used to a regular dose of adrenalin, like an addict getting used to a drug.

So he takes a late evening train to Nová Ves, not one with compartments, but an ordinary commuter train. Freddy chooses a dark, unlit, cold carriage. He sits on a cold leatherette bench near the door by the carriage platform and listens closely. His heart beats high in his chest with excitement and expectation: how will it go today?

In the middle of the carriage two Moravian girls are chatting.

"But I did tell him!"

"Well, then tell him again!"

And so on.

The train departs. It judders as it hits the points, and then it enters the tunnel. It's pitch dark. This is Freddy's moment. He has about thirty

exciting seconds before the train emerges from the tunnel on the other
side. Night vision goggles would be ideal, but they're too big and
clumsy. They'd let him down. He gets up and, holding onto the seat
rests, sets out towards the girls' voices. He puts a hand on the thigh of
the nearest one.

The girl starts.

"What?" she shouts in Moravian dialect.

Freddy embraces her with one arm; with the other he grabs her
crotch and breasts. He prefers skirts. He once groped a girl who had
nothing on under her skirt. The girl screeches and her friend can't
understand. She keeps asking in the dark:

"What's wrong with you? What's wrong with you?"

Freddy is excited, but still counts carefully. Before the thirtieth
second has passed, he retreats. Putting his hands on the seat backs, he
gropes his way back to his seat. He opens the door to the carriage
platform, but stays seated. He sits down on the leatherette bench. Forty
two seconds: just time for Freddy to adjust his appearance. The train
leaves the tunnel. The young passenger is in shock. Freddy jumps up.

"What happened, young lady?" he asks in a matter-of-fact way. He
gets up and approaches the girls as if to help.

"Some pervert!" complains the Moravian girl.

Freddy nods. He heard a girl shout, then some one ran past him and
onto the carriage platform.

"He must be in the other carriage by now," he assures her.

The girl has now recovered. Moravian girls are tough.

"I'd cut his balls off and feed them to him," threatens the other girl.

Shivers run down Freddy's spine. It's a thrill to be so close to terrible
punishment and yet be relatively safe.

"Did he hurt you?" he asks in a matter-of-fact way.

"He pawed me all over!" the victim complains.

Freddy goes back to his place. As he sits there, the buzz of excitement in his ears dies down. He's got away with it again. A pity, though,
that the Bratislava tunnel isn't at least ten seconds longer.

But perhaps he would welcome being caught and gaoled. At least a
change would yank him out of the totally pointless and aimless life that
he's leading. Without Sida and his little girl, he's just a figure staggering
through life, clinging to his habits and daily rituals like crutches.

In any case, Freddy vainly seeks for any force that would give his
confused staggering meaning. If he liked alcohol and it didn't make him
sick, he'd drink himself to death.

* * *

There have already been a number of attempted burglaries at Freddy's: each time the burglars found that they couldn't get into the house thanks to the extreme security arrangements, but they broke into his garage or his summer kitchen. The damage was never very great. Once he lost a battery charger, other times a spray gun, a pump, or cast iron wheels with winter tyres. But when the burglars took his petrol lawn mower, he was enraged. They got into the shed by smashing the door with a pickaxe.

"It wasn't professionals," said Rácz who'd just driven Freddy home from a seasonal Adrenalin Club outing: setting cooperative farmers' haystacks on fire. "It's addicts. Filthy, wretched, fucked up druggies."

"If I got my hands on one, I'd show him," Freddy fantasizes, as he counts the damage.

"Pay for security like Rácz," suggests Rácz. "My house and garden are guarded day and night by armed guards. Don't tell me you don't have the money! I'll get you some good men."

But Freddy is stingy. He's really angry with the burglars, but the thought of paying to protect property which he's already paid for is unimaginable. If he caught them, he'd gouge out their eyes.

"If the police catch them, they let them go," says Rácz. "And even if they're sentenced, the victims get nothing out of it. No one compensates them for damage. And the thieves are out in a few months."

"Not if I have anything to do with it," boasts Freddy. "If I catch them in the act, I'll cut their fingers off!"

"You can't," says Rácz. "Then you'll end up in court, too. It has to be done another way. Fuck them right away and bury them."

Freddy likes the idea.

"You know what?" Rácz says, "If you ever do catch a burglar, tie him up and call me. Rácz will show you how it's done."

Indeed, a few weeks later, Freddy notices tools for burglary hidden in the bushes by his garage entrance. The discovery excites him. He thinks about what Rácz told him. He likes the idea of avenging himself for all the humiliations that thieves have caused him ever since they stole his collection bag when he worked as car park attendant.

From his company's props department he takes a few pairs of steel handcuffs. He loads a gas pistol that he and Sida bought on their first holiday in Spain. Just looking at the pistol, a replica of an American policeman's Colt, brings home painful memories. He remembered passing day after day by the shop selling knives, replica weapons and antiques, until he finally bought it. Sida took a dislike to it, so he had to explain to her that it would be a prop for a forthcoming film.

Now Freddy stays at home for days on end. He works at home on a screenplay. His ears are pricked and his heart beats with excitement. His feelings are transferred to his screenplay. The lady of the house catches a burglar; she and her maidservant torture and humiliate him: they puncture his sexual organs and nipples with knitting needles and he is forced to drink their urine. But writing gives Freddy no fun. He has to make himself do it. The loss of his wife and daughter has taken all the pleasure out of his work and life. Everything he does is done by sheer inertia. He no longer eats, washes, picks up or answers the phone. His letter box overflows with newspapers and post. His blinds are always down and he prefers to switch on the lights so as not to be reminded by the world around him of what his mind has long since rejected.

Freddy wakes up in the night. He hears a noise. He looks through the blinds and notices stealthy movement in the yard. He runs out with his gas pistol and corners the burglars. The burglars are two underage drug addicts. They have long hair but look quite respectable. Freddy hands the handcuffs to one of them and orders him to put them on the other one. Then he handcuffs the first burglar. He calls Rácz's mobile.

"The spider's caught two flies," he repeats a phrase from some film.

Rácz hasn't seen the film: it takes him time to grasp what it's about.

"Should I call the police?" Freddy asks.

"No, no!" Rácz shouts, and all the sleepiness goes out of his voice. "They're ours now!"

Rácz's voice echoes a passion for hunting, or rather fishing. As if a fisherman suddenly found a huge fish hooked on his rod and then asked a fellow-fisherman to help him land the catch.

Freddy barely has time to put down the phone when from outside comes the impatient screech of Rácz's Mercedes sports coupé.

"So these are the ones?" Rácz asks looking at two bundles of bad luck crumpled in the corner.

The burglars are starting to realise that something's wrong. They naïvely assume, however, that as they're minors, they'll get off cheaply.

"Okay," says one, acting casual. "Call the cops; let's get it over with."

"Oh you'd like that, wouldn't you?" Rácz laughs malevolently. "Don't worry, we shan't need the police to deal with you."

The thieves fall silent. They haven't counted on this turn of events.

"Bring us something to drink," Rácz tells Freddy.

Freddy searches the whole house and finds in the fridge a bottle of champagne left by Sida. He pours two glasses.

"Have you ever killed anyone?" Rácz asks Freddy and drinks the champagne like beer. He holds out his glass for more.

Freddy pours him another glass and shakes his head.

"Not yet," he confesses.

"Not even an animal?" Rácz asks. "I mean a biggish one: a dog, a cat, a hen?"

Freddy thinks about it.

"No," he shakes his head. "The hens, geese, and rabbits were killed by our uncle who used to come to do it."

"In the village I come from," Rácz says, "everything was killed by Rácz. Even goat-kids."

"Well, I don't think I could do that," says Freddy.

"If you had to, you'd get used to it," says Rácz. "And what about Christmas carp?"

"Sida buys... used to buy frozen fish fillets," says Freddy. "I hate the bones and the muddy taste of carp."

The captive thieves listen to the conversation with growing consternation, into which a vague horror is creeping.

"I know what you're saying," says Rácz. "But if you marinate the carp overnight in milk and put it in the fridge, the muddy taste goes away. Lenka, my lovely wife, taught me that."

"I don't care any more," says Freddy. "What's Christmas to me, now that Sida's run away?"

"She'll be back, you'll see," says Rácz. "Do you want her back? Rácz will find her for you, no matter where she is. My men will get her back to you. But in my opinion, you shouldn't give a fuck about her. You need a healthy virgin who's been to university, like the one I married, not some sort of... Actually, I'd like to know, tell me, how could you stand her being fucked by so many men in your films? How could you go to bed with her, when you knew she'd had so many pricks in her already? That's what I've always wanted to know."

"It's a profession like any other," says Freddy. "It never bothered me at all."

"Or perhaps it turned you on a bit, did it?" Rácz looks impish. "There are people like that... They get excited when everyone has their woman, when they can see her tits and everything below her neck."

Freddy reflects and realises that Rácz is actually right.

"Well, this is what you get in return, Freddy," says Rácz. "As you sow, so shall you reap. After all, your wife didn't have to work, as you say. She could have stayed home and you could have made those swinish films with other little pussies, couldn't you? And you wouldn't have the problem you have. I'll tell you one thing, Freddy. If anyone saw my wife's pussy, Rácz would gouge out both his eyes for it."

Rácz drinks up his champagne and firmly puts the glass on the table.

"Well, that's that," he says. "You know yourself best. So, you've never yet killed any creature?"

"I have," says Freddy. "I've killed flies, and all kinds of vermin. I even killed a mouse once with my shoe. When I was at the car park. It got into my trailer."

"Killing a man's just as easy," says Rácz. "Only the humanitarians have invented a lot of blather about it. In reality, a human being is not much more than a mouse. And these two are even less than a mouse. What's more, they do more harm than mice. By killing them, you help humanity. Not just now, but later generations. Because these druggies could spread the revolting useless genes that attracted them to drugs and then poison humanity, which is degenerate enough as it is, even more."

"Hey, what are you talking about?" asks one of the long-haired youths. "You can't just kill us! We haven't done anything. We're minors! Call the police right away!"

"We'll pay you back for everything," pleads the other one.

"Shut his gob," say Rácz wearily, not even looking at the delinquents.

From a corner Freddy takes a greasy, wet, hairy rag used for washing the floor, tears it in half and stuffs half in each mouth. The thieves writhe and try to spit out the stinking textile.

"If you two don't shut your fucking mouths right away," says Rácz with annoyance, "we'll burn you alive. We've got the petrol."

Then he turns to Freddy.

"I'm not saying that killing a man's nothing," he says. "It's an experience that takes you to another place. Once you've killed someone, you look at everything quite differently. There's a very thin line between life and death. Just watch."

Rácz takes a pistol from his armpit, screws on a silencer, and cocks it.

"You've seen my face, so you've got to die," says Rácz to the burglar, laughs loud and menacingly and shoots him without hesitating.

Despite the silencer, the shot in the small room is deafening. When the acrid smoke clears, the burglar is twitching in his death agony; finally all movement stops.

"It did the job, didn't it?" says Rácz and hands the pistol to a shocked Freddy. "Now, you do the other one."

The other thief is trembling with horror and through a layer of rag come muffled whimpers.

"Now show me you are a man and not a piece of shit, Freddy," Rácz orders him. "Take the law into your own hands."

Freddy aims the gun at the burglar. His hand starts to shake and the barrel drops.

"I can't," says Freddy.

"Give it to me," says Rácz, takes the gun and fires again.

Two corpses lie next to each other; the room smells of burnt cordite.

"Don't worry about it, Freddy," says Rácz in a conciliatory way. "You'll cope next time. Now we're in the same boat. You're my accomplice now. Apart from our common interests, this binds us together."

Freddy can't pull himself together. He stares at the twisted corpses.

"They won't steal any more," says Rácz. "Well, Freddy: now they have to be buried. Get a pickaxe and shovel and dig a hole out in the garden. Why are you staring? You don't expect me to do it all myself?"

Freddy begins to dig. He digs at the back of the garden, under the trees. On Rácz's advice, he carefully sets aside the turf. The night is quiet, only the sounds of shunting engines come from the station. Freddy tries to make as little noise as he can, not to wake the neighbours up. Once the hole is dug, Freddy and Rácz put both thieves' bodies in it.

"Light as a feather!" Rácz is surprised by the first one. "This is what drugs do to a man. Well, heave-ho!"

They swing the corpse, throw it in the hole, then get the next one.

Finally Freddy fills the hole, packs it tight and puts the layer of turf back on top. After he's sprinkled it with water and washed off the traces of soil, nobody would guess at first sight that someone had been digging here a short while ago.

"Well," says Rácz. "Let's go in. Any champagne still left?"

Freddy pours out the rest of the bottle with his shaking hand.

"So, to us!" says Rácz and raises his glass. "And never say die, Freddy. You're slowly becoming a man. You're lucky to have met Rácz. Rácz will make something out of you."

Once Rácz is gone, Freddy takes his torch and goes to have a look at the grave. He goes back to the empty house and before he lies down, he turns the lights on everywhere. All the same, he is haunted by dreams that someone, covered in mud and with a rag in his mouth, is reaching for the front-door handle. He jumps up three times during the night to make sure the door is properly locked.

Anal Justice Part I

A young man (~~Luigi Longo~~ Bruno Tatarelli) is in a cell, naked and chained to the wall. Meanwhile preparations for interrogation are afoot in the torture room. A Grand Inquisitor (~~Siedah Strong~~ Naomi Africa), dressed in leather, with bare crotch and breasts, in fishnet stockings and metal-heeled high boots, sits on her throne. On her head is an SS cap. In one hand, she holds a whip, in the other, pliers. Her two assistants (Wanda Desire and Deep Stella) also wear corsets and fishnet stockings. They are preparing various torture instruments, which look very like surgical instruments. An enema and a catheter are both there. At the Grand Inquisitor's prompting, the prisoner is led in. They tie him to the torture rack. The Inquisitor gets up and approaches him. She lovingly observes his long member. She lifts it with her little whip. The prisoner's member immediately begins to engorge with blood. With a gloved hand, the Inquisitor experimentally moves the foreskin of the prisoner's member a few times. Then she whips him energetically. Her assistants are to find out how many ejaculations the prisoner produces without stopping. If it is a lot, then the prisoner is certainly in league with the devil. The assistants masturbate the prisoner, perform fellatio on him, put his member in several of their body openings, and he sprays his semen again and again into a glass chalice they have ready. This is finally filled, so the Inquisitor, who has been sitting there idly observing and masturbating with her hand and other long instruments, takes the chalice and drinks it all with pleasure. She finds that the prisoner is not linked to the devil: he is the devil himself. She gets up and unties his handcuffs. She kneels in front of him and asks his pardon. She recognizes him as her master and, to assuage his anger, offers him both of her assistants to torture. Hitherto she has only tortured insignificant losers and thought that the devil did not exist, though she very much wanted to be one of his faithful. Only now has her wish come true. The Inquisitor and the devil undress and tie the surprised and shouting assistants who can't understand what's going on. They are being psychologically prepared for terrible tortures. In the last shot both assistants are seen hanging from a rack, awaiting terrible pain.

(From Freddy's notebook)

* * *

Freddy remembered the main railway station from the times when he used to go to the city together with his grandfather. They rarely got back to Devínska Nová Ves before dark. As a boy, he found the station mysterious and seductive in the evening light. In the country he was used to a small village station, and here he found himself in the huge main station's hall with its gigantic fresco which covered the whole wall and made it quite a different world. It was a world of its own; a world of foreign and strange people, of blinding artificial light and mysteries. The complexity of the station design made him feel threatened: he could get lost here forever and without trace. He feared all these passengers who acted as if they'd been born and spent all their lives here. He was afraid that if he got separated from his grandfather, he would end up as one of them. About that time he had read a Soviet book, *Your Contemporary*, where three novellas dealt with the fate of homeless children in England, South Korea, and America. He could graphically imagine a homeless child's fate and, unlike other children, he didn't long to become one. He gripped his grandfather's rough hand all the harder, to make sure he would never lose it.

Now, as an adult, the main railway station seemed to him much smaller. Even with its extension it looked less metropolitan than it had in the distant past. There even seemed to be fewer platforms than before. The track now seemed to have been laid ridiculously shallow. Thirty years ago, the rails were hidden in deep canyons; if you fell down there you'd never be able to climb out. Today they seemed to him hopelessly shallow. Shallow and boring.

The only thing that was still the same was the lady's voice announcing arrivals and departures. Just as in all other big stations, here too the announcer, to judge by her voice, had been hypnotized. She seemed to be stressing, by using utterly expressionless diction, her remoteness, abstraction, fragility and an uncaring impersonality. Freddy likes to listen to her peculiar phrasing, so unlike normal human speech.

"PASSEN GERTRAINFROM, says the announcer, "ŠTÚRO VOBRATI SLAVANOVÉMESTO, DESTIN ATIONLAM AČDEVÍN SKANOVÁ VESANDZO HORKÚTY, ARRIVINGAT PLAT FORMNUM BERTWO TRACKNUM BERFOUR..."

Freddy boards the train and imagines a pale vulnerable beauty with a transparent complexion and big, deep, vacant eyes, staring into infinity as she sits at the microphone. And above her, in a black coat and a top hat, a demonic hypnotist with spellbinding eyes and bushy eyebrows keeps her in an induced somnambular state.

The train hurtles into a tunnel and Freddy, feeling the pressure in his trousers, gets up from his seat. Right from the start, while the train slowly bumped over the points as it left the station, he had singled out a tall young Moravian redhead wearing a miniskirt and manicured with light-blue nail polish. Those azure nails, as long and sharp as a predator's talons, aroused Freddy to the point of insanity. As soon as it got dark in the carriage, he prepared to act. He gropes his way in the dark along the handrail towards his chosen victim. The young woman is sitting four rows of seats away. Eight, nine, ten. Freddy jumps on her, using one hand to gag her mouth and the other to feel her crotch. Thirteen, fourteen. Between the girl's thighs his hand feels a thick sanitary towel. "She's got her period," Freddy realises, and gropes her knees and thighs. Sixteen, seventeen, eighteen. The tall Moravian girl fights back like a tigress. She presses her thighs together and uses her hands to pull her attacker's hands off her body. Twenty-two, twenty-three, twenty-four. Long nails jab into Freddy's face and painfully cut across his face all the way to his ear. One of the nails digs into his right eye.

Freddy screams. There is a flash in his eye and he feels he's been hit by a brick. A dull pain flares up somewhere deep in his skull and explodes in his brain.

"Oy!" he screams. "It hurts!!!"

In an instant he gets to his feet and clambers off the young woman. His hands clutching his face, he backs away in the darkness. Something viscous and slippery like a broken egg is sliding down his right cheek. He touches that side of his face and feels sharp pain all the way up to somewhere in his head. He panics. There's a metallic taste of blood in his mouth. The shock and pain has made him forget to count the seconds.

The train leaves the tunnel and light returns to the carriage. The tall Moravian girl yells like a banshee. Her hands and azure nails are covered in blood. Freddy, semi-blind, has to face all the passengers on his own.

"Grab him!" the Moravian girl shouts. "It's that so-called Phantom! He tried to shag me! He was touching me up!"

A bold and agile Moravian man heads past the seats towards Freddy. Perhaps he thinks the redhead will give him points for bravery.

Freddy has a feeling that he won't be able to survive this much pain. But he won't let himself be captured. The shame and disgrace!

He retreats to the carriage platform and makes for the door. Someone tries to block his path but, aghast at the sight of Freddy, backs off. Freddy spots his face reflected in the door's glass panel. One of his eyes is popping; all that is left of the other one is a big pink fleshy hole. Freddy grabs the handle and yanks the door open. The train is rushing along the embankment towards Patrónka. Freddy's pursuers run onto the carriage platform. Freddy closes his good eye and jumps in the direction the train is travelling. He tumbles down an embankment, it seems, forever, and finally he is lying at the bottom. The carriages hurtle somewhere a long way above him. Fortunately, nobody has pulled the emergency cord. Soon the noise of the last carriage dies away. Freddy falls into merciful unconsciousness.

When he comes to, he has no idea what time it is. He is blind. He uses his hands to feel where he is. He wipes his eyes. The right hand runs into a lump of unnaturally swollen flesh protruding from an empty eye socket. Freddy's left hand wipes off a layer of congealed blood that had oozed down his face while he was unconscious.

It is night. Somewhere to his left he hears cars rushing down the road to Malacky. Along the embankment an endless freight train thunders.

Freddy feels the passage of each goods wagon separately in his skull. Each wagon gives him a stab of pain. Rubbing his tongue round his dry mouth gives no relief. He has a fever.

That Moravian cow has gouged his eye out: he realises the whole naked truth with sudden dread. How is he going to live now? She must have reported him. They'll be looking for him. They'll find him from witnesses' descriptions. All the quicker, now he has an eye gouged out.

Freddy gets up. He takes out a handkerchief and covers the empty socket with it. He starts to stagger along the railway track.

After a good hour and a half, he finally reaches the gates of his house and, with shaking hands, gropes for his keys.

If only Freddy could fall asleep now and in the morning wake up to find that it was all just a bad dream; he makes this pious wish as he falls half-undressed into a bed whose sheets, ever since Sida had left him, he has been unable to change. He breathes in all Sida's pampered body fragrances, not yet evaporated from the bed, and falls into oblivion.

In the morning his nose detects an additional smell: putrefaction. He moves his head and terrible pain sweeps through his brain. Clinging to the headboard, he gets up. He remembers everything. It wasn't a dream. He walks round the room, searching for the source of the rotten smell. He can't find it. He staggers round the whole ground floor and still finds nothing. He heads for the bathroom. He looks with his good eye in the mirror and freezes in terror. His empty eye socket is full of congealed blood. He gently touches the gelatinous substance and sniffs it. The rotting smell is emanating from his eye, or, to be precise, from the thing on his face that had replaced it.

He sits down helplessly on the edge of the bath but soon leaps up in panic. He urgently needs to relieve himself. He sits on the lavatory, afraid to push. Every push of his bowels is punished by a hammer blow right in the middle of his brain. He waits for the stool to fall by itself. It takes an awfully long time. He suffers like an animal during the ordeal.

He takes a little mirror and looks into the hole in his head. After the congealed blood is removed, the hole seems to go all the way into the brain. Freddy is terrified. He decides to call an ambulance, but as soon as he picks up his mobile phone, he changes his mind. They're sure to be looking for him and he'd fall into their hands. He remembers Rácz. Rácz would certainly help. But the disgrace! The disgrace and the unpleasant consequences! Rácz would be horribly furious if he found out that Freddy had been operating off his own bat. But it's not just the initiative, but also the fact that Freddy is a pervert. He admits it to himself. He's a pervert. He'd never have admitted that to Rácz. When Rácz is around he tries his hardest to look like a completely normal man. And he is, too.

Rácz has helped him a lot. Thanks to him, Freddy has more confidence than any psychotherapist, even the most expensive one, could give him. Thanks to him, Freddy would even be able to kill next time. How could he now look the hotelier in the eye? But Rácz has two eyes; it's Freddy who only has one left. Oh, God! One eye! He's one-eyed!

In his horror, Freddy dusts his socket with some thirty-year old medicinal powder that burns him terribly: he found it in the first-aid box he inherited from his parents. He ties a white handkerchief round his head. Weak from dread, his knees buckling, he crawls back into bed. Utterly devastated, with one wide-open eye he looks at the ceiling. He picks up the mobile phone and dials the office.

"Anka," he tells his assistant, attempting as unemotional a tone as he can. "I've got some sort of illness. Everything hurts. Yes, I think it might be flu. I'm sure, my head aches, too. Listen, I have to stay in bed. My mobile will be off, so that nobody disturbs me. Everyone knows what they have to do. Are you taking this down? Tell Kurnáč to edit *Madness in Handcuffs*, and when Kulíš shows up, tell him to re-edit the ending of *Naked, Wet, and Crucified*, as we agreed. He knows how. No, no additional shooting. No more spare shots. He can go to the editing room and work. Valco is shooting the exteriors in Monte Carlo, so he won't be back before the end of the month. If Video Urban asks about me, tell him that he can... no, just tell him I've left town. In the country, somewhere; for Christ's sake, for the salary I'm paying you, you could think of something, couldn't you? I have to think something over. That's it!"

The conversation had so enfeebled Freddy that he fell asleep there and then with the phone in his hand.

When he woke up, he was hungry again. He opened the freezer and took out a pizza. Before the microwave oven bell rang, he carefully took off his bandage. The socket had turned black, but the swelling had gone down. The pain, too, had abated.

Freddy eats his fill. To wash down the pizza he opens another bottle of sparkling wine left by Sida. He likes the sweet, cold sparkling wine so much that he drinks the whole bottle. The alcohol cheers him up. He takes the last glass with him to watch television. He feels restored and quite calm. The pain of losing an eye passed faster than he'd been ready to believe. So what, he reflected: who in history was one-eyed? Jan Žižka, Ľubomír Feldek, Moshe Dayan, Admiral Nelson, Josef Lada, and look what they achieved! Maybe Freddy, too, won't miss his lost eye so very much. Life is beautiful, he thinks.

All too soon, however this state of pleasant anticipation of what life has in store for a one-eyed man reverts to an abyss of despair and hopelessness and the awareness that he has irretrievably lost something vital. Oh, what bad advice Rácz gave him then! What meaning does Freddy's life have now, without Sida?

As the television warms up, it's time for the evening news on the *Markíza* channel. It takes him a while to realise that the news is about him. That is, about someone they don't know and whom only Freddy knows about. They're looking for the Train Phantom, who assaults women travelling on the evening train from Bratislava. They show an identikit picture and Freddy feels insulted. They've gone too far, Freddy doesn't look like that at all. He's not that bad a monster! In conclusion, the newsreader puts on a stern expression and says that, according to the latest reports, the Phantom has a scarred face and is probably missing an eye. For that reason all casualty doctors are asked to report any similar persons who have sought treatment.

"Like hell, you cunt!" Freddy shouts. "Me see a doctor? You're not going to get me that way!"

He switches to a Czech TV channel, where they're not discussing him and not looking for him. They have plenty of their own problems.

Then comes the weather forecast. For some time now Freddy has been secretly in love with one of the weather girls on Czech TV. She's a slender blonde with a short sporty hairdo and a slightly receding chin. The miniskirts that she wears arouse him. But the camera seems deliberately to avoid her legs. What are they like? Are they nice? Long? As in the *Playboy*, or in *Penthouse*; even there the women are photographed mostly as torsos with no legs, at most with only the upper third of their thighs. Freddy doesn't give a shit about torsos. After all, legs, if they're nice, are a woman's finest asset. Today, the weather girl is wearing a miniskirt again, but once more the camera shows Freddy just six inches of her lively restless thighs between the hem of her skirt and the bottom of the screen. Only once does she show her knees, calves and ankles. Freddy feels like screaming. And the weather forecast ends, as usual, without any undressing. A fetishist's life is hard and full of injustice.

In no time Freddy feels sorry again for his wasted young life. And yet it had all been looking so splendid and hopeful. From absolute zero he had worked his way up to be a wealthy and influential man, a professional film-maker, setting new trends in the genre of perverse porn. He was happy and had a wife and a child. And all that has been taken away from him and he's become a hunted man, in hiding from the law. And, what's more, he's been made an accomplice in a double murder.

If this wasn't an appropriate time to make a dignified departure from this wretched life, then when?

Freddy sheds copious tears from his single eye. The empty socket has healed now: he doesn't even have a hole in his skull; matter from behind the eye has filled the empty space. It's some kind of a pink tissue. At first Freddy feared that it would protrude from his eye, but it didn't.

Every object, nook and cranny of his house reminds him of Sida and their little daughter. He feels abandoned and unhappy. After all, he never did anything wrong. He tried his best to be a good father, husband, and provider. If this wasn't good enough for his wife Sida, it wasn't his fault.

He doesn't answer the landline, and his mobile phone has no charge. There are a few messages from Rácz on the answering machine. He is worried by Freddy's absence from some excellent recent Adrenalin Club outings and, if Freddy is sick, hopes he'll recover and join them soon.

Freddy smiles sadly. He'll never get over this. His life has no more meaning. Everything is dark. Even the sun has been hiding behind clouds the last few days, and a damp chill of painful depression has descended over the whole region. Freddy feels depression literally drilling into his bones. He won't find a way out of this mess. There is no hope of waking up from this nightmare with both of his eyes and finding next to him a sleepy Sida voluptuously stretching her body, his still beloved Sida.

Worst of all, the police are looking for the Tunnel Phantom, and hunting down Freddy is only a question of time. He is literally a marked man: he has an eye missing. When they find him, they might stumble on his Adrenalin Club exploits. And if the police interrogate him, or even, God forbid, torture him, Freddy will confess to everything. He'll even tell them where the two burglars are buried, the ones he and Rácz murdered in cold blood and with such enjoyment.

Freddy looks out of the window at the garden over which autumnal mist is slowly spreading. He can't help a furtive look at the corner of the garden, the two burglars' hidden grave. No, nobody in the world would find it. They're buried pretty deep; in any case, Freddy took Rácz's advice and carefully set aside the pieces of turf before replacing them. No, nobody would think that the area had been dug.

What will happen to this house once Freddy is no more? Sida and their little girl might return. She'll get news of Freddy's death wherever she is. And they're not divorced, so she and her daughter are his heirs: Sida will stay on here. Perhaps she'll think of him now and again.

Freddy still loves his wife and suppresses his first impulse to burn down the house and destroy their common property. After all, Freddy doesn't care at all what happens once he's gone. On the other hand, why should he destroy property that will one day belong to his daughter?

Freddy looks away from the dew-covered window. Now, it's only a question of solving the problem of how to depart this world. From the start, Freddy has excluded jumping off a very high place: he suffers from vertigo and, moreover, he can't imagine the horror of those few seconds falling into an abyss. And what about the pain if he should survive, badly injured? That happens sometimes, too. He would be lying down there, on the concrete, smashed up like a pitiful rag doll, fully conscious. People would come to take a look at Freddy and turn away, repelled by the sight. Something would ooze from him. Blood? Or the contents of his burst guts? The wait for the ambulance would be endless. Freddy would, of course, want a merciful loss of consciousness, but his strong resilient constitution would betray him and deny him relief. Worse, the pain would be slow to come, as well; the monstrous pain of flesh wounded by shards of fractured bones. And then Freddy would start to scream so horribly that mothers all round would have to cover their children's ears.

No, this wasn't a solution.

How about jumping into the Danube? Freddy could throw himself into the muddy, turbulent Danube and the waters would close over him. But Danube water is smelly and dirty. Disgusting. Moreover, Freddy would, because of his obesity, float on the surface. Like a cork float on a fishing rod. He wouldn't be able to drown. Somebody would throw a lifebelt at him and someone else might even jump in to save him. That would be so embarrassing. Freddy would have to come out of the water embraced by his rescuer. They would all look at him with compassion. Somebody would quickly bring a blanket and something to warm him up. Freddy would have to pretend to be deeply grateful to his saviour. He would have to pretend that he had fallen by accident into the Danube. And what if it turned out quite differently? There would be no rescuer; Freddy would float on the dirty surface like a bloated piece of carrion, climb up the bank quite alone after the Slovnaft oil refinery. He would find himself in wet clothes on the edge of the city, shaking with cold, catching a chill. His mobile phone would be soaked, so he couldn't call a taxi. And where would he go? Back to his despair and suffering?

What about slashing his wrists? The warm water in his bathtub would slowly ferry him to that bourn from which no man returns. If he did it with a sharp enough instrument, it wouldn't even have to hurt.

Freddy goes to the kitchen and opens a drawer. None of the knives is sharp enough. But what about a razor? Freddy is a skinflint: it doesn't occur to him to take a new blade from the pack. Instead he reaches for his shaver and takes a used blade out. As an experiment, he draws the razor-blade over the back of his hand. A thin, hair's-breadth wound opens and a drop of blood appears. An unpleasant burning sensation wipes out all Freddy's courage. He can't imagine being able to cut open his entire wrist with all the veins, arteries, and muscles.

Freddy would then lie dead in the tub. The water would be red with blood. It would slowly go completely cold. After a few days the blood would start to decompose. Then Freddy, too, would start to decompose. When they found him after a few weeks, there would be fat bluebottles buzzing all over the place. No, this wasn't a solution.

And why not take a piece of rope and go somewhere far into the woods, away from all the paths, and hang oneself? Is death by hanging really so terrible? Maybe not, if your neck breaks immediately. But what if a man just hangs there, jerking his legs, slowly, really slowly suffocating? He makes a hissing sound, his tearful eyes survey the world that he's leaving, and his suffering can last for minutes. His lungs would fight to the end for a last breath of oxygen. Oh no, this is a terrible thought!

Freddy picks up the remote control. He meant to turn the television off, but the news is followed by a discussion. A Czech foreign affairs expert is explaining how it happened that a long time ago Slovaks settled Junja beyond the Arctic Circle. In the nineteenth century many Slovaks left to find work in America. A Junja Khan took advantage of this by chartering a ship in Hamburg onto which he lured Slovaks by charging only half price for a ticket to America. Once on the open sea, the ship turned out to be a slave trader taking them to Junja. The Khan repeated this trick several times and thus managed to transport several thousand Slovak men and women to Junja. He sold them all to the Junjans and they used them for slave labour. Gradually, generation after generation, more and more Slovaks escaped to the far north. Here they lived, or rather eked out an existence, as free people. In time their status was legalised. Junjans realised that if they gave Slovaks freedom, and let them do what their typical Slovak industriousness and inventiveness leads them to do, they would get more profit from them. So the Slovaks became superb hunters, reindeer breeders, and fishermen. Slovaks did not rebel against high taxes, they were content with very little. They faithfully nurtured Slovak traditions handed down from their grand-parents, prayed to Christ, made love and multiplied: the more people in a yurt, the warmer it is. A few generations later, Slovaks no longer wanted to leave Junja: they had got used to it. Since they multiplied at breakneck speed, they became an ethnic majority, unlike the degenerate Junjans who spent generations lolling about on fur, too lazy even to copulate, exploiting hardworking Slovaks.

In the nineteen-thirties Russian communists got to Junja. They set up a puppet Soviet government that requisitioned the Slovak herds, fishing boats and founded reindeer, fishing, and hunting cooperatives. Ethnic Junjans, who were lazy and thus understandably charmed by communist ideas, headed these cooperatives. After the fall of communism and the Soviet Union, the Russians left Junja. Since then the two main ethnic groups have been at daggers drawn. There are many more Slovaks, who thus have an indisputable right to govern.

Freddy is engrossed by the debate. The expert lecturer is followed by a debate among fashionable Czech thinkers who theorize about the situation. Some defend the ethnic Junjans and the official government and say that the Slovaks are merely terrorists. Only God knows what to think, since there is so little information about recent developments.

What is certain is that the civil war between Slovaks and Junjans is getting fiercer. Reports from the battlefield talk of dozens of dead combatants daily, on both sides. The fighting spares no one, including accredited journalists in the war zone. The number of journalists killed in action is considerable.

Freddy reflects on it. Death from a bullet sounds good. It is the only dignified kind of death for a man. If well aimed, death by a bullet is clean and fast. A man dies and this kind of death gives him a sort of charisma, and a whiff of heroism.

"He died in battle," or "perished on active service." That sounds completely different from "he hanged himself in his flat," or "he jumped from the twelfth floor." The former is how men die; the latter how servant girls and frustrated female pensioners die.

And so Freddy, after long abstinence, takes a bath, shaves, combs his hair and puts on sunglasses. He calls a taxi and visits the bank. He takes cash from all his current accounts and buys a ticket for the next flight to St Petersburg. At night, he goes to the office, takes the best digital camera and tripod, with a full bag of cassettes, and leaves on the desk a mysterious note for Video Urban:

URBAN, I'VE LEFT FOR JUNJA. THERE ARE OTHER THINGS IN LIFE. FREDDY

He doesn't have to say goodbye to anyone and is too cowardly even to call Rácz. It's better that way.

The next day he packs a few essentials, clothes and toiletries and takes a taxi to the airport. He checks in his camera, which is packed in a crate, and is soon in his seat in an aircraft taking him to Russia.

Only in St Petersburg does he remove his sunglasses and cover his eye with a black patch he made from black velvet and elastic ribbon. At first, he feels that everyone is looking at him, but soon gets used to it. He goes to the Aeroflot counter, buys a ticket to Murmansk and flies off.

In Murmansk, however, he finds that it is not so easy to get to Junja. There is no regular connection.

"But it's easy," says a watchman in the port when Freddy offers a fat bribe and asks to be shown a ship sailing for Junja.

The man points to the railway wagons loaded with fifty-kilogram bags of potatoes. "Look, stick with those potatoes," he says. "They're meant for Ćmirçăpoļ. And when the potatoes get there, you do, too!"

The potatoes are loaded on a rusty old ship with a wooden superstructure. Freddy does a deal with the ship's captain and for a large wad of money they give him a poky cabin behind the steersman's.

The cabin smells of a good forty years' smoking, the window won't open and the bed is covered in stains, but for Freddy this is like being on the deck of a luxury yacht.

Once the potatoes are loaded, the ship puts to sea and heads north.

Freddy stands on the deck, looking at the land vanishing in the mist.

He is not sure if Murmansk is still Europe, but if it is, this is the last time that he will see Europe.

One ability that Freddy definitely has is to be moved to tears by his own fate: ever since he left his native home, city, and country, he has been repeatedly moved to tears of self-pity. Analysis of his own sentiments tells him that he is leaving as a broken and abandoned man. The whole world has turned against him and forced him out of his country, out of life itself. No eye will shed a tear when Freddy's eye closes.

Book Two

> Junjan children are cradled by the devil.
> *Junjan Slovak proverb*

If any of Freddy's possessions were lost, broken, or damaged back home in Slovakia, he would be out of his mind for days and be unable to eat or sleep. But Junja changes all your priorities. Ever since he and the potatoes landed in Ćmirçăpoļ, his main priorities have been to preserve his life and health, to keep out the cold and to lay hands on food. As for material possessions, the most important were those that immediately helped him survive and find food: clothes, shoes and work tool, in this case his camera. And, if need be, a weapon and ammunition.

A large compact group of journalists and photo reporters had come to Junja from all over the world. Freddy quickly got in with them. Slovak and Czech reporters helped him find accommodation and gave him leads for interesting stories. When Freddy admits to them that he hasn't been sent out by any television station, but is a freelance amateur working off his own bat, they're quite baffled. When they see him moving about on the battlefield, at first they think he's mad. But when they see his battle-field shots on television in the hotel in the evening, they begin to admire him. You can't shoot that sort of thing without risking your own neck.

Soon Freddy has a reputation as a reporter with more *sang froid* than anyone else. After a while, the CNN group staying at the same hotel, or rather workers' barracks, offers to pay in dollars for his superb shots. Freddy doesn't refuse. His filming is only a pretext to get himself killed, but, if it's so good, why shouldn't it be shown worldwide?

Money doesn't matter to Freddy, since he won't benefit from it, but, of course, that's not what he tells the Americans.

Since Freddy longs for death and has absolutely no interest in living, he reacts with stoic calm during an attack when a bullet hits him and only the camera absorbing most of the bullet's momentum saves his life. Not much is left of the camera. Freddy throws it at a group of rocks which other journalists are hiding behind. Freddy gets up, blood pouring from his forehead. He turns his body to face where the shot came from. Dying is better than living like this. When one stray bullet whizzes past him, he offers his body to another. He reaches into his jacket for a small auto-matic Minolta Riva that he bought for some reason at the airport.

"Take cover!" his Czech colleagues shout at him from their shelter. "Take cover!"

Freddy ignores the insistent voices. He ignores the bullets whizzing overhead. He stands tall to photograph Junjan mercenary units finishing off wounded Slovak guerrillas with their rifle butts.

High in the air something whistles and thunders. Freddy turns round. Instinct tells him to throw himself on the ground, but his mind is made up and disobeys. The air warms up for a fraction of a second and from somewhere behind Freddy comes a dull explosion. Flames and black smoke hover over the Czech journalists' hiding place. The hot blast throws Freddy several metres from the explosion. Another round whistles in the air. A mortar round, thinks Freddy. They're firing from a mortar. He checks if his camera was damaged when he fell. About a hundred metres from him another round explodes.

Somewhere near Freddy a group of men runs by, weapons in their hands. The smoke has filled Freddy's eyes with tears, but he can see they are Slovak guerrillas. A burst of machine-gun fire comes from ruined buildings. The guerrillas fall to the ground. One of them quickly throws himself into the Czech reporters' hiding place, which the mortar round has turned into a crater. Freddy throws himself after him. The safest place in a bombardment is the crater from a previous round; rounds never fall in the same place twice.

There are several dead bodies in the crater and a mass of camera shards. The Slovak guerrilla is wounded; blood oozes from his arm through his torn sleeve. The advancing mercenaries are close. You can hear their hoarse voices and occasional shots. They're finishing off prisoners, Freddy guesses. And here it is: his longed-for death is imminent.

The Slovak guerrilla sits in the corner, leaning against the crater wall. Freddy feels that he has seen him somewhere before. Yes, he reminds him of a Czech journalist who was always high on something. The guerrilla is tattooed all over, but looks like him. Unlike the slim Doložil, the guerrilla is a big man with black braids. He does not wear glasses, even though his tattoo looks like glasses. Freddy turns round. Doložil is lying there, dead in the mud. his belly ripped open. Freddy throws himself at the corpse and rummages in its pockets. He takes out the international journalist's card and puts it in the guerrilla's hand.

"Quick!" he whispers feverishly. "Take this. You will be him from now on. They won't shoot you. But you've got to cut your braids off."

The guerrilla holds the card in his hands. He looks at the photograph and nods. He takes out a razor-sharp knife and rapidly slashes off his braids. Then he quickly combs his hair with his hand. In an instant his hair is short.

"Wow!" says the astonished Freddy, who's never seen such quick, neat work in his life.

The guerrilla digs a hole in the semi-frozen ground, buries the braids and knife and fills in the hole with his hands.

"Now put his waistcoat on!" says Freddy and begins wrestling with the corpse. "But quick, quick!"

The guerrilla helps Freddy undress the dead man. He puts on the Czech's waistcoat. Luckily, there are no sleeves, so he can wear it, even though he is three sizes too large. He still looks like Frankenstein's monster in this tight waistcoat.

"Put his glasses on!" Freddy hurries him, handing him the journalist's John Lennon style dark glasses.

The guerrilla can't see a thing now, but accepts this part of the disguise, too.

"Good: now the camera," says Freddy, picking up Doložil's Leica. "It doesn't matter if it's broken! Can you hold it? This is how. When they come, you wave your card. From now on you're a Czech journalist. But you have to play dumb, or else you'll give yourself away."

Freddy reads the name on the card.

"From now on, you're František X. Doložil," says Freddy. "Do you get what I'm saying?"

"Sure," says the guerrilla wanly. "God bless you, good man!"

There is a sound of steps near the crater.

"*Ömhünd źźŕitt!* (You two!)" shouts a killer with a machine gun. "*Mozćd karmwlltź, prgýz'g agğaä!* (Come out with your hands up!)"

Freddy and Doložil climb out of the crater. They both keep their hands above their heads, holding their journalist's cards.

"*Żżurŕnńrdğ!* (Journalists!)" the killer announces to someone behind him in a contemptuous and hateful tone.

Freddy realises that he has no further need of the cassette in his breast pocket. Nor of the Minolta. They search them and do, in fact, take his cassette and camera. Doložil also loses his broken Leica. They are escorted by guards with guns at the ready to a yard.

Other journalists are already gathered there, being interrogated one by one.

"*Du yoo speack English?*" asks a moron in Junjan army uniform. "*Zpreschen sei Dutsch?*"

"*Ein bisschen*," says Freddy.

"What are you doing here?" asks the interrogator.

"I am a CNN cameraman," says Freddy. "Here is my card."

"Where is your office?" asks the interrogator.

"I don't have one," says Freddy. "I work on my own."

"Strange," says the interrogator. "All cameramen have an office. Only Slovak spies work on their own."

"You can check," says Freddy. "If you think I'm a spy, shoot me on the spot. Don't spin it out."

"Well, we'll see about that," says the interrogator. "We'll put you in an internment camp. If CNN wants you, they'll ransom you. If they don't pay in three months, you'll be liquidated as a Slovak spy."

This reminds Freddy of the Animal Protection Law.

"Better execute me right away," says Freddy and opens his green cameraman's waistcoat, warm jacket, pullover and flannel shirt wide, showing his pink chest. "I'm ready to die."

The interrogator smiles.

"If you're a journalist we can get money for, we shan't kill you," he says. "At least not right away. If you turn out to be a Slovak spy, you won't escape death. Take him away."

The last words were said to two armed men in Junjan army uniform.

As Freddy leaves, he sees the interrogator beginning to interrogate Doložil. Freddy returns.

"He's a famous Czech journalist," he tells the interrogator. "Everyone knows him at home. His name's František Xavier Doložil. Their shelter was hit by a mortar round."

"So what?" asks the interrogator. "Is your friend dumb that he can't tell me that himself?"

"Yes, he is," says Freddy. "Their shelter was hit by a mortar round and he was the only one to survive. He was scared mute. You'll get a lot of money for him: his weekly paper belongs to a rich Swiss company!"

The interrogator checks Doložil's card and makes a note against his name. Then he nods.

"Take them both away!" he orders. "If they aren't ransomed, they'll die in the taiga. But meanwhile they'll be of some use for a time. They'll pay us back at least in part for the criminal lies they spread about us."

* * *

Radio Twist was the first to announce that a Slovak photographer and documentary filmmaker, Alfréd Mešťánek, had died on active service. The news was then passed on by the daily paper *SME*, and soon it was the only topic of conversation.

Most people had never heard of the name Alfréd Meštánek or Freddy Piggybank. A few connoisseurs and lovers of perverse pornography, perhaps, knew of him. His death on the battlefield in a war of great media interest ensured his undying fame. Soon, even those who'd never heard of him knew Freddy's name. Slovaks, a nation fairly insignificant in global developments, eagerly embraced one more son of the Slovak people who had made the world stage: he had died as a heroic war photographer.

Only now was it revealed how many shots seen right round the world had come from Freddy's camera. Fired by making and establishing the image of a new Slovak hero, people totally ignored his activity in the field of pornography. Only his fearless actions in Junja were stressed.

He becomes a legend. A posthumous exhibition of photographs from the war in Junja is organized in the National Gallery in Bratislava.

Sida emerges from obscurity: as his loving widowed wife, she takes over the job of assessing everything linked with Freddy. She contacts a highly professional PR agency and skilfully begins to build the Freddy myth, all the better to market the Alfréd Mešťánek brand. Luckily for Sida, they had not yet got round to divorcing. Dressed in black, she plays the role of the nation's hero's widow and keeps opening exhibitions of his work. She is writing a book *My Life with Freddy*. In the Nová Ves house she has an Alfréd Mešťánek Museum built; in his garden she has a symbolic marble mausoleum erected. The workers building it dig only a few metres away from a real grave. Once the mausoleum is finished, masses of tourists from all over Slovakia come to the museum and the symbolic grave, paying hefty sums for entry. Sida's influence ensures that all mention of pornography is erased from his official biography. It says only, "for a time he also devoted himself to erotic art."

Actually, Freddy, as is usual in novels like this one, is still alive. More or less. Together with other captured and kidnapped journalists he first has to record in an improvised TV studio a heart-rending message for his loved ones at home. Something to the effect that he is being held, is in good shape, but if by such and such time he isn't ransomed, he will be killed. Doložil, who has by now adopted his role perfectly, is spared this. They just show a brief shot of him. Then they herd the prisoners with yells into the frozen hold of a stinking old hulk and set off to sea.

After a few days of sailing with no food and almost no water, they land on the island of Ommdru. As soon as they leave the ship's hold, slaves in rags start loading the ship with green-grey bundles that look like moss or lichen. They ogle the new arrivals with curiosity, but the whips in the overseers' hands force them back to work. The column of prisoners is about to start a forced march from the harbour through snow-bound country to a labour camp, Kandźágtt, where they arrive at night.

The journalists are shocked. Only in films or books have they seen the like of this. They still can't believe anyone could dare to do anything like that to them, the representatives of the fifth estate.

At a distance the camp looks like any other concentration camp any-where in the world, as shown in films: several rows of long single-storey barracks, a square where the prisoners are mustered, the commandant's barracks, dog kennels — all lit by blinding lamps swaying in a blizzard. What's missing here is the barbed-wire fence with watchtowers at every corner. Only one tower rises over the camp. Pillars mark the camp perimeter, but there's no fence. All round, from the depths of the dark but snowbound tundra, come the wolves' menacing howls.

The guards herd the hostages into cold barracks filled with wooden bunks and heated only by the prisoners' farts. The barracks are full of hostages. They have been asleep, but the arrival of new prisoners wakes them up. They all turn out to be foreign journalists captured just like Freddy and his companions.

"*Witamy serdecznie Państwa w naszem hotelu* (A cordial welcome, gentlemen, to our hotel)," someone says in Polish. From another corner comes hoarse ironic laughter.

Without a word, the prisoners move over on their bunks to make room for the new arrivals. A feeling of embarrassment, a vestige of civilised habits, makes the newcomers reluctant to climb into the warm, foul-smelling heap of prostrate bodies. Finally, cold and fatigue win. They all somehow find a space, but none of the newcomers closes an eye. Only Doložil curls up in foetal position and sleeps like a log.

"I've been here two months," a journalist from the Polish daily *Gazeta Wyborcza* whispers to Freddy. "My paper probably hasn't had the news. Otherwise they'd have paid the ransom by now."

"Same with me," says the Slovak daily *SME* photo-journalist, an ugly scar from a steel-tipped boot on his forehead. "I've been stuck here six weeks. I think they're just bluffing and haven't told anyone they're holding us hostage. But it should be in their interest to get money for us."

"KRŔTÔĞĄ Å!" a squat guard roars after peeping into the barracks. They all fall silent.

"What did he say?" Freddy whispers.

"He told us to be quiet," whispers the *SME* reporter.

"It's in their interest to wear us out picking that lichen of theirs," whispers the Czech photojournalist.

"What lichen is that?"

"You'll see tomorrow," says the Pole. "And now go to sleep, so you can take it. The first few days you won't be able to fulfil the norm, but don't worry, we'll help you. Otherwise you'd go without food."

"It's simple maths," says the Czech. "If you don't fulfil the norm, you don't eat. But rations are so small you hardly notice the difference."

"Good night," says the reporter from *SME*.

Freddy doesn't respond. He is beginning to shiver with cold. Until now he has been moving and not feeling the cold. Now he can. He has a good imagination and knows exactly how he'll feel about three a.m.

Fortunately, merciful sleep has him in thrall until morning, when the guard starts banging on an iron bar hanging by a chain. Freddy guesses it is about half past four in the morning. Nobody can confirm or deny it: watches were the first things the Junjans took away from them.

With shouts and blows they organize the prisoners into rows and make them wash in the snow. Then they give them tiny loaves of bran bread and pour into their tin mugs coffee probably made from roasted fir needles. Then they herd them off to work. The road leads into a forest blasted by a freezing wind. Fistfuls of snow shower on them as they go.

"Odd," says Freddy, more to himself than to Doložil, who sticks to him like a faithful dog. "All the prisoners here seem to be from Eastern Europe. Where are the Americans, English, French, Italians, Finns and Norwegians? In another camp? Have they already been ransomed?"

"No to both questions," says a Serb marching in the same row. "Nobody's ransomed them. They simply didn't survive."

"The Westerners were the first to die," adds the Czech. "One tall Swede was broken when they found his cell phone and took it off him. But what use is a phone here anyway? He just lay down on his bunk, turned to the wall, and was dead by morning. Or do you remember those two Englishmen and a Belgian that ran away? Or, rather, tried to run away? I don't know where they thought they were running. Maybe they thought they were in the Scottish highlands with a pub in every valley to phone home from, or something. They guards were in no particular hurry to go after them. When they did start their aerosledge after a while, they went to look for what was left of them. They brought back to camp some bloody rags and a shoe with a piece of bone sticking out. Wolves."

"What's the aerosledge?" asks Freddy.

"You'll see," says another Czech. "The guards have in a lean-to this terrible corrugated iron monster on three wide skis. The front is a cabin and the rear is an aero engine with a propeller. It's a Soviet-made machine from the thirties. It makes a terrific noise and uses about two hundred litres of petrol per hundred kilometres: that's why they don't use it much, only when someone runs away. Or for executions."

"Executions?" Freddy is shocked. "What sort of executions?"

"By propeller," says the Czech evasively. "For various offences."

"There's no point running away," says the Pole. "After all, where would you run to? On this island, there's only the camp and the harbour, where the Junjans work. And the moss. One day we'll be ransomed and we'll all get home. We'll remember this like scouts' camp."

"Just do as they tell you," the Czech advises Freddy. "Don't stick your neck out. Don't be clever. If the fat man, Agapp, hits you with a cable, pull your head down and don't look him in the eye. You've only got one eye left, and you'd be sorry to lose it. Pushkin is fine. He'll just ask you if you "know Pushkin". Tell him you don't know Pushkin. He doesn't Pushkin, either: if you told him you did know Pushkin, he'd beat you to death with his cable. But the one you have to worry most about is Gorloy. That's the one with the thin moustaches. He's a swine. Don't attract his attention when he walks around. He'll kill a man for fun. Last week he killed a Romanian for nothing."

"And watch out for the prisoner Fridrych, he's a grass," the Czech warns him.

"Which one is he?" Freddy asks.

"The one walking alone," the Czech discreetly points, "with the bulging, watery eyes. The one always smiling like a cretin. He used to work in Prague in the Ministry of the Interior; then he became editor of *Resort* weekly. He came to Junja to write about the Junjans as a misunderstood minority. Now he's an informer. They promised him double rations of marmalade. But I've never seen marmalade here since I came."

"He informs on us to the guards," the *SME* reporter says with hatred. "Just like Lynař used to."

"Vladislav M. Lynař, a failed politician," the Czech explains. "When he found that the Czechs at home didn't like him and he wasn't likely to have a career in the politics, he went back to journalism. He informed on us to the guards. For this he could warm himself up for an hour at the guardhouse stove. But we got back at him. He suffocated in his sleep."

"Wasn't he the son of that communist?" Freddy suddenly recalls.

"He was," says the Czech. "His father was an informer, too. In secret. He only pretended to be right-wing."

They are by now approaching the rocks, which take up an enormous space: there seems to be no end of them. They are all covered in wet bunches of green lichen. The prisoners get metal scrapers and buckets and can start gathering it.

"Just for your information," says the Czech to Freddy and Doložil, pointing to his bucket, "ten of these buckets is the daily norm. You'll be lucky if you manage three. But it will get better in time. It's the way you do it. Stick with me; I'll show you how to do it."

Soon, women guards bring in a column of female prisoners near the journalists,.

"Who are these women?" Freddy asks.

"Various," says the Czech. "They're hostages, foreign journalists, Slovak guerrilla wives, local Slovaks caught in raids. Women's hands are smaller, so they can reach the best quality lichen in the cracks. That's why they keep them here."

For a while Freddy observes the women wrapped in quilted coats with hoods. Suddenly, someone from behind gives him such a terrible blow on his back that he almost wets himself from acute pain. With a wild and astonished yelp, he turns round.

Above him on the rocks stands Agapp, his legs spread wide.

"*Émzdrgmhh bôžžtüul gáčćmnń*!!!" the guard shouts and swings his arm to strike again.

Freddy does not care any more. He only wants to die. He straightens up and fixes his single eye on the guard's face. He grabs the guard's raised truncheon made of an offcut of cable, rips it from his hand and throws it onto the rocks.

Agapp goggles at him in astonishment.

"*Uff! Uff!*" he is nonplussed. "*Gonđcŕř! Gonđcŕř!*"

The prisoners stop gathering lichen. Shouts of admiration and amazement come from all sides.

Freddy turns to his friends.

"This is how I, Telgarth, talk to these anthropoid apes," he says solemnly.

The informer Fridrych promptly translates Freddy's words into broken Junjan.

Freddy really has no idea how the mysterious word "Telgarth" got to his lips. Maybe a distant memory of films about World War Two Slovak partisans has drifted up from his subconscious? A biting cold march over Chabenec Mountain, Ján Šverma, frozen feet, the village of Telgarth, now called Švermovo, burned down by the Germans... Who knows?

Now, now the time has come, Freddy realises in a brief moment of true insight. The moment of death. He regrets nothing. He has enjoyed his life; life was generous to him. It showed him its bright side, too: love, success, and wealth. Sexual satisfaction. From now on, it's downhill all the way. Why drag it out? Nobody's eye will weep a tear when Freddy's eye closes, etc. At least he'll die a hero. Slovak and Czech journalists, once they're released, will take the news of his heroic death to his motherland. None of them will forget anything like this.

Freddy would like to say more, something to rank as famous last words, but nothing occurs to him. While he reflects, a rain of blows hits him on all sides. The guards have got over their shock and hit him all over with their cables. Freddy grabs one truncheon, but a well-aimed blow then cracks his head and makes him lose consciousness.

When he comes to, he is lying on a bunk in the barracks. A prisoner, it is hard to see who in the dark, is making him drink some warm slop.

"He's coming to!" he shouts in semi-whisper to the others.

Someone climbs to him over the bunks. Freddy hears laboured breathing.

"Well, you really caught it," says the Czech. "We thought you were a goner. But you're lucky. They're behind with their plan, so they started worrying that they might be exchanged for others and sent into combat. That's why they need every pair of hands. They've spared your life."

Freddy lifts himself on his elbow, but cries out and sinks back again.

"Don't move much," says the *SME* reporter. "They broke three of your ribs and your collarbone. Rest, so you can go back to work tomorrow. If you don't show up for work, they'll execute you. By propeller. That's what Gorloy said."

Freddy quakes with horror. He doesn't mind being shot, or beaten to death. But not killed with a propeller! Anything but that! If only because of the unbearable noise. To die in such a noise must be twice as hard.

Doložil crawls to him.

"I've found some mushrooms under the snow in the forest, Telgarth," he tells Freddy in the strange, archaic Junjan Slovak dialect. "They're for you. We're lucky they grow here. If you chew about ten buttons tomorrow morning, you'll get up with no problem. Nothing will hurt. You'll feel pain, but it will be as if the pain was hurting someone else. And every time more pain comes, you chew more mushrooms. When you run out, tell me. I'll gather some more."

He puts a small bag of soft, white button mushroom on his chest and crawls back to his place. Freddy nods, clutches the bag in his fist and again falls unconscious.

* * *

Despite the prisoners' disparaging comments, the Belgian hostage managed to escape. In the harbour he hid himself on the roof of a warehouse and waited for the next ship. It was a ship taking a cargo of lichen to France, the perfume superpower. The Belgian crawled deep into the load of lichen. He could breathe well through the porous material and it kept him warm, too. Once in France, in Le Havre, starved almost to death, he reported to the authorities. At first nobody would believe him, but eventually the whole world found out the shocking truth about the Kandźágtt camp on the Junjan island of Ommdru.

After the visit of a Swedish representative of the Red Cross, interned foreigners are not allowed to work. But nobody has forbidden taking them with other prisoners to the moss-gathering zone. And so every day, they take them to taiga and let them stand all day long up to their knees in the snow and storm. Old and new prisoners come to know each other really well. Moreover, they are closely bonded by mutual knowledge of the secret of the violent death of the grass Fridrych, who was about to run to the guards' barrack to betray Doložil's identity, since he knew the real Doložil personally from Prague. Freddy caught up with him on the way. Fridrych the grass slipped and was unlucky enough to fall and fatally break his head on the barracks wall. Then Freddy recalled Rácz's words: *once a man kills another man it's like a window opening in the middle of his forehead and nothing will ever be the same as before.*

In other prisoners' eyes, Freddy's reputation grows even more after this act. They respectfully call him by a name that first slipped from his lips in a moment of shock. For all of them, he was Telgarth from then on.

Hostages whose ransoms are still unpaid spend whole days in the snow. In the evening, they're taken back to the freezing barracks with the ordinary labourers.

The cold is vicious. There's not a living thing anywhere around. Everything has either frozen up, or migrated to warmer coastal areas.

Agapp comes to check the prisoners. He looks around in hatred, as he'd like to try his new whip's resilience on the foreigners. He can't understand the new era, and has no idea why foreigners don't have to work. Under the Soviets they had to. Once a commercial Canadian aeroplane made an emergency landing in Junja, and before they ascertained that this was not a case of espionage, the captured foreign passengers had to go to the camp and work, too. The guards kept a stewardess for entertainment, even after they handed back all the others. They just declared her dead. Some Canadians couldn't take it: what do you expect? The foreign woman was lent to the harbour guards, but they didn't watch over her during their orgies: she ran naked into the sea. She was found a few days later, drowned, tossed ashore by the waves.

And why has the chief forbidden beating foreigners until they cry? Doesn't a foreigner deserve to be beaten just for being foreign? When a foreigner's ransomed, he goes back to his world to loll in warmth and luxury while the bosses up here divide the dollars among themselves. But Agapp will freeze forever in the work zone. What an injustice!

Agapp spits angrily, and his spit freezes on his collar. Only his angry slanting eyes look out from under the fur. He remembers the old times. Soon he sets out to herd other prisoners, those gathering lichen. Some of them will feel his harsh, casual, but precise blows of the whip.

Freddy Piggybank is used to the magic mushrooms even though his ribs healed long ago and he has no more pain. Today he found a new supply under the snow, enough for three or four fixes. Now he feels good and has no pangs of cold or hunger. His thinking has accelerated. He almost feels pleasure. He watches the women. They climb over the rocks, scraping off the green-grey cover. They are dressed in thick quilted clothes that give them a stout, mannish look. They look like the television record of the landing on the Moon. They, too, move clumsily like astronauts and scrape at rocks with the same care.

Freddy can't even remember when he last had an erection. Even though, as an interned foreigner under Red Cross protection, he doesn't have to work, he is somehow constantly sleepy. He can even sleep on his feet. It may be the mushrooms. Looking at the emaciated women, who defecate when they need to right in front of his eyes, does not excite him at all. Freddy is a civilised man. For him sex has to be served up æsthetically. It has to have refinement: make-up, perfume, stockings, and garters: in short, it has to be served with all the sauce that goes with it. Mutual rubbing of mucous membranes is the last thing, and even at the peak of his sexual activity Freddy did not really require it.

He's quite unaware that whatever comes to mind he says out loud.

Blažkovský thinks that it was addressed to him. He agrees with Freddy. He'd rather have his prick cut off rather than screw one of them.

Freddy understands that. As one man to another, he can say that even back home, in Bratislava, not everything was to his liking. Some women were dressed even worse than here, in the camp. Freddy hates especially the new disgusting fashion. Those shapeless shoes. Women walk in them as if they had a brick tied to each foot.

"And those horrible acrylic sweaters two sizes too small!" Ondrejka joins in after stomping the snow nearby.

One thing is for sure: Ondrejka hated that fashion when it appeared for the first time in the seventies. Every young woman now wants to look like a dirty drugged whore. And with that pathetic backpack on, she looks as if she is perpetually hiking.

Doložil has no opinion on these things. He listens in silence. He can't fully understand everything anyway. He remembers times when he would return from a hunting trip and his good wife would let her hair down, light five lamps, undress and warm him with her body. Warmed up and revived by her hot skin, he would enter her and make love to her. He had no idea what these men were talking about, all that painting and dressing up. What painting? Real beauties are tattooed, after all. And these men? They're like women talking about softening reindeer skin in the women's corner of the yurt. Men are supposed to talk about hunting, fighting, trade, long journeys, escapes, not about women's boots!

One of the women lichen gatherers seems too slow for the woman guard. The prisoners watch the guard greedily attack her with a whip. The female prisoner tries to escape, but in vain. She slips and falls with a thud into the snow. The female guard kneels on top of her and beats her all over. The prisoner can't feel much pain through her coat's quilted layer, but she screeches even more. Finally the guard hits her in the face, her only unprotected place and the prisoner, bleeding badly, grows quiet.

Blažkovský also hates those shoes. They are formless and disgusting. They make women's legs look grossly thick. Blažkovský likes women in classic pumps with medium to high heels. A woman should walk like a gazelle and not like Frankenstein's monster.

The female guard calls for a colleague. Together they try to put the obstinate female prisoner back on her feet and make her walk.

"But a heel should not look like a hoof," Ondrejka emphasizes.

"Definitely not," agrees Blažkovský. "It has to be a thin stiletto heel. And at least eight centimetres high!"

The female prisoner doesn't want to come back to life. She drags her feet powerlessly behind her. Tracks of blood lie in the snow. The guards drop her onto the ground and leave her lying there. Other prisoners have interrupted their work and watch everything. Whips in hand, the guards hurl themselves at them and force them back to work.

"But I don't even like that executive style," says Ondrejka. "Those stupid mini-suits. All the girls in the office then look identical, like supercharged bitches in a hurry."

The prisoner lies in the snow and even at a distance it is clear that she will never get up. The snow around her head is bloody. The guard who hit her so precisely behaves as if nothing has happened. She shouts at other lichen-gatherers and only occasionally casts a glance on the prostrate woman now being covered up by falling snow.

"It was a white woman," sums up Ondrejka, when he looks at the prostrate woman from a safe distance.

Other men look that way without much interest.

A Dutch reporter, one of a new batch of prisoners, turns hysterical. He shouts in fury. A Hungarian and a reporter from *Mladý svět* knock him down and hold him down by force. One of the two Romanians gags him. The Dutchman emits incoherent muffled noises at the guards.

Gorloy approaches, whip at the ready, his face vengeful and curious.

From somewhere in the forest comes a high-pitched whistling. The women stop working and muster themselves into a column. Gorloy loses interest in the Dutchman.

"I prefer women dressed in suits to those in modern grunge and those hooves," Blažkovský resumes the topic, to break the tension.

"Tell me, how can women make themselves look so bad?" Freddy asks. "If nobody likes it and they find it hard to walk in those hooves, why do they wear them?"

"Because they're all cows," Blažkovský closes the debate.

Gorloy runs up with Pushkin and Agapp.

"*Ünńcrzžhy! Ünńcrzžhy!*" they shout. "Line up! Line up!"

The foreigners are lined up and herded at the end of the column, behind the women.

The female prisoners eye them curiously. Some are young, others old. They drag the corpse behind them in the snow. Her bloodied face bounces on the frozen ground. From the tundra come the wolves' howls.

"I don't even like the way they paint themselves," says Ondrejka. "Every time I see a girl like that on the street, with that long hair and emphatic eye shadow and lines, it reminds me of all those ridiculous German soft-porn films they show on satellite TV."

"Ah, satellite TV," sighs Blažkovský.

The camp is not far off now, and with it the hope of warm beet soup. The men forget about women and start on another topic.

"Do you remember the milk bar in Bratislava, opposite the theatre?" Ondrejka starts. "I used to go there for their cheese salad and crunchy bread rolls. And they had draught Kofola to go with it…"

Doložil gets behind Freddy.

"We're escaping," he mumbles. "Tonight. Get ready."

This surprises Freddy.

"How are we going to escape?" he is stumped.

"Men from my unit have come for me," whispers Doložil. "They're somewhere about in the tundra. They probably sailed here on a kayak. They gave me a sign a while ago. You'll come with me."

"And what about them?" Freddy points at Ondrejka and Blažkovský.

"We'll leave them here," says Doložil. "They'd slow us up. No one will harm them. They'll be freed in good health. I'm taking only you."

"But why?" asks Freddy.

"Because you saved my life," says Doložil. "Because you're my brother. And what's more, you're a brave fighter who won't break."

"What should I take along?" asks Freddy practically.

"Nothing," says Doložil. "There's enough of everything."

"*Krŕtoğą å*! (Silence!)" Agapp and Gorloy shout in unison, but dare not whip anyone.

The dogs are nervously barking, straining at their leashes. They'd love a bite of fresh meat. The guards can barely hold them back. They let them lick at least the bloody snow left by the murdered female prisoner.

ANAL DRILL length: 60'

Another superb morsel for lovers of anal porn. Experienced and perverse Lucy (Oral Norah) organizes a course of anal sex for three interested ladies who've had problems with partners that have so far refused to satisfy them anally. To start with, Lucy and her extremely well endowed partner (Bruno Tatarelli) show what a big rod a female anus can take. When another partner equipped with an even bigger tool appears on stage (Luigi Longo) and joins his colleague, the ladies can't believe their eyes. You too won't be able to believe this: two such huge rods in one anus! You won't see this anywhere else! But everything that Lucy demonstrates will have to be learned by the ladies on the course. They'll have to match and in one case even outdo perverse Lucy!

Order Nº: 2215 4044

Price: 699.00 Czech Crowns

Club members' price: 650.00 Czech Crowns

(From the *Freddy Vision* catalogue)

* * *

That evening Freddy is tense as he lies on his bunk. He is shaking as much with cold as excitement. The time for escaping is ineluctably nigh. Freddy would perhaps even prefer to stay, he fears an uncertain future. He knows what he has here. He could easily wait here to be ransomed. If the Slovak government won't pay, CNN will. It's only a matter of time.

There is no escape from the Kandźágtt camp. All around is hostile tundra that gradually turns into an endless snowy plain. When the wind starts to blow, it turns a man into an icicle in a few minutes. The founders of the camp realised that and that is why, as we said, Kandźágtt consists of only a few wooden barracks and a square for mustering prisoners. No fence, no window bars, and only one tall tower rising up. The barracks are of a cheap sandwich construction, so inside it can be even colder than outside.

Freddy has got used to the cold in the barracks. He feels the cold, but it doesn't have a devastating effect on him. This is partly the influence of the hallucinogenic mushrooms. He is wrapped in a blanket and another one is at his feet. When he goes to sleep, he wraps himself in the other one, too. Today he realises that he has wrapped himself in it for the last time. Help is coming tonight.

He remembers the time spent in the camp and falls asleep.

It is perhaps a few hours after midnight when somebody shakes his shoulder. It is Doložil.

"We have to go," he whispers.

Half asleep, Freddy is scared: he is slow recognizing Doložil's voice.

"Move it faster!" hisses Doložil impatiently.

Freddy pulls himself together, takes the rolled up blanket and blindly follows.

"No need for a blanket," says Doložil, who can see even in the dark.

Doložil and Freddy slip out of the barracks. The gale almost knocks them off their feet. They carefully hug the wall and then turn the corner. The camp is lit up, and even in the gale they can hear the roar of the generator. The lights flicker sometimes under the force of the wind. The fugitives keep to the shadows.

Dogs start to bark wildly. Their barks shake the wooden kennel wall.

Doložil and Freddy run from the light into the darkness, to the tundra. The gale seems even stronger there. The barracks at least broke the wind. The snow is bright and lights their way. Between the snow banks stand dark figures.

"Geľo," a voice shouts, "is that you?"

"It's me," says Doložil.

"And where's your hair?" asks the man in surprise.

"That's a long story," the man who was Doložil waves his hand. "I'm bringing a friend."

Freddy finds himself encircled by men in hooded fur coats.

"A Slovak?" someone asks.

"He's one of us," says Doložil. "His name's Telgarth."

Somebody hands Freddy a bottle: "Drink up, Telgarth!"

Freddy takes a drink: searing heat seizes his guts. He immediately feels better.

"Now we have to hurry, with God's help," says someone.

They give Freddy a heavy warm fur coat and Freddy puts it over his thin quilted camp clothes.

"Now let's go!" Doložil commands.

It is hard to run over slippery snow. The men push clumsily through the scrub. Freddy is out of breath; he has never run like this in his life. He sweats and suddenly feels hot. He feels like taking off his huge fur coat and cooling himself. But unconsciously he guesses that this could be the death of him. Two of his unknown rescuers support him. The gale throws clods of snow in their faces. Frozen fir needles burn them as if the wind was hammering them into their skin.

Behind them, roughly where the camp might be in the whiteout, something lights up. A rocket is fired, and then another. A guard must have discovered the fugitives' tracks in the snow before they were covered by the blizzard. Soon, driven by murderous vindictiveness and the passion of the hunt, they will set out after them with dogs. For the camp guards, hunting escapees is a welcome, if rare, pastime.

"If they manage to start up their aerosledge," shouts Freddy, to be heard over the blizzard, "they'll soon get us."

"They won't!" shouts Doložil. "I bit through the engine cable."

Not far off come the wolves' wild howls. Between the trees flash long shadows: wolves as big as calves. One of them gathers courage and hurls himself at Freddy who is lagging behind. The thick fur coat stops the wolf biting through Freddy's jugular. Freddy falls down, the wolf hanging on to his shoulder. He frees his hands and in desperation grabs the wolf by its head and sinks both thumbs into the wolf's eyes. He presses with all his might and feels his nails penetrating soft, warm mucous tissue. The wolf howls in pain and horror. Freddy presses his thumbs all the way in and mercilessly twists his thumbs in the bloody wounds and brain matter. The wolf lets go and starts to leap about in its death agony. Its howls of pain cease. Two men help Freddy get up.

"He got a wolf with his bare hands!" the men shout in admiration. "Wow! Wow!"

One of the rescuers knifes to death a second wolf that dares to attack.

Freddy is drunk on wolf's blood, runs amok and is about to throw himself at the whole pack and kill them with his bare hands. The men have a hard time holding him back.

"Telgarth is like a wild wolf," Doložil tells others. "He was like that in the camp."

It's hard to move in the powdery, freshly fallen snow. Behind them, the wolves fight over the carrion. Their wild howling is heard all the way here. The men stop from time to time and breathe hard. There is no time to talk. After minutes of frantic running, the forest ends and then begins an extensive snow plain which ends, out of sight, at the seashore

Here in the snow three very strange means of transport are at the ready. They are huge sledges with masts like sailboats. Their sails are tucked in and the tops of the masts twist in the wind.

Freddy is amazed.

"Get on! Get on!" the voices sound all around.

The sledges begin to move over the snow with a swishing noise. Despite a side wind, the rescuers deftly rig the sails to increase steadily the speed of these strange vehicles. Freddy is alarmed by the speed.

The sledges constantly threaten to overturn. The crew hang onto cables that hold the sail and bend outward. The monotonous swish of the sledges in the snow and gentle rocking lull Freddy to sleep. So, after being on his feet and treading the snow all day in the lichen harvest zone, and after the excitement of the escape, he falls asleep.

The muffled noise of a distant aircraft engine wakes him up. Somewhere far off an aeroplane seems to be flying over the countryside.

"Aerosledge!" shouts one of the rescuers.

"So they still managed to get it started!" says Doložil. "Maybe it was the wrong cable."

The unbearable noise in the dark distance comes closer. Freddy's insides feel as if clenched in an invisible icy fist.

"Give me a rifle!" asks Doložil.

They give him an automatic rifle.

"Oh, my God!" he whistles in admiration.

"It's a Czech submachine gun, Geľo," says one of the men on the sledge. "What they showed us when we were in Prague. Model 58/V."

"Why do they call you Geľo?" Freddy asks. "That's the name of the leader of the uprising. I've always wanted to meet him and film him."

"Well, you've met him," says the pseudo-Doložil. "It's me."

"You?" Freddy is flabbergasted. "You're Geľo Todor-Lačný-Dolniak? Why didn't you tell me?"

"How could I know you wouldn't betray me under torture?" asks Geľo, extends the stock and pulls out the firing mechanism.

"You could have," says Freddy, offended. "Haven't I given you enough proof whose side I'm on?"

"You certainly have," Geľo nods. "Plenty of proof. But why should I worry you? We'd have survived even without you knowing my real identity. And can you shoot, Telgarth?"

"Can I?!" Telgarth laughs.

"Well, here you are then," says Geľo and throws him another submachine gun.

The man sailing the sledge and hanging on the ropes looks at Geľo.

"We're almost on the coast, Geľo," he says. "There's a cliff. It's about thirty metres high. There's a Czech submarine underneath, waiting for us. They have frogmen in rubber dinghies waiting to rescue us."

The sledge makes a sharp turn at an angle. So do the second and third sledges. They take the sails off the masts. The noise of the aerosledge is getting quite close.

Over crunching snow the men run to the rocky cliff edge buffeted by the wild offshore wind. The roar of the sea comes from below. Freddy looks at the shiny and phosphorescent surface stretching to the horizon. His head swims. What did they say? Thirty metres? It seems a good hundred metres to him. Just imagining those long seconds' falling down, with the wind taking his breath away, utterly freezes his loins.

One of the rescuers signals with an electric torch. A distant flash responds. Only now does Freddy notice a long dark shadow on the surface. The submarine.

"They're sending out a dinghy," says a rescuer. "We have to hold on here until they come right below us. In this cold water we wouldn't last for more than half a minute or so."

An illuminated dot appears on the snowy plain, approaching fast.

"Lie down," Geľo orders. "Don't shoot until I give the command."

The aerosledge comes closer. Freddy can now see the stained corrugated aluminium body, the cabin windows and flashes from the exhaust pipes. Its two powerful headlamps are like a fabulous animal's eyes.

"What a monster!" says Freddy.

To the guerrillas' surprise, the aerosledge does not slow down as it approaches the cliff but attempts to make a turn. At full speed it only slightly changes direction and flies over the cliff, disappearing into the depths with an awful noise. A huge explosion follows and a flash lights up the whole surroundings.

"So that's the wire you bit through," Freddy remarks to Geľo.

"Yes," says Geľo, smiling roguishly. "That was a good wire, too."

The rescuers put away their weapons. They look down into the depths. The petrol spilled on the surface is burning out.

Motor dinghies from the submarine are coming closer.

"Well, now, in God's name, men!" says Geľo. "Let's jump down! Better not to think too much: just jump in without hesitation."

"Hey, wait a minute," says Freddy, forcing himself to speak calmly. "We don't need to jump. We can use the wires from the sail sledges. We'll tie them together and lower ourselves down."

"And how will you anchor the wires?" asks one of the rescuers.

"Well, that is a problem," Freddy looks round.

"The sledges are light, they couldn't take your weight," says Geľo. And you can't drive a peg into this ground; it's solid rock under the snow. So let's jump, men, let's get it over with!"

He throws his fur coat off and hurls himself into the abyss-like depth. Freddy's eyes follow his fall of several seconds and the impact on the surface. Soon his head emerges from the water. Two frogmen are beside him, helping him into the dinghy.

"Who's next?" asks Freddy.

"I don't mind," says one rescuer and jumps off the cliff.

Others follow. Finally, only Freddy and one of the rescuers, evidently the leader of the rescue mission, are left.

"So let's go, Telgarth," says the leader. "That's all we can do. Our persecutors are also down there, with the devil's mother."

Freddy takes a few deep breaths. He realises that the guerrilla's watchful eye is on him. He tries to look casual as he stares into the depths. He'd rather stay here a while and pull himself together properly. Behind him is the camp with its everyday torment and hard work. Here, in front of him, is a freezing sea, but also the comfort of a heated submarine, the certainty of warm soup and, above all, freedom.

Freddy begins to run and takes a leap. He is surprised how brief the fall is. The water is so cold that it hurts his groin. But two frogmen fish him out before he fully realizes how cold it is.

Then he sits wrapped in an electric blanket with the others, and the dinghy rushes to the submarine's lengthening shadow. When Freddy's feet touch the deck of the vessel, they hear the Czech captain's voice:

"Welcome to the submarine *Kamýk*. Come down quickly, so that you can warm up and change into dry clothes. What was the explosion on the surface? Did you throw something down?"

"It was the explosion of the aerosledge with guards from the camp chasing after us." Freddy answers. "They didn't make the turn."

"Hey," the captain shouts. "I can hear that you aren't a local man. Where are you from?"

"From Bratislava," Freddy says. "I'm a war correspondent."

"Well, come down quickly, so we can lock up and sail off," says the captain.

They all enter the submarine, the hatches are closed, the vessel submerges to periscope depth and sets off for the open sea. The submarine has delivered its cargo, so it has a lot of vacant space. The guerrillas have the front hold to sleep in. Here they also get their supper after a badly needed hot shower and a change into dry clothing.

Geľo, his deputy Sirovec-Molnár, the rescue mission leader and Freddy are invited by the skipper, Lieutenant Commander Kubeš, to dine in the officers' mess. There they all get to know each other. Freddy uses his new name. Captain Kubeš orders a bottle of champagne to celebrate a successful mission. He raises the glass to Geľo Todor-Lačný-Dolniak.

"We've saved the most important man of the Slovak uprising," says Kubeš. "It's a great honour that I and my crew could help."

"Without you we really couldn't have done it," says Frolo Sirovec-Molnár.

"We're happy to have been just in the area," says third warrant officer Kulan, "so that we could take part in this spectacular mission."

"And what about you, Mr Telgarth?" Kubeš asks Freddy. "How did you get into Kandźágtt concentration camp?"

Freddy briefly tells his story. He doesn't feel like saying much, for fear that the captain might accidentally find out his real identity. After all, in Slovakia and Bohemia, too, he was quite a well-publicised person, if for no other reason than being Central Europe's richest porn producer.

"Well, interesting," says Lieutenant Commander Kubeš.

"I assume," says first warrant officer Lieutenant Skopšík, "that after we reach Öggdbardd, you'll part from your new friends and be our guest on the journey to Europe."

"It will be our pleasure to take you back to your homeland," confirms Lieutenant Commander Kubeš. "After this mission, we're going home on holiday. And since we've left two men in Junja, we have two airline tickets from Riga to Prague."

"Thanks for the kind offer," says Freddy.

"I assume that after the suffering of prison you'd probably want to recuperate at home," says Kubeš.

"If you'll allow me, I'll have to think about it," says Freddy. "I have to think about work duties. I assume that we're docking at Ćmirçăpoļ."

"Not quite," says Kubeš. "Ćmirçăpoļ has now fallen again to the Junjans. Or rather to Tökörnn Mäodna. But we'll land you anywhere on the coast, as you wish."

After a sumptuous dinner, strong aromatic coffee is served. But even this doesn't stop Freddy, Geľo, and Sirovec-Molnár, after struggling with fatigue, from making their excuses and going to bed in comfortable bunks near the bow.

*　*　*

"Don't think," says Freddy to the guerrillas lounging on their bunks, "that I've never come across anything like the aerosledge. I have, and it was even more terrible."

The submarine is now sailing for a second day. Freddy feels as if he's in hospital; he can sleep whenever he wants, mostly all the time, and the only thing to make him aware of time dividing the day in three parts are breakfast, lunch and supper. The Slovak guerrillas have never seen a hospital before, but they behave likewise. The submarine crew tries to disturb them as little as possible.

"Well, this is how it was," says Freddy. "One day they sent me to a distant island, where I had to investigate the activity of a very evil man."

"What's 'activity'?" asks Krčmárik-Košta-Spodný.

"Bad things," Geľo explains. "Injustices."

"I had a helper," says Freddy. "His name was… Quarell. He was at home there. He came from a neighbouring island. On that island we met a girl who collected shells. She was a beauty. Her name was Zlatka Ryderová. She told us a story about a dragon who came out at night and then went around the island with fire coming out of its mouth."

"What's a dragon?" asks Krčmárik-Košta-Spodný.

"Something like *Ökötöm-kökötom* snow monster," says Geľo.

"And sure enough, this vehicle like the aerosledge showed up at night," said Freddy, "except it had wheels. They shouted at us to surrender and come out of the bushes. When we declined, they burned Quarell with a flamethrower. So Zlatka and I surrendered. We turned out to be prisoners of a Chinaman, a doctor. He intended to destroy the whole world. I escaped from him and stopped him doing what he wanted. Then I saved Zlatka, too, when she was tied down on the shore so that the crabs could eat her alive."

"Wow! Wow!" The men were amazed.

Freddy spoke quietly, so that none of the crew could hear him, even if they were listening right behind the massive door.

"I knew right away that you were the right kind of man," says Geľo. "The very first time I saw you. When you saved my life. And the day before yesterday, with the wolf, too. That was something else!"

Geľo runs his hand through his hair that has started to grow during his stay in the camp.

"You know," Geľo says, "everyone advises me to follow my reason. But I'd rather follow my heart. The heart can see even what reason can't."

"Hey, Telgarth, tell us another of your experiences," asks Sirovec-Molnár from his bunk.

"All right, then," says Freddy. "One day I and another man were trying to collect money that was stolen from us. There were only two of us and there were more of them."

"What was the other man's name?" Sirovec-Molnár interrupts.

"You don't know him," Freddy says.

"It doesn't matter," Geľo smiles, "What was his name?"

Freddy knows of the almost sacred importance that Junjan Slovaks attach to names. For them, a name mirrors the personality, and is a sort of talisman. If someone commits an ugly act, he has to change his name to atone for it. Similarly, if someone gets seriously ill, he has to change his name to get better. Sometimes it helps, sometimes it doesn't. That's why the guerrillas wanted to know the name of Freddy's companion: to be able to imagine him better.

"Urban," Freddy says without thinking.

Men begin to whisper. They respectfully nod their heads. Urban is a good name.

"Telgarth and Urban," says Geľo with respect.

"We only had handguns," Freddy continues. "I've always insisted that you need a shotgun for this kind of work."

The guerrillas sitting round Freddy mumble in agreement and nod their heads in admiration.

"When we entered the flat where the thieves were hiding," Freddy continues, "they were just having breakfast. They almost shat themselves with fear. I shot dead right away one of them who was relaxing on a sofa, so the others were clear whom they were dealing with. I made another one very nervous by eating his breakfast and drinking his drink."

"Ho, ho, ho!" roared the men with understanding laughter.

"A suitcase full of gold was in the kitchen dresser," Freddy recalls.

"And then they slew them all." Freddy uttered this sentence from Holy Scripture every time he filled someone with lead. When he began the sentence, Urban would already know that the baddies were doomed. But finally, another of the baddies ran out of an adjoining room and shot the whole magazine at Freddy and Urban, without hitting any of them even once. So they killed him, too. "Thou shalt not steal! He who takes with his hand... and so on!"

Freddy's single eye looks at Geľo's group.

"And you?" he says. "You're too merciful. You won't win like that. You have to be unfeeling and fanatical! Why do you shoot in the head? It's too small a target. Besides, you only put one enemy out of action. Shoot in the belly, so that he stays alive! Then you get rid, as well, of two others who have to carry him away. And besides, the cries of the wounded in a campaign destroy a unit's concentration and damage its morale. What's more, they give away its location, too."

"The mercenaries don't care about their wounded," says Geľo. "They leave them where they fall. We often have often finish them off."

"Don't," says Freddy. "Let them suffer and yell. I'd make propaganda use of them, I don't know... I'd impale them on spikes so they yell even louder. Let everyone see how our enemies end up. Everyone has to be afraid of Slovaks. Yes!"

The men mumble respectfully. They nod in agreement.

"Tell me, Telgarth," Geľo suggests shyly. "Would you like to stay with us and help us until we finally win? We need someone like you. You're a Slovak by birth, but you're different from us. You're experienced. We're just simple hunters..."

"Don't underestimate yourselves," Freddy says. "You're great fighters, you're just too nice to your enemy. And you lack combat experience. I've got the experience, but, on the other hand, I don't know how to deal with the local harsh environment. You've made an ally of it, as you've always lived here. Teach me what you know and I'll teach you what I know. Otherwise, you and your fighting morale remind me of the boys I commanded years ago in my special unit."

Freddy blushes, but when he sees the hunters hanging on his every word he continues with more courage: "It was a rescue mission, too. Terrorists were hiding their hostages in a fortress on a high mountain.

There was only one road leading there not guarded by the terrorists: straight up this vertical rock, about two hundred metres high. There were patrols all over the place."

The men only understood every third word, but their hearts caught the thread.

"We had to climb to the top up this vertical rock, use the element of surprise, enter the fortress and rescue the hostages. Before the climb, I gathered my boys and told them: 'Ahead of us is a dangerous climb and the enemy is listening. The slightest noise gives us away and means death to the hostages. So I beg you: if anyone can't make it up the rock and falls down into the chasm, he mustn't make a sound. Otherwise he'll give us away. I believe we'll all make it to the top safe and sound, but I want to be sure. Anyone unsure of himself should step forward: I won't reproach him.' Nobody stepped out."

The guerrillas respectfully mumble and nod.

"The climb took us over two hours," Freddy continues. "We often had to take a rest, so that our hands wouldn't get cramped and we could use our weapons right away. Of twenty men, only eleven made it. Nine of my fellow fighters slipped from the rock and were lost in the bottomless abyss. None of them made a noise. Falling to certain death, they were as silent as the grave. Thanks to them, the mission was a success."

Freddy pauses to drink tea.

"Well, you remind me of those men," ends Freddy and keeps looking at the ground with his single eye, lost in thought.

"You haven't answered my question," Geľo interrupts the heavy silence with his mild voice. "Will you stay with us?"

"I'll gladly help you," says Freddy, recovering from his reverie. "I'll be with you through thick and thin. My life has been worthless until now. Except, of course, for various heroic exploits I've done at home. Together we'll triumph!"

The men are happy. Finally they have on their side someone who is as big a swine as Tökörnn Mäodna!

"Tökörnn Mäodna?" Freddy burst out laughing. "When the Slovak guerrillas catch that man, they'll gouge his eyes out and put him in a cage to show him to the hunters', reindeer herders', and fishers' settlements along the coast and in the tundra. They'll just show him to the people. Nobody will be allowed even to touch him. They'll feed him well, he'll be healthy and his face will glisten with fat. And then a committee will sit down and decide how Mäodna is to leave this world. Freddy has a few good ideas. But no matter how, his execution will take a long, long time. Tökörnn Mäodna will be dying in unimaginable torture for entire weeks. His howls will reach all Junjan Slovaks on the coast and deep in the tundra. Everybody will know that the man who hurt the Slovaks so much will now, in small, carefully measured doses, part with his black soul."

* * *

The hostage video with Freddy pleading never gets to Slovakia.

That Slovakia is going from bad to worse has long been clear to Urban. For a few years he consoled himself with the vain hope that when the right kind of people won the elections and got a chance to rule, things would start to get better. In the meantime, there were several elections, end-of-term and mid-term, but nothing improved. It is worse and worse not just for poor, simple people who own nothing, but for businessmen. All right, Urban isn't starving, naturally, and can afford to dress well, but he too finds it hard to give so much money to the state only to see that nothing is achieved. Deductions are higher and higher, the business tax burden more onerous. Only a stupid Slovak can work under such ridiculous business terms. A German, Englishman, or Frenchman wouldn't give a toss for business on those terms. Urban can see it by looking at the owners of the video rental outlets, sex shops and video and multimedia shops that buy from *Freddy Vision*. They keep going only because they started long ago and can't give up now. They have put too much of their own money into it and nobody would pay that much to buy the business.

Urban can't understand why Slovakia has to be such a bewitched country. Maybe it is because its people are hard working, but stupid. Again and again, they let politicians pull the wool over their eyes. They always fall for it. Urban knows something about it.

He got caught up in politics once, and even became a member of parliament. After his professional and personal break with Rácz, he soon left politics, too. It was an enlightenment, in its way. A former hustler, money-changer and occasional pimp, he was sickened by the things he had to do as a politician. In the porn business he found far purer characters and far straighter people.

Lucky for him, he broke up with Rácz amicably, even though they didn't stay very close friends. But they'd never been that close anyway. Since he was always straight with Rácz, Rácz was straightforward with him. But Urban realised this only very recently, so he had some anxious moments waiting for Rácz to pay him his share of the holding company.

Rácz guessed that Urban was slowly roasting over the coals of his own doubts, so just for fun he fed those doubts a little. He invited Urban to all kinds of senseless events and Urban, panicking about losing Rácz's favour now that he really depended on it, assiduously attended these events, even though it affected his family life badly. His two live-in lovers, Wanda and Eva, sensing that the flagship of wealth and luxury was about to founder, made an attempt to detach themselves from him. They didn't want to walk the streets again, being used to a married lady's life. So they set up a telephone service and went out servicing clients interested in luxurious erotic offerings. Thus they stopped depending on Urban. He was getting deeper and deeper into his paranoia that Rácz would steal his money and not pay him his share of their prosperous company. He spent very little of his energy on the relationship with his two common-law wives. Moreover, Wanda and Eva had for some time known that they did not need a third person for their erotic life, and the occasional presence in their bed of Video Urban, a hairy, panting intruder who grabbed their tits and other intimate places, invaded these two fragile fairies' gentle romantic idyll with his disturbing urgency, inconsiderate penetration, gasping tension and messy spray of semen.

That was not the only reason why one fine day they stole all the foreign currency and gold, which he improvidently kept in the flat, and vanished to follow their own destiny.

At the time Urban hit bottom, psychologically speaking; Rácz played a game of cat and mouse with him and Urban told himself that perhaps he did not deserve such treatment for so many years' loyal behaviour. Of course, he did not say so to Rácz. He went on smiling at him and kept up a pretence of being his good friend. Finally, Rácz was bored with it and Urban was paid all the money due to him from shares in Rácz's businesses. Without a word Rácz bought his shares at the top price and organized a small company leaving party for some five hundred guests. There he gave him a personal parting gift, a platinum Omega watch. Yes, Rácz could be a model at one and the same time of pettiness and of magnanimity; he was a banal person as much as a tycoon.

For his part, Urban never abused any confidential information he was privy to during his years of close collaboration with Rácz. He knew only too well that he could do something like that only once in his life.

Urban travels round Slovakia and never ceases to be aware that this part of the world is beyond help. This nation will not learn to work properly; it was screwed up by decades of a communist regime. The Czechs are in much the same state; there is no great difference. Czechs may even be a bit lazier and more pensive than Slovaks. But unlike a Slovak, even the stupidest and laziest Czech has a prodigious gift of the gab, so he can verbalise everything and thus sound more viable. Slovaks will just drop everything and not do a thing. Czechs also do nothing, but they keep talking. It makes no real difference, but a Czech gives a superficial and ill-informed westerner an impression of greater dynamism.

Urban has long been toying with the idea of selling his share of *Freddy Vision*, transferring the money to the Czech Republic and even moving there himself for good. Not because things were progressing so radically, but because the Czech State is nearer the West.

He has shed all his other business acquisitions and real estate in Slovakia. He sold everything at a time when he could still get a good price. Today he couldn't do that: anyone with real estate in Slovakia is automatically a hostage to that property. He can't sell it; he can only helplessly watch the price steadily dropping. Like the value of anything else located in Slovakia that can't be moved to a happier part of the world. Urban is one of the lucky ones with a good nose for disasters both small and great, so he has managed to divest himself of everything at a time when things were looking up, after the election victory of a coalition that portrayed itself ostensibly as rightist. By the time people found out that this was another group of cynics and crooks with right-wing rhetoric, but left-wing hearts, everything was sold and Urban had moved into a modest bachelor flat that he rented temporarily. All his precious things and antiques he smuggled out to Bohemia and packed them into one of the rooms in his cousin Tina's villa. All his disposable funds were transferred there. He invested them in Tina's company.

She immediately increased production. She rented or bought new premises and had them *optimised*. This is what Tina calls the conversions that give her a maximum number of working places for her slaves, who are stuck for whole days at their knitting and sewing machines.

If only Urban could now sell his share of *Freddy Vision*, he would be completely happy and could move to Bohemia and slam the Slovak door shut for good. There's no point going on without Freddy. In any case, Urban was never interested in the porn industry, only in the company's economic results. Conceptual and artistic issues were totally in Freddy's hands, and Freddy is now most probably dead.

When Freddy left for Junja, Urban thought it was the whim of a millionaire who would soon get over it. For the time being, the company could carry on under its own momentum. However, after Freddy's disappearance was definite and his death probable, Urban had to take over the running of the company, and that almost makes him break out in a rash. The only solution seems to be to sell his share of the company and move to a more benevolent and promising business environment. As a shareholder in Tina's company he could start numerous ventures to establish her brand name better in the world, or at least in Europe.

Selling *Freddy Vision* is no problem: there are plenty of interested parties. The problem is that Urban is not the firm's sole owner and thus, without Freddy's agreement, he can do nothing. Not even unload his share. After all, if Freddy were alive, he could buy his share himself. If he were dead, his widow could buy it. And perhaps, together with Sida, Freddy's heiress, they could sell the whole business and have peace and quiet. There's no point to it without Freddy's imagination.

But Freddy is still missing without trace and nobody is in a hurry to pronounce him officially dead.

* * *

But Freddy is not dead at all: quite the contrary. After successfully fleeing the internment camp, he finally refuses Commander Kubeš's offer: he lands with Geľo's group on the coast. He's one of them.

Ever since then he's felt that now at last he's really begun to live. What he's enjoying is just what he longed for in his childhood: to have a group of friends who respect him, and to have adventures with them.

As a boy, he had no friends. He grew up in a factory settlement and as his parents were building a house, he could not have a bicycle. His contemporaries would go off on their bikes for adventures, and Freddy would awkwardly huff and puff behind them on foot. When his friends decided to go to Devín Lake, Freddy ran after them as far as he could. Once they were out of sight, he sat on the edge of the road. He was not even half way there, and the gang was on its way back. The boys whizzed past without noticing him. He was not worth stopping for. No one even offered to give him a ride on the bike's carrier. When the dust settled, Freddy set out back, towards three high brick chimneys you could see on the horizon, towering over the greenery. When he got back to the settlement, the children had dumped their bikes in a heap and were grilling corn-cobs they'd stolen from the collective farm. When he joined them, nobody apologized to him. He was invisible to them. And yet he so much wanted to be one of them, to be a real member of the gang.

Now, an older man, he is one. The looks of admiration that his new friends give him as they discreetly observe him almost embarrass him.

"That's the one who killed a wolf with his bare hands," they say of him. At the same time, Freddy realises that he knows nothing and is no use to them. Except for the advice he gives them. But he doesn't think this important, though for the Slovak combatants his advice is of great help.

"Why do you kill only Junjan soldiers and mercenaries?" Telgarth asks Geľo during a dinner.

Geľo stops chomping over his mess tin and gives Telgarth a baffled look.

"You have to kill civilians, too," says Telgarth, licks his spoon and puts it inside his boot.

"Why?" Sirovec-Molnár is also puzzled. "They don't shoot at us."

"We'll have no peace until we get rid of all the Junjans," declares Telgarth. "Every Junjan is our enemy, whether he wears a uniform, or not; it's all the same. In Europe we have a saying: 'one corpse in civvies is worth more than ten in uniform'."

Geľo nods. He slowly grasps the idea. He doesn't yet agree, but he knows that Telgarth has more experience.

Sometimes the guerrillas have a problem: mercenaries have mined the only pass that the guerrillas could use to pursue them. Two Slovaks are wounded and one cries for an hour because of a torn-off thigh, until he asks for a *coup de grâce*.

"What now?" the men ask Geľo, their commander. Geľo is helpless, though he does not let on. Inside he rages helplessly. He doesn't want to retreat, but he can't advance. These are special mines; some leap up to the height of a man and then explode, hurling steel arrows all round.

Telgarth has advice.

"How far is it to the nearest Junjan settlement?" he asks.

"Right here, just over the pass," a man points behind. "It's where a fur processing plant used to be."

"How far is it?" Telgarth asks.

"It's not far," says the guerrilla. "You'll work up sweat five times."

"How many souls live there?" Telgarth wants to know.

"Three official clans live there," the priest says. "That makes about hundred and fifty Junjans."

"That's enough," says Telgarth. "Half of the unit can stay here, just in case of a counter-attack. The other half goes to the Junjan settlement and bring a hundred Junjans back here."

"What are they for?" wonders Geľo.

"We'll drive them ahead of us through the minefield," says Telgarth. "All the mines will be set off by the Junjans. Nothing will happen to us."

The men stand in silent awe.

"But they'll all die there," Čižmár counters.

"So?" Telgarth laughs. "Those mines were laid by their own people, so let their own people be blown up by them, not us, right? At least it stays in the family!"

This strange argument silences them all.

"As I said," he says. "One corpse in civvies is worth more than ten in uniform. When the Junjans and mercenaries find them, they'll realise that we know no mercy and they'll be frightened."

And this is what happens. The herded Junjans, whimpering with fear, clear a way for the Slovak fighters through the mined area, and thus the retreating mercenaries lose the advantage. Geľo's unit locates them and attacks them at night.

Telgarth takes part in this action, too. He fights in the vanguard and his fellow fighters can see his contempt for death. He is now used to the sound of bullets flying past his ears and his life is taking on a new quality, although he still does not fully realise it. This time he's not just a passive witness of bloodletting. This time he's holding not a camera, but a weapon, a Czech 58/V submachine gun that he was given by Geľo the day they fled the labour camp together. He shoots right and left, but as he does not know how to shoot, his firing is pretty ineffective.

After the battle, a few trembling prisoners lie tied up on the ground. The fighters took them prisoner at Telgarth's prompting.

"We need squealers," Telgarth explains.

"What are squealers?" ask the baffled fighters.

"That's what you call prisoners who tell you something about the enemy units' plans," says Telgarth.

The prisoners, who at first sight look like Russian mercenaries, are smiling arrogantly. They despise death and even more they despise the Slovaks. They have no idea that they are now Telgarth's squealers and that, for that reason, a quick death would be the best outcome for them.

Before Telgarth joined the guerrillas, the Slovaks were mild and good-natured, almost naïve you could say. They would let prisoners go after the latter promised to be good and not to fight the Slovak people. The Junjan Slovaks had this reputation, so the Russians are arrogantly grinning. They're sure of being released.

"Where's Mäodna's hiding place?" Telgarth asks them, smiling amiably. "How many soldiers are defending Úŕġüllpoļ?" The Russians have close-cropped hair, as if the hairdresser used a chamber pot on them all; their faces are black from smoke. They look at Telgarth arrogantly.

"They won't say," Geľo shakes his head. "I know them. They'd rather be shot."

"Why shoot them outright?" asks Telgarth with a smile. "There are other means."

He adopts the persona of a nonchalant SS-man, played by the elegant František Dibarbora in a Slovak film *Wolf's Lairs*.

"Pain," says Telgarth meaningfully.

He looks like a professor giving a lecture. His words are addressed not only to his fellow-fighters, who stand by bored, their weapons ready, but also to the stubborn prisoners. He has hated them from the start: those Russian turnip heads with their "chamber pot" haircuts. Hatred slowly permeates his heart. He shudders.

"Unspeakable pain," says Telgarth, not caring whether anyone understands him, "pain that puts someone on the brink of madness. Pain that engulfs the entire mind and ousts all other ideas. It burns out the nervous system in unspeakable ecstasy."

"Slovaks don't do torture," says Geľo proudly, but hesitantly.

Geľo has been unsure of his own words ever since he cleared the mined pass by using Junjans.

"That's right," nods Telgarth. "They don't do torture. No need to. We won't touch these Russians. Nothing tortures a man more than his own body. Coil them up! All of them! Let them torture themselves."

Some guerrillas, ropes in hand, approach the Russians and, perplexed, look at Telgarth.

Telgarth realizes that these simple men have never in their life read Karl May. That is why they have no idea how to coil somebody up.

He shows them how. He has them lay the Russians prone and gag them. He forces one to stretch his tied hands out forwards. He uses the rope to tie the handcuffs and leg cuffs together as tight as he can. The Russian is now lying only on his belly. His tied arms are raised over his face, almost in a begging gesture. His bound ankles are tied to his arms. The rope connecting them is about half a metre long. The Russian has trouble breathing.

"Tie them all like this," Telgarth orders. "When their tendons relax a bit — in about fifteen minutes — tighten the rope. When their feet touch their hands, call me. They'll be ready to talk."

Telgarth leaves the Russians and sits down by the fire. He looks at Geľo wrapped in his furs. He reaches into his pocket for a bottle. He takes a sip and throws the bottle to Geľo. "In an hour we'll find out everything," says Telgarth. "We'll know everything they know."

Geľo is silent.

"This is not torture in the real sense of the word," says Freddy, detecting a silent reproach in Geľo's eyes. "Nobody's slashing them with a knife, burning them with fire, or flaying them. They're torturing themselves with their own bodies. When we untie them after interrogation, they won't have any wounds, any traces on their bodies."

Geľo takes a drink and throws the bottle back to Telgarth.

"I'm not saying anything, for God's sake," he says. "I see you know what you're doing. God himself sent you down here. I don't like fighting women and children. I don't even like humiliating an enemy prisoner. My heart says no, but my reason says yes. Ever since you came, we've begun to have success. And if we're successful, more Slovak men leave home and join us. I know of a large unit that the Slovak fishermen have formed on the northern islands: it's on its way here. We'll strike Űŕġüllpoļ together. Slovak people are rising up across the land and fighting bravely. And we have you to thank for that, too."

Geľo finds it hard to get the words out.

Telgarth is quiet for a while.

"I'll find out for you how strong Űŕġüllpoļ's defences are," he finally says. "At least you'll know what you're up against."

"And then what?" Geľo asks. "What if we make it into the city?"

"Then we'll have to proclaim a free Slovak State," says Telgarth. "And defeat the remnants of Junjans."

"You know how to do that?" Geľo asks. "Because I don't."

"Necessity teaches us everything," says Telgarth. "First, the world has to learn of our just struggle. We'll take Űŕġüllpoļ and then we'll shout about our cause to the world. That's the only way. We have to get the support of world opinion. That's the strongest weapon these days."

"We've got support," retorts Geľo. "The Czechs are for us, after all."

"The Czechs?" Telgarth laughs. "Do you want to know something about the Czechs?"

"I'm a simple hunter," says Geľo. "I can fight boldly and can also think about that fight. But thinking about several battles is something I can't do."

"That's what's called tactical and strategic thinking," says Telgarth. "You, Geľo, are an excellent tactician. And I'll be the strategist. I'll sell our truth to the world."

"No selling, Telgarth!" says Geľo. "We won't sell anyone our truth."

"I didn't mean it like that," laughs Telgarth. "I meant that I know what to do to get more respect from the world. And also to make them fear us. As you said the other day, deep in the tundra, lakes of mineral grease have burned ever since the world began. Well, that mineral grease is the most precious thing in the world. It's worth more than gold."

"But there's plenty of gold here, too!" says Geľo.

"It's because of the mineral grease that the Czechs are so keen to help us," says Freddy. "Whoever has mineral grease is the master of the world. Everything you see round you, ships, aerosledges, electricity generators, aeroplanes, all run on mineral grease. Without mineral grease all life on the earth would come to a halt. That's how it is."

The men look in the fire in silence for a while, occasionally taking a nap. The bottle keeps circulating.

"I didn't know that," says Geľo after a moment.

In about an hour, Geľo's son Juraj shakes Telgarth's shoulder.

"The feet have touched the hands," he whispers. "Hurry, Telgarth!"

"What's happened?" asks Telgarth without understanding, woken from a semi-conscious chilly nap.

"The feet have touched the hands," Juraj repeats. "One Russian has stopped breathing. The others are all blue, too."

Telgarth gets up and pisses against a rocky wall. Then he approaches the tortured mercenaries. He selects one of them who is still conscious.

"Well, listen, *tovarishch*," he addresses him in broken Russian. "Tell us now how many of your soldiers are waiting for us in Ůŕġüllpoļ. A few? A lot? A great number?"

The Russian mumbles something. His mouth is gagged, and you can't make it out. His eyes shine madly and his forehead is dripping giant drops of cold sweat."

"I know you can't wait to tell me," says Telgarth sympathetically. "But take it easy. I'll go for a short walk and when I return, I may listen to you. So consider your answer carefully. Think about it."

The Russian can see Telgarth leaving and begins to emit muffled shouts of desperation. Telgarth smiles angelically. On purpose, he walks slowly across a stony plain with a thin covering of scrub. He walks to its edge and focuses his eyes. In the distance lies Ůŕġüllpoļ. You can guess its location by its few lights. This is no Bratislava shining from afar.

This world is not only wild, but beautiful, thinks Telgarth fondly. He will have a good life here. It is not only that the simple rules of this world will be easy for him to keep, but also that he will be present at their creation. This will be Telgarth's world. It will be a substitute for the Meccano set that he never got from his parents as a child, since they had to build a house and had no money to spare for him.

When Telgarth ambles back from his circuitous walk, the Russian is ready to talk. His voice keeps breaking; at every second sentence he demands that they release the rope tying his wrists to his ankles. Freddy magnanimously ignores his desperate demands. The guerrillas learn all that they need to know. The position of the mercenary army in Ůŕġüllpoḷ makes it extremely favourable for a rapid attack by Slovak units.

"And what if it's a trap?" Gel'o frowns.

"What trap?" Telgarth laughs. "Just look at him. He would even tell you what milk he sucked from his mother."

"What are we going to do with them now, Telgarth?" asks the armed Slovak who has been guarding the Russians all this time. "Shoot them?"

"Why" Telgarth is puzzled. "No need to waste bullets. Why kill them? They'll die on their own."

He turns his back on the interrogated Russian and misses the mad expression in his eyes when the guard gags him again.

Early in the morning, Gel'o's unit meets up with a unit of fishermen. Besides rifles, they also carry harpoons, terrible weapons in the hands of anyone who knows how to use them. Altogether, that makes about five hundred men ready for anything.

The following night they attack Ůŕġüllpoḷ. The battle is brutal, and there are losses on both sides. Finally, the Slovak guerrillas take the city.

Telgarth consolidates his reputation as a brave fighter who is cruel to conquered enemies. He teaches his people yet another way of getting information from prisoners: hanging them by one foot.

"It's very effective," he explains to his fellow warriors. "To hang someone by both feet is nothing. But if he hangs by one foot, he doesn't know what to do with the other one. For a while he can lock it with the one he's hanging by, but he can't do that for long. If he lets the free leg just hang there, he'll go mad from pain. And when we untie him after interrogation, he can do splits like a ballerina for a few hours."

The guerrillas admire him, though they fear him a bit, too. His hatred of Junjans, both civilians and mercenaries, is incomprehensible to simple Slovak hunters, fishermen, and reindeer herdsmen. Men who have all lost a relative during the Junjan rule, whose wives, daughters, or mothers the Junjans may have raped, find this hatred incomprehensible. But their respect for Telgarth is unbounded and constantly growing. "Telgarth kills wolves with his bare hands and is like a wolf himself," they say of him.

Telgarth's authority increases especially after he alone, at the risk of his life, liquidates an encircled mercenary commando who took hostage a group of Slovak women and children from their shelter. It is true that, apart from the mercenaries, five civilians died during Telgarth's action, but they all saw Telgarth advancing as tracer bullets flew round his head.

"Believe me, that was the only way," Telgarth assures Geľo, after taking the remaining hostages to safety. "They'd never have let them go. They'd have shot them all. This way, at least three women survived."

Nobody dares ask how many hostages were shot by Telgarth because of his legendary wide aim. Telgarth resolves to learn to shoot perfectly.

"A bit of exercise never hurts," he explains to Geľo. "I used to be a crack shot once, back home. But that was long ago. I need practice."

And so Telgarth spends entire days practising and amuses himself by shooting captured Junjan mercenaries.

He sits on a raised platform with a telescopic hunting rifle in his hands. When he gives a signal, the guards release a mercenary.

"Run!" Telgarth tells him. "You're free."

The mercenary looks round like a coyote caught in a trap. Then he starts to run zigzag across Megalomania avenue, wider than Moscow's Red Square. He runs and the greater the distance he puts between Telgarth and himself, the more energy he gets from the illusion of freedom. But not for long. Freddy takes aim and fires. The prisoner spins round and falls to the pavement, next to the others. Yes, practice has made Telgarth an excellent shot.

A few days later, Geľo and the whole army, joined by enthusiastic town Slovaks, moves on.

"You'll stay here, Telgarth," he tells Freddy before he goes. "I'll leave you a strong unit here. And, as you know, every day more of our brothers from every corner of the south coast are coming to join us. Soon a mighty army will be here. It will be at your disposal. But don't get bogged down by military affairs, I'll leave you Sirovec-Molnár to deal with them. He'll take care of order in the city and of training new recruits. You do what you know best. Receive foreign visitors and journalists. Explain to them patiently that Slovaks are only fighting for freedom. Show them who we are and what we're after. If you need to requisition anything, like a car or something, just do it. You're one of the most important men in our revolution. Remember that. We'll stay in touch. Keep your spirits high and fight your battles. They may be even more difficult than destroying enemies with a weapon in your hand."

Friends till death do them part, they embrace. Then Geľo does a soldier's about-turn and leaves the room without looking back.

Freddy sits at his desk. The feeling is indescribable. He has not sat at a desk for over two years. He passes his hand over its textured surface. It is a desk from a different world than the world Telgarth comes from. This desk was born and has spent its entire life here, in Junja. Who knows who used to sit at it? Freddy has a very special feeling. There's something missing on this desk. He has to think for a while what it might be. A computer! Yes, he needs a computer and printer to write and print all the proclamations of the Provisional Revolutionary Government that he hereby proclaims, including all orders and regulations. The same applies to all materials for journalists, so that they know what to think and write about Junja. About Junja? All geographical names will change. Junja is a word invented by Junjans. Using this word amounts to legitimising the Junjan regime. For Slovaks and the whole world from now on the name will be the Slovak Archipelago. And Öggdbardd? No! New Liptov. Űŕġüllpoļ will henceforth be known as New Bystrica. And Ćmirçăpoļ will be known as New City. And this applies to everything. Each river, island, hill, valley, and settlement. Only after we name it, will the place really begin to belong to us and become a part of us!

Indescribable pride seizes Telgarth. Yes, he, once the fat boy from the brick-making settlement, whom nobody wanted to play with and who as an adult was rejected by every woman, though he later became Central Europe's porn king, has now touched power that he never held before and that few people hold on this planet. People who believe in him have vested that power in him. And he'll never betray them or let them down. Part of this power is the right to rename places. Telgarth almost trembles with excitement. If he now renames an island, the size of two Austrias, New Liptov, it will stay that way forever. Centuries after Telgarth departs this world, New Liptov will be on all world maps, American, French or Ugandan. Freddy gets out a new leather-covered, flat hip flask and takes a swig. That's right. And now, let's get a computer.

He takes a submachine gun, checks the magazine and steps outside the building. The guards click their boots. They are new volunteers from the city. They've never seen Telgarth in action. Never mind. They will.

"You two, come with me," he orders them. "We're off to get something."

"And what sort of thing, Telgarth?" asks a guerrilla who looks at first sight like a simple fisherman from the North.

Telgarth reflects for a while. Then he waves his hand dismissively.

"You wouldn't understand anyway," he says. "Hurry up! Even if we have to turn the whole city upside down, we have to find it and requisition it in the name of the Slovak people, for God's sake!"

* * *

Video Urban can't be said to have missed Freddy Piggybank that badly. But the company misses him as scriptwriter, director and producer. After Freddy disappeared to Junja, Urban had to take more interest in the day-to-day running of *Freddy Vision*. He gets no pleasure from it. After the original enthusiasm aroused by the success of this type of pornography, Urban now suffers more and more distaste from communicating with people who spend days within the company. Just to find out what everyone does there seems beyond human powers for Urban. He'd rather sell his share to Freddy or somebody else, take the cash and move it to Prague. Instead, he has to sit in the office at Freddy's desk and solve his subordinates' idiotic or disgusting problems, and wait until Freddy is declared dead, so that he can do a deal with Sida and either sell his share to her, or jointly sell the whole company to a third party.

But Sida has her own worries. She has adapted to her position as the nation's widow. She wears mourning with an elegant hat and veil. But Urban is unconvinced: he knows the whole story. Sida dressed as a black widow only reminds him of yet another a pornographic film role. All her sophisticated mourning outfits from the best designers' studios are to him just film costumes to use in the first five minutes of a porn film, before the screwing starts.

However, Sida is utterly at home in her new social position. She organizes and personally opens an exhibition of Freddy's photographs from Junja. With the help of a venal writer who usually writes about hockey players, she pens a book about Freddy's life. Understandably, whole episodes from Freddy's real life are missing and even when the authors can't avoid mentioning his years of involvement in the porn industry, they make him into another Larry Flint, a perverse guru of perverted porn. Yes, Freddy's cult is becoming a reality.

One day Urban is in his office, wondering what to do next, casually leafing through the latest issue of *Stern* magazine. There is a big article about Junja there. One photograph captures a guerrilla commander with an eye patch standing amidst a group of his fighters, as he looks gravely straight into the camera lens. Below the picture is a caption which, translated from the German, reads: *One of the most fearsome revolutionary leaders of the Junjan Slovaks, Telgarth, who has become deified in his own lifetime. The Slovaks' struggle may be just, but their uncompromising stance hinders the peace process in Junja.*

Urban freezes, dumbstruck. He recognizes Telgarth as his Freddy Piggybank. Is it possible? Freddy's alive! And if Freddy is alive, so are Urban's hopes of shedding the nasty burden now hanging round his neck now like a millstone.

Stern goes on to say:

... on the coast road by the airport we get to Űŕġüllpoĺ, taken about two months ago by the guerrillas and renamed New Bystrica. We slowly approach the buildings. Right by the first buildings we see patrols of Slovaks. On the road are barricades patrolled by Slovaks who check our documents. Nearby is a group of foreign photo-journalists with cameras ready to shoot. They are dirty and the stress of their everyday work is obvious. One of them tells me in broken German that there is no more fighting in the city. While he is saying this, a constant noise of shooting comes from the streets. People walk by as if nothing was happening. We pass through the city. The streets are full of armed men. They shoot only in the air. Slovak guerrillas are celebrating.

"Three helicopters carrying mercenaries came yesterday," a cameraman from the Czech weekly Reflex *announces. "The Slovaks fought back. Some mercenaries in the commando were killed; the rest flew away. A group of mercenaries fearing capture committed suicide by shooting. Two helicopters were left burning on the tarmac."*

Nobody knows why the helicopters came and flew away. "They came to rape Slovak girls," is the rabble-rousing claim of the commander of the city, Telgarth, a living legend among the Junjan Slovaks and at present the most famous guerrilla leader. Foreign analysts believe that after the Slovak forces' final victory Telgarth will be head of state.

It is certain that the population, mostly of Slovak and or part-Slovak race, has joined the guerrillas. The government invaders had to retreat. Residents of Junjan origin have fled the city. Those who failed to do so were beaten and had their heads shaved. After taking the city, the Slovaks, led by the guerrillas, raided the Junjan army stores where they found a supply of handguns, so that everyone is armed to the teeth.

We pass a burning airport building. Everywhere are traces of fighting. Nobody is putting out fires. Everyone is trying to steal whatever he can use. Doors, tables, chairs, metal rods... Under our feet we hear the crackle of dozens of cartridges. We visit the rebels' headquarters in the main railway station building, about a kilometre from the airport. Junja has about three hundred kilometres of railway, but the main station is a monumental marble building erected in the best traditions of socialist brutalism. The road is littered with giant concrete blocks and wrecked cars. The guerrillas move about in cars that can only be called "wrecks". One wreck looks particularly ugly. As if a napalm bomb had exploded in it. "There were four of them inside," an American CNN cameraman says. "One fired an anti-tank weapon at a helicopter trying to land. The helicopter exploded, but the reactive gases burned everything in the car. They're crazy."

In the new masters' car park we see old Volga, Moskvich, Pobeda, Kharkov vehicles, and military GAZ jeeps. It looks like a working open-air museum of the Soviet car industry. The cars are in a dreadful state, with no doors or bonnets, their bodywork bullet-ridden. The broken windows bristle with gun barrels. Even a month after the conquest of the city, there is no calm and the guerrillas rush about to mop up the last bits of dying resistance. This is a war not of tanks and armoured personnel carriers, but of obsolete Moskviches, driven roughly by people who a month ago had no idea what a car was.

By the building's entrance we see a few prisoners tightly tied in a coil. This punishment is commander Telgarth's speciality. He uses it as an educational tool and as an ingenious way of executing people. No wonder this enigmatic and charismatic guerrilla leader gets such respect from his men and arouses such horrible panic and hatred in his enemies.

We are expected. Escorted by guards, we enter the hall. We walk through offices. All the doors are open. In one of office we meet commander Telgarth who has been expecting us. He is a stocky middle-aged man. He looks ordinary and normal except for a black eye patch over his right eye, which gives him an extremely combative look. He is dressed in a fur jacket and trousers. He wears fur boots. He sits at a desk in the middle of a looted room. On the right of the desk lies his submachine gun, on the left is a pistol: both are Czech made. He smiles and in broken German offers us tea. He is evidently proud of his linguistic ability. He waves his hand and an armed men hand us envelopes. I open mine: it is an ordinary press kit, as if we were somewhere in Europe, attending a press conference with the manager of a successful company, not in the middle of a raging civil war. The kit includes an information bulletin divided into chapters:

Who are the Junjan Slovaks?
Who are Junjans?
Who are the mercenaries fighting for Junjans?
Why have Junjans forfeited their right to live?
What will Junja be like after the Slovak Liberation Movement's victory?

There are also colour slides attached to a page. I hold them to the light of a paraffin lamp. One shows atrocities by foreign mercenaries against Slovaks. Another shows Telgarth holding a weapon, looking into the distance with clear eyes. Yet another shows a group of Slovaks in typical fur outfits: one is Telgarth — probably a commanders' meeting.

An armed man brings tea; Telgarth is ready to take our questions.

Q: Mr Telgarth, was Űŕǵüllpoļ conquered under your command?

A: I am one of several leaders of the Slovak resistance. The supreme commander of the guerrilla unit that took the former Űŕǵüllpoļ, now New Bystrica, four weeks ago was Colonel Todor-Lačný-Dolniak, a Slovak national hero. I am his deputy with my own command authority.

Q: In the political staff of the resistance you play an important role. What is your function?

A: First of all, I am a soldier of the Slovak revolution and any political functions today, while combat continues, have little meaning. After the final victory, I will, however, hold the office of chief administrator.

Q: What does that mean?

A: I shall be responsible for creating the independent Slovak state's power structures; for maintaining order and security against internal and external enemies; for the purity of language and of the Slovak race; for education, culture, and trade; for foreign policy; for everything.

Q: Ah, that seems quite a demanding role.

A: Yes, I enjoy the confidence of the Slovak people.

Q: There are voices in the Slovak resistance that point out that you are a foreigner in Junja and should not have such an important position in the leadership of the resistance.

A: I'm not aware of any such discussion. I have proved my devotion to the national cause so many times by risking my life, that nobody can have any doubts. I even suffered for the national cause in a labour camp where I would be to this day, if I hadn't managed to escape. Today I have enormous power, but also great responsibility. It is true that I was not born in the Slovak Archipelago, but I'm as good and true Slovak as my fellow combatants. Napoleon was a Corsican, not a Frenchman. And Stalin was not a Russian, but a Georgian. If you think about it, all Slovaks are foreigners here.

Q: Do you think of yourself as a modern Napoleon? Is Stalin someone you'd like to emulate?

A: I am the servant of my people. I am one of those who will permanently liberate Slovaks from Junjan oppression.

Q: Since you're a Slovak and you're not from Junja, are you perhaps from Eastern Europe?

A: No comment.

Q: Your German is surprisingly good, but your accent reminds me of a city on the Danube...

A: No comment. You'll have to excuse me, but history is strict with my time, so if you have no further questions...

Q: I'm sorry. Your methods of combat are incompatible with all UN conventions. Western observers reproach you for excessive brutality. What is your attitude to this, as a European?

A: Our methods are above all effective. UN conventions are of no interest to us. If the conventions help my men to kill more enemies, I'll take an interest in them. I don't care at all about western observers' opinions. Where were the western observers all those decades when the genocide of Junjan Slovaks was in full swing? You must admit that you first came across the word Junja two years ago, when the Slovak nation's sacred war broke out!

Q: Are there among your people many Slovaks from the continent? They say that many murderers and violent offenders have fled from the nations of the former Czechoslovakia to Junja.

A: Among my people are many courageous Slovaks risking their lives for the people's cause. They are very useful to us, as they have combat experience. All the blood they spill here is hot and red. It is Slovak blood from which our freedom is born. I need no other information about our heroes.

Q: Where does all this hatred you harbour come from?

A: I see what the Junjans have done to the Slovak nation. First, they drag them here against their will, then enslave them and mercilessly exploit and mistreat them for a hundred years. Now they are painfully paying for all that. And so are their children. That's how it is. We members of the Slovak resistance aren't sportsmen who meet for a beer after a match with rivals. We don't play at chivalrous noble warfare. We are underhand, vindictive and bloodthirsty. But we're no cowards. We know how to die with a scornful smile on our faces and a merry song on our lips. We fight for our existence, our living space and the extermination of the entire Junjan nation. We reckon on death, but not defeat.

Q: Why don't the Slovaks return to the Carpathian Slovak Republic?

A: Why should they? They've lived here, in the Slovak Archipelago, for generations. They're at home here and here they'll put matters in order. Anyway, who'd want them in Carpathian Slovakia? The govern-

ment there supports the regime of Hüğottynünđ Űrğüll. No, we're not seeking asylum. To say nothing of the absurdity of seeking it now, when victory is within our grasp.

Q: Have you ever thought of making peace?

A: You mean, drawing a line under the past and pretending that nothing happened?

Q; Yes.

A: Well, I've never considered it personally and I don't know of anyone in my circle of fellow fighters who'd be able to do so. We hate Junjans. We hate their language, their culture, children, and women. We'll never stop hating them.

Q: How does that fit in with the fact that the majority of Junjan Slovaks are Christian believers?

A: Our faith is deeply rooted in our hearts. Sometimes we set it aside and behave apparently at odds with the teachings of Christ. But then comes a time for repentance. We fight for the sheer survival and God is helping us in this endeavour.

Q: However, Christ is the symbol of forgiveness, of making peace. Would you be able to stop hating?

A: Only if all Junjans to a man committed suicide. I'd value that.

Q: There are few Slovaks in Junja who are racially pure. Almost all of them have some Inkirunnuit and even Junjan blood. How does that square with your nationalism?

A: For me the man is the most important thing. If he feels like a Slovak, then he is a Slovak. While the Junjans enjoyed unlimited power, they always liked to rape Slovak girls. That is why their blood runs even in our veins. But to be a Slovak is not just a question of blood. It is above all a question of will and feeling. There are many Slovaks who have accepted Junjan ideas and have thus become white Junjans. They have accepted Junjan nationality and acquired Junjan citizenship. Some even have gone and had plastic surgery on their eyes and lips in order not to look like Slovaks. That is a disgusting betrayal.

Q: What is your political aim?

A: Victory.

Q: In your future state you take no heed of the Junjan population. Or does it only seem like that to me?

A: Junjans will be our slaves. They, their children, and their children's children will serve the Slovaks as the Slovaks once served the Junjans. Forever. I'm no opponent of slavery. Junjans are so primitive that they had no Middle Ages. Now they'll feel what it's like.

Q: So you'll have a slave state?

A: To a certain extent, yes. But, leaving aside the Junjan slaves, we will, of course, try to have a classic parliamentary democracy of a West European type.

Q: The civilized world today recognizes the just cause of your fight, but is unlikely to agree with your inhuman plans for the future. Aren't you afraid that you'll be isolated?

A: Let's discuss that after victory. After we kill and enslave all our enemies, we'll be the most peace-loving and the most democratic nation in the world. We want nothing else. We'll certainly enrich world culture significantly. We have talented people. Junjan Slovak heroic epics, handed down orally from generation to generation, are a real treasury of beauty and wisdom and are sure to serve as an inspiration for creators of modern songs and literature. We are not only good poets and soldiers. We're good hunters, fishermen, herders and merchants, too.

Q: I'm afraid that a Europe on the brink of a new millennium will not be very interested in your fishing and herding abilities. And then, after the news of the slave state reaches the world, you'll lose much of the world's good will.

A: Believe me, we have something to offer the world, not just lichen for the perfume industry. We're not going to beg the world: the whole world is going to stand at our door and wait for us to let them in.

Q: Those are brave words. What do you have to offer beside your famous lichen? A diamond as big as the Ritz?

A: I'm not at liberty to talk about it yet. Believe me, straight after victory we'll be members of the European Union, despite the fact that we have geographically nothing in common with Europe. And despite the fact that we believe in the slave system and will never abolish it. Europe will be glad to accept us.

At the time of our arrival in Junja, Slovak rebels controlled only a few settlements in the north of the main island, a small part of the tundra and a few small islands. The Slovak uprising is, however, spreading like wildfire on the Junjan islands. We are leaving Junja. Some settlements in the south-west of the island of Öggdbardd, renamed by the Slovaks New Liptov, have also fallen to them. These are unconfirmed rumours. According to diplomats, Slovak guerrillas control a third of the railway between Ćmirçãpoļ in the south and the northern ports. Some diplomatic family members are being evacuated early this morning. We wonder how to leave Junja. Should we try the suicidal early morning flight from

Űŕǵüllpoḷ-New Bystrica, on Air Junja's only aircraft, where we could, at best, get standing room only, or take a Norwegian businessman's dilapidated and rusty ship, due to sail in two days? Both ways are equally expensive, but the Norwegian ship promises more comfort. Finally, because of the pressure of time, we decide to take the plane.

We find lodgings for the night. The only functioning hotel in Űŕǵüllpoḷ-New Bystrica is filled with journalists. They tell us to go to the bar next door and ask for lodgings. In a smoky room there are about eight men. They're all Slovak. When we ask about lodgings, one gets up and indicates that we should follow him. He gets into a luxury SUV with a broken window and the engine running, so he does not have to connect any wires under the instrument panel, and motions to us to get in. He evidently comes from Carpathian Slovakia and he came to Junja looking for adventure and big money. When he found out that we had talked to Telgarth himself, he can't believe it. At the hotel it takes him some time to find the keys to his room. He vainly searches for a light switch. In the end he can't find the main power switch, so we spend the evening in his new hotel in the dark. But the room is free. Karol, as the new hotelier introduced himself, would not take money from Telgarth's friends.

The morning plane is packed. Passengers stand in the aisles between the seats. On the flight we find that we have left Junja just in time. The aircraft's Russian crew has decided to stay in Russia with the plane and not to return to Űŕǵüllpoḷ-New Bystrica. Right in the cockpit they organize a little party to celebrate their final home trip. One pilot then comes out to molest the female passengers. A female journalist, the New York Herald Tribune *reporter, takes his fancy so much that he invites her into the cockpit while over the ocean, to witness the landing manœuvre. The naïve American agrees. What happens behind the closed cockpit door we can only guess. We get into a tailspin a few times, but all ends well. At noon our An-24's wheels touch down on Polyarny airport runway.*

Two days after we landed in Polyarny, Slovak guerrillas commanded by Telgarth moved by rail to the other end of the island and attacked Ćmirçăpoḷ. They mortared the airport and adjacent buildings. Mercenary units repelled them from the city and forced them to take refuge in the inhospitable tundra. Another chapter of the Junjan conflict is over.

What will the future bring?

Urban is completely stunned. For a fraction of a second it seems to him that this evil Telgarth, the uncompromising avenging angel, cannot possibly be Freddy Piggybank, "his" Freddy. He studies the photograph closely for a long time: Freddy, or Telgarth, sits there at his desk, his bleary single eye looking at the camera. That single eye perplexes Urban. Freddy never had any eye trouble. And Telgarth's figure, stocky but not fat, is very different from Freddy's. On the other hand, Telgarth's facial features and his rather theatrical speech suggest Freddy. Finally, Urban overcomes all his doubts and is certain: Telgarth *is* Freddy!

He nervously gets up from the desk: he needs a drink. In Freddy's shabby globe bar only the half-empty bottle of Cointreau takes his fancy. Urban is glad. He opens the fridge in the hall to see if there's any ice. There is. He reads the article again and again, and downs the contents of the bottle of tasty distillate in three swigs.

If all this is true, then what is there to stop Urban, except for his unadventurous nature, from flying to Junja and explaining to Freddy the situation he's in and either persuading him to agree in writing to the sale of Urban's share of *Freddy Vision*, or even to buy it, possibly?

* * *

The road to Junja leads, alas, through Russia. There's not much to describe. We all know what it looks like. When Video-Urban arrives in Polyarny in northern Russia, he finds his assumptions were far too optimistic. The Junjan archipelago is as good as cut off from the rest of the world: there's no scheduled connection. Only Russian polar pilots sometimes risk their necks to make money taking food and alcohol to Junja. The profits are big, but on landing in Ürgüllpoļ, there's a serious danger of one side confusing them with the enemy and shooting them down.

"I don't give a fuck," a Russian in a pilot's cap waves his hand, after Urban starts talking to him in the airport bar, housed in a derelict trailer, where you can only get charcoal-filtered vodka or stale Petersburg beer. "Who'd want to live for ever? Either I live and get rich, or I go to the devil's mother, fuck it all."

Urban buys him a few vodkas and a bottle of coke for himself. It's a glass bottle, something he hasn't seen for years. The metal cap is rusty, but the coke is still all right.

"Hey, you, Czech brother," smiles Kostya. "I'll take you to Junja and you'll travel like an American president with me. You'll sit alone in the cabin, drink vodka, and look out of the window. Everyone knows Kostya and his aeroplane. They won't shoot Kostya down, not the Junjans, or the Slovaks."

"And how much do you want for that?" Urban enquires.

"So you're one of those?" Kostya squints at him sternly through his pilot's goggles. "A man offers you his heart on a plate, wants to help you and you ask how much? So, this is what Czechs are like: always the same. They measure everything in money. They don't even talk to you, they don't kiss you twice properly, and they only ask 'how much'. What can I say? Give me a thousand bucks and wait for me here at ten."

Kostya points out of the window.

"That's our plane," he says. "Oh my dear little grey dove, how many flights we've flown together over the taiga."

The old An-2 biplane is dark green, but Urban gladly overlooks Kostya's vagueness. He is more shocked by the price. In the end he gets it down from a thousand to seven hundred dollars.

"But cash in advance," Kostya says hastily, and his eyes rest hungrily on the rough greenish bottles of vodka above the bar.

"I'm used to paying only at pay time," Urban objects.

"And what about airport fees?" Kostya rounds on him. "And fuel? If you want to fly tomorrow, I have to get the aircraft ready right away, so nothing goes wrong. It's a question of trust, Urban Urbanovich."

Urban Urbanovich sighs, opens his wallet and counts into Kostya's proffered hand seven one hundred-dollar notes.

"So, tomorrow at ten," he takes leave of the pilot and goes to get some sleep in the caravan site hotel *Zarya*.

The next day he packs what little he's brought and at ten he is at the airport. Some men are lurking round Kostya's plane, loading something into it. Urban looks closer: mailbags.

He approaches the plane and clears his throat.

"What is it, mate?" asks one of the loaders. "What are you looking at?"

"Excuse me, please," Urban hesitates. "But do you know where Kostya is? We were supposed to meet here at ten."

"What Kostya?" a man with a stern moustached face seems puzzled. He looks like Stalin's grandson.

"Well, Kostya," says Urban. "The pilot of this plane."

"I happen to be the pilot of this plane," says the man and jumps down from the ladder. "I don't know any pilot named Kostya."

Urban turns pale.

"Yesterday, over there, in the bar, I met a pilot," he says with a lump in his throat. "He asked seven hundred dollars to take me to Ürġüllpoḷ in this plane. I paid him and now I'm waiting for him."

The pilot looks at his colleague and shakes his head.

"You fell for it, mate," he laughs. "Oh, how you fell for it! But how could you be so stupid?"

"Don't you have eyes to see?" asked the second man.

"This plane is too small; how could it fly to Junja? It would crash in the middle of the ocean without fuel. God, you're stupid, brother!"

"And what did that Kostya look like?" asks Stalin's grandson.

"About this tall," Urban gestures. "In a leather pilot's cap."

"A leather pilot's cap?" the other man shouts. "That was Konstantin Trifonovich. A geologist, a doctor of science! Yes, the geologists were here with their samples. We're taking them now to St Petersburg with the mail. Oh, so you were conned by Konstantin Trifonovich?"

The men stop loading the mailbags. They laugh so hard that they bend double. When Stalin's grandson notices Urban not laughing with them, he is abashed and becomes serious.

"Konstantin Trifonovich is a member of the Academy of Sciences," he says. "He's a famous scientist. At least in the airport bar."

They both break out laughing again.

"His only problem is that he's a boozer," says Stalin's grandson. "But he's got his wits about him, the son of a bitch! He's always conning someone. He said he was a pilot!"

Despite their fits of laughter, Urban remains grave. He has nothing to laugh about.

"And where can I find him now?" he asks formally.

"Try to find the wind in the tundra!" says the second man. "They all left at five in the morning in a launch."

"Look," says Stalin's grandson. "My plane can't make it to Junja. You need a bigger machine for that. A plane like a Lisunov, a Yak, or a Douglas. With extra fuel tanks to make it across the ocean. This is not a one-hour flight, mate. And no one will take you there for seven hundred bucks. If you need to get to Junja, you pay for it. No ordinary tourist goes to Junja now. But look, I know all the pilots this side of the Kola peninsula. I can find you one who might be willing to take you to Junja. Where are you staying?"

"Hotel Zarya," says Urban.

"Right, I'll leave you a note to tell you who to look for," says Stalin's grandson. "But it's your baby afterwards."

"And what do you want for it?" Urban asks distrustfully.

"Nothing," says Stalin's grandson. "I'll get my percentage from what you pay the pilot. Don't you worry about me, matie. And I hope you find what you're looking for in Junja."

Stalin's grandson raises his eyebrows meaningfully, gets into the cabin and starts the engine. From the exhaust comes thick smoke, the propeller begins to turn. A second man bangs the cargo door shut and sits next to the pilot. The aircraft begins to move, rolls out onto the runway and is soon a mere dot in a clear sky.

* * *

Telgarth gets straight down to his meticulous macro-political and community work. He is grateful to the guerrillas for making him supreme commander of Űŕġüllpol—New Bystrica, because New Bystrica is only his first aim, the first conquered fortress. It is a microcosm, a laboratory crucible in which he can try everything out in miniature before doing the same for the whole country. Yes, Telgarth sees himself as the whole archipelago's future leader. So far he's made no mistakes in pursuing this aim; anyway, the local Slovaks have no one else like him.

All ethnic Junjans have to wear a white ribbon on their arms and to work all day clearing the ruins. They live together in the city market hall. Their flats have been requisitioned and given to Slovak families who were previously forced to live in shanty towns.

After the conquest of the city, Czech submarines anchor right in the city harbour to unload their cargo. Likewise, Czech transport planes begin to land at New Bystrica airport. Besides crates of humanitarian aid, the Czech aeroplanes also bring journalists, military instructors and observers. Telgarth has polite relations with them, but he is not overly friendly. For the time being he keeps to himself his negative attitude to the Czech plan to restore Czechoslovakia. The railways are in Slovak hands. Part of the humanitarian aid stays in New Bystrica; the rest goes by rail up north, where savage fighting is raging. Young Slovak commanders then fly in Czech planes back to Bohemia to take an intensive commander course; others take a course in sabotage and explosives. That, too, is a part of Czech humanitarian aid. Telgarth now limits it after seeing young commanders returning from Bohemia full of harmful Czechoslovak ideas.

Telgarth is seriously ambitious for power. Each day he devotes half an hour of his time to journalists from all over the world. Improvised press conferences are held in his office. He feeds journalists fresh news from the battlefield. If he has none, he makes it up. He answers their questions, even what the journalists consider unpleasant ones — on human rights, treatment of prisoners, and discrimination against ethnic

Junjans. Telgarth responds with a smile, but radically. It's a question not of cosmetic changes, but of a huge national movement. Slovaks will get their rights and there's no power on earth to stop them. The Russians? They have nothing to eat. NATO? They have their own problems. UN? They're happy if they can take a piss without too much pain. And so on.

Work on outlining the shape of the future Slovak state consumes Telgarth so much that he sleeps at most four hours a day. He sleeps in his office on a stark military bed. He eats modestly; every day he opens a tin of Czech humanitarian aid. His only hobby is hunting in the tundra outside the city limits.

Nests of Junjan resistance in New Bystrica are successfully suppressed. Soon the time seems near when no one will have to be coiled up.

One day, as Telgarth together with three armed men in a *Pobeda* car are on their way back to the city from a hunting trip, he is stopped in the suburbs of New Bystrica by a unit of armed men. It's immediately obvious that they are Junjan mercenaries. Telgarth's driver tries to reverse quickly and get clear, but a well-aimed bullet kills him. Telgarth and his two guerrillas run out of the car. Both guerrillas are shot down by bursts of submachine fire. It seems to be a well-laid trap. The mercenaries know only too well who has fallen into their hands.

Telgarth is swooning. Horror makes his forehead break out in cold sweat. For a fragment of a second he wishes this were a dream: he wants to wake up in his cosy office at the main railway station. Alas, this is no dream. There is no point thinking. Telgarth pulls out his pistol, but before he can turn it on himself and pull the trigger, the armed men throw themselves at him, handcuff him and knock him out with a well-aimed blow to the back of his head.

When he comes to, he is lying, trussed like a rolled ham, in someone's flat.

"He's awake!" an armed man guarding him shouts in Russian to the others in the flat.

Soon two mercenaries show up. The older one, probably a commander, is smiling.

"Well, well," he says in Russian. "So we've got you, One-eye. You know we've been waiting for you for days, planning for it. You didn't expect that, right? The great Telgarth himself, the commander of Ürġüllpoḷ: and now you're nothing. You're a piece of shit. And now we'll give you a taste of what you give our people. We'll tie you into a coil, too, and see how you like it."

Telgarth turns pale. They can't be serious.

"Release me right away!" he says in broken schoolboy Russian. "I promise that none of you will be hurt. I'll say nothing to anyone."

The mercenaries laugh.

"If you don't let me go, I'll be freed by my own men soon," says Telgarth. "And then you'll be harshly punished. Just consider the situation. You're almost defeated. There are more of us. Be sensible. We can always do a deal."

"So now you want to do a deal?" snaps the mercenary commander. "And why wouldn't you do a deal with our friends when you coiled them up and used them to perfect your shooting skills? Now you're in trouble, you want to do a deal. You're doing no deals with us. We want nothing from you. We only want you to croak, but as slowly as possible."

"They'll avenge me," says Telgarth darkly. "Oh, their vengeance will be terrible."

"They won't," says the commander of the mercenaries. "They'll be happy to escape with their skins intact. The attack is planned for today. They're already fighting in the streets. Can't you hear?"

Telgarth tries to listen. Yes, from a distance comes the sound of muffled shots and explosions.

"Úŕġüllpoḷ is surrounded and nobody will help you," laughs the mercenary. "The Czechs took off like rabbits the moment the shooting began. By air and submarine. The harbour and the airport are deserted. Well, where are your allies? Only the journalists are left in the city. And you'll croak here slowly, in agony, alone and abandoned."

Telgarth is quiet. Icy horror slowly permeates his soul. He'd like to say something, but he can't control the twitch in his mouth.

Soon they mercilessly and brutally coil him up. The pain in his spine and abdominal muscles takes his breath away and stops him breathing properly. A long time ago he experienced this fear in *Rivers of Babylon 2*, when he was in early puberty and girls in an enemy gang caught him, tied him up and whipped him with stinging nettles. He even felt a strange pleasure then. But there are no girls here, only mercenaries armed to the teeth, stinking of tobacco. No pleasure is coming, only deadly horror.

Soon it's unbearable. Telgarth begins to moan aloud and plead. The mercenary commander comes in.

"So how are we doing?" he asks ironically. "Look at the coward! He's even pissed himself with fear. It's not that pleasant, is it? To pass the time before you die, try to count how many of our men you finished off this way. Put a gag in his trap, his squealing annoys me!"

He is about to leave the room.

"Hey, listen," Telgarth shouts behind him with his last bit of energy, drenched in mortal sweat. "Let me say a word."

The commander stops. With a gesture of his hand he stops the mercenaries about to gag Telgarth with sticky tape.

"Well, what do you want to say?" he asks.

Freddy weeps. Big tears fall from his eyes; his face is wrinkled like a statue of the Buddha.

"I've always basically admired you," he says in tears. "I wanted to switch to your side a long time ago. And you've done this to me…"

The mercenary commander looks at him with contempt.

"Yes," says Freddy. "I really want to join you and fight the Slovaks. Untie me quick, so I can join the fighting. I'll show you how I can fight."

"Shut his trap," says the mercenary commander on his way out. "Before I throw up."

"Just a moment!" Freddy shouts desperately. "I know how to help you in a big way. I know a secret that will help you defeat the rebels. If you untie me, I'll tell you."

"First tell us," says the commander. "Then we might untie you."

"No, first untie me!" Freddy insists.

"Shut him up!" orders the commander.

And despite his noisy protests, Freddy is silenced.

He closes his eye. He tries to think of something else, but his mind keeps reverting to his painfully stretched tendons, dislocated joints and pinched nerves that he now feels like white-hot light bulb filaments in his body. Time has stopped and no longer moves.

"What will I die of?" Freddy wonders. A man who is shot dies because his heart stops, or because he bleeds to death; a hanged man dies because he suffocates, a beheaded man dies because his spinal cord is cut. But what will he die of? If it were of pain, then he should have by now at least lost consciousness. But he's still aware of everything round him. If anything, he is even more sensitive than ever.

Only cold water brings him back from his swoon. They've brought him round by drenching him with a bucket of water.

"No sleeping," says the mercenary commander. "I want you to enjoy it, like all the men you disposed of this way. You wanted to tell me something?"

At the commander's signal, an armed mercenary rips the tape off Freddy's mouth. "You were saying something about some secret that might make our victory over the rebels easier?"

"First, untie me," moans Freddy.

"We will, we will," agrees the commander. "We'll even give you a rifle and we'll fight the rebels together, as you wanted. But first, talk!"

"But will you really accept me?" Freddy asks sceptically.

The commander looks at his armed men. They all nod their heads.

"Of course we will," says the commander. "We need every real fighter as much as we need salt."

"Apart from the propaganda effect," says Freddy, "you've no idea of the devastating impact my changing sides will have on rebel morale."

"Yes, that will be the transfer of the season," agrees the commander. "And now the secret."

"All right, then," says Freddy and licks his dry lips. "Listen: I know where the rebels hide their women and children. If you go there and take them hostage, the rebels may surrender, or they may not, but in any case, you'll have hit them very hard."

"That sounds interesting," says the mercenary leader, draws up a chair and straddles it. "So where are they hiding?"

"In the tundra," says Freddy, "on the pastures of a reindeer herder Kresan, a Slovak."

"Have you been there?" the commander asks.

"No, never," says Freddy. "But the men have been talking about it a lot. I know exactly where it is."

"Where does this Kresan live?" asks the commander.

"His pastures are some five hundred kilometres inland from a hill the Slovaks call Stormy Tooth," says Freddy. "Kresan is not only sheltering the rebel leaders' families, but he also stores the cargo from the Czech submarines. He knows all the signals for the submarines. If you put pressure on him, you could learn the signals and catch at least some submarine crew members in the act."

"So, his name's Kresan, you say?" the mercenary commander nods. "Well, we'll take a closer look at this Kresan of yours. Thanks for the information."

"By the way," says Freddy, "they say the Slovak guerrillas' wives and the older daughters are really good looking, at least so they say. We could have some fun with them before we torture them all and kill them."

Freddy cackles frivolously and voluptuously, as far as the pain in his stretched tendons allows him.

"Well," agrees the mercenary commander of the mercenaries, "we'll certainly have some fun with them. *Spasibo*, thanks for the tip. But not you, Telgarth. You know, I've changed my mind. You'd betray us, just as you've betrayed your friends without batting an eyelid, just to save your pathetic life. We don't need people like you. Now you just croak here in silence."

"At least shoot me!" Freddy begs. The soldiers burst out laughing.

"It'd be a waste of ammunition," says the commander. "You'll croak on your own, anyway. Now stuff his big mouth shut."

Freddy again loses his consciousness from pain and despair. You can't call it merciful unconsciousness. That's only a literary phrase. Writers often imagine that unconsciousness is something like sleep or anæsthesia, when a person can't feel anything. This is not the case. It is more a semi-conscious state, when a person has no control over his limbs, still feels pain, hallucinates and can't distinguish hallucination from reality. And so it was with Freddy. His laboured breathing is coming to an end, his entire body is in pain, and he longs only for a quick death. But death is in no hurry.

* * *

Video Urban had to endure a long and boring wait, as he did a few days before. He mostly slept through them in his room in hotel Zarya, his head turned to the plastic wall. His situation filled him with despair. Seven hundred dollars have gone, and he's still in Polyarny.

He's made a habit of taking long walks in the town. He watched fishermen catching fish in the Kola river's wide estuary. He bought a fishing rod in a tackle shop, together with hooks, landing net and other accessories. He never caught a fish, and was sure that he must look ridiculous. He didn't even know how to throw the rod and bait. So he now avoided other fishermen and searched for deserted places. He never caught anything, but that was not the point anyway. All his ideas went through his head, leaving no trace. Only now and again, at moments of extreme visualisation, he was amazed by his weird life. Just a few weeks ago he sat at a desk in a stinking Bratislava office and longed to be sitting in a Prague pub or having sex with his cousin Tina. And now he's sitting at the northernmost point of Russia, fishing in the Barents Sea.

Five days pass. One day, when he gets back from fishing, the woman concierge tells him that someone from the airport has phoned him. They said they had another aircraft for him. Urban thanks her. He goes to the airport. Stalin's grandson turns out not to have forgotten him. In the bar two men are waiting for him: stout, with weather-beaten faces, dressed in camouflage outfits bought from a discount store. Urban joins them. The men have a modified Il-14. The aircraft has Arctic modifications to adapt it for longer flights. They agree to take Urban and transport him safe and sound to Junja, perhaps directly to Űŕġűllpoḷ.

"But if we find they're fighting again over there, then we'll land outside the city, on the plain," the chief pilot warns him.

Urban is glad that they don't want money up front.

"Not until the plane touches down on Junjan soil," says the co-pilot.

So Urban packs his things in the evening, and the next day at six in the morning comes with his backpack, bag and fishing rod to the airport. This time it's for real. The plane is ready, its engines running.

The cargo space is full of boxes of consumer goods: cigarettes, tins, and bottles of vodka. How nice of them to smuggle all this using Urban's money, he thinks.

"Make yourself comfortable, Urban Urbanych," the co-pilot says and points to a bench under the windows. "Don't move the boxes during the flight, as it's balanced, more or less. Better sleep."

Before the pilot draws the curtain dividing the cargo space from the pilot's cabin, Urban catches sight of a crate of vodka. Soon the smelly, nicotine-stained curtain parts to reveal the co-pilot's red face.

"Come and drink to a successful flight, Urban Urbanych!"

Urban doesn't mind. At least it'll help him get over his fear. He has never flown like this. The pilots drink a toast with him. After the first bottle they open another.

"And what brings you to Junja, Urban Urbanych?" the co-pilot asks.

Between two glasses each holding two hundred grammes of vodka, Urban briefly explains to the two Russians who he is, what his relationship to Freddy is, and what he has to sort out in Junja.

"Oh, you've chosen a bad time to visit your friend, Urban Urbanych," the captain shakes his head.

He has now managed to take off. Urban is sitting at a little table, in a place for the absent flight engineer, with a full glass of vodka in his hand, following a steep take-off manœuvre. He becomes a bit nervous.

"Who's going to pilot the plane?" he asks when he sees the second half litre of Stolichnaya vanishing.

"Don't worry," says the plane's captain. "One of us is on duty and doesn't drink."

But there's no such person on board. The flight proceeds normally. By the time the plane's at cruising altitude, heading for Junja, both pilots are drunk. They switch to autopilot, set their alarm clock and fall asleep.

Urban is sitting behind them, watching their regular breathing and the joysticks moving synchronously and seemingly chaotically now right, now left. He clenches his teeth and finishes his glass of vodka. His throat tightens, not knowing whether to swallow or spew out the vodka. He is goggle-eyed and keeps half a glass of vodka in his mouth for a long time. Finally, using all his willpower, he swallows it. Immediately, he feels like vomiting. He overcomes this feeling and finishes the rest of vodka in the third bottle. He blanks out for a moment. With a last ounce of energy, he stumbles back and stretches out on a bench covered by slashed leatherette. He falls asleep instantly.

They wake him when the archipelago is in sight.

"Bad news, Urban Urbanych," says the captain. "Úŕġüllpoļ has been taken. Junjan units are there again. They've occupied the airport, too."

"What does that mean?" Urban does not understand.

"For me and Vanya, nothing," says the captain. "Everyone will be glad to see us and our goods. But for you, as a Czech, it means that if you fall into their hands, they'll shoot you like a dog. You Czechs are working against the Junjan government, aiding terrorists. We can't land in Úŕġüllpoļ with you, pal. They'd even punish us because of you."

From behind captain's shoulder, a red face peeks out. It's Vanya the co-pilot, holding a dirty backpack. When Urban takes a closer look, he sees that it's a parachute. Urban is clear what the two are thinking about.

"I'm not a Czech, but a Slovak," says Urban and shows the co-pilot his passport. "My government supports the Junjans."

For the first time in his life, Urban is happy to have such a far-sighted government.

"A Slovak?" the captain shouts.

Both Russians' faces express almost mortal horror.

"Oh my God," says the captain. "If Junjans get you, they'll torture you to death!"

"But I'm not a bad Slovak from Junja," argues Urban. "I'm a good Slovak from Europe. The Slovak Republic doesn't recognize the rebels."

"You can't get that over to them," says the co-pilot. "Look, the captain and I are educated people, literate people. We graduated from institutes. Yet we don't know who the hell you are. Do you think that stupid Junjans will care?"

"They won't ask questions," the captain joins in. "Are you Czech? We'll hang you, because you support the rebels. Are you Slovak? We'll hang you, because you're a rebel. And what's worse, they'll hang us along with you, because we're your companions."

"Don't make it hard for us, Urban Urbanych," says the co-pilot with a pleading voice and shakes the parachute. "We'll drop you off somewhere in the tundra where the guerrillas will find you. And if you are, as you say, a friend of that Telgarth of theirs, nothing can happen to you. We're honest people, civilised people. Look, we don't even want your money. Keep your bucks! We brought you here completely free, that's how nice we are to you. Just put this thing on, for God's sake, and we'll push you out of the plane ourselves. We're flying low; the parachute will open by itself. It'll be like landing in your bed."

"We simply can't land in Ůřǧüllpoļ with you," the captain adds categorically. "We're businessmen, not heroes."

They hurl themselves at Urban and force the parachute on him. Urban in a panic fights back like a lion. In the heat of battle, he pushes both pilots against a crate. All the crates fall down. The automatic pilot can't recover from such a loss of equilibrium. The plane is in a tailspin.

Vanya lets Urban go and fights his way through the crates to the cockpit. The captain is wrestling with Urban on his own. Urban almost seems to be succeeding in staving off the humiliating drop, when someone hits him over the head from behind. He sees stars in his eyes and then there's only darkness.

When he recovers consciousness, he is lying in the snow and someone is slowly pulling him from behind. He looks round. Nobody is pulling him, it's just the wind blowing into his half-collapsed parachute and pulling the strings. In the distance there are echoes of the muffled noise of the plane. Urban gets up and unbuckles the parachute. He finds his wallet and counts his money. The Russians kept their word: they took him to Junja and didn't take a single penny from him. He even gradually finds his backpack, bag, and even the bag of fishing tackle that the Russians threw behind him in the snow. God, such honest people, Urban thinks. You'll have a hard time surviving, pals!

Urban collects all his modest possessions and with heavy heart sets out across the snowy plain. On the way he encounters the fog. Urban is walking down hill. The snow line ends, but Urban has no idea where he's going. For three days he keeps wandering among mountain pines and has no idea if he is going north, or south. He periodically climbs a tree, locates another tree in the fog and sets out towards it. He uses all the food he brought along in Polyarny. He drinks clear and cold water from a stream. He tries again to catch fish, but again with no luck. He chews on roots and gathers berries. He is afraid of wolves, but doesn't see any. He is wet to the skin. At night he sleeps in trees.

After three days he gets to a railway track. He can't believe his eyes. The rails have a shiny surface, evidence of regular train traffic. Urban collects dry twigs from all around and piles it on top of the track. It takes him a whole day. Exhausted, he lies in the low grass and chews on the roots that he has dug out somewhere. That's it. He's not moving from here. He will either die, or wait for rescue here.

* * *

On their eighth journey, returning from Junja, at one thirty in the morning the *Kamýk* radar operator identifies a vessel on his screen coming towards them at almost 33 knots. Only a warship can be that fast.

Kubeš orders a dive to periscope depth.

"What's the status of battery charging, Mr Kolesa?" he asks, observing the surroundings through the periscope.

"We've charged only half of them," reports Lt. Commander Kolesa.

"Oh, well," sighs Kubeš. "It'll have to do. Dive to 100 metres."

The boat dives rapidly.

"One hundred metres," says Kolesa. "The boat is steady."

"Turn off the engine," commands Kubeš. "Leading Rating Anděl, analyse the sound of the vessel."

In the sudden silence a weak buzz, gradually getting stronger, can be heard coming from the surface.

Anděl, the electronic systems operator, loads the sound into the computer and then runs it through a programme that analyses it.

"It's the sound of a Russian *Sovremenny* class anti-submarine destroyer, sir," he soon reports.

"Fancy that," says Kubeš. "Here we go, gentlemen. We've been noticed at last. About time, after eight trips by the *Kamýk* and six by the *Albatross*."

"Ping," the sound echoes.

The men are startled.

"Asdic," says Kubeš. "Anti-submarine detector. You all know it from Lešany, so please don't look so surprised."

"Ping," the sound is back.

Then there is silence.

"Ping," it goes again. "Ping…ping…ping."

Silence.

Then they hear a sound as if someone had thrown a fistful of pebbles at the boat's hull.

"The submarine is within the destroyer's search cone," reports Anděl.

"Good," Kubeš can't help saying.

He issues several orders to the helmsmen. He is trying to position the submarine with its back to the destroyer, to hinder the search. But the submarine's speed is low now, so it does not react to the rudder turning.

"The destroyer is heading towards us," Anděl notes.

"Let him," says Kubeš.

"Its position is 120 degrees, and approaching quickly," adds Anděl.

"No problem," says Kubeš.

In his mind he is calculating his own course, the enemy's, the evasive manœuvre; if he miscalculates, the submarine will sail into the charges. The men realise that and stay silent.

"Sharp right, left engine full speed ahead," says the commander.

The noise of the destroyer's screws gets louder. It is approaching the submarine. Suddenly the destroyer is directly above them. Its fast turning screws make an awful noise.

There are two thunderous explosions, much more powerful: the lights in the submarine go out. Battery powered lights come on.

"Water leaking through the water metre glass," reports the chief engineer.

"Seal it," orders Kubeš.

"The destroyer is leaving," says Anděl.

There is silence.

Only a stream of water entering the submarine through the water metre's cracked glass hisses, now in a high, now in a low pitch.

The destroyer stops. They can't hear it, but they are all clear that it's searching for them.

There is a long silence.

"Maybe they've lost us," says Skopšík.

"Ping," they hear again.

After a few seconds, again.

Then the pauses in which the searching cone misses the submarine become shorter and the little stones again drum on the hull.

"He's lost us and found us," says Kubeš.

The ship's screws begin to turn; the turns get faster, closer and louder.

The men on the *Kamýk* can hear everything: the destroyer passing above them and quickly taking off at full speed to stop it being damaged by its own charges.

This time the Russians set the depth charges for greater depth and all ten explosions therefore go off above the submarine, pushing it still deeper.

The commander points an electric torch at the depth gauge. They are one hundred and eighty metres deep.

The destroyer sails away.

When it stops, Kolesa asks: "Should we empty the chambers, sir?"

"No," says Kubeš.

"The submarine is sinking, sir," says Kolesa.

"I can see that, too," says Kubeš. "Is the main pump mended?"

"We can't see well enough to repair it, sir," someone answers from his post at the main ballast tank.

"Turn the emergency light on, then," orders Kubeš.

"The depth is 250 metres," says Kolesa.

The hull of the submarine makes a cracking noise. Then comes the sound of scraping, as if a strong steel cable were being dragged against its hull. The submarine has reached the limit of its stress resistance.

The emergency light is on in the command centre.

"I've had enough of this," says Kubeš. "Do you think, Mr Kolesa, that you've programmed the chips on the Stingers properly?"

"I guarantee it, sir," says Kolesa and there is a hint in his voice of devilish joy and excitement.

The destroyer sets out for a third attack. This time the charges explode quite far from the boat.

"Perhaps they've lost us," says Skopšík.

The reply is a familiar ping and the sound of pebbles hurled at the hull.

"This is how I see it, gentlemen," says Kubeš and puts his foot on a crate of spare parts. "Mr Kolesa will change into his neoprene suit and take oxygen tanks with him. He will prepare one missile. We're going to surface now. As soon as the pressure is equalised, Mr Kolesa will climb the bridge, tie himself to the bridge and fire a Stinger at the Russians. We'll then dive fifty metres. If one missile doesn't do the job, I'll have another one ready."

"But why you, sir?" asks Kolesa. "It's enough if someone passes the second missile to me when I re-surface."

"They won't pass it to you, Kolesa," says Kubeš, "because you'll stay under. Don't forget about pressure sickness. You can't surface in a few seconds from a depth of fifty metres."

"Well, I suppose you can't," says Kolesa. "But there's another option."

"Which is?" the commander enquires.

"For me to climb up with two missiles and if I miss with the first, I'll use the second," says Kolesa. "But, of course, the submarine would have to stay surfaced a few seconds longer."

"Fine, we'll take your suggestion," decides the commander. "Go and change and prepare two missiles."

"The destroyer is waiting but not moving," reports Anděl, his earphones on. "They're looking for us."

"They're looking, looking, and have no idea of the fate we're preparing for them," says Kubeš. "Senior helmsman! Prepare secret documents for destruction."

"Yes, sir," says Sub-Lieutenant Petrovič.

"Mr Mikuš, we're going up," Kubeš tells the second senior engineer, when Kolesa appears in the command centre in a neoprene suit with scuba diving equipment, an anti-aircraft Stinger missile in each hand.

"Empty all tanks simultaneously," says Kubeš. "Equalise the buoyancy in time. And you, Kolesa, don't forget to tie yourself to the bridge. Make sure to aim well, because if you miss, the next depth charge bombardment will tear you to pieces outside a pressurised submarine."

"I'm rather aware of that, sir," smiles Kolesa and climbs up.

"Someone help him with those missiles," the commander says. "When he gets to the bridge, hand them to him fast, and close the hatch."

The submarine rises towards the surface.

"Surface to periscope depth," Kubeš says impatiently.

"We've reached periscope depth, sir," says Mikuš.

The periscope slides from its bed; Kubeš observes the surroundings.

"Yes," he says. "They're some 200 metres away, 120 degrees. Mr Kolesa, he's aft of us, across. It's a nice target. Let's do it. Good luck, Rudolf."

Kolesa notes that the commander has called him by his first name for the first time, but has no time to reflect on it.

"The submarine has surfaced," reports Lieutenant Mikuš. "Pressure is equalised."

Kolesa climbs to the bridge. The surfacing of a mysterious submarine stirs the Russian destroyer to busy activity on board.

"They seem about to launch a boat," Kolesa reports to those below.

Besr and Zapletal quickly pass him the two Stingers and close the hatch. Kolesa ties himself to the bridge and squats down. He puts the first firing mechanism on his right shoulder. He pulls down the visor and turns on the targeting module. He prays that his slight software change to the targeting regime will work.

He raises himself enough to put the optics of the targeting module above the bow of the bridge. The targeting lozenge roams the field of vision and when it crosses the image of the destroyer, it stops and begins to flash. Kolesa raises himself, takes a breath and fires the missile. In fascination he watches the Stinger fly out of the tube, cover a few metres and, at a safe distance from the firing tube, ignite the rocket engine and disappear in a flash: there is a fire and explosion on the distant destroyer. Bits of metal, displaced by the explosion, fall in the water.

Kolesa throws away the empty firing device, arms a new one, cursing the slow sighting lozenge, takes aim and fires the second missile.

"Let's go down!" he shouts down the speaking tube and locks it.

He does not wait to see the outcome, puts on his mask and takes the scuba mouthpiece in his mouth, and then holds onto the bridge rails.

The submarine seems to dive forever. But Kubeš ordered all the tanks to be flooded and started both engines even before the second missile hit.

The way down to a depth of fifty metres is for Kolesa like a horrific journey down a roller coaster. When the submarine stabilises at its right depth, horrible sounds are heard: the sound of the damaged and sinking destroyer's partitions cracking. Kolesa thinks that the second missile must have hit their ammunition or missile stores.

Even at a depth of fifty metres, the light of a giant fire on the surface illuminates the water. Lt Commander Kolesa can now see all the way to the surface: burning fuel spreading round the destroyer in widening circles, lighting up a whole column of water. In the transparent water round Kolesa move bizarre shadows. If he hadn't had a mouthpiece, he would have shouted with joy. He grabs the firing tube and bangs it with all his strength against the metal cover of the bridge.

Around him are long columns of pressurized air bubbles.

They're clearing the tanks and surfacing, Kolesa thinks. He unties himself from the rails and with powerful kicks of his flippers swims away from the *Kamýk*. He sees the submarine's giant dark shadow majestically rising. He realizes that others will see the result of his work before him. He sighs, if sighing is possible at fifty metres under water, and then also begins a controlled surfacing, keeping his eyes on the depth gauge.

It is hell up above. The Russian destroyer has broken in half and is sinking quickly. The sea around has turned into a fiery inferno which puts survival out of the question for anyone overboard.

The deck of the *Kamýk* is now crowded by men following this extraordinary event through their binoculars.

"I've never seen anything like it," says senior bosun Schäffer.

"We'll wait for Kolesa, then we're off," says the captain. "Everyone down except for those on duty. Officers may stay on the bridge."

The sailors obey the command with quiet muttering.

Silence reigns on the bridge, broken occasionally by explosions from around the sinking destroyer.

"Commodore, sir. May I have permission to give my opinion?" asks Lt Commander Ondriáš, the medical doctor.

"I'm listening, doctor," says Kubeš, watching the fire.

"In my opinion, this was a mistake," says Dr. Ondriáš.

"Oh, really?" Kubeš is intrigued.

"Yes," says Dr. Ondriáš with resolve. "After all, we could have got away without a fight."

"What fight are you talking about, doctor?" the captain asks. "There was no fight. The Russians were annoying, so they paid for it."

"Well, exactly," says Dr. Ondriáš. "They thought we were surrendering. They were already lowering a boat. What if they managed to report our coordinates?"

"Those will soon change, doctor," says the captain. "Next time, please, don't criticize your commander's military decisions. Better get the medical station ready to check Commander Kolesa over. I'd like to know if he's all right after that superhuman effort. You can leave."

Dr. Ondriáš climbs down. Kubeš turns to Kraus.

"And what do you think, Commander Kraus," he asks in a menacing tone. "What do you want to tell me?"

"Just one thing, sir: how many re-programmed Stingers do we still have?" asks the second warrant officer with a smile.

Finally Kolesa surfaces, blowing a column of water from his air pipe.

"Deck guard, launch a boat," orders Kubeš.

Kolesa is soon fished out and taken into the submarine.

"Put the boat in the cargo hold and let's go below deck," says Kubeš. "We need to get out of here."

Kolesa watches in fascination the remnants of burning fuel and the mighty vortex on the spot where only recently a destroyer stood.

"They'll be after us now," he tells himself.

"Get in, Mr Kolesa," says the captain. "You're shivering with cold. Report to Dr. Ondriáš, I want you to have a full check-up."

A chunk of sea rises with a muffled noise and then settles back. The submarine shudders.

"Shit, what was that?" Kraus says in alarm.

"That was the explosion of the depth charges they'd already set to our depth, but hadn't managed to launch or lock, Mr Kraus," says Kubeš. "At the set depth they exploded, and so did the locked ones."

The men climb down to the command centre.

"Dive to snorkel level, release the radar antenna: I want to see two men on radar duty. Full speed ahead, course 200!" says Kubeš. "Prague's ahead of us, gentlemen!"

* * *

Telgarth regains consciousness when a shot is fired in the room. He blearily turns round. Someone is releasing him from his bonds. Telgarth straightens out, moaning. His tendons, stretched to the limit and inflamed, now react to being relaxed. Telgarth comes to completely. Geľo is bending over him.

"It's all right now," he tells him.

"Geľo," whispers Telgarth. "Is that you?"

"Can you walk?" asks Geľo.

"I don't know," says Telgarth. "I'll try."

Only now can he see where he's been held. It's a low suburban house made of unbaked brick, of which entire city quarters were built around Ürgüllpoļ. The ground is covered with mercenaries' corpses and the whole house is full of Slovak guerrillas in their typical fur hats.

Shooting continues in the neighbourhood.

"Move it faster, men!" somebody shouts from outside.

"Let's go, Telgarth," says Geľo, helping his friend.

It's hard, but finally Telgarth, his teeth clenched, starts to move.

Outside a fight rages for every inch of ground.

"We have to retreat," says Geľo. "The mercenaries have surrounded the city and are penetrating it. We can't hold them off much longer!"

Telgarth still can't pull himself together. He stumbles like a drunk.

"RETREAT TO THE STATION!" shouts Geĺo to his men, waving his submachine gun. "WE'LL MEET IN THE STATION HALL."

"How did you get here?" Telgarth is puzzled.

"We discovered they were about to retake Ű́r̊g̊üllpoḷ," says Geĺo, "so we moved here to help defend the city. They told me you hadn't got back from hunting."

"But how did you find me?" asks Telgarth.

"By chance," says Geĺo. "You had the luck of the devil. The mercenaries didn't move your car. So that's how we traced you. We stormed the house and shot everyone."

Telgarth sighs in relief, but does not let on. This way, at least, his cowardly betrayal will stay forever secret.

"They tortured me," he says, "but couldn't get anything out of me. I spat in their faces."

"Sure, Telgarth," Geĺo nods. "You're one of us. But move faster! We must reach the station before the Junjans get through our defences."

"Too bad you've killed them," says Telgarth, "I wanted to get the commander alive so I could play with him for a while until he curses his own mother for giving birth to him."

"Tökörnn Mäodna?" says Geĺo. "He gave us the slip."

"That was Tökörnn Mäodna?" Telgarth is amazed. "The mercenary leader himself? If I'd known, I'd have strangled him with these two hands!"

"When we had them surrounded, he tried to negotiate with me, but I wasn't having it," says Geĺo. "I'm not as good at it as you are. I don't want to listen to any stories, and so I whacked him right away. But he had a bulletproof vest under his jacket, the bastard. He played dead for a while, and took off when no one was looking."

Telgarth is quiet. He has such a bad conscience that he can't even look Geĺo in the eye with his single eye. He can only look at him sidelong, or with his peripheral vision. When he talks to him, he looks at his chest. He's upset that a witness to his temporary loss of will and morale has escaped.

Running is hard for him, but he can do it. He had been right about one thing: this sort of torture does no permanent damage. Now he has an opportunity to prove it on himself.

Somewhere nearby a mortar grenade explodes.

"There are coupled locomotives with ten carriages at the station, ready to go," says Geĺo. "We'll all board and force our way through the encirclement with the locomotive. The mercenaries left the track intact, they've no idea that we've got two locomotives left. By the time they work that out, we'll be in the taiga."

There is no mortar bombardment round the station. Relative calm reigns here. The station hall is filled with guerrillas and civilians. They all are getting into the passenger carriages and goods wagons. The locomotives are bathed in steam and smoke. They radiate heat and power. You can hear the locomotives' hissing and regular rhythmic breathing.

"If there's anything that you need in your office, go and get it," says Gel'o to Telgarth. "But hurry."

"Of course I do," says Telgarth. "I have a computer there. All my work's on it. Even a bit of constitution that I started devising just a few days ago."

"Right," says Gel'o, though it's clear he has no idea what Telgarth is on about. "Put it in the HQ carriage. It's the one just behind the locomotives. But be quick. The mercenaries will be here in a few minutes."

Telgarth runs to his office. He takes the computer and printer and puts them in the HQ carriage. Then he goes back for a few pieces of clothing and a hunting rifle. An explosion comes from outside. Telgarth looks out of the window. From every street leading to the railway station square the guerrillas, pushed out by the mercenaries, are retreating.

"Move faster," shouts Gel'o in the corridor. "We leave in a moment."

Telgarth runs through the hall and into the empty station hall. Guerrillas are getting on the train through every door and window and settling onto the flat beds of the goods wagons. The whole train bristles with weapons. The locomotive sounds the long departure call. Freddy gets into the HQ car.

Shooting now comes from the immediate surroundings of the station. The noise of the shots echoes among the station hall columns, veneered in fake marble. The last guerrillas run in. The locomotives puff and the creaking train begins to move. Armed men jump on the train; they grab proffered hands, handles and railings.

Pulled by two locomotives, the train gathers speed and shoots out of the station hall. Freddy can see a group of mercenaries entering the empty hall. A flash of fire comes from their weapons. A few bullets drum on the carriages. One guerrilla clutches his belly and falls onto the track. But the other shots miss.

The train hurls through the suburbs of New Bystrica, rattling over the points. Then the rattling stops. A long straight track opens up in front of them, aimed at the very heart of taiga. The city and its columns of smoke stay far behind them.

"We'll be back soon," Geľo stubbornly threatens the vanishing silhouette of the city. "And then we'll stay for good!"

Freddy finally has time to collect himself. The guerrillas have managed to load all the important equipment onto the train, including a generator. Nothing is missing.

"And where are we going now?" Freddy asks.

"Up north," says Geľo. "As far as we can. The mercenaries may pursue us, but they don't stand a chance. At least not on the track. There are no working locomotives left in Űŕġüllpoļ. We chose the most powerful ones and blew up the boilers of the others with hand grenades. We'll leave the train on the north coast. It'll be fine there. Local hunters will lend us sledges to get us to Kresan. He's got weapons, ammunition, and other supplies. Whatever the Czechs brought to Űŕġüllpoļ by submarine and by air has had to be left there. Now we're short of munitions."

"To Kresan?" Telgarth asks: dark foreboding comes over him.

"Yes, to Kresan," says Geľo indifferently. "We'll wait for the mercenaries there."

"How do you know they'll come?" Telgarth asks.

"They'll come," Geľo says. "You lured them into that trap."

"How do you know?" Telgarth is shocked.

"Mäodna told me before he played dead," replies Geľo. "The Junjans will think that we fled to the northern islands to hide. Some of them will follow us up there and some, led by Tökörnn Mäodna, will set out for Kresan's settlement, as you thought they would. And we'll be lying in wait for them. We'll destroy them and take Tökörnn Mäodna prisoner."

"He'll be mine," Telgarth's eyes flash.

"Have it your way," says Geľo and looks Telgarth in the eye with a gaze that forces him to lower his eye.

The track meanders like a snake through picturesque hills. The locomotives, climbing uphill, hiss with fatigue. Geľo is silent, looking out of the window. One day all this country will be free.

Telgarth lies down on one of the benches. He rolls his coat, makes a pillow out of it, wraps himself in furs and lies down. The exhaustion of the last days has left its mark. Soon he falls into a restless, intermittent sleep.

The guerrillas drink rough moonshine and clean their weapons.

The train puts the mountain ridge behind it: now it flies at maximum speed across the endless taiga. Suddenly the brakes squeal and the bottle of moonshine falls off the table. They all have to hold on to their seats.

Geľo looks out of the window.

"There's a fire on the track ahead of us," he says and turns to Telgarth. "We were talking about traps; it may be a trap for us there."

But Telgarth does not even wake up. His hands and face twitch inconspicuously, as he tries to get over his horrible experiences.

Geľo reaches for a submachine gun and gets ready to shoot. The burning fire has already caught the attention of the guerrillas. The train stops, its brakes squealing, forty or fifty metres before the burning twigs.

"Careful," shouts Geľo; he get out, aims his weapon and, using the hot and hissing locomotives for cover, stealthily approaches the fire. The others follow.

The fire turns out to have been lit by a ragged, hairy man in dirty European clothes. He is lying by the track with matches in his hands. He is shivering with cold; his cracked lips and burning forehead suggest high fever. The stranger has a backpack and a bag with fishing tackle sticking out. The guerrillas reconnoitre the surroundings, but can't see anyone else.

The man can't talk. They put him in the HQ carriage and search his luggage.

"Telgarth," says Sirovec-Molnár and shakes Telgarth's shoulder.

Telgarth opens his eye with an effort. His entire body is aching.

"Look what he had in his backpack," says Sirovec-Molnár. "This could be of interest to you."

He gives Telgarth a dirty Slovak Republic passport and a crumpled and much folded piece of shiny paper. It is the article from *Stern* about Telgarth with photographs and an interview.

"Who had what in a backpack?" Telgarth is bewildered.

"There was a fire on the track and a man lying next to it," explains Sirovec-Molnár. "So we put him on the train. And he had this in his backpack."

"He's sure to be a Junjan spy," says Telgarth without thinking and still half-asleep. "Shoot him and throw him off the train."

He closes his eyes and goes back to sleep.

"I think you should take a look at it anyway," says Geľo obstinately.

Telgarth sighs. He starts casually going through the things that Sirovec-Molnár gave him. The green Slovak passport attracts his attention.

"Look at that, a fellow-countryman," he thinks.

For a moment he thinks about the fate of his own passport. He must have lost it when the Junjans imprisoned him as a reporter. He didn't have it in the labour camp.

Telgarth opens the passport and he thinks he must be dreaming. He fixes his eye on it and then leaps off the bench.

"URBAN!" he shouts.

Grimacing painfully, he hobbles to the man. He looks at his face.

The man uncomprehendingly looks into the one eye.

"URBAN!" he shouts and shakes his shoulders. "It's me, Freddy! How the hell did you get here?"

Urban lifts himself up on the bench. A mixture of astonishment, recognition and relief runs over his face.

"Freddy..." he breathes out. "I... was looking for you..."

He closes his eyes and again loses consciousness.

Telgarth turns around with a burning look.

"This man is my best friend," he says. "I don't know how he got here, but he's come to see me."

He looks at the medic Stano Čierny-Orkiš-Horniak.

"Take good care of him!" he tells him. "Your own life is at stake."

Then he stumbles towards his own bench and again falls asleep.

Soon not just the whole carriage, but the entire train is asleep. Only the men in the two locomotives are up, stoking their engines and trying to penetrate the thick fog with their sharp eyes.

* * *

A host slices reindeer meat in thin slices; a guest puts four in his mouth at a time.
Junjan Slovak proverb

The moon appears between the hills. It climbs higher and higher up the sky. At times the fog veils it and then the stars shine brightly.

Silence reigns all round. Only occasionally can reindeer herds on the tundra be heard. They run fast. The stomping of hooves drowns out the herders' shouts. The herds are moving south, deeper into the tundra; the silence returns, interrupted only by the monotonous and distant murmur of the sea behind the ribbon of the ice field.

"They were that close?" Urban is astonished.

"They are and they aren't," says Telgarth. "In the tundra sounds carry a long way. Anything can be ten kilometres away and yet you can hear it as if it were just here, round the hill."

Geľo impatiently waits for Freddy to finish.

"Let's go faster!" he orders. "We can't waste time!"

The guerrillas' dog sledges turn sharp right, into the snowy tundra.

Further from the coast, deeper in the tundra, a wild wind blows. It knocks the dogs off their feet.

Telgarth takes a shiny bottle from under his fur jacket. He takes a long swig and then gives it to Urban. Urban takes a sip. A pleasantly sharp heat invades his body. Freddy takes another sip and then puts the bottle back in the furs.

"It's not Martell, but it warms you up just as well," he laughs.

Video Urban nods.

"What's going on back home?" Freddy asks. His voice suggests that he's not that interested.

"No change," says Urban. "There is no point doing anything over there. That's why I've decided... to move to the Czech..."

"You know," Telgarth starts talking, "at first, I felt differently about it. I took pictures, made films, and filed reports. But I felt I didn't belong here, that I was a foreigner. I felt I'd come to Mars. Junjan Slovaks? They were as interesting as guinea pigs. Like meeting a distant relative, so distant that you feel nothing for him. But then the Junjans captured me. They didn't care that I was a reporter. They put me in a camp. And Junjan Slovaks helped me escape. So I've stayed with them. I taught them how to fight and rob goods wagons. And now I'm one of them."

"YOU taught them how to rob goods wagons?" exclaims Urban. "And who taught YOU?"

"It's a long story," says Freddy evasively. "You don't know much about me."

For a moment, Urban feels a special kind of respect for his old friend and business partner, a kind of remote admiration. The dizzy transformation of the clumsy, stingy, perverse, stupid fat slob in one year in Junja has taken his breath away.

"I've been meaning to ask you for some time..." says Urban. "Where did you lose an eye?"

"This war is cruel," says Freddy, thoughtfully scanning the white horizon indistinctly outlined far off in the dark. "It spares no one. And sometime you have bad luck. I've been in a labour camp, too, but I got away from them. And just a few days ago, I was a prisoner of Tökörnn Mäodna himself and escaped!"

Urban nods with understanding. Freddy fixes a burning gaze on him.

"But a few Junjans have paid for that eye now," he says, his mouth wildly contorted. "They'll pay for everything! I won't be coming home. You can keep the whole company. Sell it, strip it, do what you like with it. I'm giving you my share. I'm not a businessman; I'm a fighter. If you like, I'll put it in writing. The main thing, that whoring bitch, you know the one I mean, is not to get any of it. Considering she let me down so terribly, she's doing fine. She cleaned out my accounts, kept the house, so she has somewhere to live. And the child? Who knows if it's mine, anyway? In any case, I belong here now. This country needs me."

Suddenly Geľo stops the dog sledge, flings himself onto the ground and examines the reindeer droppings. They tell him when the reindeer herds passed by. He clears the snow with a stick, and removes moss, grass, and willow leaves: they tell him which way the reindeer passed.

"I have nobody in Slovakia now," says Freddy. "My family's been taken from me. My parents are dead. And my friends? You've always been my only friend."

Urban is quiet. If he weren't a cynic, he'd have said he was moved at that moment. A man has to fly thousands of kilometres and trek through hundreds of kilometres to know someone whom he thought he had known for so many years.

And again the guerrillas' sledges rush into the wind. The lead dog finally smells human habitation and turns sharp left, rushing ahead, straining its last remnants of energy.

A man's silhouette appears in the dark.

"Who are you, in God's name?" shouts Geľo and gets ready to fire his submachine gun.

The unknown man recognizes Geľo's voice and comes up.

"Geľo?" he shouts, "Is that you, brother? Don't shoot!"

"Martin!" shouts Geľo and jumps off the sledge.

They introduce each other, and Telgarth passes round his bottle of moonshine.

Urban is amazed again to see what respect and admiration Telgarth commands among these people. Everyone knows his name.

"In this weather, wolves get at the herd," says Martin. "They attack the deer every night. We don't have enough herders. So I'll help them. I, too, have ten times ten reindeer over there!" he adds, not without pride.

"Is the herd far away from here, brother?" asks Geľo.

"Not far," says Martin. "If you run, you'll sweat only eight times. That's why I'm walking. There's no point taking out the wind sledge."

"And where are your yurts?" Geľo asks.

"Here, quite near," says Martin. "You'll sweat only three times."

"Are my children and wife all right?" asks Geľo.

"They're fine," says Martin. "Kresan's made them their own yurt."

"And how about your Maria?" asks Geľo about his sister-in-law.

"Oh, she'll be glad to see you!" Martin says.

"And Zuza and her child are fine?" asks Geľo after his sister-in-law and future wife inherited from his brother. He feels as if something has moved in his crotch.

"All's as it should be," Martin assures him. "They're with your family."

"And our father?" asks Geľo.

"He died a few weeks ago," says Martin. "He went out at night to take a shit in the tundra and the wolves tore him apart."

"So the wolves did it," Geľo nods. "And is Kresan at home?"

"He is," nods Martin. "He's been waiting for you for a long time."

"Take us there, brother, and then one of us will take you to the herd," Geľo proposes.

"Wise words, in God's name, brother!" agrees Martin, takes another sip of moonshine, shoulders his rifle and hops onto Geľo's sledge.

* * *

Kresan's herds are numberless. His wealth cannot be counted. Where his reindeer pass, no moss will grow even after three warm summers. They're divided into ten herds. In each herd, there are twenty times twenty, and twice more twenty times twenty. That's how many reindeer old Kresan has. You can't keep them in one herd: they get restless for lack of moss and will run away from you.

Each herd comes with ten tents where the herders and their families live. Ever since the guerrillas' women and children from the coast joined them, that makes more than a thousand souls. They're all employed and fed by Kresan. But nobody is idle. The children help the herders with the herds; the women process the meat, milk, and skins. They smoke the reindeer cheese, salt, mix, and preserve the reindeer feta in round wooden churns. Every pair of hard-working hands is needed.

Kresan lets each of his herders keep a pair of their own reindeer. Then the herdsman sees himself as a small farmer and runs round exhausting himself, protecting at the same time Kresan's huge herd.

Kresan is a good Slovak, but he likes to get on with everyone. When the Junjan extortionists come, he complains, but gives them whatever they ask for. If they raise their demands, he gives them more. He doesn't want trouble. He's hard on his own people, but yielding to Junjans. He's not cowardly, just reasonable. He knows that if he made enemies of the Junjans during a civil war, they'd send their mercenaries to destroy him.

The reindeer in the tundra are easily harmed. Junjan revenge would starve, as well as Kresan, a thousand people: a thousand good Slovak men and women. Kresan can't fight for the whole Slovak nation. It's enough for him to fight for his employees. So he yields. His commitment to the Slovak cause is met by supplying Slovak guerrillas with dried meat, reindeer cheese and other foodstuffs behind the Junjans' backs. In the tundra he makes and maintains secret storage places for weapons, ammunition, tins and medicine brought by Czech submarines.

So when Junjan mercenaries come to requisition reindeer, he gives them, without a word, as many as they ask for. Only he knows what he's thinking then. The positive side is that he can also supply the guerrillas with fresh information on the mercenaries' movements in the taiga.

"Let's be true Slovaks, but not everyone has to know about it," he's glad to repeat when his close relatives are around.

As soon as news spreads of Geľo's and his men's arrival, the whole Kresan settlement comes to life, as if night were over and it was time to get up.

Kresan, too, wakes up. He lies on soft reindeer skins, covered by a fox-fur coverlet. He looks blank for a moment, but then he gets up. He calls in both daughters and his bride and gives them each an order:

"Anča and Cila, cook a full pot of walrus meat. The lean one! These slant-eyed Slovaks from the coast are mouse-eaters! They don't understand good reindeer meat. You needn't keep serving them the best. And you, Mária, light another lamp. Light two! Three! Kresan's not a poor man, he's not going to welcome special guests in the dark."

Geľo, Telgarth, the priest and Urban clamber into the warm corner.

"Is that you, Geľo?" Kresan asks.

"Yes, it is," answers Geľo.

"And Telgarth himself!" an amazed Kresan shouts, recognizing Telgarth by his black eye patch. "Oh, what an honour for an ordinary poor reindeer herder! Oh, how many brave heroes in my unworthy yurt!"

The men sit down round the reclining Kresan.

"This is Urban," Geľo presents his guest. "He's from overseas, too, from the Slovaks' country. He came to see Telgarth; they're old friends."

Urban bows awkwardly.

Well, I can see that we can't lose if even foreign Slovaks support us," exclaims Kresan. "Slovaks must stick together! This is how, look!"

Kresan clenches his dry hands and presses them to his chest so everyone can see.

"Slovak brother, embrace your mother!" he adds.

"Do you know why we've come, uncle Kresan?" asks Gel'o.

"Yes, your messenger arrived three days ago," Kresan confirms.

"We were held up on the coast, until we found the number of dogs we needed," says Gel'o.

"It's all ready, as you asked," reports Kresan. "Yesterday the herders brought the ammunition and tinned food. One storage place was found and looted by *Ökötöm-kökötom,* the snow monster, but he left the tins alone. And we'll give you lots of reindeer cheese and dry meat. After all, you fight for us, too, my heroes. And what's new? How is our cause?"

Gel'o was about to open his mouth, but Kresan interrupts.

"Žofa!" he orders his bride. "Are our guests to talk with dry throats? Where's the tea? And you, Jakub, where's the booze, damn it all!"

The youngest son reaches for a carefully cleaned plastic bottle and treasured plastic cups. Kresan pours the drinks.

Gel'o tells him about the situation at the front. The old herder listens with interest. Now he asks for explanation, now he nods sympathetically.

All this time, women in the kitchen corner use a hammer to break frozen raw meat into small pieces, slice the roast, take smoked tongues out of the pot, and make a salad of mushrooms, green herbs and roots cooked in fat. Soon Kresan's yurt wafts a tempting aroma of delicacies.

"So the mercenaries seem to be resisting hard," reflects Kresan when Gel'o finishes. He pours more drinks. "Are they on your tracks?"

"They're pursuing us," says Gel'o. "But they'll be looking for most of us on the northern islands. We've swept our tracks clean."

"They won't look for you here," says Kresan. "I put on an act for them and pretend to be on their side. One of their units may wander over here, but we'll know long in advance. The herders on the pastures won't miss a thing."

"But they'll come," says Gel'o. "They will. A unit of mercenaries will come here for certain. It's been planned to happen."

"Who planned it?" says Kresan with fear.

"We'll discuss it later," says Gel'o. "Telgarth has come up with an excellent plan to capture Tökörnn Mäodna alive. But tell him yourself," he asks Freddy.

Freddy blushes. They all look at him. So he starts to talk. Even though he's learned quite a lot of Junjan Slovak dialect, he still uses a lot of fast Bratislava language. Gel'o, who more or less understands him, occasionally has to interpret for him.

Freddy's plan is simple. When the Junjan soldiers caught him a few days ago, he deliberately told Mäodna that the guerrilla leaders' women and children were hiding at Kresan's. So Tökörnn Mäodna won't miss a catch like that: he'll come here in person. In the meantime, Kresan will send all the women and children to safety in distant pastures. The settlement will be full of Geľo's men dressed as herders. It will be a trap God would wish for. When the mercenaries come, the guerrillas will overpower them and wipe them out. They'll take Mäodna alive.

Kresan shakes his head in disbelief. He utters incomprehensible shouts of amazement. He falls to the ground and jerks his head and arms and legs only to freeze suddenly, his eyes staring wildly. His expressions of admiration and respect are so exorbitant that Freddy is embarrassed.

"Without Mäodna, the Junjans are lost," exclaims Kresan, when he takes his place and recovers from his astonishment.

"Yes, indeed," says Geľo. "Victory will be ours."

"And when are we going to do it?" Kresan enquires.

"We must wait," says Geľo, "here, at your place. The mercenaries are on our tail, but we're well ahead. But I know they'll show up."

"My herders have eyes everywhere," says Kresan. "If just one mercenary appears within a thousand kilometres, we'll be the first to know."

Kresan orders another bottle of spirits and pours for everyone. Freddy's cup is filled to the top.

"I'm already looking forward to life after victory," says Kresan. "We'll be the masters here. Nobody will be able to seize my modest property. If a Junjan comes near my settlement or my herd, he'll get a bullet. There'll be no pity. Let them all starve to death."

"Yes," says the priest. "We'll be the masters here. Life will be happy. We've never known a life like that. We'll have to get used to it."

"It's easy to get used to good things," says Kresan.

"But we'll have to get used to responsibility, as well," the priest points out firmly.

"And what about you, Geľo?" Kresan asks. "What will you do after victory? Will you go into politics?"

"What an idea!" says Geľo. "First of all, I don't understand politics and secondly, I'm doing it right now. After victory, others can take over. People who are true fighters and have education!" He looks at Telgarth.

"Will you go back to the coast?" Kresan asks.

"Maybe I will," says Geľo. "I'll trade fur and mineral grease. I was always good at trading. And I'll hunt just for pleasure!"

"You've planned an excellent life for yourself," Kresan adds.

"I only miss reindeer," says Geľo. "Live reindeer. I have no herd. We're poor at the coast. When hunting's good, we eat. When it's bad, we starve. And reindeer don't have to be followed across ice floes. So, as soon as the war ends, I want to have a herd. I want to be like you."

The old Kresan becomes more attentive.

"Well, we in the tundra are poor, too," he says evasively. "The herd is attacked either by wolves, or disease. It must be better for you on the coast. The wolves certainly don't attack seals and walrus as they attack reindeer. But if you like, I'll help you. After all, we're family! For every ten Junjans you or your men kill, you'll get one reindeer from me. Just bring me their right ears, that's all I need."

Kresan reaches into his jacket and shows them ears on a thread. Some are fleshy, others as transparent as parchment. Big male ears and small soft female ones, too.

"They're from the times when we settled accounts with the collective farm officials and their families." The women hurriedly bring plates with various dishes. Kresan tries a little bit from each course.

Urban takes smoked reindeer tongue in a spicy sauce as this reminds him of a speciality from Prague's *Domažlice Room.*

Geľo just toys with the delicacies and soon takes his leave. He'd like to see his family: he hasn't seen them for such a long time.

* * *

Elena is waiting in her yurt with the children. Her hair is cleverly braided in a complex hairdo of thin plaits anointed with reindeer fat. She is wearing a festive dress made from skins of unborn reindeer calves, embroidered with coloured threads. The children are also well dressed and they're excited to see their father.

Geľo opens the curtain and looks at his family.

"Is that you, husband?" asks Elena.

"Yes, it's me," says Geľo.

He puts away his weapons and comes to his children.

Jurko follows him into the yurt wearing ammunition belts and carrying a machine gun in his hands.

Geľo caresses each child and kisses its forehead. He gives them the modest gifts from Prague that he has been carrying all this time. He embraces and kisses his wife.

"And what happened to your hair?" asks Elena.

"It's a long story," says Geľo.

Elena discreetly points to a fur curtain dividing the yurt.

Geľo goes to the curtain and opens it.

Behind the curtain kneels Zuzana, his brother Adam's widow, holding a child in her arms. She is also dressed for a special occasion. Around her eyes are tattoos of orange suns, so that she looks as if she had huge eyes. She looks at the ground.

"Get up and join us," says Gel'o.

Zuzana humbly gets up and, her gaze lowered, moves with tiny steps to join Elena.

"I've decided," says Gel'o, "to accept you as my wife once my sister-in-law. I accept your and Adam's daughter Kristina as my daughter once my niece."

"She's a good wife," says Elena, "and she's sure to win your love, husband. We got along well in your absence."

"My sister-in-law Elena was a good support for me during my unspeakable sadness, sir," says Zuzana. "If it weren't for her, I'd have died of sadness after Adam's death."

"Why the 'sir'?" Gel'o shakes his head and sits down. "If you want me as your husband, call me Gel'o. If not, call me Gel'o, anyway."

Zuzana blushes.

"So?" Gel'o wants to know. "Do you agree?"

"Oh, yes," Zuzana says quickly. She throws herself at Gel'o's hand and covers it with kisses.

"In that case," says Gel'o, "and if my wife Elena also agrees, we can be married tomorrow by the priest."

"I agree," nods Elena. "At least I won't be so bored here."

Gel'o gives Zuzana a gift of perfume from Prague.

"You won't have to wait for me much longer, my wives," Gel'o assures both women. "Victory is near. Then we all go back to the coast. We shall live as never before. And now, let's have some food."

Between courses, Gel'o drinks moonshine and lovingly watches his children play with their new toys. They don't even want to eat. Jurko helps his mother and Zuzana.

"And you, Jurko, sit here, by me," Gel'o addresses him. "You're a real fighter and guerrilla. You've been through fire and blood with us. You took Úŕġüllpoļ and fought in the encirclement. You've always been at my side. From now on, you sleep in the men's corner. And take this, and drink it! A man needs a drink of spirits, not to hold on to his mother's skirts!" The boy, flattered by the compliments, sits next to his father. Soon another course arrives, fish baked with herbs in the ashes.

"Well, in God's name!" Gel'o sighs and loosens his belt. "It's good to be home! And it will be even better!"

* * *

The party at Kresan's yurt really gets going only with the third bottle of moonshine.

Urban expresses an interest in being introduced to the ladies.

Kresan nearly chokes on his food: mixed company is not the custom in the tundra. Finally, not to offend the special guest from afar, he agrees. He claps his hands to call the women of his family to the men's corner.

The women come. They blush and cover their faces as they giggle.

"Why don't you sit nearer us?" Urban enquires.

Freddy chews a bit of meat. He burps and rubs his ear. He knows something of local customs.

"In the country Urban and I come from, it's customary for ladies to sit at the same table," he says in explanation. "Not just at weddings and funerals, like here."

"Then who cooks the food and serves?" asks one of Kresan's sons who has until then been quietly eating and drinking.

"Everything is cooked in advance," says Urban. "And then they consume it."

"Then they what?" Kresan can't understand.

"Then they eat and drink," says Freddy. "Men and women together."

"And after the meal?" asks the youngest of Kresan's sons, Jakub, who is still single.

"After the meal, the party goes on," says Freddy.

"With women present?" Kresan is astonished.

"Yes, with the women," Freddy confirms: his voice suggests that he withdrew his moral support from this custom a long time ago.

"Then your country's men are pitiable," the old reindeer herder concludes. "Don't they know that a woman's tongue is a hundred times faster than the fastest dog sledge, but to no avail? That a woman's garrulousness is like the tundra wind: it stops you speaking, steals words from your mouth and, if your constitution is weak, can even drive you mad."

"Can men have a real talk if women are sitting with them?" says a baffled Jakub. "Don't women keep interrupting? How does it work?"

Kresan sees that the man from afar is embarrassed by the questions.

"Oh, well," he says, lifting his precious plastic cup for a toast. "Other lands, other customs! Have it your way, Urban! Women, you can drink, too; come and join us. Today the world is upside down, so be it! As we have such special guests, even the old ways can all be topsy-turvy!"

Urban gallantly pours for the ladies. The ladies giggle; it's a very odd situation for them. They squat round a little table, their postures hinting that they're ready to leap up at their master's slightest gesture, and they get on with their work.

"Let's drink to our friends, the foreign Slovaks!" says old Kresan, raising his cup. "To the great leader Telgarth, who shed his blood in the fight for our Slovak cause and who made our small, but heroic nation world-famous! And let's drink to Urban, his friend, who's also come to help Slovaks! He, too, must be very brave."

Urban is even more embarrassed.

"Yes, he's very brave," Freddy agrees. "Almost as brave as me."

The women feel their presence is unwanted and move to the kitchen corner. Unused to strong drink, they feel cheerful and animated. They slice meat for the guests and giggle madly.

"And what sort of work do you do in your country, Urban?" asks Kresan. "What do you live on?"

"I'm in business," says Urban and he too finds this word somewhat strange. "I own a company."

"What's that?" Kresan asks Freddy.

"He leads people," says Telgarth. "He has lots of people under him. Not as many as you do, but plenty. These people work for him and he looks after them."

"Oh," nods Kresan with approval. "Then we're the same. And how many people does he look after?"

Embarrassed, Urban sips his drink. Now Kresan and Telgarth are talking about him as if he were deaf and dumb, or mad.

"About two score," says Telgarth. "And besides, he also has under him people that he doesn't look after directly, but who work for him."

"Independent herders," Kresan shows he understands.

"Right," Freddy agrees. "A long time ago, before I came here, I used to work with him. We owned a company together."

"We still do…" Urban remarks.

"We still do," Telgarth concurs. "But I'm giving it up. My place is here. I want to fight our beloved freedom. And then for recognition for our nation by the whole world."

"You speak wisely, by God!" shouts Kresan and puts a delicacy in his mouth. "They'll see what Slovaks are made of!"

Urban feels sick. He's bathed in cold sweat and wants to vomit. His eyes pop; he hopes to quell the storm in his guts by sheer willpower. In the end, he can't hold back: a hand over his mouth, he runs from the yurt.

Outside, a blizzard rages. Urban vomits and the wind blows it away from his mouth. It knocks him off his feet; his head lands in sour-tasting snow. It is hard to get up under the wind's attack, but he finally manages to clamber back to the yurt.

"That's all right," Telgarth tells him. "Do you want to go to bed?"

Urban shakes his head. He has got drunk suddenly, not gradually as after drinking good quality distillate. A big wheel is spinning him round. Even with his eyes open wide, he feels in danger of plunging into the deep darkness. He holds on to Kresan's hand even while sitting.

"Good drink, isn't it?" the old Kresan laughs. "It shakes you up real good, doesn't it?"

"And how many Junjans have you killed so far, Urban?" Kresan's youngest son Jakub asks admiringly.

Urban shakes his head. He wants to say something, but only wheezing comes out from his mouth.

"None so far," says Telgarth. "But he's helping us in another way. And when we retake Úrġüllpoļ, he'll be indispensable to us."

At the urging of his host's family, Urban has to recount his anabasis from Polyarny to here, including the characters of Kostya and Stalin's grandson. He tells it like a funny story and his inebriated listeners do in fact laugh merrily. This encourages Urban and he invents grimaces and voice distortions that the real characters did not have. His days spent waiting by the track are re-enacted like a Chaplin turn.

"Oh, by God, Urban, you're a riot," says Kresan when Urban's account is over: he laughs as he pours another round.

The women serve them and can't help giggling now and again, stifling the giggles in their furs.

The alcohol has got into the blood of Cila, a bolder nubile girl, as strong as a mare, with snow-white teeth, a free spirit.

"You're more fun than those government mercenaries a few weeks ago who tried to fuck all our girls in a row."

Urban's chokes: he is still not used to such words not being thought obscene by Junjan Slovaks.

Freddy calmly gnaws at a bone.

"Are you saying," he asks, striking while the iron is hot, "they were after you, too?"

"Not me," says Cila. "I hid from them and they didn't see me. But they nearly fucked Žofa here. And they nearly fucked Mariena, too."

"And where were your menfolk?" asks Urban, automatically adopting the Junjan Slovaks' archaic language.

"Out in the tundra, hunting wolves," says Maria. "By the time Cila had warned them, we'd almost been fucked. They were Russians paid by the Junjans to fight Slovaks."

"We ran back; we were late, but still in time," says Jakub. "It was only a small unit."

"They're buried out in the tundra," Kresan adds between two helpings, not taking his eyes off his plate of reindeer meat, "shoved into a leather sack, and then straight into the ground."

"It must have been hard work, digging a pit in this frozen ground," Urban notes in admiration.

"Well, it took them two days to dig it," laughs Kresan.

"And you could hear them whining under the earth two more days," says Jakub.

"True," sighs Kresan. "Russian mercenaries are tough."

"How many times has Geľo told you, 'No heroism'?" Freddy says angrily. "We need you for other things, uncle Kresan. What if Tökörnn Mäodna found out? He'd come and wipe out the entire settlement."

"He hasn't found out a thing," says Kresan. "He'll think they've vanished without a trace. The tundra is big. Wolves may have attacked them, or perhaps *Ökötöm-kökötom*, the snow monster."

"What if they'd radioed that they were at your place?" asks Urban.

"Radios don't work here in the tundra," says Telgarth. "Something underground and in the mountains here bends and jams the waves."

He turns to Kresan and says sternly, "But you took pointless risks."

"Should we have let them fuck our women and daughters?" says Kresan defensively.

"Better fucked than dead," says Freddy. "Tökörnn Mäodna wouldn't play games with you. He'd shoot everyone in the settlement. He's done it more than once. I know him, I was captured by him, but I got away. But never mind. Let him come now. We're ready for him!"

There is a moment's silence. Kresan is quiet. Urban reaches for the roast meat and cuts off a piece.

"Help yourself!" Kresan becomes a host again. "Nobody's suffered. The mercenaries just vanished in the tundra. Who'll find out we did it?"

"And we've given you their weapons," says Jakub. "They're quite new, never used. They just fell in the snow once."

Jakub gets up, goes to the nearest corner screened by a fur curtain and soon returns with a Kalashnikov in his hands.

"They're no good to us," says Kresan. "They jam in this cold. On your way back, just throw them in an ice hole. Nothing good comes from a Russian. We've kept some Czech weapons, just in case. Czech weapons are good quality, and here you never know what can happen."

Kresan wipes his mouth and gets up. He takes Telgarth and Urban outside to a neighbouring yurt. He draws the leather from the entrance and shows them what's inside. The cold space inside is filled with a stack of wooden crates. Some have their covers open and all kinds of weapons can be seen packed in them.

"The herdsmen brought these yesterday from storage," says Kresan. "If you like, you can start loading tomorrow morning."

Urban spots a typical tin of Prague ham in one crate. He picks it up.

"What?" Freddy asks. "You feel like some?"

"How about you?" asks Urban. Just imagining eating or drinking anything makes him feel sick again.

"I don't fancy those things any more," says Telgarth. "I prefer the local food. There's nothing tying me to your country. I've no one there."

"But what about coffee and milk?" says Urban, pointing to a case of condensed milk.

"I don't know," Telgarth shrugs his shoulders. "I haven't tasted it since I've been here. I prefer tea. Local tundra herb tea."

"And wine?" Urban tests him.

"This is my wine," Telgarth taps his fur coat that hides a flat bottle of moonshine. "That's enough for me. Junjan Slovaks are modest."

"And I suppose you're a Junjan Slovak?" says Urban with a tiny hint of irony.

"I certainly am," says Freddy.

He turns away from Urban and checks the ammunition in the crates.

Kresan joins Telgarth and Urban.

"Oh, there's a lot of good food in the tin boxes," he nods with admiration. "We've tasted everything. We liked this one best of all."

Kresan grabs a half-kilogram tin of pork in its own gravy and shows it to them.

"What sort of meat is it?" he asks. "It's delicious."

"It's pork," says Urban.

"What?" Kresan hasn't heard right.

"Pork," says Freddy. "From a pig."

"A pig?" Kresan is dumbfounded. "But that's an insult to us. Do the Czechs have such an animal in their country?"

The reindeer herder shakes his head incredulously.

"Take it, uncle," says Telgarth. "Take all the tins you like."

Kresan is abashed.

"How could I?" he objects. "All this is for the guerrillas. I'm not going to deprive those who fight for me? We have our own reindeer meat. But to tell you truth, the tinned meat is different somehow, finer."

Freddy makes him take two tins of pork. A piece of paper falls out of the case; the draught blows it into a crack in the wall.

Urban bends to pick it up.

"Leave it there," says Kresan. "We get a lot of these papers. I can give you some. The paper says the Czechs want us to fight for them, for some sort of Czechoslovakia."

"For what?" Urban is apprehensive.

"For Czechoslovakia," Kresan repeats: clearly the word is awkward on his lips. He is someone unused to saying it every day.

Urban picks up the flyer.

Telgarth puts a finger to his lips. He looks at Urban meaningfully.

"We are sitting on the biggest oil reserves in the world," he explains in a whisper. "When drilling starts, the Arabs are finished. And somehow the Czechs have found out. When they began bringing humanitarian aid, they brought geologists by submarine. They hired native guides and surveyed every square metre in the taiga. According to them, we're the richest country in the world. I talked to them in Ûŕġüllpoļ, before they flew back home with the samples. They were quite beside themselves. They never saw anything like it. Oil, gold, uranium, diamonds."

Urban laughs.

"So that's why you're here, Freddy!" he says. "Well, I have to admit I've rather underestimated you. This is a different business than making porn films. Freddy Piggybank, oil sheikh!"

Kresan looks at them meekly. The newcomers are laughing, so he is too. He understands nothing of the fast Bratislava prattle.

"Papers like these are packed in every crate, he says. "But here nobody understand these Czech signs and squiggles."

Urban reads:

Dear Slovak brothers.

It's only recently that the Slovaks' and Czechs' common state was treacherously destroyed after almost 70 years of history. Today the time is coming which our nations have been waiting for so long: a common state of Slovaks and Czechs will be restored under its original name The Czechoslovak Kingdom! This time, however, the state will do without the degenerate population of the Carpathian Slovak republic, who also call themselves Slovaks. We have had enough of their quarrelsome and yet servile nature. This time we shall enter into a state union with you, good and forthright Slovaks of the Junjan archipelago, who follow in the steps of the heroes of the glorious works of Ondrej Sládkovič, Stano Chalupka, and Jan Botto. The former khanate will be renamed after our glorious victory <u>Slovakia</u>. *After the liberation of the entire territory of Slovakia from the barbarian yoke and Junjan oppression, the brotherly Czech kingdom will extend all possible economic and cultural help, so that the living standard of our Slovak brothers will rise and will rapidly become full fledged citizens of a newly restored union state of Czechoslovakia.*

Hurrah for the eternal friendship of the <u>Czechoslovak nation</u>*!*
Hurrah for <u>Slovakia</u>*!*
Death to the <u>Junjan occupiers</u>*!*
Hip, hip, hurrah!!

The Royal Czechoslovak National Committee in Exile
The Slovak National Council in Exile

Urban finishes reading the flyer and gives it to Freddy.

Freddy shakes his head. "I know that flyer very well," he says.

"When did the Czechs get submarines?" wonders Urban. "The country's landlocked! Our newspapers say nothing at all about this."

"It's no big deal to buy a few submarines, is it?" asks Freddy. "Today anyone will sell you an old World War Two submarine. If the Czechs could have a merchant navy, why can't they have submarines now? Who cares? The main thing is that they bring weapons and ammunition here. If you like, I'll show you one of those submarines one day. From inside. You like those Czechs and I'll introduce you to one of the captains. They're interesting, outgoing people. They like having visitors and they'll have a drink with you."

"You've seen such a submarine already?" Urban asks.

"Seen?" Freddy brags. "I spent a week on board one. It was called the *Kamýk*. And ever since I became commander of New Bystrica, I've made friends of all the Czech captains that come here. How many times I've been there when the cargo is unloaded! I know them all. We used to have such parties together…"

"In New Bystrica?" Urban is at a loss.

"Yes, New Bystrica," says Telgarth, "the new Slovak name for Ŭṙġüllpoḷ!"

"You know," says Urban, "there are places I'd like to see. I've been to the US. I shan't go to Mars. But I've always wanted to be in a submarine."

"When we've finished everything we have to do here," promises Freddy, "we'll go back to the south coast and attack New Bystrica. After we conquer it, Czech submarines will be docking there again. They'll like you, since you are a Czechophile. They like us too, since they're sure we're fighting for their cause."

"Well, aren't you, Freddy?" Urban asks.

"We're not fighting for any Czechoslovakia," says Freddy. "We're fighting for freedom, that's what we're fighting for. But our aim isn't a 'state union' with the Czechs, but a free Slovak state. A Slovak empire. And, by the way, Urban, I've told you five times now that they don't know me here as Freddy, Freddy Piggybank."

There's a hint of reproach in Freddy's voice.

"Please don't use that name. Here I'm Telgarth, the feared guerrilla leader. Yes, Telgarth! Telgarth the First!" he adds quietly, and blushes.

Telgarth doesn't wait for Urban to reply. He scans the crates. He grabs a shoulder-firing anti-aircraft missile and puts it on his shoulder. He tests it by aiming at the yurt's ceiling.

"With this we'll defeat the government mercenaries in no time," he announces. "They've bought a few decommissioned Mig-24 combat helicopters from the Russians. Well, let them try hassling us with them. We'll shoot them down like clay pigeons! And you, uncle Kresan, try the chocolate now. This one, look: *Kofila*! It won the gold medal at the 1958 Brussels Expo. Oh, Brussels style! Urban used go on and on about it!"

Telgarth pats Urban's back in a friendly way.

"It's like coffee, uncle Kresan!" he tells the old man. "It won't hurt you, for God's sake!"

* * *

In the middle of the night Gel'o is woken by a woman's sobs coming from Zuzana's corner.

"Can you hear?" he whispers to Elena who, tired after several hours of wild lovemaking, has fallen asleep in his still lusting hands.

Elena mumbles something and turns over.

Gel'o leaves his den of furs; naked, he goes to the curtain separating him from Zuzana's corner. He listens for a while with bated breath. Cold and excitement paralyses his limbs. He finally resolves to lift the curtain.

"It's me," he says and slips like lightning under Zuzana's fur cover. "Don't be afraid."

The widow turns her tearful face to him.

"Why are you crying?" Geľo asks.

"I don't know," says Zuzana. "From happiness and sorrow. You're so good to want to take care of me."

"Adam would have done the same if anything had happened to me…" says Geľo with a lump in his throat.

He touches Zuzana's powerful, lithe, sleep-warmed body.

"How beautiful you are!" he whispers, his throat tightened, gazing on the gorgeous tattoos on her belly, underbelly and thighs.

Zuzana closes her eyes and as if by chance touches Geľo's manhood, as hard as a stick. She withdraws her hand as if scalded.

"No, no," Zuzana whispers. "It's a sin!"

"Why sin?" Geľo argues, grabbing her tattooed breast. "We belong to each other. The priest will marry us tomorrow. That's in a few hours!"

He firmly embraces Zuzana's body and pushes between her legs.

Zuzana does not fight him off, but moves her face aside, as if afraid that Geľo's increasingly insistent kisses might defile her. She spreads her legs and completely opens up to him.

Geľo enters her and moves around powerfully.

Finally comes relief. Geľo throws off the covers. He withdraws his wildly pulsating member from Zuzana and with a firm hand aims it away from her bed. Hot streams of his semen quickly leave his insides, but only whitish frozen chips fall on the ground.

"Cold!" Zuzana says through her chattering teeth and covers herself with fur. She's asleep in a moment. There is no trace of tears.

* * *

The coming days will see a big memorable social event: the wedding of Geľo Todor-Lačný-Dolniak to his brother's widow Zuzana.

Kresan orders a few of the fattest reindeer to be butchered. The women search all day for the tastiest herbs and spices to make fine dishes. Great amounts of sugar and flour are set aside to ferment to distil spirits and make a drink which inspires the human soul to flight.

After a Christian rite, celebrated by the priest with his two sons as altar boys, the feasting begins. The tables groan under the weight of roasted delicacies and bottles of alcohol. Geľo sits at the head of the table; on his right is his first wife Elena, and on his left Zuzana, the bride. She is dazzlingly beautifully dressed. To honour the guests from afar, she has put on the perfume Geľo brought from Prague. She's used half the phial and now all the guests near her have tears in their eyes. But that doesn't dim anyone's cheerful mood, and the closer they are to the bride, the more they laugh through their tears.

There is no end to the toasts. Music begins: the accordionist Treful'a, two musicians terribly screeching on instruments resembling primitive violins, and someone playing a wooden harp that, under his nimble fingers, produces dark base tones on gut strings drawn over a reindeer skull soundbox. Some of the wedding guests begin to dance. Others have already lost consciousness and are in various immobile states.

Kresan's very old father has been getting ready all day long to recite the folk epic which foretells even the armed conflict in Junja, as well as the coming of a hero from a distant country overseas. He dresses for the occasion in ceremonial costume. He appears before the gathering with fragile, but lively steps. He bows smoothly like a schoolboy celebrating the Soviet revolution.

"HIPP BOWDURF!" he mumbles the title of the epic poem.

"What was that?" Urban asks Telgarth in a whisper.

"It's a traditional poem," says Telgarth. "No one understands it, because it's handed down orally. It always misses one generation. Children learn it by heart from their grandfathers before they can understand its meaning. So, over the years the meaning has been totally lost."

"That's a bit awkward for them, isn't it?" Urban smiles.

"It's the jewel of their folk literature," says Telgarth with conviction. "It's our entrance ticket to the club of the world's most cultured nations."

"I see," says Urban and, pretending to listen with interest, turns away from Freddy.

Kresan's old father, obviously, will soon have to join the People Above. He recites with arms akimbo, like a visionary. Sometimes he makes small funny dance steps, sometimes his jerky motions mimic throwing a harpoon and other basic actions. He recites:

For no begraal!
Crownpont turmmissed,
Mork pinch crumdown.
Bont hazzerissed!

Chuk mahn bestage choosenu:
"Bergo! Falush? Inmead?"
Farbow no brokarah:
"Woolab acban winmead!"

Try slantban mordant,
Ment kaar da mamalpont,
For chinslob gordant,
Der punk soon gravlapont.

"Frick ent feer!"
Uthers feelsen mooleh.
Priktahn fan sholobahn,
Someken non bin fooleh!

"Bonga!" sant den pasha.
"Longa," retorp masha.
Skrooni bot bagputen,
Vrooni muck lickputen!

"Has no one tried to work out what it might mean?" Urban whispers to Telgarth.

"No," Telgarth shakes his head. "Why should they? After all, that mellifluous old Slovak is a great enough artistic experience. We Slovaks have the world's loveliest language. Why bother about meaning?"

"I see," Urban nods. "I understand."

The old man is now slowly coming to the finale. He clenches his dry brown hands and shows them to the public like two wrinkled walnuts. His ecstatic gaze rises heaven-wards.

"Now Kresan's grandson Jakub will take over," whispers Freddy. "It's a tradition that the last stanzas are recited by a new reciter."

And indeed, to enthusiastic shouts, Kresan's son relieves the old man. He loudly sets out to recite the rest of the epic:

Ona my heelah
Yola nigh meelah.
Minah sant krah,
Tunah ban krah!

Wollah na bluh
Boolah na fluh.
Meen ken forau
Forbrow bowdurf

Eh, Voylah!!
For lengsine.
Hipp Bowdurf!
Hipp Bowdurf!

Jakub's performance sparks off spontaneous shouts of approval and admiration. They all congratulate his proud father. The groom toasts the grandfather and the grandson Kresan. He is evidently moved.

"But he said far less," Urban criticises young Kresan's performance.

"Why this constant fucking bitching?" Telgarth rounds on him. "It's as if you were mocking the very essence of the Slovak nation. You know who you remind me of? The bloody Czechs. Yes, you have a Czech character!"

* * *

Indeed, Urban shows precious little appreciation of Telgarth's newly discovered devotion to the ideals of the Slovak resistance and to the Junjan Slovaks' national cause in general. But the thought that Urban could soon leave him and return to Europe is disagreeable to Telgarth.

Urban becomes Telgarth's more or less involuntary companion. Any writer or journalist would have been happy to be so close to events talked about by the whole world, but not Urban. He is neither a writer, nor a journalist; the discomfort, the dirt and, in particular, being unable to get a table in a good café and order something nice is gradually getting on his nerves. Moreover, he misses his cousin Tina's long, slim legs.

A few days after Geľo's wedding he witnesses an unsuccessful attempt to catch Tökörnn Mäodna in Kresan's settlement. Although the guerrillas shot all the mercenaries who came for easy pickings, Mäodna was not among them.

Urban then takes part in a legendary attack on the capital Ćmirçăpoļ, that Telgarth renamed New City. The guerrillas enter the city at night by train, and by morning they occupy the whole centre. After two days' fighting, the guerrillas are surprised to get reinforcement from a Czech Army élite paratrooper regiment and capture the whole city for good.

The mercenaries are weakened: those who did not perish in combat, or weren't hanged by one foot from street lamps, have run off into the tundra. Now that the Slovaks have imprisoned the Junjan Khan and his entire government, the mercenaries have lost any reason for loyalty. They were not going to get paid, anyway. And so they try to leave the archipelago in small scattered groups. Small mobile Slovak guerrilla units pursue and destroy them.

Freddy soon orders the prisoners to be released from the Kandžágtt camp. Freddy firmly rejects Geľo's proposal to destroy and burn down the camp, so that not a trace remains. After all, who can tell if a correctional institution, from which escape is impossible, might not be needed?

"I've got no one here, Urban," complains Telgarth, when a few days after victory they sit alone in some gruesome snack bar in the city's port and pour themselves drinks from a well-stocked bar.

Telgarth's personal guard is patrolling outside.

"But you're surrounded by guerrillas waiting for any order you might give them, Telgarth," Urban objects.

"Well yes, but you're the only thing linking me to a civilisation I've abandoned over in Europe," says Telgarth.

"What do you need a link for, when, in your own words, you've parted company with that world?" Urban enquires. "And especially if I have that bloody Czech character, as you've told me?"

"Look," says Telgarth, "don't take everything I say so literally. Here we are, just after a victorious war, facing terrible chaos. Keeping this up is a risky, deadly business. I have enormous responsibilities. I have a daily press conference and in the evening I give briefings to journalists. I'm writing a Constitution of the Slovak Archipelago Republic. I'm creating a new concept of the state. And I know nothing about all this. You were in politics, even in parliament. Why not be my adviser?"

"No, Freddy," Urban laughs. "What advice could I give you? You've made your bed, so lie in it."

"You've got experience," says Telgarth. "All you need to do is put the brakes on me occasionally and tell me if such and such can't be done. I need someone with an overview, someone I can fully trust."

Telgarth pours himself and Urban a glass and gulps his down.

"Try and understand me," he says. "Maybe I'm a bit depressed. I'm facing unimaginable duties. I have to make a free and sovereign Junjan Slovak state out of this wild country. And I also have other plans which I have to keep quiet about. And do you think anyone but me could see this through? Geľo? Frolo? Šebo? They're simple hunters who bow to anyone who gives them a better gun than the old ones they shot walrus with."

"You mean the Czechs?" Urban asks.

"I mean the Czechs," Freddy nods. "A Czech won't stop at screwing people who screw him."

"Actually, I think that Czech aid was substantial all through the war," objects Urban, "and still is. For example, everything we eat comes from the Czech Republic."

"You've seen their flyer, haven't you?" Freddy asks. "That's the reason they're doing it all."

"But nobody's told them yet that they're not welcome," says Urban.

"Their help was welcome," says Telgarth slyly. "After we've finally liquidated the enemy, they can leave with our gratitude and good wishes. So? Will you agree to be my adviser? At least for the first few months?"

"What do I get for it?" Urban asks.

"Good question," says Telgarth. "You'll be paid in gold. And you'll get shares in our oil industry, too. That's a fair offer, don't you think?"

"It is," says Urban. "I could stay here a few weeks. But let's have a written contract."

"Fine," Telgarth laughs. "If you want a contract, you'll get one. To your health and our collaboration!"

* * *

The weeks turn into months. Soon it's Christmas, and then New Year. The New Year celebration turns into a great celebration of victory for the Junjan Slovaks. Freddy prepares a great celebration in the New City, with Czech representatives present. He gives an impressive speech from the balcony of the former Khan's Palace. He wrote it alone, the night before, and wept as he wrote:

"Dear Slovak men and women! Brothers and sisters! When I set out on the sorrowful path of war, I promised to take off my uniform only after final victory. Now, as you see, the day has arrived. Slovak men and women! From today we're no longer a nation in retreat! We've rediscovered our pride and self-confidence. It is born of all the streams of blood that we have shed for our God and nation. So we can rejoice today at our success and be proud of what we've achieved. For I tell you: today we are not cheering just over a tiny trembling flame that might go out one day. I say, in the name of those who have fallen on the road here, this will never happen. Slovak men and women! Together, we've resurrected the flame of the restless conquering spirit that moved your forefathers many years ago to leave their homes and go into the wide world to seek a new future. Even though they ended up somewhere they did not originally choose, that flame has warmed them over many years of slavery and oppression. Today that flame burns bright. Just as bright, untamed and full, as it burned in them many generations ago. Brothers and sisters! In this cruel struggle, we've found ourselves as well as our place in the world. The time for weapons and killing has ended at last and now comes a time of love and procreation. A time for peaceful building. Therefore, let us love, procreate, build, live and get to know freedom! But we must never turn our backs on the victory that we've achieved by sacrificing our blood. Those of our ranks who have fallen would never forgive us! Thank you for your attention."

After the speech begins a festive banquet and then the evening festivities continue in a free entertainment, which means unrestrained drinking. It cannot be otherwise, for the company is almost entirely male. It consists of prominent Slovaks guerrillas, now the free archipelago's supreme representatives, and of representatives of the Czech Army and some foreign journalists. The handsome Czech officers lay siege to the few foreign female journalists, so all the rest of the guests can do is indulge in an unrestrained drinking competition.

The guerrilla commanders, in badly cut suits requisitioned from ethnic Junjans, feel ill at ease in this environment, but they bravely surmount that feeling. This is how it will be from now on. Their families are still on the tundra pastures, as it is not safe here yet. Shots are heard at night every now and again.

The guerrilla commanders drown their frustration in alcohol. The supply of wine and delicacies in the former Junjan Khan's palace seems inexhaustible.

Here Telgarth and Geľo meet several of their fellow prisoners from the Kandźágtt camp, journalists from Hungary, Romania, Poland, the Czech Republic and Carpathian Slovakia. They have to drink a toast with each one of them. The journalists particularly recall Telgarth's heroic, unbending attitude to the guards. This warms Telgarth's heart. All puffed up with his own importance, he busily urges everyone to eat and drink.

Then Telgarth introduces to Urban an officer in a perfectly tailored uniform, Commodore Kubeš. Both Urban and Kubeš look at each other without a word for a moment and then firmly shake hands.

"I'm glad to see you again," says Urban. "How long has it been?"

"And so am I," says Kubeš. "Well, it's been almost two years. And how is your beautiful cousin?"

"Thanks, she's probably fine," says Urban. "I haven't seen her for a long time. I've been in Junja for half a year already."

"And what brought you here?" Kubeš wants to know.

"We've known each other for many years," Telgarth speaks for Urban. "He came to visit me and offer his services to the young Slovak Archipelago. As a former federal parliament member he advises me on legislative questions, including how not to suck up to the Czechs."

Kubeš nonchalantly ignores the last sentence. After all, he's not a politician. He's a sailor.

Urban squirms, but finally decides to bite his tongue.

"And where did you meet the commodore?" Telgarth asks Urban.

"In Prague," says Urban, "on a summer cruise on the Vltava."

"Now I can say it; it's no longer secret," Kubeš tells Urban. "This is the new job I was telling you about on the *Mayor Pfitzner*. My last voyage, when I met you and your beautiful cousin, was on Friday and on Sunday I left for the submariner course. Do you know I still have her business card?"

"Really?" Urban asks.

He often thinks of his cousin Tina, too. The longer he is away from her, the more he longs for her.

"After this voyage, I'll have an extended holiday," boasts Kubeš. "I'd love to phone her and visit her. After all, I promised to tell her more about magic Prague."

"Yes," says Urban with a crooked smile. "She'll be very glad."

"I'll be very glad to see her," says Kubeš. "She's a superb woman."

"What's the uniform you're wearing?" Urban asks, changing the topic.

"It's a Czech navy uniform," says Kubeš. "We got it just recently."

"It's handsome," nods Urban. "Better than the one you wore on the *Mayor Pfitzner*."

"I wasn't a Czech navy commodore then," says Kubeš.

"The Czech navy didn't even exist then," concludes Telgarth. "Gentlemen, you talk a lot and drink very little. Here's the champagne; please let me have your glasses."

Soon midnight comes and with it an improvised fireworks display over the city, then new toasts. Those with guns fire bursts into the sky.

Telgarth is moved to tears. He is not merely moved, but a while ago, in the lavatory, he ingested another dose of his much-loved mushrooms. And topped that off with champagne. Genuine tears spring from his eye:

"This will be a great year for Slovaks! Oh, it will be a great year for Slovaks, indeed! A great year!!!"

* * *

One Czech drives another, and their own stupidity drives them.
Junjan Slovak proverb

Playing Soldiers, or *Watch Out, a Junjan Soldier's About!*

The settlement Horná Náprava can't be found on any map of the Junjan archipelago. It's not even on the military map hanging in the hall of the former fur trading post. Welcome to the residence of one of the many Czech units that have come to defend the interests of the Czech Kingdom on this piece of frozen land.

"Over there, it's over there." "What, where?" "Well, over there. Can't you see the flag flapping on that pole?" We thought that it would take forever looking for the Royal Czech Paratroopers in Junja.

Sunday

So this is the Royal Czech Army élite. This army was a few years ago, for a record brief period, part of NATO. An army now meant to help keep peace and order on the Junjan archipelago and also to defend Czech (or rather Czechoslovak) interests. Meanwhile, the élite unit amuses itself cleaning the mud off its boots and cursing the weather.

"It's hard to get used to this weather. It's rained non-stop for two days; last night the rain came down so thick I've never seen anything like it. It pours into the tents. And not far from here, in the tundra, there's two metres of snow," worries a man sent by the Czech Kingdom to bring peace and progress to an archipelago that may soon be part of it.

In Horná Náprava they bring humanitarian aid and progress to dozens of migrant herders and a number of reindeer grazing behind the barbed wire of the military base. The Slovaks are apparently doing fine; the Czech soldiers seem to them, now they've helped the Slovak guerrillas conquer the capital, a welcome distraction. But that doesn't mean that the Czechs are no use to the local population: a military doctor tends to their injuries. Sometimes a herder cuts his hand, or boys who've been throwing rocks at each other come. Soldiers have to be tended to, as well: sometimes they hit themselves with a hammer or get abrasions at work.

"Hey, when do you go back home? Will you take our letters?" ask the tattooed rough fellows with submachine guns on their backs and shovels in their hands. (It's the weather. They have to clear mud left by the melted snow from the base.)

"They haven't assigned us an address in Prague yet. Nobody knows where we are. We'll collect the letters ourselves. And we'll give you money for the postage," say the soldiers eagerly.

"If I tell anyone in Prague that I went to Horná Náprava, they'll all just laugh at me. After all, you can't find it on any map. General Tvrdý thought that we were taking the piss and that we invented the name for his sake," is the rough soldierly reply of the Czech company commander Pavel Vodička in the officers' mess, formerly the warehouse of the Russian fur post. "The power's on for several hours a day. There's no more fuel for the generators. And they told us that Junja is floating on oil."

But the Czech soldiers are not in Horná Náprava to cater to local Slovaks. They are mainly here to signal to the whole world by their presence the will of the Czech Crown to remain here and realise the dream of so many people of a restored Czechoslovakia, but this time with Slovaks who want a common state as much as the Czechs do.

We're told that they'll take us to Ćmirçăpoļ, or New City. We're happy we're going to see something at last: watching soldiers reading porn magazines, or digging ditches in the mud seems boring now.

Day D, Hour H

On Monday morning we set out for Ćmirçăpoļ, New City. At the crossroads we wait for other military vehicles to join us. At last another jeep and an army truck come. We wait a while. Soldiers shout something to each other. The truck vanishes in the dust and two jeeps go on to the city.

The city, as it turns out, is not muddy and the corpses don't smell so bad here. There are burnt out houses, but not that many. We agree that we've seen much worse in Junja. The soldiers show us what a proper patrol looks like. Fingers on the triggers of their submachine guns, they proceed cautiously down the road. They don't talk, but signal with their hands. This impression is somewhat spoiled by the press spokesman of the company, Tomáš Branický, who walks as he is, unarmed and dressed in a bulletproof vest.

Suddenly, a very old Junjan appears on the road, leading two reindeer behind him. He looks at the behaviour of the soldiers with surprise. He has been quite alone in his burnt out village for weeks. Since members of the Czech Army are supposed to "collect information from the population," the commander Vodička talks to the old man. The Junjan tells him what happened at night: "There were mercenaries here. They were shooting. Shooting right behind the hill. With submachine guns. Ta-ta-ta-ta-ta. You understand?" Vodička says he does. "If you have any problems, stop my soldiers, they'll help you. We patrol here." The old man who has had quite a night, asks an innocent question: "And where were you at night then? I didn't see you anywhere."

Up Your Arse!

Patrolling the city is the only way for a soldier to get out of the base. Otherwise, Czech soldiers are not allowed out. This means that most of them haven't seen anything outside the base. Hope for the prisoners in green comes when a new plant is built in Horná Náprava. Soldiers occupy the old one. Before anything gets done, most soldiers will have to cope on their own.

"For example, I read erotic literature, but only soft porn, nothing hard. The boys read crime novels or war books," Radek admits. Almost everyone reads porn magazines on the base. What else can you do? Josef, whose nickname is Shovel, who has a golden necklace with a blue elephant from a Kindersurprise chocolate egg, is reading Forsyth's The Fist of God.

His best friend, Lety (real name Pavel) gladly tells us what the book is about: "It's about the Gulf War. How Saddam Hussein tried to build a big cannon so that he could hit even America, but the British found out."

After a walk among the tents it is clear to me that porn is much more popular than any other literature without pictures.

But reading doesn't satisfy. You soon get bored with cards as well. And a soldier's day is monotonous. Reveille, breakfast, work, lunch, work, free time, sleep. If God so chooses, then there are two duty shifts in between. Guarding the base. Those are entertaining at least, because you can play with the children.

"Hi, how are you, I'm fine, thanks, please, you're welcome," a ten-year-old Slovak herder's daughter with big slanting eyes repeats the Czech words. The Czechs educational effort in Junja is bearing fruit.

The most popular entertainment is the so-called "broom." When I ask what it is, the soldiers laugh madly: "It's a really popular favourite game." My curiosity grows and finally, after a minute's hesitation, it's satisfied. "Well, one man takes a broom handle and the others hold the one who deserves the broom and together they really clean him out. His arse," he adds, so there's no doubt where the broom handle goes. They usually play the broom once a week and they say that every new soldier has experienced it.

Rambos

When the Czechs were in NATO they were new soldiers, too. And God knows: if they hadn't left the organization in record time, they might right now be getting the broom.

"I used to clear mines in Bosnia. But not here. We're not allowed to do anything. If we find munitions, we have to call in the Slovaks. We're not allowed to clear anything," says the explosives expert Marek.

"I think Slovaks don't want Czech blood spilled in this land," says Ota, his friend. "Then we'd have a claim to it. But the Slovak representatives treat us like guests."

"Yet they learnt it all from us, at sabotage courses in the Czech State," says Marek. "They say we're guests too precious to risk our lives. What guests? When they were up shit creek in Ćmirčápoļ, they had a use for us, didn't they? Didn't our politicians promise us that this here would become a Czech colony?"

When I listen to Marek's stories I wonder if a man like him isn't more dangerous in his own surroundings than when defending peace and order. He has a lot of weapons and a big bomb at home (not functional, unlike his guns). His dream is not just to clear mines, but to lay them. *"For example, I'd lay an anti-tank mine so it was visible. And when you came to pick it up, you'd have to kneel with both legs on two mines."* Marek is in his seventh heaven when he shows me the refined traps he'd lay on the road.

But this explosives expert is not the only man on the base to complain of lack of work. *"Higher authority"* denies there are problems. *"Cooperation with the Slovaks is excellent,"* claims Vodička.

"We're glad we have the Czechs here. They're true professionals; they know what it's all about," says Colonel Anton-Molnár-Gajdoš-Krátký of the Slovak National Front for Liberation, the political wing of the Slovak Liberation Army.

"I'd be very surprised if the Slovaks sidelined our soldiers in any way," says the Royal Czech Army commander in Junja, General Tvrdý. *"After all, we fought on their side, doing the hardest tasks, and in fact helped them win. For the whole war, we trained their soldiers and sent them humanitarian and — today I can reveal — military aid."*

"Well, over there is a military airport that was mined. The Slovaks are clearing the mines, but we're not allowed to even look in that direction," claims one Czech soldier on the way to Ćmirčápoļ. *"The only aircraft that managed to land there, they say, was an old Ilyushin piloted by two Russian chancers. They were both blown up unloading their cargo. The whole airport was strewn with cigarette cartons they brought."*

Going Home?

Radek complains that his girlfriend found his going to Junja hard. *"She didn't agree to my going anywhere. I hope she's finally got used to it."* I ask him if he knows how long he would stay in Horná Náprava. *"I don't know, nobody does. They said until February, perhaps."* Marek's wife said nothing when he was leaving. But she still wanted to know when he was coming back. *"So I told her, 'The commander's over there, go and ask him.'" "And did she?" "She did." "And what did he tell her?" "He said half a year and a bit." "And how long is that bit?" "Nobody's told us."*

The soldiers believe that the contracts they signed before flying beyond the Arctic circle made no mention of how long they might spend here. Although they admit that they're afraid and have families at home, they don't want to go back. For some it's the *money, for others the adventure. "I want to make enough money to buy a flat. Yes. If I stay here six months, I'll have enough for a flat in Prostějov," says Josef. "You can't do this work for money," says an agitated skinhead giant. "A man has to like it." Then he goes outside his tent to show us how he gave himself a special injection against pain. "If you step on a mine and it rips off a piece of your foot, it's great. You can crawl for another hour without feeling any pain." This Goliath explains that there are all kinds of ampoules for injections available, that he doesn't know them all. His friend on the next bunk, in a tent that sleeps 17, keeps stressing that he can survive in the taiga with just an emergency box containing matches, hooks, and a fishing line that can be used to trap animals. He had something else as well, but we didn't get to see it because of the superb camouflage scarf known as a barracuda.*

Attention!

No, these people don't want to go home, whether they're in Junja for money, or for fun. And many of them certainly like soldiering. So far, they've only been playing soldiers under the ægis of a future Czechoslovakia. But boys have always liked playing soldiers. And nobody gets paid for playing, do they? This play, paid for as if it was serious, has one basic drawback: loss of personal freedom. When I ask one of them if he doesn't mind having to stand to attention whenever someone orders him, he replies: "I don't mind standing to attention at all. You see, I know why I'm doing it!"

ONDŘEJ TARÁBEK, Lidové noviny (The People's News)

* * *

> For a man, nothing is certain.
> *Junjan Slovak proverb*

As soon as the sound of champagne corks popping and of gunpowder celebrating New Year subsides, the country has to be put into some sort of an order. As early as January, Telgarth resumes the export of lichen: its price on the world market has now reached dizzy heights. The world's perfume industry breathes a sigh of sweet relief. Ethnic Junjans are used to gather lichen. Telgarth doesn't want them in the cities anyway. It's best if they're overseen and centred in concentration camps. Telgarth recalls the months he spent in such a camp. So he orders three more to be set up on Ommdru island. His experience as an inmate and escapee now helps him improve these camps' security system. When the lichen puts money in the state treasury, Telgarth will implement further steps.

For example, he'll transfer the seat of government and all state organs to New Bystrica, the former Űŕġüllpoļ. Its location in the south of the country is better suited for international sea and air links.

* * *

Junja—the End of the Idyll?
Ćmirçăpoļ (New City), Prague. Just a few weeks ago the Junjan Slovaks were welcoming Czech soldiers as liberators and brothers in arms, bearing them on their shoulders and throwing them flowers. Today, they often curse them, throw rocks at them and sometimes even shoot at them. One patrolling soldier was even wounded by an angry mob of Slovaks in the former Ćmirçăpoļ, today's New City. Trust between representatives of both sides has been harmed. Serious incidents are reported almost daily when the Royal Czech Army and Marines forces (brought, of course, to the Junjan archipelago on planes, rather than ships) have to deal with armed attacks. The main reason for enmity is that the soldiers are trying to implement in Junja a multiethnic environment and protect the remnants of the ethnic Junjan community from attacks by vengeful Slovaks.

Those who know local conditions are not very surprised. "It's understandable; the euphoria is gone and suddenly there's a mutual recognition of people's expectations," says intelligence expert Petr Kopečný. "The Slovaks understood their victory side by side with Czech soldiers as liberation and expected the Czechs to go on helping them; the Junjan Slovaks did not quite understand that the Czech presence would also mean the first steps being taken for a civil society and tolerance."

This causes the Czech command anxiety. The situation in Junja has changed rapidly since spring. If this state of affairs continues, there is a threat that Junja could become hostile territory for Czech forces. This would not just make their activities unacceptably risky, it could, at worst, prematurely scuttle the mission, some foreign observers note. This would also put an end to hopes of creating a common democratic state. The joint command of the Royal Czech Army and Navy so far officially ascribes tension to post-war chaos and apparently fights shy of open conflict with the Slovaks. They say that the Slovak National Front of Liberation (SNFL), the most powerful Slovak organization, may have lost control over some of its members.

But privately, some western diplomats express the opinion that the situation is quite the opposite: the political leadership of the country headed by the legendary and controversial Telgarth, is working against the Czechs, while the position of open support for Czechoslovakia is now held only by a group around Geľo Todor-Lačný-Dolniak, another respected fighter for freedom. Some Czech commanders are unofficially extremely displeased and have no confidence in the leadership of the military wing of the SNFL.

"We have problems with some isolated extremist elements. But we'll deal with that," General Evžen Tvrdý, commander of Czech forces tried to make light of the situation.

Hundreds of incidents belie this statement. Tvrdý himself soon challenged the leadership of SNFL to explain to its countrymen that Junja today has nothing in common with Junja before the fall of the Khan's fascist regime. "Junjan Slovaks have achieved many of their aims, above all independence, thanks to us. It would be madness if they now went on to attack Czech units," said Tvrdý.

However, it is obvious today that the political leadership of the Junjan Slovaks is in no hurry to build a multiethnic state and is perhaps not even interested in having Czech forces stay on their territory. Foreign experts worry that the SFNL leaders, particularly Telgarth (in fact, his real name is Alfréd Mešťánek), are playing a double game: they pretend to cooperate and disavow attacks on Czechs; in reality, however, they support all anti-Czech activities and, according to many reports, sometimes even organize them. All those who know the local situation stress that any change for the better will take time.

The enormous pressure that the Slovak community has now put on Junjans is understandable given the terror once organized by the Junjans: it will take some time for the situation to calm down. "Incidents luckily don't affect the whole territory of the Junjan archipelago. This situation will eventually stabilise," says Petr Kopečný.

But Czech soldiers realise that they cannot let the situation get out of hand. General Tvrdý yesterday sharply warned the Slovak Liberation Army leadership, the SNFL's military wing, not to try to create artificial tension between Czechs and Slovaks in Junja.

The forthcoming weeks will be critical, according to diplomats. It remains to be seen if Czech forces will succeed in mollifying the Junjan Slovaks' extreme positions, bring their supreme representatives back to reality and force on Junja an atmosphere conducive to a democratic restoration of the country and then creating a restored Czechoslovakia.

PETR DAVID, *Respect*

* * *

The real world has completely vanished under a patina of interpretation, Urban said philosophically to himself one day, after reading one of dozens of newspapers that, besides fishing, were his only distraction, as he hung about between breakfasts, lunches, and dinners with Telgarth. He still lived in the only more or less luxurious Ůŕġüllpoļ, or New Bystrica, hotel Murgdźżbb, recently renamed the Ambassador. Telgarth keeps emotionally blackmailing him, begging him to stay on. He keeps upping his offer. Urban has always been an irresolute opportunist and still is. With an open option of leaving at any time, that's tolerable.

When, a few days ago, with a thousand apologies and deep bows, he was kicked out of his suite and moved to a smaller room, it seemed that his patience was exhausted. He began to long for civilisation, for Stuffed Steak à la Lamminger in the *Domažlice Room*, for well-tapped Pilsen beer in the *U Pivoje* pub, for his cousin Tina, for Prague trams, for the rubber-smelling Metro, for the view of Charles Bridge and the Vltava from the *Hanavský Pavilon* restaurant, for the labyrinth of lanes under Jánský Vršek. Here, in Junja, he's fed up with everything.

"You mustn't!" Telgarth pleads desperately. "You can't abandon me. Such terrible people surround me, now that my only salvation is my old guard of guerrillas and you, my longstanding friend. You've no idea what our lunches and dinners together mean to me. With all the terrible duties I have, and I'd rather not talk about them, our meetings are the only bright spots in my life. Urban, stay a bit, it'll be worth your while. I'll reward you generously. And when it's time for you to go home, I'll send you home in a special plane, like a president, except a bit richer!"

"I'm wealthy enough, Freddy," Urban objects weakly. "I don't need your rewards. My reward is seeing how well you're doing."

For a while, Urban freezes anxiously, but Telgarth magnanimously overlooks the irony. He is strutting like a peacock. He is surrounded by Italian tailors measuring him for an elaborate new uniform; an official Russian portraitist wants to paint his portrait, commissioned by the politburo of the SNFL; he has petitioners whose relatives have been imprisoned without trial, and he's besieged by secretaries who ask him to sign all kinds of documents.

"Aren't I doing well?" Telgarth laughs at Urban through the crowd. "I just serve the people, the Slovak nation. Selflessly. You know I set myself no salary. I work for board. lodging and clothing."

Urban slowly follows Freddy and his suite. Freddy gives orders; he's like a choleric hyperactive fusspot. With firm gestures, he shoos away the arselickers and sits down at his modest desk. He looks up at Urban.

"Tonight, dress formally," he says mysteriously. "We're going to have dinner here, in the palace. There'll be three of us."

"Could the great Telgarth have fallen for the allure of some beauty?" Urban expressively raises his eyebrows.

"No, Telgarth has no time or energy for that," is the reply. "When all my work's done, then, maybe. Even a fighter like me longs for love. But you know that my own wife has left me. I'll make sure I don't get burnt a second time."

"So who's coming to dinner?" asks Urban, sits on Telgarth's desk and takes a short Cohiba out of the humidor.

"It'll be a guest from afar," says Freddy. "From very far away."

"Come on, Freddy! Don't fuck about, tell me," insists Urban.

"Surprise!" says Telgarth dryly and raises his hands.

"So, be here at eight, in the palace. And now, please go, since I have to receive a delegation of fishermen from Sangäägg, who want to rename their island Telgarth. I always enjoy talking to brave Slovak fishermen."

Urban shrugs, and leaves Telgarth's office. He walks out through the huge hall of columns. It is daytime, but the palace hall, built when there were still Soviet advisers, is dark. Urban passes by guards in grey-white-black camouflage uniforms with fur hats: the mark of élite guerrilla units. His steps echo on the marble floor. He stops to light his cigar and throws the match away. He checks his watch. It's still only half past two. Oh, God, what is he going to do until the evening?

He returns to the hotel and lies down on his bed for a while. Maybe being moved out of the suite to a more modest room had something to do with the mysterious visitor, he speculates. Finally he gets up, changes into fur trousers and jacket, takes his fishing rod and landing net and goes to his usual place near the port. He's never caught very many fish here, but ever since he discovered this spot, not far from the docks, he's come up with so many good ideas that the hours spent at the water's edge have paid off.

Somehow he has to kill time before dinner, and they say that hours spent fishing don't counted towards your age. The fish won't bite and a bleary-eyed Urban watches the port traffic. Two Czech submarines are at anchor on one side of the port. Their slender grey hulls majestically toss on the surface of the bay. Urban looks closer. *Seagull* and *Albatross*. Neither is Kubeš's *Kamýk*.

Finally a fish bites. After a long, exhausting duel, Urban pulls it ashore and lifts it up with the landing net. The fish shines all the colours of rainbow. It's big, and Urban has his hands full landing it. When he's satisfied looking at the majestic creature helplessly fighting for air, he undoes the hook and releases the fish into the turbid port water.

He does not know why, but he thinks of his three greatest desires: to be healthy, to be rich, and, finally, to get out of Junja. But the third one is not really a desire, he can do it at any time: after all, he can say good-bye to Freddy-Telgarth, and leave. A desire should involve something that you can't affect by your own will; something that requires a supernatural agency. If he could influence things around himself that way, then he would ensure that cousin Tina was his, that she didn't just treat him as a horny cousin whom she has to help occasionally like a good Samaritan and then be pursued by remorse, because she, too, got pleasure out of it. Instead, he would ensure her messy private life was ordered and that she understood that Urban was the best man for her, so that she could surrender to him with joy, without the senseless stress and reproaches afterwards. She should belong only to him, simply by becoming his wife. That's what Urban would desire most of all. But who knows what she is up to? Who is she whoring with? Kubeš?

Urban sighs, picks up his tackle and slowly sets off back to the hotel. It is time to prepare for the dinner.

As usual, there's no hot water. And even several bangs on the pipes with a blunt object won't change a thing. Never mind, Urban will take a cold shower. And gladly. He only has to think of the months spent with Telgarth, Geľo and their regiment in the inhospitable tundra. Then he couldn't shower or bathe at all. He suffered like an animal. Geľo and the other Junjan Slovaks were used to it, they'd never bathed much. At most twice a year, they'd heat up stones in the bath, but at other times they would just roll in the snow. Freddy never had any particularly rigorous hygiene routine, so he did not mind. When Urban's entire body and head began to itch, then he would force himself to undress, go out into the snow and thoroughly wash his body with it, like the other men. Each time he had a small heart attack and his body went into convulsions. So a cold shower in the Hotel Ambassador does not bother him at all.

After his bath, he wraps himself in a sheet and lies down for a while. He falls asleep and only by chance wakes up at half past seven. He quickly puts on his suit. He bought it himself at Telgarth's prompting a few days after victory. The SNFL leaders needed to wear something other than fur and camouflage; foreign visitors and journalists had turned into a flood after victory. Freddy again showed more resourcefulness than the simple hunter Geľo. He asked Urban ("You were always so fashion-conscious.") to fly to Norway in a requisitioned Yak 40, quickly repainted as a government plane, and buy each leader a good quality suit, tie, shirt, shoes, belt, hat, and a coat. For himself, too. Urban obeyed. He was given gold to pay with. Two Slovaks from Košice, ex-military pilots who'd been kicked out of the air force, flew the plane. Like other adventurers, they came to Junja and fought in the Slovak Liberation Army. As pilots, they bombed Junjan mercenary positions from the air, using planes taken from the mercenaries. One man was pilot, the other stood tied to an open door, throwing bunches of hand grenades on

295

mercenaries' heads. Urban flew in the pilot's cabin, listening to their incredible stories.

They landed on their last drops of fuel at Kirkenes airport in Norway. Urban went to town, to sell the gold in a jeweller's, and then they went to a small department store near the airport to shop. Urban had a rough idea of the quantity and size of the suits he had to buy. In the end he was happy to have bought the necessary number. Just to be sure, he bought extra shirts. They didn't have very many coats, and he bought just all the hats they had, that is, eight in all. The pilots kept carrying it all to the plane and Urban just kept buying. In the grocer's he bought three thousand dollars' worth of delicatessen items. There was a bigger problem with alcohol. The woman in the store was reluctant, but when she got a hundred dollars for her own pocket, Urban could choose whatever he wanted. A few cases of champagne, a case of bourbon, a case of whisky, a case of cognac, and ten cases of vodka crowned Urban's successful day's shopping.

When he got safely back to New Bystrica, on the last drops of fuel, the leaders of the uprising tried on their suits. Some found a jacket that fitted, others trousers. Finally everyone had something. Urban had to tie everybody's ties: his fingers had cramp by the last tie.

Next came formal picture taking. The leaders of the uprising were smiling proudly, but amiably. In the middle stood Telgarth and Geľo, the two supreme representatives of the free Slovak Archipelago. Around them stood the others: Geľo's brother Samo and his son Juraj, Šebo, Sirovec-Molnár, Turanec-Štefánik, Kyselica, Jakub Kresan, the priest, Ondrej Jančo-Divný, Fero Premieň and other front leaders. It was the first group photograph of the Provisional Government of the Slovak Archipelago Republic.

"How about you, Urban?" Telgarth shouted, as the photographer was already setting his aperture and focusing.

"Why me?" asked a puzzled Urban, putting away the cases, boxes, and bags in which the clothes and shoes had been packed.

"Come and have your picture taken with us!" suggests Telgarth.

"Why me?" Urban smiled. "I'm not a politician at all."

"You fought with us, for God's sake!" Geľo joined in. "You're one of us!"

"Sure," said Telgarth. "Come over here! Make room for him!"

"But I'm not a government member…" Urban tried to wriggle out.

"You're my adviser!" claimed Telgarth. "My adviser on… integration."

"Well, in that case..." Urban shrugged, threw the boxes aside, checked his tie and stepped into the frame.

The photograph flew round all the world's media.

And this is the suit that Urban is now wearing, as he dashes to the former Khan's palace, where he is expected for dinner.

His steps echo down the wide avenue. Strange country and strange city, he tells himself, looking at the megalomaniac buildings among which, here and there, a pedestrian figure in a hurry emerges.

A surprise awaits him in Telgarth's palace.

When he hands the servant his coat and scarf and enters the room, Telgarth and his mysterious guest are already having an aperitif.

"Rácz!" says Urban in shock.

Rácz turns to Urban with a smile.

"Urban," he says. "I'm glad to see you."

"Man..." Urban catches his breath. "I really wasn't expecting you."

"And are you glad to see Rácz, or not?" Rácz enquires.

"Now that I don't depend on your good will, I'm glad," says Urban.

Rácz takes it as a joke and starts to laugh. An obviously tense Telgarth joins him, forcing a smile.

"Yes," Rácz concurs. "Rácz was always a man of good will."

He interpreted it his way again, Urban tells himself. As always.

"So the old company is back together," says Telgarth cheerfully, as if there ever had been any kind of old company.

"Rácz is glad to see his good old friends doing so well," says Rácz menacingly.

The servant by the drink table gives Urban a questioning look.

"I'd like champagne and a drop of vodka," Urban tells him.

Urban gets his drink. He looks at the bottle like a connoisseur. They are the same bottles he brought from Kirkenes some time ago. Soon it will be time to do more shopping.

"Listen," Rácz continues jovially. "Rácz has found you two getting up to no good without Rácz, so he's flown straight after you. You'll get nowhere without Rácz."

Urban feels shivers going up his spine and into his ears. Whenever he heard Rácz try a clumsy joke, he had shivers right down to his behind.

"Rácz has come to help us, Urban," Telgarth tells Urban, apparently reciting lines Rácz has drilled into him. "The Slovak Archipelago is awash with oil. When extraction starts, the Arabs are finished. But huge capital sums are needed for that. And I don't want to let any fucking foreign capitalists here. No multinational conglomerates. We're against globalisation. We want a market society compatible with the rest of the civilised world, but we want to get there in our own special way. All the profits have to stay here, in the Slovak Archipelago Republic that we shall soon proclaim."

"And you're going to put in the capital?" Urban asks Rácz.

"Well, I've saved up a little bit," says Rácz. "And if need be, I'll sell all my companies in Slovakia. That would be a beginning."

"You don't need much to begin with," says Telgarth.

"Nobody will steal that oil from us," says Rácz. "We're in no hurry. Rácz is doing everything with forethought."

"And shouldn't Geľo be here, too?" Urban asks. "As far as I know, he is the Prime Minister."

Telgarth looks at Rácz and frowns.

"Geľo has been led astray," he says. "He fell for Czech propaganda. I've talked to him. He wants to stick to all the deals we've signed with the bloody Czechs. He's a fucking Czechoslovak. I don't think he's a good Slovak. I see no loyalty in him."

"Why are you blathering on about that republic?" Rácz asks. "I think you can level with Urban about what's going on."

"Right then," Freddy agrees, fixing his one-eyed gaze on Urban. "Look Urban. We've been talking, Rácz and I. A republic is shit. Take Slovakia: look how it ended. I don't want that. The Czechs are smarter."

"And what's your alternative?" asks Urban. "To do it their way?"

"Yes," says Freddy and his eye shines. "Monarchy."

"But the Czechs haven't improved things that way," objects Urban.

"Look, they all obey me and are devoted to me," says Freddy. "I'm the resistance hero. No one's done more for freedom than me. They owe me a lot. And moreover, I'll make them all rich. No local Slovak will ever have to work hard; not even their descendants. What did Havel promise the Czechs when they crowned him Czech king? Democracy. That's what no one here knows or needs. I'll promise them wealth."

"Human gratitude is as volatile as love," says Rácz. "You have to keep topping it up. Promise them wealth and they'll even go to hell with you. They'll even go against Geľo, or whatever his name is. Promise them another Switzerland. Another Monaco. It's all the same whatever kind of a system you proclaim. You, Freddy, can do anything."

Freddy puffs up like a peacock. His cheeks turn red with self-importance.

"Telgarth the First," says Rácz. "Emperor of Slovakia, Telgarth the First. Listen, Urban, we'll ennoble you with a title of prince."

"Consider it done," says Urban and asks for another drink.

"Cigar?" Rácz asks and offers him one from a wooden case.

Urban takes it. Rácz lights it for him.

"Do you remember, Urban, how we began in the Ambassador hotel?" asks Rácz, "in *Rivers of Babylon*. How we wiped out the Albanians? How we bought the hotel at auction? Well, we were young, bugger it all! We've achieved everything we planned."

"The west watched the Slovak nation suffer and stayed passive," says Freddy sternly. "And now, after victory, everyone wants to know us. They'd all like to invest in the Slovak Archipelago. I'm sorry, my European gentlemen! Where were you when Telgarth suffered as a political prisoner in a labour camp? When thousands of Slovaks suffered under the Junjan regime? We won't give our oil to any capitalist."

"But the Czechs weren't passively watching," says Urban. "They helped from the start. They even sent their soldiers. I think you're being unfair to them."

"To the Czechs?" Freddy laughs. "They did it all with the aim of taking over our natural resources, Slovak natural resources. But Slovak natural resources are not like the Bojnice altar the Czechs borrowed from the Slovaks and refused to return to Slovakia. You've miscalculated, Czech brothers!"

He shouts the last words through the open window towards the port where the two submarines are anchored.

"Even their plans to found a new Czechoslovakia with us were not sincere," he tells Urban and Rácz. "I've read the Czech newspapers they occasionally brought me. There wasn't a word about Czechoslovakia. They were only writing about the Slovak Archipelago becoming a part of the Czech Kingdom. A colony! Like Transcarpathian Ukraine in Beneš's time. We don't want that."

"Right, Freddy," says Rácz. "Rácz is really in favour. I told you you can always count on me. I'll help you and you'll help me. You sign my monopoly rights to drill and extract oil in Junja and I'll help you become emperor. The Slovak nation needs an emperor, bugger it all!"

"I think you should have invited Geľo here, too, Telgarth," Urban insists. "He trusts you and relies on you."

"And have him here slurping and chomping?" Freddy gets upset. "He can't even use a fork. He'd even eat soup with a hunting knife. Don't worry, I'll sort him out neatly some other time."

The door opens to reveal a Russian servant whom, together with the rest of the staff, Telgarth inherited from Khan Hüğottynünđ Ůřğüll.

"Your Excellency," he says with a slight Russian accent. "Dinner is served."

"Thanks, Vasin," says Freddy and turns to Urban and Rácz. "Gentlemen, may I invite you to table. Talk is one thing; food is another."

The dinner has several courses, mostly fish cooked in various ways. This is accompanied by Crimean sparkling wine from the khan's cellars.

The discussion carries on over dinner, but only Freddy and sometimes Rácz speak. Urban sinks into silence and speaks only when asked something.

After dinner Rácz shows them the gift he's brought: a bottle of Martell XO.

Urban tries it, Telgarth doesn't: he's had enough. He sits there babbling. The hallucinogenic mushrooms he got used to eating in the camp, added to champagne, is a devastating combination. In any case, Telgarth can't take alcohol. He finally falls asleep in the armchair when Urban and Rácz return to the hotel.

The next day Rácz tours the city, then takes a helicopter to the taiga.

"Here Rácz will go hunting!" he declares looking at an endless, snow-covered wilderness, criss-crossed by scores of fox and wolf tracks.

On the third day, Rácz leaves in his own plane, promising to return soon. He leaves Telgarth half his security team, eight men, saying that they'll give Telgarth better, more professional security than the primitive seal hunters.

Urban is relocated in his hotel suite with many bows and apologies.

Freddy avoids him. He doesn't request his company for several days. Urban doesn't mind. He slowly packs his bags. He has nothing more to do here. He knows that every Thursday at ten a special Czech Army plane leaves the airport for Prague. Urban knows that if he boards it, the next day he can have lunch at the *Domažlice Room*.

At the airport, just before he boards the plane, men from Telgarth's new security team stop him. The hotel must have informed them. They don't stand on ceremony. They take him to the car, force him inside and drive him to see an enraged Telgarth.

"What are you doing to me?" Telgarth asks him. "Why are you tormenting me? Why did you try to leave me? And in such a cowardly way, without even saying goodbye?"

"I'm fed up to the teeth with it all," says Urban. "You've got into bed with Rácz. As if you didn't know who he was... and you go and invite him to Junja!"

"But why try to give me the slip?" asks a bewildered Telgarth.

"I knew you wouldn't let me go," Urban shrugs.

"Get out!" Telgarth tells his guards.

Then he turns to Urban.

"I didn't invite Rácz," he says. "He came off his own bat. He's offered me help. Thanks to him, all the profit from Slovak resources will stay with Slovaks. We shan't bow to the West European capitalists, or to the Russians, or even the Czechs. We'll rule the country ourselves."

"I don't like it, Freddy," says Urban. "You've never worked with Rácz. You know him only by what he does on his days off. Rácz will rule here, get that into your head. You'll be a puppet emperor signing documents on Rácz's behalf."

"And I don't like you betraying me like this," says Telgarth. "Just when you see that I'm in a tricky situation."

"I want to go home, Freddy," says Urban. "It's no fun now. Anyway, I have an insatiable craving for stuffed steak at the *Domažlice Room*."

"The steak can wait," says Telgarth. "You must see that now that you're privy to my plans I can't just let you go, especially not in a Czech military plane. Are you mad? What if they torture you and get information from you about my agreement with Rácz?"

Urban can't help laughing.

"I can imagine them torturing me," he says. "And now what? Do I consider myself your prisoner?"

"Prisoner's too strong a word," says Telgarth. "In any case, you can go on moving about freely. You remain my adviser. However, since you are a person at risk, I'm assigning you protection. They're tough experienced men who won't move an inch away from you. Some of them my be familiar to you from when you worked for Rácz. They'll patrol in front of your suite and go everywhere you do."

"So I will be a prisoner, after all," says Urban.

"This is just a temporary arrangement, believe me," Telgarth promises. "Scout's honour: as soon as there's no reason for a heightened alert, I'll personally escort you to the airport and, as a goodbye present, give you shares in our oil industry as a reward for what you've done here. In the meantime, I'll keep them as safe as in a Swiss bank. A bank can be robbed, but nobody robs Telgarth."

Urban is unhappy: he's been visualising disembarking at Ruzyně airport, taking a taxi to his cousin Tina. At the same time, he's a weakling. He is unable to resist Telgarth's will.

He decides to sulk. For a few days he stays in his suite. If he has to be a prisoner, then he will act like one. By the third day he's tired of it, takes the fishing rod and decides to go fishing. When he comes out into the hall he notices that his guards have already settled in: they've brought out a little table and chairs into the hall.

Two of them accompany him to the harbour. Urban sits down and looks at the float, which does not even move. Occasionally, he lifts his gaze and observes the entrance to the bay. He is going to run away from here, that's certain. Even if it's in a Czech submarine.

* * *

> Is he hungry? Promise him bacon.
>
> *Junjan Slovak proverb*

Rácz has done as he said. When he returns to the Slovak Archipelago in a few weeks, everything is arranged and paid for. Soon a ship with drilling equipment arrives in the harbour. Presently, an oil field appears in the north of Öggdbardd island, and the purest oil in the world begins to flow through a new pipeline to a terminal near New City.

At the same time, in New Bystrica, Freddy has himself crowned Emperor Telgarth I. The priest will place on his head an emperor's crown that Rácz ordered in Europe, modelled on the Hungarian crown of St Stephen.

The priest has just returned from the Vatican, where it became apparent that the Junjan Slovak understanding of Christianity was as remote from the Roman Catholic faith as the faith of a tropical African witch doctor. The priest has learned that everything proclaimed by him, and by his forefathers and other priests spread over Junjan Slovak settlements of hunters, fishermen, and herdsmen, was nonsense. What he was told about Jesus Christ clashed sharply with what the priest had known. He could not accept it at any price. It seemed to him that while Slovaks in Junja suffered, cut off from the outside world, the Catholic church had gone off at a strange tangent. Even if the priest spent time in some mountain monastery undergoing re-education, his own flock would throw him down an ice hole for this interpretation of gospels.

It turned out to be impossible to unite with the main body of the Roman Catholic church, or with any other Christian denomination. Instead of Christ the triumphant warrior, all the other so-called Christian religions present him as a weakling who let himself end up caught by his enemies and crucified, instead of fighting like a lion and dying on the battlefield. How could the priest explain to his flock that, according to the Vatican, the cross is the symbol of Christianity not because Jesus punished evildoers by nailing them to a cross, but because he himself let them crucify him, without defending himself? The priest could foresee the objections of simple Christians of his parish. Why did Christ, about to be taken, not fire all his bullets at the Romans and keep the last for himself? And why didn't the apostles help him? Twelve adult Slovaks could wipe out a whole Roman army. But this lot, on the contrary, not only let the Saviour be crucified, and did nothing to defend him, but let themselves be caught and destroyed one by one in an even more humiliating way. Were these men Christians, Catholics?

In a nutshell, the priest returned from the Vatican disappointed, but confirmed in his own faith. He was convinced that one can rely only on oneself and on God.

Freddy heard the priest out and offered to proclaim him Metropolitan of a True Catholic church that would be the official church of the Slovak Archipelago. It would teach its believers faith and obedience to the emperor. The priest agreed and so it came to pass.

Next, in recompense, the priest, now Archbishop and Metropolitan of all True Catholics, crowns Freddy Emperor. For this he receives a promise that the first oil dollars will be spent on building a huge True Catholic basilica in New Bystrica and a cathedral in New City.

* * *

My patience is at an end, General Tvrdý warns
"Slovak Emperor" Alfréd Mešťánek

Úŕġüllpoĺ-New Bystrica (Czech Press Agency CTK). The commander of the Royal Czech Army temporary located in the Junjan Archipelago, Major General Evžen Tvrdý on Saturday warned the self-proclaimed political leader of the Slovak National Front of Liberation (SNFL), the Carpathian Slovak adventurer Alfréd Mešťánek, who recently had himself crowned Emperor "of all Slovaks" Telgarth I, that his "patience is at an end. It's inconceivable I'd allow in the future ten or fifteen Junjan foreign mercenaries to be lynched even if it puts me in conflict with the SNFL," said General Tvrdý.

"Our priority is security, but unfortunately we are not able to give ethnic Junjans and defeated members of the former Junjan foreign legion full protection. The hatred is such that we'd need one soldier for each Junjan, and that's impossible," he stated. "I will be non-partisan, but I cannot be passive. My aim is to support in the archipelago a multiethnic Slovak state aware of its history, but not tied to its past; one that would become an integral part of the Czech Crown. If we are to be forced to leave the Junjan,

now Slovak, archipelago, then we shall be defeated and our help for the Slovaks will have been wasted. In addition, according to our information, certain criminal elements have penetrated here from Carpathian Slovakia, which tremendously complicates an already tense situation," stressed General Tvrdý, adding that he saw "an encouraging signal" in the return of the moderate Slovak leader, Todor-Lačný-Dolniak, to the former Űŕġüllpoļ, today's New Bystrica. "Of course, he is residing somewhere secret," he added.

Václav Fischer, Czech Minister of Foreign Affairs, spoke in a similar vein. Talking to the newspaper Word for Today, *he said the Royal Czech Army had not stepped on Junjan soil "to give up a global treasury of natural resources to cut-throats of the Slovak Liberation Army and their sponsors from the East European underworld."*

* * *

At some point then Telgarth is visited by his old fellow fighter, in name still a top leader of the SNFL, Geľo Todor-Lačný-Dolniak. Telgarth welcomes him with a brotherly embrace and offers him a drink, while keeping a certain distance. Telgarth has for some time considered Geľo to be a political corpse. He has virtually no powers, any more than his followers Turanec-Štefánik, Čižmár-Turoň and others. Most other veterans are loyal to Telgarth, since he's succeeded in persuading them that the Slovak Archipelago is in good hands under his leadership. Telgarth is now reaping the fruits of patient and diligent political work.

Geľo's stubborn insistence on cooperating with the Czechs has lowered the respect felt for him by all his followers and supporters from the first day of the civil war. He became Prime Minister of the Slovak Archipelago Republic, but before he could properly exercise office, the republic became an empire. Suddenly Geľo had no idea whether he was still Prime Minister, or not. He did nothing for days but sit in his office, getting bored and dreaming about hunting walrus among the ice floes.

Telgarth, extremely busy, will receive him none the less, perhaps out of curiosity about what his former fellow combatant has to tell him.

Geľo is no orator. From the outset he says that he is a man who can gut and skin a dead walrus faster than say what he thinks. He realises that the ability to win, weapon in hand, seemingly hopeless fights and the ability to offer a nation drunk on victory a concept of a future political system are two different things. On one hand he still trusts Telgarth, who saved Geľo's life and fought bravely at his side. On the other hand, Geľo is confused by present developments. If this is to be the inevitable outcome of any newly acquired freedom, then he sees no point in staying in the capital and in the transitional government. After all, Telgarth does not need him for anything, nor, it seems, does the new Slovak Empire. That is why he's decided to leave politics and New Bystrica, too. Geľo is sure that now he's won freedom for the Slovaks, he can go back to the north coast and live there with his two wives and children and make a living hunting fur animals. Everyone is meant for something and he feels that he's meant for this. When the common enemy had to be fought, he fought. And the same goes for other fellow fighters, with whom he leaves for the New City tomorrow by train and from there on dog sledges or aerosledges, further north, home.

For a while, Telgarth is quiet. He realises that Geľo is making way for him and that he couldn't wish for anything better. On the other hand, his former fellow fighter takes the wind from his sails by being so frank. Telgarth is startled by his openness.

If that's how it is, Telgarth won't stand in his way. Telgarth understands that everyday political reality is not an ideal life for everyone. After all, what is politics? An everyday fight for compromises. Telgarth seems to be apologizing to Geľo for what he's done.

However, Geľo doesn't reproach Telgarth for anything. He's found that he couldn't understand those things at all. He doesn't know what's right. He knows what it is to breathe freely, but he doesn't know why friendship with the Czechs can't continue. Geľo was in the Czech lands long before Telgarth came to Junja, that is, to the Slovak Archipelago, and made unforgettable friends. The Czechs helped the Slovaks from the start. Fine, Telgarth says that it was only pretence and that the Czechs are calculating swine, but Geľo likes them anyway. Now he's leaving. He'll live like a simple hunter again, and when a Czech submarine rounds Cape Sleeping Walrus, he and all Habovka settlement will wave to it.

Telgarth nods. He, Slovak Emperor Telgarth I, understands Geľo's decision and fully supports it. If Geľo needs anything, he must come. The door to the emperor's palace will always be open to him.

Geľo thanks him and offers thanks on behalf of the fellow fighters leaving with him. But there's one more thing that he'd like to discuss before they part. He doesn't know where to begin. In the mercenary offensive, before his apparent death, Tökörnn Mäodna warned Geľo about Telgarth. He told him that Telgarth, out of fear, betrayed the whereabouts of Geľo's and his friends' wives and children. That's why Geľo wanted to kill Mäodna, so that the latter could not pass this on to others captured with him, or Telgarth's honour would suffer. Now, after the war, Slovaks need positive models, exemplary heroes, and Telgarth's person combines the Junjan Slovaks' tradition with European sophistication. He is the most celebrated person of the resistance, an honoured hero, and His Imperial Highness. Should his betrayal, committed out of fear of torture, become public, it would harm not only Telgarth, but Geľo, who trusted him and enabled him to achieve higher standing than any other Slovak before. And so, should anything happen to him — anything — Geľo has made sure that the whole Slovak Archipelago would hear of this secret. Telgarth's minutes on the throne would be numbered. He wants nothing from Telgarth for this, just a quiet life in freedom.

Telgarth does not know where to focus his one eye.

Luckily, he does not have to think very long, as Geľo gets up, bows and quickly leaves Telgarth's imperial office.

Long after Geľo's visit, Telgarth finds it hard to pull himself together. He runs nervously up and down his office, with foam in the corners of his mouth. He has no idea whether to laugh or cry. Finally, he opens his desk and takes a few mushrooms from the bottom drawer. He chews them and lies down on a sofa for a few minutes.

A few days later he has another bitter pill to swallow. In an unguarded moment Urban manages to escape.

* * *

Despite maximum vigilance, the guards failed to prevent Urban's desperate escape. Accompanied by his guards, he went every day to fish in the New City harbour. No one knew that he was discreetly watching the movement of ships in the inner harbour. When the Czech submarine *Albatross* makes for the open sea, Urban leaves his fishing rod and shocked guards behind and jumps head first into the icy water, swimming with mighty strokes to intercept the vessel. Before the guards can gather their wits, the submarine slows down and changes course. The crew throws Urban a lifebuoy from the deck. When they lift him, wet and half frozen, onto the submarine's deck, both guards are still helplessly standing on the shore. They watch the dirty, oily harbour water foam again astern, as the boat heads for the exit from the bay.

Urban gives them a victorious smile and a rude finger gesture, and is then taken below deck. He was a celebrity in Junja, so he doesn't have to explain anything to anyone. Captain Kylar personally welcomes him aboard and offers him asylum.

"We've known for some time that you were Telgarth's hostage," one of the officers told Urban. "But we couldn't do anything about it."

After Urban has changed into dry clothes, he can take a rest in a bunk in the bow cargo hold, now an improvised cabin. First of, Urban ensures that his most precious possessions are undamaged: personal papers in a waterproof plastic cover, money and also Freddy's signed affidavit making over his share of *Freddy Vision* company to Urban. That's all he needs. Everything else: clothing, personal effects, and so on, were left in the hotel suite. He leaves just as he came.

This time the *Albatross* has a lot of passengers: Czechs are hurrying out of the Slovak Empire. Those who could not get a seat on a plane were glad to travel by submarine, so the trip passes quickly. The boat's captain invites individual passengers to lunch and dinner at his table in the officers' mess, there are all kinds of communal games to play, and there are videos in the evening. Urban takes no part in the communal activities, but spends most of his time in his own bunk behind a drawn curtain, in a sort of semi-slumber. He prefers to read a Bible borrowed from the boat's library. He'd never have guessed that it was such a readable book.

The boat sails most of the time on the surface and dives only when the captain wants to raise the adrenalin level in his passengers' blood. There is nothing to keep secret any longer: it's all over. The entire world knows now about the Czech submarines.

For that reason, there is a whole welcoming committee waiting for them in Riga, including the Czech ambassador to Latvia and the military attaché. All the civilians are to take a military plane to Prague. Around midnight Urban takes a taxi from Ruzyně airport and gets off in Střešovice, two streets away from cousin Tina's house. He does not want to wake her up. He wants this to be a surprise, if she's at home.

He walks a few streets. He unlocks the gate quietly and carefully, then the house door and enters the hall. On the coat rack by the French window there's something shiny. Urban goes closer to the coat rack. He gropes and touches an officers' overcoat with epaulettes and stripes on the sleeves. He's stunned. It feels as if someone has stabbed him in the heart with a long knife and then twisted it slowly in the wound.

Urban leaves the house and his head spins as if he were drunk. Under a cover in the courtyard his BMW is parked. Urban opens the gate and drives the car into the street. He drops the house keys in the letter box. He spots the curtain in Tina's bedroom window twitching.

He has no reason to wait: he starts the car and drives towards Letná to get a room in the Hotel Belveder.

It's near morning when he falls asleep in the hotel room, sleeping nervously, waking up every once in a while, desperately jealous, only to fall asleep again for a moment, tired by the journey home.

In the morning he has breakfast in the restaurant, drinking plain black coffee, and in the Slovak daily *Práca* that he chanced to find on the newspaper table, he reads an interesting article:

The Slovak Archipelago and the End of the Czech Dream

Three years ago, a gang of Junjans treacherously raided a peaceful fishing hamlet Habovka, populated by Slovak immigrants, or rather, kidnapped hostages, and murdered several dozen local inhabitants, mostly women and children, when the men were away fishing. The Slovak population of the Junjan Archipelago went on a mass protest against this crime and their demonstration ended in a massacre. The coastal Slovaks rose in an uprising against the dictator Hüğottynünđ Ûrğüll, and Slovaks from the city slums joined them. The dictatorial couple, Hüğottynünđ and Karķla Ûrğüll, were on the run. At their instigation, specially trained mercenary regiments paid out of the profits of the Junjan mafia spread over all the states of the former Warsaw Pact, began a reign of terror in Junja. Units commanded by Tökörnn Mäodna shot some 500 people, including 80 children, in Ćmirçăpoļ alone. The dead were taken out of the city and thrown on heaps. Anyone still alive was burnt alive. In Ûrğüllpoļ, today known as New Bystrica, it was even worse. Slovaks, lead by the legendary guerrilla leaders Todor and Telgarth, now the self-appointed ruler of the Slovak Empire, chanced to arrest the Khan and his wife. Mäodna's well-armed units literally went out of their minds. Murdering Slovaks without mercy, they tried to re-conquer the capital with the aim of freeing the Khan. It was only due to a superior force of the Slovak units, reinforced at a decisive moment by a surprise appearance by the Royal Czech Army and Marines, that these highly trained killers were overwhelmed. The mercenaries comprised Russian and Ukrainian veterans from Afghanistan, former IRA terrorists, Arab veterans from Hamas and the PLO and Romanian Securitate killers, in other words, humanity's élite. Isolated mercenary units continued to terrorise the whole country, knowing that they had nothing to lose. Therefore, in March, the Slovak Front of Liberation, shortly after a brief trial, had the former Junjan Khan Hüğottynünd Űrġüll and the former Prime Minister Okhlann Üncmüñć executed in front of television cameras. The Khan's wife Karḳla Űrġüll was sentenced to life in a labour camp. As Emperor Telgarth I stated, the anger of the Slovak people was great. In a television commentary to this outlandish and shocking execution it was said that any mercenary Junjan soldier caught would be executed in a manner to make them envy Hüğottynünd Űrġüll and Okhlann Üncmüñć their easy and relatively painless death.

Results were quick. Terrorist resistance weakened considerably and the Slovaks gained the upper hand for good. Members of mercenary units knew that if the Slovak people captured them, they would die a horrible death: they tried at all costs to escape from the archipelago. However, this was prevented by a blockade of the island set up by the provisional Prime Minister Geľo Todor-Lačný-Dolniak. No aeroplane could take off or land on the former Junjan, now Slovak Archipelago without thorough inspection. The air space around Junja was under 24-hour surveillance by the Royal Czech Air Force. Aircraft that for any reason did not heed coded messages were shot down without mercy. Ships were prevented from sailing in either direction by a sea blockade of the archipelago, operated by Czech submarines. Telgarth's régime gradually rounded up the scattered mercenaries and executed them in a manner that outdid the wildest imagination. The Czech side vainly protested against this, as they pursued their strategic aim of restoring the former Czechoslovakia, this time not with Central European Slovaks, but with Junjan Slovaks. After a bankrupt and broken up Russia, no longer capable of anything, not even effectively defending its interests in the northern seas or in China, which distanced itself from the conflict, a new significant superpower was intended to emerge as an effective counterweight both to the USA and to a united Western Europe.

The Czechs Protect the "Shark"

Tökörnn Mäodna (real name: Paraskiv Cojanescu) was before 1989 a captain in the Securitate, the Romanian Secret Service. After the demise of the Ceauşescu regime, he left Romania and became a hitman and a mercenary. He was finally appointed Hüğottynünd Űrġüll's chief of security. During the civil war in Junja, he led the mercenary units and was the Slovak guerrillas' most serious adversary. Even his name horrified people. His nickname was "Shark," because he loved capturing Slovak fighters and brutally torturing them. According to witness state-

ments, he himself tortured and killed several people, including a Slovak priest. After the mercenaries' final defeat, he disappeared into parts unknown. Soon a hunt to capture him was organized.

The news that Tökörnn Mäodna had been living in strict secrecy in the Czech Kingdom almost all the time since the government mercenaries' defeat was not so surprising in the light of preceding events. The Czechs caught the Shark when he tried to leave the archipelago in a fishing boat. In the period of "friendship," the Czechs would hand over all captured mercenaries and prominent Junjans to the Slovaks for merciless, even bestial punishment, Mäodna fell into their hands at the time when tension and enmity reigned between the allies. So Mäodna was not handed over, and even his capture was kept secret.

The future fate of Mäodna may be controversial. It is certain that he will escape punishment. At the moment, the Royal Czech Secret Service is interrogating him. Mäodna is planning to undergo plastic surgery and will return under a new name to his original homeland, Romania, where he would like to live on modest savings deposited in Switzerland.

Untraditional Methods in the Service of the Securitate

We now broach a topic that has nothing to do with Junja, but is the reason for Mäodna's interrogation by the Royal Czech Secret Service. "Look, back then nobody in Romania had to be tortured or killed," Shark begins his narrative. "It wasn't our aim. Quite the contrary. We had to win a man over to our side and persuade him of the justice of our cause. We used all available methods, which is normal. It's always has been, is being and will be done, under any government, no matter how democratic. We even used non-traditional methods, such as parapsychology. Professors and specialists of the famous Bucharest School of Sabotage have studied paranormal phenomena. Their graduates are truly dangerous, since they use paranormal phenomena for their work. The most skilful of them are the Arabs. Even in Junja we used hypnosis, brainwashing and African witch doctor practices. They say that a person leaves his body during those sessions and in spirit, he can go wherever he wants and see whatever he wants. Then he returns to his body as if nothing happened. We would not shirk even from Saharan magician practices. They can control their people over distances of thousands of kilometres and order them through their thoughts. You know, Ceauşescu was a great lover of gold, precious stones, but also of paranormal phenomena. Entire teams of Securitate were researching strange things that would seem almost laughable to a layman."

310

The Securitate Searched for Dracula's Grave
"Ceauşescu believed that in the Transylvanian Alps a mechanism must exist to keep vampires immortal and give them unbelievable power. That's why we searched for Count Dracula's grave. We have also searched for descendants of the witches who have lived in Hunedoare and the surrounding mountain since time immemorial. I don't know if they found anything, it wasn't my assignment. Even if people thought what they liked about such things, they never said anything aloud, since that could mean treason. We had to obey orders, no matter what. But sometimes we didn't feel like laughing. For example, when the Securitate got people into a state of clinical death to send them down the famous tunnel and then tell us about it. Who would do that? We were never short of volunteers: prisoners, Securitate members, or simply volunteers for anything. And if we didn't have any volunteers, then we'd always find someone. We spent almost five years trying to find out if you could dodge a bullet. Several people were involved and finally we found one who was really good. During a demonstration, there was an accident. He really did dodge a bullet, but despite his excellent health, he had a heart attack. We also experimented with the energy people radiate at a moment of mortal danger. For example, when they fall under a car, they manage to stop it for a fraction of second, though, in reality it doesn't mean anything, of course. As far as I know, among the East European states, Czechoslovakia played a prominent role in this kind of research. Arab saboteurs in Sahara trained some of us. There they taught us various things you don't like to talk about. Some Securitate men are said not to have survived this; others lost their minds..."

Living Lie Detectors
"It was interesting when we searched for and tested people who could recognize a liar by his smell. They were living lie detectors. With people it works the same as with the animals, except for the suppressed olfactory and animal instincts. When a wolf is hunting, animals get scared, since they know that he's out to kill. That's how nature works. If they weren't afraid of the wolf, he wouldn't merely leave them alone: they'd make him run, since he'd be the one afraid. This is how it works unconsciously with people, though they don't realise it. These fear and superiority pheromones can be activated and intensified by training. Our specialists have worked on it. You can recognize a man who is afraid by his smell, since he knows you're after him and his conscience isn't clean.

This special science is ideal for counter-terrorism and other investigators. With that sense of smell, you can discover a corpse, no matter where it's buried. Some people are born with it, others can get it by an operation, but it's dangerous, since one small mistake changes a person into something completely different. Besides, I know that almost all police forces and armies in the West use similar 'noses'."

Politicians Change, but the Methods Stay

"We also researched telepathy. Ceauşescu had a special team of scientists and specialists in the Securitate that tried to discover and communicate with beings from parallel worlds. Apparently, it worked quite well, but I don't know much about it except that they managed to enter a parallel world a few times, but I've heard that beings from parallel worlds come to us much more often. They communicate with us telepathically. To research their existence, the Securitate used newborns, animals, and Down's syndrome people. A person has to have a blank mind for this kind of communication. Madmen are mad from our point of view, but they can communicate with beings from parallel worlds quite easily. You can see it in their eyes. You suddenly find they're normal, since their eyes begin to shine and they behave like human beings. Maybe they behave differently, but with intelligence. And when beings from other worlds leave, they again turn into demented people and their eyes turn off like lamps. As for animals, they say that fish, pigs, and cats react best. Dogs can be great, too, and strangely enough, even snakes..."

Is the Junjan Snow Monster a Phantom, or a descendant of Extraterrestrials?

The mysterious Ökötöm-kökötom, the snow monster, has been an object of terror for the inhabitants of the permanently snowbound tundra in the interior of the islands of the Slovak Archipelago. He is very shy, but at the same time extremely powerful and rapacious. Nobody has yet seen him, or if he ever did, then he couldn't tell anyone about it. In the distant past, the snow monster was responsible for culling whole herds of reindeer, and for the mysterious disappearance of groups of fur trappers.

"Of course, as soon as I arrived in Junja, I got interested in Ökötöm-kökötom," claims Mäodna in his Czech exile. "We made several attempts to catch him. Alas, they all failed. Eventually, I stopped believing in his existence. It's the same as the Loch Ness monster. Among the Inkirunnuit, the original population of the Junjan Archipelago, there is a legend about gods who came down from the heavens and then could not

get back. They were said to be evil gods who threatened people. It's possible that unknown arrivals were forced to adapt to life in inhospitable regions of Junja and gradually lost their technological advantages and became wilder from generation to generation, until they became the feared Ökötöm-kökötom. I think this is a puzzle awaiting a solution. When European companies start to mine uranium and gold intensively and drill for oil, the interior taiga will lose all its secrets."

Dream and Reality

During the nineties the Czechs tried unsuccessfully to join the European Union. In the process they were constantly humiliated and bullied by Eurocrats who kept upping their senseless demands. This went on with the assistance of the home-grown Euro-suckers, such as the former government appointee Pavel Hul, who later committed suicide after being voted the Most Hated Man on the Czech scene in a New Year poll.

Not surprisingly, it was the EU that was supposed to have regretted most the restoration of Czechoslovakia. After assisting the Slovak victory over the Junjans, the top Czech politicians openly boasted of their aim of "giving it to the European Union". The unimaginable wealth of natural resources in Junja (above all oil, uranium, gold, and natural gas) gave this basically justified bitterness the semblance of a probable threat.

"A few years from now, all Europe will be fatally dependent on Czechoslovakia," the Czech Prime Minister Petra Buzková told a press conference. "Of course, we'll be ready to consider helping in exchange for accepting our political and economic conditions. And they will be unusually severe, I can tell you that now."

The Czech King, Václav V, in his "Speeches from Lány", tried, as is traditional, to smooth out the unfortunate undiplomatic rhetoric of his Prime Minister: "The natural resources found on the Slovak Archipelago could help the economic problems of the whole world. The lands of the Czech Crown will merely manage this wealth and distribute it according to both need and merit. Help will be determined by rules that we will draw up. Every superpower has a right to make such conditions and if my memory serves me right, so far no superpower, former or present, has renounced that privilege."

The Czechs dreamers' plans and calculations met the resistance of the majority of Junjan Slovaks. They approved of the Czechs when they needed them to defeat the Junjans, but afterwards they were no longer needed. And so behind the Czechs' backs they crowned the freshly named provisional chief administrator of the Slovak Archipelago republic, Alfréd Mešťánek, known under his nom-de-guerre Telgarth, as Slovak Emperor. Todor-Lačný-Dolniak, a devoted supporter of cooperation with the Czechs, the provisional Prime Minister in the first days of the free state, had to give up office and was de facto sent into exile on the north coast, where he had begun his victorious march on Űrġüllpoḷ.

"A Czechoslovakist simply cannot hold any high government office in our young state, which is both Slovak and national," argued Emperor Telgarth I, giving a signal for other personnel purges in the imperial government. Soon the new state, now called the Slovak Empire, asked the Council of Europe for membership of the EU. Despite the fact that the Slovak imperial leadership has openly proclaimed that human rights will not be a political priority on the Slovak Archipelago for a long time, the Eurocrats received the application very positively.

After tragicomic bullying of poor Central European countries like the Czech and Slovak republics with absurd demands for human rights (the EU for example set both countries a quota for proportional representation of their Roma population among university educated citizens, scientists and private businessmen), the EU's highly welcoming attitude to an application by the Slovak Empire, holder of 80% of the world's supply of oil and uranium, seemed all the more paradoxical.

After expulsion from NATO and outright rejection by the EU, the Czechs received a third humiliation on the eve of the new millenium, this time from the Junjan Slovaks. Anti-Czech demonstrations, and the cooling, even rupture of diplomatic relations, made a Czech military presence on the archipelago untenable and it had to end. Any eventual resistance from the large Czech military garrison on the Slovak Archipelago was pre-empted when the Slovak Empire asked the EU for military assistance, which was promptly granted. Some 900 days passed and another Czech dream collapsed: the dream which led the Czech Kingdom to invest unimaginable means in founding its now so unnecessary navy. The Czech people will feel the economic consequences of this risky investment for four or five generations, according to experts. The yearning of a poor, but very sophisticated Czech Kingdom for superpower status and prosperity through Slovak oil and uranium has vanished and turned into an even bigger abyss of economic recession.

There is a Czech fairytale about easily acquired ducats that, with the coming of morning, turn into crocks of clay. The Czech Crown now weeps over the crocks of clay of its imagined future.

Viktor Cheležnikov

Urban stops reading. He doesn't know why, but he recalls that every spring and early summer Tina's villa crawled with ants. They sometimes crawled over him at night. Do they crawl over Kubeš, too?

One spring morning, when Urban opened the window of the guest room to air it, he noticed the ants carrying their eggs to the windowsill. He had nothing against ants. Their hard work and organization seemed attractive to him: after all, he was of the generation that spent Sunday mornings watching the puppet *Fred the Ant* on television. On the other hand, he found crawling ants disgusting. He decided that he'd take the ant eggs and use them as fish food in Tina's pond. So he placed the beige eggs on a little plate and noticed that the ants tried to escape quickly. It embarrassed him, but he continued. He noticed that some eggs had already hatched, and on the windowsill sat a few freshly hatched winged ants. He took the little plate of eggs and ants trying to save them and swept them into the pond. He watched the lazy red veil-tail fish cautiously sampling them. They'll never know how much suffering is behind their delicious lunch, he thought. But is it any different to any industrially prepared food?

Once, there used to be a hunter and his prey. Sometimes this was reversed and the hunter became the prey. That's how it's meant to be.

At that time, a long ago, Urban went go to bed a bit earlier than usual. He patted his pillow and found a winged ant underneath. He never thought about it: it seems odd to him that he should recall it right now.

He killed that ant without thinking. He perceived nothing then, only now, when he remembers it, he feels a chill round his heart.

The ant must have hidden in the dark for hours under the pillow. It was certainly waiting to be rescued. But no help came from the anthill: the ants were totally crazed after absorbing doses of ant-killing powder that Urban gave them.

Only today, after much time and experience, is Urban able to imagine in real terms the horrifying loneliness of the little ant, freshly hatched and immediately abandoned in a strange world, so incomprehensible and horribly foreign.

The little ant then bore his fate stoically. He waited for death passively under Urban's pillow, having understood that he would die without a chance to taste the gift of life that we each receive only once. He knew that no pleasant company of new friends was waiting for him, that he'd never walk even a centimetre of the corridors of an anthill that was supposed to become in his short ant life a home and fortress. That he would never have the exciting adventures of exploratory expeditions into the depths of a house or a dark garden. He knew he was lost.

That equanimity seemed moving to Urban even then. Yes, he killed him. But it was a mercy killing, done as fast as possible. It was a fraction of a second even in accelerated ant time.

And today something tells him that he was only fulfilling a partial action in some great, thought-out plan. Today he, the former blasphemer and atheist, realises that it is simply impossible for this world to exist without God. Nothing exists just for its own sake; not even Urban, not the lonely and abandoned ant whom he will never ever forget. That is quite a feat for one short ant life. Or could this ant have existed just for Urban? He did as he was supposed to and then vanished irrevocably?

Urban knows: any suffering, even the least comprehensible, in the world has its deep meaning reflected in a larger whole, which, so far, we can't see for various reasons. The meaning is revealed to us bit by bit. If, by an unimaginable failure in this world's logic, all backdrops vanished and we glimpsed His image, we'd be burnt to cinders by what we saw.

That is why it's proper that we get the whole truth in carefully measured doses, Urban believes. Of course, the disadvantage is that some things we perceive out of context, which results in a feeling that this world is meaningless, spoiled, an automated toy abandoned by its creator. And this is a mistake, Urban realises.

Under an awning of logic and materialism, Urban senses discomfiting features of something more and more mysterious and at the same time vertiginously dazzling, pure and liberating.

* * *

After Urban's departure, Telgarth rages like a man possessed. He has to be given a cold compress to prevent another vein bursting in his brain. He is raging not because Urban could in any way seriously damage him. In a few days the situation in the Slovak Archipelago has got so tense that it is no longer a secret that Junjan Slovaks do not want a common state with the Czechs. He rages because he realises that he meant much less to Urban than Urban did to him. And that has hurt him.

Thank God Rácz is still around! They are linked by many common experiences.

By the way, Rácz has decided to change his life. He sells his property, hotels, factories and even his beloved brewery, ensures his family is well-off, and then moves for some time to the Slovak

Archipelago. He decides to act like a man: he'll start again from scratch. Well, not really from scratch, but still, it's a courageous decision. He plans to wait in New City until the political situation calms down and then to go up north, to oversee personally the construction of oil fields, a pipeline, and a terminal for big tankers. He's never done this before, but he's paying for experts, oilmen from Baku.

In both cities of Slovak archipelago hostile inscriptions, like "CZECHS, GO HOME," and so on, appear. There are regularly popular demonstrations, enthusiastically recorded by journalists and TV crews from all over the world, against the Czech military presence.

Despite these unstable times, Rácz sets up and registers a commercial trust called *Oil Junja*. Telgarth dislikes the name, but finally agrees to it. He agrees to anything that Rácz suggests. He also agrees that the few dissidents daring to protest at Telgarth's decisions will have to be sent to a camp to expiate their guilt by working on the rock lichens.

The Czechs have found themselves in a difficult situation in the Slovak archipelago. From a diplomatic point of view, talking to Emperor Telgarth is out of the question. He stubbornly insists on all Czech troops leaving the territory of the Slovak archipelago. He won't accept any arguments. Yes, other people signed contracts, but His Imperial Excellency Telgarth I did not. Those people no longer represent the Slovak nation and are no longer in New City. Finally, the Emperor refuses to talk to the Czechs and locks himself in his rooms. A spokesman, whom the Emperor trusts absolutely, Rácz, represents him. He knows how to deal with Czechs. He spent his military service with the Czechs. He was in an artillery regiment, Unit 5963, in Lešany near Prague in 1981-1983. His commander was Major Konečný; the political officer was Major Dürr. Rácz was a model soldier. He had the Czechs sussed: coffee and beer.

Since *Oil Junja* has now signed strategic contracts with France, Germany, Spain, Italy, China and Japan, the Czechs fear an international row and decide to leave the scene in a huff, but without a fight. The Royal Czech Army and Navy's departure *en masse* is the Czechs' final military operation on Slovak archipelago territory and a indisputable proof of the failure of Czech diplomacy.

Telgarth I gives Rácz the title of prince and stuffs parliament with obedient and stupid fishermen, hunters and reindeer herders to elect him Prime Minister of the Slovak Empire. The new Prime Minister immediately goes north, to oversee personally the final touches before the giant and rich oil fields start up.

Attention, dear reader, this is a decisive moment! Here Freddy Piggybank vanishes not only from our story, but from our life. We will never hear of him again. And so, just as a weekend ends with Sunday dinner, not at midnight, our book pretty well ends here.

What is there to add? Geľo Todor-Lačný-Dolniak's dream of a peaceful life with his family, relatives, and friends from the hunting settlement of Habovka was only partially, or — to be precise — temporarily fulfilled. At first Geľo stayed at home for a while, hunting, checking his traps, going to meetings in the men's house with his coævals; sometimes he went to Stormy Tooth to get mineral grease. Recent events have had an impact on his life, too. The north of the New Liptov Island has been settled. As if by the stroke of a magic wand, huge oil fields appeared with thousand of drilling rigs spreading all about as far as the eye could see. There were fewer animals to hunt, and the walrus moved away, too, when huge tankers took over their living space.

One day Geľo came to the sea and the whole shore was black from an oil spill after the first wrecked tanker.

Then he, too, concluded that the old life was finished. So he set out together with his son Juraj, his brothers, Sirovec-Molnár and other men from the coast to find work in the oil fields. There they met only foreign workers, from all over the world. Nobody knew Geľo or his glorious past. The Habovka men got jobs and began work. They were now paid in a new currency introduced by Emperor Telgarth I, *vindras*. When Geľo became a foreman of his drilling team, his annual pay was 3000 vindras. One vindra was worth two dollars. The Slovak economic miracle was becoming a reality.

The salaries of our Slovaks turned out far higher than their income from selling trapped fox hides; so they stayed there forever and so did their children and their children's children.

* * *

Dear Tina,

What blinding flash of happiness is it that has suddenly hit me and paralysed me? Why does a man have to go so far away to find himself? Why does suffering have the power to endow a man with new life energy?

Will you be ever able to pardon me for not getting in touch for such a long time? For not being able to perceive anything, to understand anything for so long? I had no idea what you were talking about when you mentioned spiritual growth. My eyes have seen things which I will never be able to tell you about, since you wouldn't believe me anyway.

My dearest Tina, I've been freed and born again. I've come back from purgatory. It seems as if everything has acquired new meaning and order. Yes, it will be a me who will win your favour. What sense would all my wealth have without your smile?

Once you told me that you loved the man buried deep inside me. If I understood it all properly, I think the man you spoke about is now out there, liberated. I am as I am. Though I'm still not the kind of man I'd like to be, I no longer fear recognizing the truth. The truth about myself, but also about what I don't yet know and what I'm only seeking.

I'm not afraid of being weak sometimes, or making mistakes, or even being ridiculous. I used to be sure that I couldn't win love or keep it by being sincere, that a woman like you needs a strong and successful man before she can love him. I was wrong. Only now I understand everything. You need someone who would be at all times truly genuine.

Yes, yes, I want to be like that! Our life could be beautiful and calm. What a pity that it's so short. This is what I'm offering you: let's spend our allotted time together.

I can't write to you any more. Take me as I am, but also, as I'd like to be. And I'll respect you, too, because I love you.

If you still feel something for me, come next Friday, at any time, to the Domažlice Room. *I will be there from opening time to closing time. If Commodore Kubeš is so dear to you that you won't come, then I'll understand and won't be angry with you. But I want to drop for ever the role of being your cousin. Either — or.*

Your Urban

* * *

No, when Urban looks back, he doesn't feel bitter. He's met many interesting people. He's seen many strange lands. He's undergone and, above all, survived adventures for which anyone else would need at least two lives. He's lost a lot, but he's also gained a lot. He finally knows that he's in love.

After all, it was an excellent adventure, he realises, as he stands by the bar in *Domažlice Room* on the last Friday of June.

"Would you like another beer with a shot?" a waiter asks.

Urban nods gratefully. He's tense, not surprisingly, but, given the delicious feeling of running his own life, the outcome is not so very important. The important thing is that Video Urban has taken a decisive step on the road to his goal of being a better person. What he's undergone will always stay with him.

All right… suppose he's lost more than he's gained?

Well, of course, that happens, too.

But you won't see him crying in any book.

also available from the Garnett Press

Д. Рейфилд, О. Макарова (ред.). Дневник Алексея Сергеевича Суворин (*Dairy of Aleksei Suvorin, the 19th C. Russian magnate, in Russian*). 1999, pp xl+666 ISBN 0 9535878 0 0 £20.00

D. Rayfield, J Hicks, O Makarova, A. Pilkington (editors) *The Garnett Book of Russian Verse. An Anthology with English Prose Translation* 2000, 748 pp. ISBN 0 9535878 2 7 £25.00

Donald Rayfield, editor in chief (with Rusudan Amirejibi, Shukia Apridonidze, Laurence Broers, Levan Chkhaidze, Ariane Chanturia, Tina Margalitadze) *A Comprehensive Georgian-English Dictionary*, 2006. 2 vols. pp xl + 172. ISBN 978-0-9535878-3-4   £75.00
(*a few seconds [8 replacement pages inserted in volume 2] are available at £40.00*)

Peter Pišt'anek, translated by Peter Petro. *Rivers of Babylon* 2007. pp 259. ISBN 978-0-9535878-4-1   £12.99

Peter Pišt'anek, translated by Peter Petro *The Wooden Village* (*Rivers of Babylon 2*) 2008. pp 206. ISBN 978-0-9535878-5-8   £11.99

Nikolai Gogol, Marc Chagall *Dead Souls* , a new translation by Donald Rayfield, *with 96 engravings and 12 vignettes reproduced from the 1948 Tériade edition* 2008. pp366. ISBN 978-0-9535878-7-2£29.99

forthcoming
in 2009:

Otar Chiladze *Avelum* (the fifth novel by Georgia's greatest living novelist)

Donald Rayfield *The Literature of Georgia — A History*, the third revised and expanded edition

in preparation

a full translation, the first into English, of Avicenna (Ibn Sina) *The Laws of Medicine* (*Al Qanun fi at Tibb*)

for enquiries, or to buy any of our books, contact:
d.rayfield@qmul.ac.uk
or write to:
Garnett Press, School of Languages, Literature and Film, Queen Mary University of London, Mile End Road, London E1 4NS, UK

website under construction: **www.garnettpress.co.uk**

Kandźǵgtt

OMMDRU

Stormy Tooth

Hromový Zub

Habovka

Cmirčă

MGDRÄAG

Ö

Úrĝüllpoḷ

SANGÄÄG